Flesh *for* Fantasy

Books by Joan Elizabeth Lloyd

THE PRICE OF PLEASURE

NEVER ENOUGH

CLUB FANTASY

NIGHT AFTER NIGHT

THE SECRET LIVES OF HOUSEWIVES

NAUGHTIER BEDTIME STORIES

HOT SUMMER NIGHTS

MADE FOR SEX

THE MADAM OF MAPLE COURT

TAKE ME TO BED

TEMPTING TAYLOR

FLESH FOR FANTASY

Published by Kensington Publishing Corporation

FLESH *for* FANTASY

JOAN ELIZABETH LLOYD

KENSINGTON BOOKS
http://www.kensingtonbooks.com

KENSINGTON BOOKS are published by

Kensington Publishing Corp.
119 West 40th Street
New York, NY 10018

All Kensington titles, imprints and distributed lines are available at special quantity discounts for bulk purchases for sales promotion, premiums, fund raising, educational or institutional use.

Special book excerpts or customized printings can also be created to fit specific needs. For details, write or phone the office of the Kensington Special Sales Manager: Kensington Publishing Corp., 119 West 40th Street, New York, NY, 10018. Attn. Special Sales Department. Phone: 1-800-221-2647.

ISBN-13: 978-0-7582-1279-5
ISBN-10: 0-7582-1279-8

First Kensington Trade Paperback Printing: November 2009
10 9 8 7 6 5 4 3 2 1

Printed in the United States of America

CONTENTS

SLOW DANCING

Chapter 1

"Maggie mine," Paul Crowley's voice echoed through the phone, "please marry me."

Maggie Sullivan's laughter warmed the miles of wire between them. "Paul, you're so sweet and you know I love you, but be real." She spread her voluminous purple silk robe out on the wide satin-covered bed and pressed the phone against her ear.

"I am being real. Marry me. Or, if not, let's run away together. We'll find an island with no one there but the two of us. We'll live on fish and mangos."

Maggie pictured Paul's deep brown hair and could almost feel its softness. He was in his midthirties and had a body that told everyone he worked out and prided himself on his physique. "Lord, after a bad day that's such a tempting offer." Maggie tangled her fingers in her black curls. As she twirled one strand around her index finger, she remembered when her hair had been that color without the help of her stylist. "But sweet, you're who you are and I'm what I am."

"That doesn't matter, Maggie mine. Let's forget all that and do what makes us happy for a change."

"Paul, we've been over and over this. I'm a prostitute. A hooker. Very high priced," she added, tucking the phone between her ear and her shoulder and leaning back against her collection of primary-colored pillows. She flipped one Mondrian-print curtain from in front of the air conditioner with her toe so the fan blew more cold air in her direction. "But still a hooker. And you're a banker. Very straight."

"I don't care. I just want you." She heard his sigh.

"And what about our ages. I'll begin to collect Social Security just about the time you reach forty."

"Sweet thing," he moaned. "We were just born at the wrong time. Anyway, what difference do a few years make?"

"What are you wearing, Paul?" Maggie purred, stretching her long, shapely legs and crossing her ankles. She spread the sides of the robe and looked at her body beneath it. Still slender, with muscular thighs from working out daily, and full breasts that sagged only a bit.

"What difference does that make?"

"I just opened my robe and underneath it I'm wearing a lilac teddy. It's a smooth satiny material and I'm running my palms up and down my side right now." Maggie's hands were, indeed, rubbing the slick material.

"Oh, sweet thing," Paul groaned.

"I had my nails done today, you know," Maggie said, gazing at her hands. "They're extra long and bright red now. The color's from a series called Romance. This shade is called Slow Dancing. Like we do when we're together. That's why I chose it. Now I'm running my nails over the front of my thigh. It feels really good."

Maggie could hear Paul drag air into his lungs. "The inside of my thigh is so soft, but I'm making bright red marks with my nails." She smiled. "Talking like this always makes me hot. I wish you were here." Paul was on a business trip and was calling Maggie in New York from his hotel room in Denver.

"I do too. But . . ."

"What are you wearing?"

"Jeans and a blue shirt."

"Take them off, baby. Please." She could hear his resigned sigh. Again she had deflected the conversation. Maggie could hear the rustling of Paul moving around his room.

"I'm pulling off my jeans and shirt even as we speak. You always do this. I propose and you reject me in the nicest way possible." There was a pause, then Paul said, "Now I'm only wearing my shorts."

"What color are they? I want to be able to picture you."

"Black. With a white waistband." Paul's voice was ragged.

"Is your cock big and hard?"

"Oh, Maggie," Paul groaned. "Why do you do this to me?"

Her smile broadened. "Because I love to make you hot. It's one of the things I do best and enjoy most. Now tell me. Is it hard?"

"Yes, he groaned.

"Do you want to touch it while we talk?"

Silence.

"Tell me, Paul. Do you want to touch it? Tell Maggie."

"Yes," he whispered.

"Wrap your fingers around it and I'll slip my fingers under the crotch of this teddy and rub all those spots you know I love. Come on, baby, do it for me." After a moment she continued, "Are you touching your cock through your tight black shorts? Does it feel good? Sort of muffled through the fabric?"

"Yes."

"I'm sliding my fingers over my slit. I'm very wet." Her fingertips danced over her skin as she pulled the thin strip of fabric aside and explored her wetness. "Ummm," she purred, "it feels so good. And I love knowing that you're touching yourself, too." She stroked her clit with her index finger, listening to Paul's heavy breaths. "Yes, baby. Do it to your hard prick while I rub myself." There was a long silence during which the only sound was rapid breathing. "Do you know what I'm going to do?" Maggie asked, opening the drawer of her bedside table.

"What?" His voice was raspy and hoarse.

"I'm getting that big dildo, you know the one, the really big one that fills my pussy almost as well as your cock does." She pulled a large, flesh-colored penis from the drawer. "I'm going to rub it over my pussy while you slide your hand under the cotton of your shorts and hold your naked cock in your hand." She rubbed the artificial cock over her wet skin. "Ooh, that's cold. I'm going to push it inside. Hold your beautiful prick while I fill myself. We can pretend that you're here beside me."

Maggie heard Paul moan softly and she pushed the dildo into her cunt. "So full," she whispered. "So full of your hard shaft." She rubbed her clit faster as she moved the dildo inside her body. "I'm so close. Are you close, too?"

"Yes. Oh, yes, sweet thing."

"I'm going to come soon," she purred. "Come with me. Soon. Soon." She felt her climax building, flowing up through her, curling her toes and arching her back. "Yes," she cried as the heat flooded her body. "Yes." She could feel the clutching movements of her muscles against the artificial phallus as waves of pleasure engulfed her. "Yes."

"Yes," Paul called. "Right now."

For a while the only sound through the phone lines was panting and a few low moans. Then Maggie slowly withdrew the dildo from her body, reveling in the soft relaxation that always followed a good, hard climax. "That was so good," she said, her heartbeat slowing. "Not as good as having you here, of course."

"Oh, shit, sweet thing. I got goo all over the bedspread."

Maggie giggled. "It probably isn't the first time. It will wash. Just leave the chambermaid an extra-big tip."

"It never ceases to amaze me how easily you do that to me."

"That's what I'm good for. I love giving you pleasure, but," she said, not allowing him to interrupt, "that's not what you build a marriage on. Good sex is wonderful, but it's not enough."

"Oh, Maggie mine, it's not just good sex. We have great times together."

"I've got to go now, Paul. Call me when you get back."

"I will. Good night, and please think about marrying me."

"Good night, Paul." Maggie placed the receiver on its cradle and sighed. Maybe if I'd found someone like Paul twenty years ago, she thought, but things are as things are. She rubbed the heel of her hand up and down her breastbone trying to ease the sudden feeling of pressure. But I'm truly happy, she thought. I have regrets as everyone who is human does, but I enjoy making love and I'm well paid for it. And why not?

Maggie took a hot shower then climbed into her wide bed, already wondering what Carl would enjoy the following evening. Carl had the most creative mind. Maybe she'd use the handcuffs and spreader bar. She fell asleep, unconsciously rubbing her breastbone.

Maggie was totally confused. She was standing in a large room, now wearing a soft, flowing white garment. "What the hell . . ."

"Not exactly," a voice said through the heavy white mist that covered the ground and swirled about her waist as Maggie took a step forward.

"What's all this?" Maggie asked, her arched eyebrows almost meeting the middle. This is a very strange dream, she thought.

"You like the mist?" the woman's voice continued. "We had it added a few months ago. Gives the place a bit of atmosphere, don't you think?"

Unable to make out the speaker, Maggie took another couple of steps forward. "Real nice," she said dryly. This is the most bizarre dream I've had in a long time, she thought.

"It's not a dream, Margaret Mary."

"Lord, I haven't been called Margaret Mary since grammar school."

"That's right. Forgive me," the voice said, sounding genuinely sorry. "Maggie. Right?"

"Yes. Maggie. I hate to ask the obvious, but where am I?"

"That's a bit hard to explain," the voice continued. It was soft, melodious, and somehow soothing.

Maggie thought she should be afraid, but somehow she wasn't. Maybe she should be angry at whoever was playing a joke on her. But instinctively she knew it was no trick. A dream, she told herself again. This is all just a dream.

"No," another, sharper, voice said. "It's not a dream. We're quite real. Well, not real exactly."

"Lucy," the soft voice said, "let me do this. You'll just confuse Margaret Mary unnecessarily. Sorry. I mean Maggie."

"According to the record, she's Margaret Mary Sullivan. We should call her by her true name."

"Don't pout, dear," the soft voice said. "Let's just get this done, shall we?"

"You know I hate it when you take over," Lucy said.

"I know you do, but when you do the introductions, you tend to get pushy and scare people to death, so to speak."

Maggie took another few steps and was finally able to make out the shapes of two women seated at a long table. "Maggie, my dear," the soft voice said, "do sit down."

The speaker was a blonde, with shoulder-length hair that waved softly around her ears. She was extremely attractive with a perfect, heart-shaped face, tiny, sloping nose, and beautiful lips. Her most arresting feature was her eyes, sky blue and fathomless, making Maggie suddenly picture calm seas or featureless blue skies. Those eyes should look cold and distant, Maggie thought, but they gazed almost lovingly at Maggie and made her feel warm, somehow. The woman motioned Maggie to a folding chair at the table, her long graceful fingers almost hidden beneath the sleeve of the diaphanous white gown she wore.

"Yes, yes, sit. Please." The harsher voice came from a dark-haired, dark-eyed woman, dressed in a tight black scoop-necked top that showed off her deep cleavage to its greatest advantage. She wore heavy makeup that accentuated the slight catlike tilt to her deep-set eyes. Her eyes, like her tablemate's, were her most amazing feature, so dark brown they were almost black, with long curling lashes and magnificently arched black brows. As Maggie looked into this dark woman's eyes, she fleetingly pictured a deep, bottomless well. "I'm Lucy," the dark woman said.

"She already knows that," the woman in white said gently but firmly to her neighbor. Then she turned to Maggie. "And I'm Angela."

Maggie took a seat at the table, and crossed her legs in a businesslike fashion. "How do you do. Now, if it's not too much trouble, would one of you two ladies tell me what this is all about?"

"Yes, yes," the one called Lucy said. "You see, you've presented us with a considerable problem."

"I'm afraid Lucy's right," Angela said. "A considerable problem." She checked the computer monitor at her elbow, pressed a few keys and continued. "Most people are easy. One or two keystrokes, a peek at their history and the decision's made. Actually, we're going to introduce a system whereby the computer actually makes most of the decisions. Very straightforward. Usually."

Maggie looked at the two women, so different, yet unconsciously mimicking each other's motions. Patience, she told herself. I will understand this eventually.

"You, on the other hand," Lucy said, clicking a few keys on her own console, "are a real dilemma."

"I'm really sorry about that," Maggie said, having no idea what was going on but willing herself to play along with this dream or hallucination or whatever it was.

"No, dear," Angela said, "it's not a hallucination either."

"No, no, of course not." Lucy turned to Angela. "I told you that the mist might be misunderstood. But no, you had to add it. 'Gives the place an ethereal air,' you said." Lucy grumbled, "Now you see? It just adds to the natural confusion."

"It might help if you'd begin," Maggie said, "by telling me where we are. That might end some of the confusion."

"That's a bit hard to explain right off," Angela said.

"Well, why don't you try," Maggie snapped, beginning to get a bit impatient despite all her best efforts.

"You won't believe it," Angela continued, shaking her head.

"Just get on with it, Angela," Lucy snapped. "Oh, never mind. Look, honey," she said, staring at Maggie, "you're dead."

"I'm what?" Maggie shrieked, jumping up from her seat.

"Lucy, don't do that," Angela said. "It just scares people unnecessarily. You have to break these things to them gently. How many times have I told you?"

"If you had it your way," Lucy said, "we'd be here for hours, breaking the news so gently that I'd starve."

"Ladies!" Maggie yelled. "Could you please stop arguing and just tell me what's going on."

"Of course, dear," Angela said. "Now sit back down and try to open your mind to new experiences."

Maggie dropped into the chair, her wobbly legs suddenly unable to hold her weight.

"Actually," Angela said, "although she said it crudely, Lucy is right. You are dead. You died quietly in your sleep of a massive heart attack."

Maggie tried to grasp what she was being told. "I did what?"

"It's always hardest to understand," Angela continued, "when you've had no warning. The chronically ill. They understand. They've been expecting it. But you. You appeared to be in perfect health."

"But your coronary arteries," Lucy said. "Shot. Too many french fries and rare steaks." She gazed at the ceiling. "Actually, right now, a thick sirloin with a baked stuffed potato. . . ."

"Dead?" Maggie whispered, unable to make any louder sound come out of her mouth. "I'm dead? Really, truly forever dead?"

"I'm afraid so, dear," Angela said. "Remember that pain right here?" She pointed to her breastbone. "Just before you went to bed that night?"

Numbly, Maggie nodded.

"Well," Lucy said, then snapped her fingers loudly. "That was the beginning of the end."

"But," Angela said, "being dead is not bad. Really."

"Dead," Maggie muttered. "And what is this place?"

"We call it the computer room. It's kind of a decision station," Angela said. "You know, up or down." She motioned with her thumb.

"You mean heaven, hell, that sort of thing?"

"Exactly," Lucy said.

"I'm finding all this a bit hard to believe," Maggie said.

"I can understand that," Angela said. "But I think we can convince you." Angela stood up and turned her back to Maggie. Two glittering white wings extended from her shoulderblades through an opening in her gown. "Angela, angel, you get it. Right?" The wings quivered and Angela rose about five feet, then gracefully settled back down.

Lucy stood up and turned. The tight black catsuit had a small opening just above her buttocks, through which a long sinuous black tail extended. "Lucy, Lucifer. Okay?" She extended her index finger and a narrow shaft of flame shot out, then, as quickly, was extinguished.

"Shit," Maggie hissed.

"Don't curse," Angela said.

"Let her say what she wants," Lucy snapped. "After all, it's her life, or death, as it were."

Slowly, Maggie was starting to accept the unacceptable. "Does everyone come through here? And what happens now? Do I meet someone like Mr. Jordan in that movie with Warren Beatty?"

"Ah, yes, *Heaven Can Wait.* That movie has led to more misunderstandings than anything in the last fifty years," Lucy said. "People expect some kindly old gentleman, a mixture of God, Santa Claus, and James Mason. Nope. No one like that. Just us."

"Actually," Angela said, "very few people get to see us at all." She clicked a few keys on her computer keyboard, then continued. "It's usually very easy. People die and the decision's already made. Good, bad, up, down. It's usually pretty straightforward."

"But, as we told you before," Lucy said, "you are a problem."

"Really," Maggie said dryly, staring at the two women clicking away at their terminals.

"We have a decision to make here that will affect you for all eternity," the women said in unison. "Heaven," Angela said. "Or hell," Lucy added.

"And what's it like," Maggie asked, looking into Lucy's deep black eyes, "down there? Is it like the movies, all fire and brimstone?"

"Nah," Lucy said, "actually it's been air-conditioned. The staff couldn't bear the heat any longer. It's not pleasant, however.

Everyone has tedious tasks to perform, like the rock up the side of the mountain thing or cleaning up after the trolls or collating a thousand copies of my daily, hundred-page report.

"Or reading it," Angela said dryly.

Lucy glared at her, "Yes, lots of hard work and constant, blaring rock music." She rubbed the back of her neck. "And recently, we've added some rap. But you have the evenings off and the food's not half bad. Very hot, of course, vindalu curry and four-alarm chili at every meal." Lucy hesitated, then added, "What I wouldn't give for a steak, medium rare." She shook her head and grew silent.

"I see." Maggie turned to Angela expectantly.

"Oh, heaven's wonderful," she said, beaming beatifically. "There's sensational organ and harp music all the time, and we have little to do but relax on fluffy clouds and think wonderful thoughts. There is a constant supply of ambrosia to eat and nectar to drink and wonderful intellectual people to talk to." She sighed. "Ah, the talks we've had about the meaning of life and the future of mankind."

Maggie thought that hell sounded much more like her type of place, but she hesitated to say so in front of Angela. There was a lot at stake here. She waited for the two silent women to continue, but when long minutes passed, Maggie brought them back to the present. "And I'm a problem for you."

"Yes, yes, of course you are," Lucy said, her head snapping back to her console. "You're a prostitute, a hooker. You have sex with men for money. And you're unrepentant."

"I guess that's true," Maggie admitted. "I don't apologize for what I do." Suddenly a bit uneasy, she said, "Does that mean . . ." She made a thumbs-down signal with her right hand.

"It should," Lucy said. "It certainly should."

"But," Angela jumped in, "you're a truly nice person. Kind, considerate, loving. We checked your record." She turned the monitor on her computer toward Maggie and clicked a few more keys. "Remember Jake? It was just a month or so before you, er, died."

On the screen, Maggie could see a view of her apartment. Jake. She remembered that evening well as the scene played out.

The doorbell rang. Maggie rose gracefully from her chair, slid the crossword puzzle she had been working on under the seat cushion, straightened her simple yellow tennis sweater and rubbed her hands down the thighs of her jeans. "Coming," she called. She crossed the large living room and opened the door. "You must be Jake," she said, careful not to touch the young man who stood awkwardly before her. "Please come in."

She backed up and motioned for Jake to come inside, but the young man didn't budge. She looked him over quickly, noting his carefully combed sandy-brown hair and his gray tweed sport jacket and black slacks. She knew from his father that he was seventeen, but at that moment he looked about twelve, with large ears and skin deeply scarred from childhood acne. She tried not to smile at the nervous twining and retwining of his fingers and his deer-in-the-headlights expression. There had been so many similar young men over the years and most of them had looked like Jake.

"You don't look like . . ." Jake swallowed hard, his eyes uneasily flicking from her face to her breasts. "I mean . . . You look nice. I don't mean . . ."

"Jake," Maggie said, "I know exactly what you mean. Come inside. I promise it will be just fine." She reached for his arm, but he entered the lavish apartment without the need for her to touch him.

Jake stopped, standing restlessly in the center of the room. "This is really nice," he said, looking anywhere but at her.

"Thanks. I've collected lots of treasures over the years. I enjoy having things around me that have special memories." She crossed to a small white linen-and-lace butterfly that seemed to have settled in the corner of a framed photo of an old European village. "There's a town in Belgium called Bruges. It looks like it hasn't changed in four hundred years." Jake walked over and looked over her shoulder, and she sensed his effort not to let any part of his body touch hers. "Wonderful old buildings," she said softly, "churches that were old before our country ever thought about George Washington. I was there about six, no, seven years ago. They cater to tourists, of course, but the city is an old center for lace making and they still make some." She ran the tip of her finger over the butterfly's white lace wings.

"That's real nice," Jake said, tangling and untangling his fingers.

"And this," she said, pointing to a smoothly carved statuette of a seal perched on a rock, "is a soapstone carving that I got in Anchorage a few years ago." She picked up the six-inch-high stone piece and placed it in Jake's hand. "I liked the shape, but what sold me was the way it felt in my hand the first time I held it." She stroked the back of the seal. "Cool and so soft," she said as Jake imitated her movement without actually touching her hand. She took the seal from him and replaced it on the mantel.

"Come on, Jake, let's sit down. We can talk for a while. About anything you like." Deliberately, she sat in a chair rather than on the long sofa. She watched Jake's face relax as he sat on the end of the sofa nearest her chair, keeping his knees from touching hers. "Would you like a drink?" Maggie asked. "I have soda, wine, beer, whatever you might like."

"Could I have a beer?" he asked, then cleared his throat.

"Sure. I have Bud, Miller, Miller light, and Sam Adams." She grinned. "I sound like a waitress. Actually, to be honest, I did wait on tables many years ago."

"What are you having?" Jake said.

"I thought I'd have a Sam Adams," Maggie said.

Jake smiled tentatively. "Okay. Me too."

Maggie walked into the kitchen of the large Madison Avenue apartment, knowing that Jake was watching her retreating ass, which was barely contained in the tight jeans she wore. Not bad for a broad on the far side of fifty, she thought as she opened two beers. She placed them on a tray, pulled two mugs out of the freezer, balanced the tray on her palm and returned to the living room. "See," she grinned, holding the tray at shoulder level. "I used to be very good at this." She twirled the tray, set it down on the coffee table and deftly poured two beers.

She handed Jake his drink, took a swallow of hers and resettled in her chair. She smiled as Jake took several large gulps of the cold liquid. "Gee," he said, "this is nice."

"Tell me about you," Maggie said. "Your father tells me you're at Yale."

For the next fifteen minutes, as Jake visibly relaxed, they talked about Jake's classes, his plans for the future, his social life at school. When they had finished their first round, Maggie went into the kitchen for two more beers. "I guess I don't date much," Jake admitted as Maggie reentered the living room, the two fresh bottles on the tray, along with a large bowl of popcorn. "I'm not very good-looking either." He ran a finger over his chin and through a few deep pits on his jawline.

"You'll never be Paul Newman," Maggie said softly, putting the tray on the coffee table. She prided herself on never lying to anyone. "But you do have his eyes." Jake's eyes were sky blue, deeply set, with long sandy lashes.

"I do?" Jake said. Then ducked his chin and quickly added, "Don't bullshit me."

"I'm not," Maggie said, keeping her voice soft. "You've got beautiful eyes." She moved to sit beside him on the sofa. "Would you like some popcorn?" She picked a piece from the bowl and held it in front of her mouth. "It's very garlicky so I won't have any if you're not going to."

Jake reached out to take a piece of popcorn, but Maggie held the one in her hand out for him. "Here, take this one," she said.

He reached for it, taking it from her while barely skimming his fingertips over hers. He popped the piece of corn into his mouth. "This is really good," he said, reaching for a handful.

"Aren't you going to return the favor?" Maggie asked, raising one eyebrow. "You took my popcorn . . ."

Slowly he took a piece of popcorn from the bowl and held it out to her. She leaned over and took it from his fingertips with her teeth, nipping his index finger lightly. She watched him pull his hand back as though burned. "Do you know," she said, swallowing, "that I met your father through a few of his friends when he was in college?"

"You're kidding. That was a hundred years ago."

"I was in business even then, back in the dark ages. I fought dinosaurs with one hand while keeping track of my customers on clay tablets."

Jake looked sheepish. "I'm sorry."

Maggie laughed, no trace of scorn, only rich warm enjoyment. "Don't be. I know it seems like centuries, and maybe it was. But I did meet your father kind of like this."

"He never told me how he knew you. I guess I thought he met you after Mom died."

"He hadn't even met your mom when I first knew him. A few of his fraternity brothers were, let's just say, friends of mine. They dared him to visit me, even paid his way." Maggie sat back on the sofa and rested her head on the back. She kicked off her shoes and, at her glance, Jake did the same. She ran her long fingers through her tight black curls. "My hair was naturally this color back then," she remembered. "He was so cute. Scared to death, like you are now."

"I'm not scared," Jake protested.

"It's all right to be nervous," Maggie said. "I was living in a small apartment in Greenwich Village and he came to my place that first evening." She giggled. "He spilled an entire bottle of Scotch on my sofa, as I recall."

Jake laughed. "He did?"

"He offered to pour us each a drink, but his hands shook so much that he couldn't get the top off the bottle. He twisted one last time, the top came off in his hand and, of course, the bottle was upside down. It took weeks to get the smell out of the upholstery."

"I can't picture my dad as a nervous teenager."

"No one can picture others having the same fears, the same feelings of inadequacy they have. I remember a certain rock star who, well let's just say, couldn't get it up."

"Who?"

"I never reveal any of the secrets I learn," Maggie said. "But, if these walls could talk. . . ."

"What did he do?" Jake asked, his eyes widening. "The rock star, I mean."

"We sat and talked. Once he was comfortable with the fact I didn't want anything from him, that he could do what he chose, he relaxed." Maggie giggled. "We actually played spin the bottle. Then we made love. Several times, as I remember.'

"And my dad?"

"Uh, uh. No tales about anyone like that. How would you feel if I told him about you?"

Jake flinched. "Okay. Point made."

"Is it warm in here?" Maggie asked, pulling her sweater off over her head. She smiled as she felt Jake gaze at her erect nipples, clearly visible through her white stretch tank top. "Why don't you take off your jacket?"

Maggie didn't move while Jake removed his sport jacket, his eyes never leaving her ample breasts. Without lifting her head from the back of the sofa, she turned to Jake. "You know what I'd like to do? How about some slow dancing." She sat up and leaned forward, giving Jake a good view of her large breasts and deep cleavage. She reached for the remote control on the coffee table and pressed a button. As Michael Bolton's voice filled the room, Maggie stood up and held her hands out to Jake. "Come on. Dance with me."

Hesitantly, Jake stood up and walked around the coffee table. "I don't dance much."

"That's really too bad," Maggie said as she moved into Jake's arms, keeping space between them. "I love slow dancing. It's like making love to music."

Jake placed one arm gingerly around Maggie's waist and held her hand with the other. He slowly shifted his weight from one foot to the other.

"Relax," Maggie said, leading him, helping him to move more gracefully. "You're doing fine." She pressed her body closer, so the tips of her nipples brushed his shirtfront. She felt him shiver, his hands trembling. She hummed along with the music, slowly moving closer until her mouth was against his ear, her chest pressed fully against his. His excitement was evident against her lower body. "This is so nice," she said into his ear.

"Ummm, he purred, moving his feet with increasing sureness. "This *is* nice."

"And we're in no hurry," Maggie whispered. As the songs changed, the two moved around the living room, locked in each other's arms. She could feel his growing hunger and nursed it until she knew the time had come. "Would you like to kiss me?" she whispered, leaning away from Jake's body.

Unable to answer, Jake pressed his mouth hard against Maggie's.

"Soft," she murmured as she cupped her hands against his cheeks and pulled back slightly, gentling the kiss, her feet still moving in time to the music. Her lips whispering against his, Maggie said, "Kissing and dancing. So good. So slow and soft." She could feel his heavy breathing against her mouth and she kissed his cheek gently. She murmured soft nonsense words, kissed his face and ran the tip of her tongue over the skin of which he was so self-conscious. He tried to pull away, but her hands and the pressure of her body held him immobile.

Without breaking contact with his mouth, Maggie slid her hands between them, unbuttoned his shirt and pulled it off of his shoulders. His chest was hairless and surprisingly smooth as she slid her palms over his skin. "I know you would like to feel my breasts against your body." In one swift motion, she pulled her tank top over her head and, as they continued to dance, she rubbed her nipples over his skin. Minutes later, when she knew he was ready, she took his hands and placed them on her ribs. Her palms covering his, she guided his hands up her sides, to her breasts. "Yes," she putted. "Hold them, feel them. Yes. Like that."

His eyes watched his hands as his fingers played with her nipples, his breathing ragged, his feet still moving to the music.

Maggie helped him, showing him where she wanted to be touched, how she liked to be pinched gently but firmly. Then she placed one finger under his chin and raised his face. She held his gaze and said, softly, "We will be a lot more comfortable in the other room."

Both naked to the waist, the two walked into Maggie's bedroom, Michael Bolton's voice following them through the apartment. The bedroom was large, dominated by a king-size bed covered with a soft off-white satin spread and a dozen pillows in bright reds, blues, and violets. The thick carpet was white, covered by an area rug of a bright geometric design in the same colors. There were two white leather side chairs with matching hassocks and a lounge chair with a chrome frame and black leather webbing. Jake's eyes widened. "I know," Maggie said, her arm around Jake's naked waist, "it's a bit flashy. But it makes me happy."

Jake turned to face the older woman. He tangled his fingers in her black curls. "You're quite something," he said. "And not what I expected at all." He pressed his lips to hers, now more sure in his motions. "I want you." He reached down and started to unzip his pants.

"Let me," Maggie said, running her fingernails down his chest and moving his hands aside. She deftly unfastened his pants and, in one motion, pulled down both his slacks and his shorts until he stood naked except for his socks. She knelt and pulled them off, her eyes level with the stiff, hard erection that stuck straight out from Jake's groin. She resisted the urge to take his hard cock into her mouth, knowing that their first time together should be plain vanilla. There would be time later to introduce Jake to the dozens of other pleasures she enjoyed.

"Would you like to undress me, or should I do it?" she asked.

Jake grinned and held his trembling hands in front of him. "I think you'd better."

Quickly she pulled off her jeans, panties and socks and led Jake to the bed. She stretched out on the spread and patted the space next to her. "Come here, darling. Let's try slow dancing this way." He lay beside her and she placed the soles of her feet against his insteps. Slowly she slid their feet over the satin spread, keeping the rhythm they had established in the living room. "Slow dancing isn't just for standing up." She wrapped one arm around him and took his hand with the other, holding him just as if they were dancing. She moved against him until the length of her body was against the length of his. Quickly she took a condom from the bedtable drawer and deftly unrolled it over Jake's throbbing cock. Then she maneuvered so her body was beneath his, her legs spread, the tip of his erection against the soaked folds of her entrance. "Yes?" she whispered. "Do you want me?"

"Oh, yes," he moaned.

"Then you know what to do."

He pushed his hips forward, sliding his cock deep inside Maggie's body. Maggie cupped his buttocks and held him still for a moment, then moved, still in the rhythm of the music. "Yes, sweet," she putted. "Dance with me. Do it. Make it feel so good."

It was only moments until Jake came, his hips pounding against Maggie's. "Oh, Maggie," he bellowed. "Oh, yes." He collapsed against her, then rolled onto one side, his cock sliding limply from her body. "Oh," he groaned, clutching her against him. "Too fast."

"Now comes the first lesson," she said, taking his hand and guiding it to her wet pussy. "You came, but I didn't. I need you to help me, to give me the same pleasure you just got."

Suddenly tense, he said, "I don't know how."

"Of course you don't," Maggie said. "How could you unless someone showed you?" She held one of Jake's fingers and rubbed it over her swollen clit. "This is where most of a woman's pleasure comes from. Rub like this." She showed him and found he was a fast learner. "Yes," she said, "like that." As she arched her back, she said, "Put two fingers of your other hand inside me. It will feel so good for me and you will feel what it's like when a woman comes."

Jake inserted his index and middle finger into Maggie's cunt and slowly stretched her hungry flesh. "Don't stop rubbing right here," she said, reminding his fingers where she got the most pleasure. "Yes," she purred. "And I like it if you suck my tit, too."

With his mouth on her nipple, his fingers filling her and his other hand rubbing her clit, Maggie could feel the familiar tightness start deep in her belly. "Yes," she said, "like that. Oh, baby, don't stop." The heat grew and filled her lower body until it exploded. "Feel what my body does when it comes," she cried. "Feel it. Share it." Waves of muscular spasms clenched at Jake's fingers.

"I've never felt anything like that," he said, his voice filled with wonder. "It makes me so hot. Can I fuck you again?"

"Of course," Maggie said, barely able to talk through the waves of pleasure. She felt him withdraw his fingers, put on a fresh condom and slide into her again. Still coming, the waves of orgasm engulfed both of them as Jake climaxed again.

Later, as they dressed, Jake said, "I never knew."

"I know, and that's what I love about doing this. I can introduce someone as sweet as you to a joy that will continue for the rest of your life. There's a lot more, too."

"I know. Can I see you again?"

"Of course," Maggie said. "Call and we'll make another date. And we can work out finances then."

"Thanks, Maggie," Jake said. "I never dreamed that this evening would be this wonderful and so," he winked, "educational. When he first approached me about this, I thought my dad was nuts."

"Give him my love," Maggie said as she guided Jake to the door.

"I will." Jake kissed her good-bye and grinned as she closed the door behind him.

"You see," Lucy said, looking up from her computer terminal. "You're a nice person. I hate that."

"But, you also have sex with married men for money," Angela said sadly.

"But I never do it without first suggesting that the men discuss things with their wives," Maggie said. "Men don't realize that their wives might be just as interested in some fun and games as they are." Maggie had little use for timid women who didn't understand the pleasures of lovemaking.

"I know that," Angela said. "But remember this evening? It was just last winter."

As Maggie stared, the monitor showed the face of Gerry O'Malley. A sales representative for a computer software firm, Gerry had been recommended to her by an old friend. She recalled their first evening together and how she had tried to convince him to share his fantasies with his wife. Adamantly refusing, Gerry and Maggie had made love in his hotel room, then arranged to meet there the following Wednesday. "I want something special," he had said, his hands clenched tightly, his fingers twined. "Dress up. Would you wear white . . . ?"

Chapter 2

Maggie had dressed in a white knit dress, short enough to show off her long, well-shaped legs and low cut enough to highlight the shadowed valley between her breasts. She added light gray thigh-high stockings, held up by elastic lace at the tops, and gold strappy sandals with four-inch heels. Long gold earrings that brushed her shoulders and a heavy gold necklace completed her outfit. She was not overly made up and her lipstick was soft pink.

Dressed in gray slacks and a light blue shirt, Gerry opened the door to his hotel room and stared, his face flushed. "You look wonderful," he said to Maggie. Gerry was medium height with thick brown hair with a hint of gray at the temples. Clean shaven, his jaw was tightly clenched and he stood filling the doorway.

Maggie smiled. "May I come in?" she asked, her voice soft and melodious.

Almost stumbling, Gerry backed away from the door. "I, uh, ordered some champagne," he said.

"Good. We both need to relax," Maggie said, patting Gerry on the arm. "It will all be fine. Really."

Almost bonelessly, Gerry dropped onto the sofa in the sitting room of the two-room suite. "I know."

With a practiced hand Maggie opened the champagne bottle

and half-filled two flutes from the tray. "Here," she said, handing Gerry a glass, "sip this."

Gerry emptied the glass. "I guess it shows," he said. "That I'm really nervous. About this, I mean."

Maggie laughed. "It does show. But what are you so nervous about? We were together last week and it was very pleasurable."

"I want something different from what we did last week."

"That's fine with me. What would give you pleasure?"

Gerry took his wallet out of his back pocket and withdrew ten fifty-dollar bills. "I understand that I can pay extra for something special." He counted out four more fifties and handed all seven hundred dollars to Maggie. "I want to have you completely in my power. I want to feed you a potent sex drug. I mean," he hesitated, "I mean that I want to be able to do everything to you and have you beg for more." Maggie could see his throat muscles work as he swallowed hard.

"You do remember my rules. No real drugs and if you decide you want to have sexual intercourse, you will use a condom."

"Of course. I remember everything you told me last week and I will abide by your rules. No problem."

"And I get no pleasure from serious pain, so whips and things like that are not for me."

"I understand."

Maggie looked up at Gerry from beneath her long lashes. She smiled. "How will you give me this drug, or have you done that already?"

Gerry hesitated, then grinned and said, "Yes. Yes. I did give it to you already. It was in the champagne."

"Is that why I'm feeling so warm?" Maggie said, slipping into the role Gerry wanted her to play.

"It certainly is."

Maggie stretched out on the sofa and fanned herself with her hand. "I'm so hot, baby. So hot."

"Yes, you certainly are. Maybe you'd better take off your dress."

"Oh, yes," Maggie said, standing up and turning her back to

Gerry. "Would you help me unzip? I seem to be all thumbs. I can't seem to make my hands work right."

Maggie could feel Gerry's cold fingers on her back as he fumbled with the zipper. As he slid the zipper down, Maggie began to move her hips. "I don't know what's wrong with me," she said, her voice low and breathy. "I can't seem to stand still." She wiggled out of her dress, let it fall around her feet and stepped out of it. Maggie had selected a pale pink satin bra and matching bikini panties. Although her age couldn't help but show, her frequent aerobic classes kept her figure tight. She rubbed her palms over the tips of her breasts. "God, I can't stand this. I'm so . . . I don't know."

Gerry stared at Maggie's breasts which more than filled the small cups of her bra. "Are you uncomfortable?" he asked with mock innocence.

"I don't know," Maggie answered, undulating her hips and rubbing her nipples. She watched Gerry's eyes, and from the gleam surmised that the fantasy was playing out to his satisfaction. "I just want something."

"I know exactly what you want and only I can give it to you."

"Please. Do it. Help me. I'm so hot."

"I know. You're hot all over, aren't you. Especially between your legs. Hot and itchy. Do you need to rub yourself?"

"Oh, yes," Maggie moaned.

When Maggie's fingertips started to slide under the elastic of her panties, Gerry pulled it back. "Well, you can't. Not yet. Not until I give you permission. Do you understand?"

"Yes. But . . ."

"No buts. You are mine to command and I say you may not have any relief yet."

Maggie played the game. "Please. Don't make me suffer like this. I need to rub and touch and stroke myself. I need to make myself come."

"I will let you when you've been a good girl and done your chores."

"What chores?"

"First you must undress me."

"Oh, yes. May I undress you very slowly? May I kiss and touch you, caress you and make you as hot as I am?"

Gerry spread his arms wide, wordlessly indicating she could begin. Maggie closed the distance between them and pressed the length of her body against his. Sinuously she rubbed her chest and thighs against his as she licked his lips. Then she unbuttoned his shirt, licking his chest as she exposed it. Slowly she pulled the tails from the waistband of his slacks, rubbing her pelvis against his erection as she did so. With her entire body pressed against his, she worked the shirt down over his arms and tossed it on a chair. Her hard nipples pressed against the fabric of her bra and she sensuously rubbed them across his lightly furred chest. "Oh, baby," she purred as she moved around behind him, constantly rubbing her body against his side, his arm, his back, stroking his skin with her satin-covered breasts and mound.

She moved completely around him until she was again in front of him. She knelt at his feet and put her fingers on his belt buckle. She gazed up at him, a silent question in her eyes.

"Say please," Gerry said.

"Oh, please. Let me." Slowly she pulled the end of his belt through the loops and unfastened the buckle. With fumbling fingers she unbuttoned and unzipped his fly. "Oh, baby," she putted. "You're not wearing anything underneath." Careful not to touch his large, fully erect cock, she pulled his slacks down and, at her signal, he stepped out of them.

"Are you hot enough to suck my cock?" Gerry asked.

"I don't have to be hot to want to suck such a beautiful cock," Maggie said, sensing these were the right words at the right time. She looked up at him. "Please. May I?"

Gerry wrapped one hand around his erect penis and aimed it at her mouth. His grin said that this was progressing exactly the way he had imagined.

"Do you have to touch it?" Maggie asked. "I want to hold it and suck it myself."

"Even better, Gerry said, his mouth open and his breathing quick.

Still kneeling at Gerry's feet, Maggie placed one finger on the tip of his cock and rubbed the tiny drop of pre-come around the head. "I want to taste you." She flicked the tip of Gerry's cock with the end of her tongue and watched him shiver. Afraid his knees would buckle, she said, "I would like to go into the bedroom, if that's all right with you."

"Yes," Gerry said, breathless. "Of course." Quickly they moved into the other room and Gerry stretched out on the bed on his back. "Now, he said, "continue what you were doing."

Maggie spread his legs, then climbed onto the bed and crouched between his thighs. "Right here," she said, wrapping her hand around the hard staff that stuck straight up into the air. "And right here." She licked the tip, then, making a tight ring with her lips, she sucked him into her mouth.

She looked toward his face and saw that his eyes were closed. "Look at me," she said, "and watch me suck your cock." She watched his eyes open and the glazed expression as he looked at her head, bobbing on his cock.

"Good," he moaned. "Good." It took only moments until he shot his come into Maggie's mouth. "Good," he yelled. "So good."

Maggie fingered his balls until he was completely drained.

Not even thinking about the fact that Maggie was unsatisfied, Gerry disappeared into the bathroom and Maggie heard the sound of the shower. "That was wonderful," he called from the bathroom. "I need to get cleaned up now." His tone was dismissive, so, with a sigh, Maggie dressed, wandered into the living room and poured herself another glass of champagne. It was far from the first time she had been asked to perform oral sex on a man who believed that it was such an onerous task that his wife wouldn't want to satisfy his hunger for fellatio. Nibbling on some of the peanuts from the champagne tray, she gathered Gerry's clothes and walked back into the bedroom. "I will leave now, unless there's something else you want." She folded his slacks and shirt and put them on the foot of the bed. She put his wallet on the dresser.

"No. That was fantastic."

Maggie counted out four of the fifty-dollar bills he had given her and put them on the dresser with his wallet. "It was wonderful for me, too," she said. "You know, oral sex isn't a chore at all. I really enjoy it."

"I guess your kind does."

Stung, but understanding, Maggie left the suite.

As the scene faded, Angela said, "See what I mean? He was a married man and you did what you did for money. That's adultery and it's a sin."

"Oh, lighten up, Angela," Lucy said, clicking the keys on her terminal. "Get real. It's done all the time. Sex is fun stuff and everyone should have his or her share."

"Yes. I suppose you're right to a point. I do take this sin thing a bit too seriously. But that still leaves us with a problem." She turned to Maggie. "You."

"Okay. So what does that mean exactly?" Maggie asked.

"Well," Lucy said, "I've talked Angela into giving you a way to help us make the decision. A task for you to do. Like the labors of Hercules and all that."

"Yes, Lucy did come up with an idea. We have someone for you to teach about sex. Someone who's so ignorant, it's shameful even to me."

Maggie grinned. "Teach some guy about sex? That's what I do best and enjoy the most."

"That's not exactly what we had in mind," Lucy said. "It's not a guy, it's a girl."

"I have to teach a girl about sex? A little girl?"

"A grown woman. Actually, she's thirty-one," Angela said. "And she's never had a good experience in bed. A few bad experiences since high school and no real boyfriends."

"Is she a nun? A total dog? Come on. Give me a break here."

"Actually," Lucy said, "she's a nice woman, which makes me dislike her from the start."

"She's sweet," Angela continued, "and she cared for her dying mother for eight years. During the final two, Barbara moved into her mother's house and tended to her almost nonstop. She had a nurse come in during the day while she was at work, but Barbara was with her mother almost every other minute."

"What does she do?"

"She's a secretary to a big-time lawyer type," Lucy said, "and she's half in love with him. But during all the time she lived with her mother, she had no time to consider dating. Now that Mom's no longer around, she has no clue where to start, and no self-confidence at all."

"And why do you two care?" Maggie asked.

"Well, actually it was her mother who got us interested," Lucy said. "She came through here about six months ago and asked us for help before we told her where she was to go." Lucy and Angela looked at each other and made the thumbs-up signal. "She was a good and caring woman and regretted what she had put her daughter through. Ugh. Self-sacrifice. I hate that, too." Lucy made a face.

"Anyway," Angela said, "we haven't done anything about it until now, but this seemed to be a great opportunity to put you to work to help us decide about which way you go, and do something for that nice mother, too."

"And," Maggie said, "put off the decision about me."

Lucy grinned. "And there is that as well."

"Okay," Maggie said. "If that's the only way to get a bit more time to play, it's okay with me. Do I get powers?"

"Powers?"

"Yeah. Like Michael Landon on *Highway to Heaven*. Remember, he had the *stuff*."

"The *stuff*? Oh, yes, I remember, Angela. He did little magic things. Tossed bad people into swimming pools and made flowers bloom for nice folks."

"I do remember." Angela sighed. "I always loved that show.

Sent that nice Mr. Landon straight upstairs when he came through."

"Sorry but no *stuff*, Maggie. Only Barbara, that's her name by the way, only Barbara will be able to see and hear you. You can appear to her and converse with her when the two of you are alone. In public, she'll be able to see you, but no one else will."

"As to powers," Angela said, "I think not, although if we see that you're getting into trouble we may, and I emphasize may, help you out."

"This is sink or swim for you, girl," Lucy said. "If you succeed and help Barbara become a sexually whole person, you'll get to go up there." She raised her eyes heavenward.

"But," Angela said, "if you louse this up, it's . . ." She aimed her thumb at the floor and Lucy grinned.

"I'm not so sure where I want to be or, for that matter where I belong." Maggie sighed. "Okay. Tell me more about this hardship case of mine."

Angela and Lucy looked at each other, then Angela began. "She's not a hardship case. She's a very nice woman who has just gone through some difficult times."

"I know. Her mother and all." Maggie tapped her foot on the soft floor. "So what's her problem. Men?"

"I guess that's the heart of it."

"Is she still in mourning for her mother?" Maggie asked. "That will make my job much harder, you know."

"She's not really in mourning," Angela said. "Her mother's death, when it finally came, was a blessing. It had been a long and very rough time."

"She lives in Westchester County," Lucy continued, "in the house that used to belong to her mother. Her father died when she was only four."

"No brothers or sisters?" Maggie asked.

"No. And no other close relatives either."

"How do I meet her?"

Lucy's fingers clacked the computer keys. She swiveled the monitor so Maggie could see. Slowly the picture crystallized.

Maggie watched the image of a plain-looking woman materialize. "That's Barbara," Lucy said, "right now." There was momentary sound, but Lucy tapped what must have been a mute button.

Maggie looked at the screen. A nondescript-looking woman sat beside a desk, typing furiously on a laptop computer as the hunky-looking man behind the desk talked. She saw him pick up the phone on his desk, press the receiver against his ear and swivel his chair so his back was toward the woman, who continued to work on the laptop.

Maggie watched Barbara tuck an errant strand of her shoulder-length medium-brown hair behind one ear while her boss talked on. "Look at that woman," Maggie said. "She's not even wearing makeup. And that blouse . . ." Barbara was wearing an orangy-yellow blouse and a brown tweed skirt. "It's so wrong for her coloring. And sensible shoes, no doubt. Who's the guy?"

"That's Steve Gordon, one of the partners of Gordon, Watson, Kelly and Wise." Angela gazed at the screen. "He's rich, bright, successful, and very eligible. And as I said, she's crazy about him."

Maggie watched Steve hang up the phone and turn back toward Barbara. He opened a desk drawer, propped his feet on it and began to talk. Lucy tapped the button and the three women could hear the sound.

"That was Lisa," the man said. "Make me a reservation for eight o'clock tonight at Enrico's and send her a dozen roses. No, on second thought, make it just an arrangement."

"Of course," Barbara said. Maggie caught the heat of the woman's gaze as she looked at her boss, while he seemed oblivious.

"Well, that's your job, for starters," Lucy said, tapping the mute button again. "First a physical makeover, then the rest."

"Yes," Angela said. "I think she should end up with that gorgeous Mr. Gordon. I can see it. A large house in the country, kids, horses, dogs . . .

"Actually," Maggie said, "he reminds me of Arnie Becker on *LA Law*. A real ladies' man and just a bit sleazy."

"Yeah," Lucy said, "me too. But Barbara really likes him."

"She would," Maggie said, rolling her eyes.

"Well, I think he's perfect," Angela said.

"Does it have to end up with them together for me to succeed?" Maggie asked, thinking that Arnie was all wrong for Barbara.

"Oh, no, of course not," Lucy said. "Actually, I think she should get out, see the world, maybe end up like you did."

"Free will," Angela said. "That's what we advocate here. Her life is her choice. It's just that she has no real choices now. We want to grant her mother's request and see what happens."

"Do you think you're ready for the task?" Lucy asked.

"I guess so." Maggie shrugged her shoulders. What choice did she have? This was kind of like the Mad Tea Party in *Alice in Wonderland*, but her options were few. And, of course, this project did buy time for her back on earth. Wondering how long she could stretch this out, she uncrossed her legs and waited for the magical zap to transport her to meet Barbara.

"Well?" Angela said, raising an eyebrow.

"I'm waiting for the magic," Maggie answered.

Lucy motioned in the direction from which Maggie had entered the room. "The elevator's that way. Just press the ground-floor button."

"Oh, Maggie said, standing up. She looked down at her diaphanous white gown. "And do I get clothes? This is a bit overly dramatic, don't you think? I'll scare poor Barbara to death."

"Hmmm," Lucy said. "You're right. We'll see to it that there are proper clothes in the waiting room on the ground floor. It's on the right just this side of the front door. Change, then go out the door and you'll be just where you should be."

Maggie nodded, then turned toward the door. "Good luck," Angela and Lucy said in unison.

"Thanks," Maggie said over her shoulder. "I guess."

As the computer room door closed behind Maggie, Lucy held out her hand to Angela. "It's a bet?"

Angela took the proffered hand. "I firmly believe that Barbara will end up settled and happy in six months. Mrs. Steven Gordon. It has a nice ring to it, doesn't it."

"And I believe that once she discovers sex, there'll be no stopping her. Whoever invented it, it's the strongest drive we have, thank Lucifer. She'll get into no end of trouble and she'll love it. I'll bet on it."

"You know, people would never believe that you want anyone to be happy. You're supposed to represent misery, suffering, and hardship, and here you are betting on happiness of one sort or another."

"I know. But happiness isn't all it's cracked up to be either."

In the room on the ground floor, Maggie found a pair of well-washed jeans, a soft light gray turtleneck sweater along with underwear, socks, and slightly worn running shoes. She dressed, leaving the almost-transparent white gown on a hook behind the door. Then she left the room and walked across what appeared to be a marble lobby toward the revolving door. When she pushed the brass handle, the door turned and she exited on the other side, right into what she somehow knew was Barbara Enright's bedroom. Fortunately, Barbara wasn't in it at the time. Maggie could hear sounds from the kitchen below. "God," she muttered, recognizing the unmistakable sound of a food processor, "I'll bet she cooks, too." She shook her head, then crossed to the large walk-in closet, pulled the door open and flipped on the light.

Oh, Lord, she thought, riffling through a collection of slightly dowdy dresses, blouses, and suits. Way in the back, she found a soft chiffon dress in shades of blue. She lifted the hanger from the rod and held the dress at arm's length. It was slightly out of style, but beautiful nonetheless. "Now this is more like it," she said, putting the dress back where she had found it. "There's hope yet."

Suddenly she realized that she had been moving things and feeling things just like she had when she'd been alive. Phew. Been alive. That sounds awful. I don't feel dead. Actually, she thought, pinching her arm, I don't feel any differently than I did yesterday. She looked at the darkened window. It must be evening now, she thought, but I thought it was morning when I was with the gruesome twosome up there and I was on the phone with Paul last evening, I guess.

She looked at Barbara's bedside table and spotted the clock. "Five-thirty and it's pitch dark," she said aloud. "But it should still be light. It's midsummer." She crossed to the window and looked out. There were small areas of snow on the ground and the stars shone brightly in a blue-black sky. "I guess time doesn't work for the girls the way it works here on earth." She thought about Lucy and Angela and marveled at how sanguine she had become about something so impossible. "I feel like a character in a play and soon the curtain will go down or we'll break for a commercial and all this will all make sense." She shrugged again. "Oh, well." She crossed to the door and started down the stairs. "Better get this over with."

Dressed in a baggy sweat suit, Barbara Enright scooped the butter-and-garlic mix from the food processor and carefully spread it on the slices of French bread she had laid out on the cutting board. Meticulously she covered the bread to the edges so it would toast properly under the broiler. As she finished the second slice, she reached out and almost without looking swirled a spoon through the small pot of simmering marinara sauce. She popped the bread in the oven, then lifted a strand of spaghetti with the clawlike device and snipped off about an inch. She popped the piece in her mouth and chewed thoughtfully. Still just a bit too firm, she thought, remembering when she had to get it almost mushy so her mother could chew it.

As she mused, she realized that her mother's death didn't hurt anymore. With almost seven months gone by, she could remember the wonderful life her mother had led before the pain.

Barbara tucked a strand of hair behind her ear, stirred the sauce and checked on the bread. She pulled one of her mother's good Límoges plates from the closet, poured a Coke and set herself a place on the large kitchen table. With perfect timing born of years of cooking for herself and her mother, Barbara removed the bread from the oven, drained and served the spaghetti and poured sauce over the top. She flipped on the TV on the counter and watched *I Love Lucy* fade in from the darkness.

"Some red wine would really go better with that."

Barbara jumped and tipped over her chair at the sound of the voice behind her. With one hand reaching for the phone, her fingers ready to dial 911, she turned slowly. "Who the hell . . ."

"It's okay," the jeans-clad figure said. "It's really okay. I'm Maggie and we're going to be spending quite a bit of time together for a while."

"Get out before I call the police," Barbara said, trying to make her quavering voice sufficiently forceful.

"Don't do that or you'll look like a fool," Maggie said, crossing the kitchen and leaning over the pot on the stove. "Nice sauce. I always loved a good marinara sauce." She lifted a strand of spaghetti and dangled it over he mouth. Nipping off the bottom, she said, "Vermicelli. And properly al dente. Not many people know how to cook pasta correctly."

Barbara stood, mouth slightly open, with her hand on the phone. For some reason she couldn't quite fathom, she hadn't lifted the receiver yet.

"I know," Maggie said, picking up a slice of garlic bread, "this is something of a shock, but believe me, it's taking me a little while to adjust, too." She took a large bite and chewed thoughtfully. "You know, I don't even know whether I can eat." She swallowed. "I guess I can, but I'm not very hungry." She pulled out the chair opposite Barbara's and sat down. "Wouldn't you know it. I can probably eat what I want and not gain weight, but I'm not hungry."

"Would . . ." Barbara cleared her throat and tried again. "Would you kindly tell me what the hell you're doing here?"

"I'm not here to hurt you," Maggie said, swallowing the chewed mouthful. "But before I try to explain, you'd really better sit down."

Barbara thought she should be afraid, but she was more baffled than frightened. This woman had arrived in her kitchen unannounced and had made herself totally at home. She shook her head, righted her chair and dropped into it. The woman had, Barbara admitted, warm, honest eyes that looked directly at you when she spoke and an open, friendly smile. Wasn't that what made con artists so hard to resist? "Okay. Tell me what you're doing here. And if you're a salesman with a very peculiar way of getting my attention, I'm not buying."

"I'm not selling anything," Maggie said, "but if I were, you'd be buying. I've actually come to change your life."

"Out," Barbara said. "Get out. I don't know how you got in here with your 'I'm not selling anything' sales pitch, but if you don't leave I *will* call the cops." She reached over and moved the phone from the counter to the table beside her right hand. "Now get out."

"Hmm. How to explain? Let me begin by introducing myself. My name's Maggie Sullivan and I'm dead." She reached over and flipped off the TV.

Her mind whirling, Barbara reran all the six P.M. sales pitches she'd heard over the years. It had gotten so she didn't answer her phone between the time she got home from work and eight P.M. *Hi*, they all started, *my name is Maggie.* She'd heard them on the phone hundreds of times. She glared. "Sure. And your next line is 'And how are you this evening, Ms. Enright,' " she parroted as the last words of Maggie's speech penetrated, " 'and I'm calling on behalf of . . .' You're *what*?" Had she heard correctly?

"I'm afraid you'll find this hard to believe, but I'm dead."

"Sure and I'm Minnie Mouse."

"You're not Minnie Mouse, but I *am* dead." Maggie hesitated. "How can I convince you? You know, I'm really new to this and I don't know what I can and can't do." She reached for the bread knife that Barbara had used earlier. "I hate this, but I think it just might work. I mean a dead person shouldn't be able to feel pain and I shouldn't bleed. Right?" To test the first part, Maggie pinched herself in the arm. Hard. "Well, I didn't feel that." She picked up the knife and held it poised over the index finger of her empty hand. "Do I really have to prove this to you? It may not be pleasant if I'm wrong."

Barbara raised one eyebrow. "This is certainly the most original pitch I've ever seen. I can't wait to see how you'll get yourself out of this." Strange, Barbara thought, but I actually rather like this ridiculous woman.

"Okay then," Maggie said. "Here goes." She took the knife and drew it slowly across the pad of her finger. "Amazing," she said. "I really didn't feel that at all." She held the finger toward Barbara. "See? No blood. And you can see I made a really deep cut."

Barbara could see that there was a deep cut across Maggie's finger that wasn't bleeding. "What's the gimmick? Are you selling artificial limbs? And why would that interest me?"

"Cut me some slack, will you?" Maggie said, putting the knife aside. "I'm really dead." She stood up. "Have you got any wine? I find I need something to fortify myself."

Barbara motioned toward a lower cabinet, and when Maggie opened the door she saw a reasonably well-stocked wine rack. "I guess it will have to be red since white wine should really be chilled." She pulled out a Chianti classico. "Corkscrew?" Numbly Barbara motioned to a drawer. While Maggie quickly removed the cork from the bottle, Barbara walked into the living room and returned with two glasses. Maggie quickly half filled the glasses and raised hers in silent toast.

As Barbara watched, Maggie took a sip, swished it around her mouth and swallowed. "Not bad, but a bit harsh. It really could have breathed for an hour or two, but it's okay." She waved at Barbara's glass. "Drink."

Barbara took a sip and swallowed. "I'm not much for wine, but my mom used to enjoy a glass with dinner." She put her glass down and took her seat. Maggie took a few more sips, then again sat opposite Barbara. "You know," Maggie said, "I don't even know whether I will have to pee as the evening progresses or whether this just goes into the ether somewhere. I have no blood, so I can't get tipsy. I wonder."

Without thinking, Barbara took another swallow. "Okay. You've been here fifteen minutes and I still have no idea why."

"I'm here for you. God, that sounds like a line from a bad sci-fi drama. Actually, I'm here because of your mother."

Barbara bristled. "What does my mother have to do with this? She died a while ago."

"I know. About seven months ago to be precise. And after she died, she asked a favor of two women I know. She wants you to be happy. Get out in the world. Date. Fuck. You know."

"I don't know anything like that at all and I'll thank you to leave my mother out of this."

"But she's an integral part of it." Maggie reached out to pat the back of Barbara's hand, but the younger woman pulled away. "Let me explain." Briefly Maggie told Barbara about her heart attack and how she had suddenly found herself in the Mad Tea Party with Lucy and Angela. "They can't decide whether I'm to go . . ." Maggie made a thumbs-up with one hand and a thumbs-down with the other. "So they gave me a project. You."

"I don't for a moment believe any of this," Barbara said, drinking more of her wine, "but why me?"

"I told you before," Maggie explained. "It was your mother. On her way through, she asked the girls to help you out." Maggie's head tipped to one side and she gazed into space. "Actually, I don't quite understand how your mother ended up in the computer room. According to Angela and Lucy, the interview process is only for the undecideds. Your mother's goodness seems to have left the girls little choice. Maybe it was a special request of some kind." She refocused on Barbara. "Anyway, I'm now here for you."

"Your reference to the Mad Tea Party is accurate. I still don't believe you."

"Well, that's neither here nor there, actually. I assume you want to get out more. Date. I saw the way you looked at your boss this afternoon."

Barbara's head snapped up. "How the hell do you know how I looked at my boss earlier?"

"The girls have a monitor and they can tune in on people. We watched you at work today so I would know who you were."

"This gets crazier and crazier," Barbara said. "Do you mean that they could be watching us right now?"

"Probably not. With the millions of people they have to check on as people come through for approval, I doubt whether they have time for idle peeping."

Barbara shivered. "It gives me the creeps nonetheless." She found she was actually playing along with this fantasy. Or was it a fantasy? "So you're supposed to give me a makeover. What's this going to cost me?"

"Nothing. And it's more than a makeover, it's a whole change of attitude. According to your mother, you're . . . How can I best say this? You're a bit of a prude."

"Nonsense. I'm just selective. Just because I don't let every Tom, Dick, and Harry into my bedroom doesn't make me a prude. Not in the least."

"Selectivity is good, Babs, but it's not life."

A handsome face suddenly flashed through Barbara's mind and her patience snapped. "Don't call me Babs. I hate it."

"All right. Don't get huffy."

"I'm sorry. I just really hate Babs. Anyway, you were telling me about my makeover."

Maggie sipped her wine. "Well, as I understand my job here, I'm supposed to teach you about yourself and sex and men and dating and all that. In the end, you're supposed to get out more, go dancing, make love."

Barbara toyed with her fork. "And what makes you such an expert?"

"I am, or was, a . . . Again how to put this. I was an expert at making men happy. Let's just say I did it professionally."

The fork dropped out of Barbara's hand. "You were a hooker!"

"I prefer call girl. Very highly priced, I might add."

"But you look like you could be my mother."

Maggie winced. "Ouch. That hurt." She walked into the hallway outside the kitchen and looked at herself in the ornate mirror that hung just inside the entrance. She studied her face for a moment, then returned to the table and sat down. "I don't look that bad, despite my current circumstances, I'll have you know." She paused. "But I guess I am almost old enough to be your mother."

"So why would some man . . . ?" Barbara suddenly realized that without being totally insulting she had no way to finish the sentence.

"Why would some man want to make love with me? Because I know how to make men happy, how to fulfill their fantasies, how to make them feel strong or weak, brave or pitiful, whatever they want. I'm damn good at what I do and I have a client list as long as your arm."

"What do you . . . I mean, *did* you charge?"

"I was worth the five hundred a night that men paid me."

"Five hundred dollars? For one night?" Barbara's mouth literally hung open.

"Not the whole night, of course." Maggie ran her long fingers through her hair and fluffed it out at the sides. "And more if they want something special."

"I don't want to know about that part," Barbara said. "Look, I don't pretend to understand any of this, but I really don't need your help. I'm happy just the way I am." In response to Maggie's raised eyebrow, Barbara continued. "Really. My life is just what I want it to be. And I'm just the way I want to be."

"Sure," Maggie said, her voice dripping with sarcasm. "Listen. You've heard enough for one evening. You really need to take a day to digest all this. Let me run along now so you can think about what we've said." Maggie paused, then asked, "By the way, what day is it?"

"It's Tuesday," Barbara said, her head spinning. She was sitting in her kitchen having a conversation with a dead prostitute. She certainly did need some time to digest this. But she didn't need any help with her life. None. Absolutely not.

"What date? What year?"

"It's Tuesday, March 4, 1996. What did you think?"

"I'm totally disoriented. This bouncing from time to time. The last date I remember was July 18, 1995." Pain flashed across Maggie's face as she recalled Paul Crowley and their phone conversation that last evening. *I wonder how he felt when he found out about me.* "And where are we? It looks like New York, but everything wonderful looks like New York to me."

"We're about twenty miles north of the city, in Fleetwood."

"I know the town well." Paul lived in Bronxville, the next town up. With a sigh, she emptied her wineglass and shook off her negative feelings. "I'm not sure how this time thing will work, but I think I can manage to be here, same time tomorrow."

"I don't want to seem rude, but I don't want you to come back. Just go away and leave me alone."

"Sorry, but I can't. I have a job and my ultimate future depends on doing it well. And remember, this is what your mother wanted."

"I'm sure my mother didn't want some whore giving me makeup tips," Barbara snapped. Then her head dropped into her hands. "I'm sorry. That was uncalled for."

"Yes, it was. But I am what I am. I am—I was—a woman who made men happy for money. I did my job well, and got a lot of pleasure myself as well. And I was highly paid for my talents."

"I'm sorry. But this whole thing is so ridiculous."

"Just think about it. Consider what you have to gain. Think about looking appealing to your boss and having him ask you out. Dream about what your third or seventh date could be like. Think about all this and I'll see you tomorrow." Maggie crossed the room and walked into the hall.

Suddenly the house was silent. Having not heard the front door open, Barbara got up to be sure this crazy woman wasn't lurking somewhere waiting to pounce or something. "Maggie? Where are you?" She searched the house, but Maggie was nowhere to be found.

Chapter 3

Later that evening, Barbara lay on her bed, the romance novel she had been trying to read now discarded beside her. It had been foolish, she realized, to even try to think about anything besides the weird visit she had had with the ghost of a sort of motherly, utterly charming prostitute. Images had whirled in her brain as she had tossed her uneaten dinner in the trash and methodically washed the dishes and cleaned the kitchen.

She considered what Maggie had said. Her life wasn't dull, it was just predictable. She went to work five mornings a week, arriving in White Plains, barring car trouble, at almost exactly eight o'clock each morning. Gordon, Watson, Kelly and Wise was a small but elite firm, run by Mark Watson and John Kelly, two aging lawyers, and Steve Gordon, the thirty-five-year-old sexy-looking lawyer for whom Barbara worked. Barbara brought her half-sandwich and salad with her each day and ate her lunch at her desk. Steve Gordon junior, son of one of the founding partners, wasn't overly dependent on her so Barbara usually left at four-thirty and was home before five.

Most weekends she did odd jobs around her two-story raised ranch. In the summer she mowed the lawn, in the winter she shoveled the driveway. Her kitchen and bathroom floors were clean enough to eat off of, and at the first sign of mildew she attacked her tub and shower with cleansers and brushes. She was an active member of her local church and could be counted to cook and bake for every benefit, chaperone the youth events and join parishioners in holiday visits to local nursing homes.

My life's not dull. It isn't. But when was the last time she had been out on a date? Carl Tyndell's face flashed again through her brain. He was the last, she realized, and that was . . . She counted on her fingers. Let's see. Mom got really sick and moved in two years ago and it was a few months before that. Maybe more than a few months. Phew. Had it really been more than three years since she had had a date? Well, after that last debacle, it was just as well. Anyway, she was happy. Wasn't she?

She thought about Steve. He was almost six feet tall with piercing blue eyes and just enough gray at his temples to be distinguished and sexy. He had a strong jaw, and large hands with slender fingers and well-sculptured nails. Frequently Barbara would find herself watching his hands as he signed the correspondence she typed for him.

Was Maggie right? Barbara sighed and popped an M&M into her mouth from the open bag on her bedside table.

She slept little that night and, the next day since Steve was in court, she typed, arranged and organized several important briefs, two wills and a few mortgage documents. Without too much thought, she opened Steve's mail, dealt with the items she could handle herself and arranged the others in folders on his desk. She answered the phone, made and confirmed several appointments for her boss and gave him his messages and took copious notes about his responses each time he called in. She nibbled on her American cheese sandwich and salad at lunch and left the office at four thirty-five.

As she drove home, she realized that, although she had thought about her life and the things Maggie had said most of the day, she had made her decision the previous evening. If this whole thing wasn't an elaborate hoax or some kind of boredom-induced hallucination, she would go along with Maggie, at least for the moment.

* * *

When Maggie had walked out of Barbara's kitchen the previous evening she suddenly found herself back inside the revolving door. She pushed her way to the other side and stepped out, only to find herself walking back through Barbara's kitchen door.

"I didn't know whether you'd really be here," Barbara said as Maggie entered the kitchen.

"This is really disorienting," Maggie said, rubbing her forehead. The kitchen was different, with two plates on the table, each with a hamburger on a toasted bun, mixed vegetables, and rice. "When am I?"

"That's an interesting takeoff on the typical question. It's almost six-fifteen. I wasn't sure you'd be back."

"Did we meet last evening or just a few minutes ago?"

"We met yesterday." Barbara sat at one end of the table and pointed to the second place setting. "I cooked some dinner for you, but I remember you told me you didn't get hungry. I can put it away and eat it for lunch tomorrow if you don't want it."

"This is all new to me, too," Maggie admitted. "I don't know exactly what I do and what I don't." She sat down and sniffed, enjoying the slightly charcoal smell of the grilled burger in front of her.

"Is this the first time you've helped someone?"

Maggie nodded ruefully. "I'm not like Michael Landon in *Highway to Heaven*. This isn't my job, you know. It's just a test to see where I go."

"I love *Highway to Heaven*. Michael Landon is so adorable."

Maggie raised an eyebrow. "Well, it's good to know you notice things like that." She picked up the burger and took a bite. "Delicious."

"Thanks. I did all the cooking for my mother and me until she died. Good wine and good food were her only pleasures toward the end, and I did what I could to make special things for her."

"Well," Maggie said, her mouth full, "this is really wonderful."

Barbara found herself delighted that Maggie liked her cooking. "What does an angel do all day? I mean, what did you do today?"

"I'm certainly not an angel as anyone who knew me in my old profession can tell you. That's the problem that puts me here with you. And for me, there was no today. I walked out of your kitchen and just walked back in." She blinked, then took another bite of her burger. "I guess I'll get used to it. Tell me what's been happening in the world since I left. Did the O.J. Simpson trial ever end?"

For the next hour Barbara caught Maggie up on what had occurred in the last eight months. Strangely, Barbara realized as she poured coffee for each of them, she had completely accepted the fact that Maggie was dead. She also realized that she hadn't enjoyed an evening this much in a long time.

"I think it's time we got down to business" Maggie said as she sipped her coffee. "I'm here to see that you get out, date, have some fun."

Barbara stretched her legs beneath the table and sighed. "It won't work. I am what I am."

"Do I hear self-pity? A bit of 'poor little me?' "

Barbara sat upright. "Not at all. It's just that you can't make something out of nothing."

"All right, let's get serious here. Do you have a full-length mirror somewhere?"

"I guess." Together the two women walked upstairs and into the guest bedroom. It was a simply decorated room with a flowered quilt, matching drapes, and a simple dresser. The room looked and smelled unused. Maggie walked behind Barbara and together they stood in front of the long mirror that hung on the closet door.

"Now, look at you," Maggie said, looking at Barbara's reflection over her shoulder. Barbara was wearing a pair of nondescript gray sweat pants and an oversize matching sweat shirt. "You look like you've just come from a ragpickers' convention."

"But this is just for comfort," Barbara protested.

"Comfort is one thing but dressing in sacks is another." Maggie grabbed a handful of the back of the shirt and pulled. The fabric stretched more tightly across Barbara's chest. "There's a body under this," she said. "Nice tits." She pulled the pants in at the seat. "And you've got nice hips, a small waist. Yes, there's actually a shape under all this material."

Barbara looked, but remained unconvinced.

"Look at your face," Maggie said, grabbing a fistful of hair and pulling it back, away from Barbara's face. "Nice eyes. Actually, *great* eyes. Good cheekbones, good shape. A definite nose, but not too much, and nicely shaped lips. Your skin's not great, but nothing that a decent foundation wouldn't cure." She released Barbara's hair and the two women stood, gazing into the mirror. "There's really a lot of potential. We just need makeup, a good hair stylist, and a new wardrobe."

"I don't need a new wardrobe," Barbara said, almost stomping toward her own room. She crossed to her closet, opened the door and flipped on the light. "Just look. There are lots of really nice clothes in here."

"Nice for a dowdy moderately shapeless old maid, but not for you. You need high shades, sapphire and emerald, deep claret and purple. Oh, you'd look sensational in eggplant."

"I have all the clothes I need."

"But not the ones you want. You seem to want to slide through life virtually unnoticed. Nonsense. Make a statement. Be a real person."

"I am a real person."

Maggie made a rude noise. "In attitude, you rate a D and in self-esteem you get an F. In looks, I'll give you a 'needs improvement.' And with the improvement will come a change in attitude as well. Are you game?"

Barbara dropped onto her bed. "I don't know, Maggie. Part of me wants to be adventurous, stick out in a crowd, have men notice me. But the rest is terrified. It's such a risk."

Maggie sat beside Barbara and put her arm loosely around the younger woman's shoulders. "Why is it a risk?" she asked softly.

"It just is."

"Think about the worst thing that could happen if you walked into a room in a bright red dress with black stockings and black high heels, with golden highlights in your hair and a 'here I am, come and get me' expression on your face. What's the worst thing?"

To her surprise Barbara burst into tears. Helpless, Maggie handed her a handful of tissues and, with her arms around Barbara's shoulders, let her cry it all out. It took fifteen minutes for Barbara to get calm enough for Maggie to attempt to talk to her again. "You have to tell me what's eating you."

Barbara wiped her face and shook her head.

"I can ask Lucy and she'll find out with that computer system of hers." Maggie explained Lucy's ability to replay events in her life at will. She had no idea whether she could even get to Lucy or whether Lucy could bring up bits of Barbara's past, but she thought it was a decent bluff.

"Oh, no. That would be too humiliating."

"Well, then, let me get us each a glass of wine and then you tell me what it is that frightens you so much. Where's the rest of the bottle we were drinking last evening?"

"In the closet next to the refrigerator, and the glasses are in the hutch in the living room."

"Lord. Unless I was entertaining I left dishes in the sink for days and in my drainer even longer. Okay. You think about how you're going to tell me the ugly details while I fetch for us." Maggie left the room.

Barbara listened to Maggie's footsteps on the stairs and slumped onto her back. Maybe I can just run away. Maybe I can tell her to go to hell. Maybe I can slit my wrists. She sighed. Maybe it will feel good to tell someone about Carl and Walt. But maybe Maggie would just give up on her if she did. Didn't that serve her purpose anyway, make Maggie go away? Too soon, Maggie returned and thrust a glass of wine into her hand.

"Drink this like it's medicine," Maggie said, brandishing the bottle and her glass in the other. "There's enough here for another half-glass for each of us."

Staying flat on her back on the bed, Barbara awkwardly emptied the glass, then held it out for Maggie to refill. Maggie emptied the bottle into Barbara's glass, then stretched out beside her on the bed. Softly she said, "Tell me about him."

"How did you know it was a him?"

Maggie chuckled. "When a woman has an ego that has been smashed as flat as yours it's always a man—or a woman. And from the way you gazed at that boss of yours yesterday, I assumed the asshole who flattened your self-esteem was a man."

"Oh, yes," Barbara said. "Carl Tyndell was definitely a man, and I guess an asshole, too."

"That's the attitude." Maggie stared at the ceiling, giving Barbara time to decide where to begin.

"I met Carl at a party. It was about four years ago and I had just had my twenty-seventh birthday. Notice I didn't say I celebrated, because, for some unknown reason, that birthday hit me very hard."

As she set the scene for Maggie, Barbara could almost see the room, hear the incessant babble of suburban conversation, smell the cold cuts on the dining-room table. A couple she knew slightly from her church had given the party to introduce some new neighbors. She had put her coat on the bed in the master bedroom and as she walked back down the stairs she saw a sensational-looking man talking in low whispers to Walt McCrory, a neighborhood bachelor whom she had dated a few times a few months earlier. The two men laughed loudly, then the stranger worked his way through the crowd and engaged her in conversation.

"I should have suspected something was up the way Walt leered at me," Barbara said.

"You and this Walt didn't part on good terms, I gather."

"We went out for a few weeks. We had dinner a few times, then one warm evening he invited me back to his place to check out his new above-the-ground pool. One thing led to another, but obviously not fast enough for Walt. After I told him I didn't want to be groped, he called me a cold bitch, incapable of giving a man a decent wet dream much less a hard-on."

"So he presumably talked this Carl person into picking you up."

"I guess that's true, but I was so naive that I didn't make the connection until much later."

"We never do," Maggie said sadly.

"Anyway, Carl and I made dinner plans for a few days later. We had a wonderful meal and a few too many drinks. He was attentive and seemed interested in everything I had to say. His eyes were so deep brown as to be almost black. His hair was also dark brown and he had nice hands. I'm a sucker for men with great hands."

"Me too." Maggie smiled, thinking about how many men's hands had touched her over the years.

"After dinner, Carl suggested a drive along the Hudson. We used my car, parked in a darkened area he knew about and kissed like teenagers. One thing led to another and suddenly my blouse was off and my bra was open. His mouth was on me and he was whispering, 'Babs, sweetie, oh, Babs.' Suddenly Walt pulled the car door open and snapped a flash picture of me, naked from the waist up.

" 'You win, Carl baby,' Walt said. 'I can't deny it when I have the proof and a great shot of Babs' tits right here.' I watched the picture spit out of the front of the camera and slowly appear before my eyes."

"Win what?" Maggie asked, annoyed by the pain inflicted by something that to those two probably amounted to nothing more than a prank.

"They had made a bet that Carl couldn't get my upper body exposed on the first date. Right there in the car Walt counted out a hundred dollars and handed it to Carl. Walt said that he didn't think anyone could get the ice bitch out of her clothes in under six months. They laughed, pounded each other on the back, then the two of them walked to Walt's car, and took off."

"Oh."

"Yes, oh."

"Well that wasn't the end of the world, was it?"

Barbara just stared at the ceiling. "I never told anyone about that night and, I guess, Walt never did either. I spent the next few weeks waiting for the picture or the story to circulate, but for some unknown reason, nothing happened."

"Did you ever see them again?"

"I never saw Carl again. He must have been 'imported talent.' " She said the phrase with a sneer. "I see Walt once in a while, but he's not a church type and I stick almost completely to church gatherings."

"Safe stuff. No risk of anyone getting sexual." Maggie took Barbara's hand. "Wouldn't you like to get him back sometime?"

Barbara smiled. "I'd love to, but there's no hope of that."

"I wouldn't be so sure. It just gives us another reason to make you over and get you some experience." She paused. "Are you a virgin?"

Barbara sat upright. "What a question."

"Well . . ."

"No. I've had relationships." She slumped back down onto her back. "But not recently."

"And Steve? Wouldn't you like him to notice you?"

"Of course."

"So you'll let me help you? For your mom and Steve and maybe even Walt and Carl."

Barbara sighed. She wanted to let Maggie help. It was all so bizarre but it was a chance to get some of the things she wanted. It might be her only chance. "I guess."

"Good," Maggie said. "First, call in sick tomorrow and we'll get your hair done, get someone to help you with your makeup and see what we can do about some clothes for you. I need to know something that's a bit embarrassing. Is money a problem? I'm a bit short of funds, you realize."

Barbara laughed out loud for the first time since Maggie had appeared the previous evening. "No. My job pays well and I don't spend much. I'm not Saks Fifth Avenue-well off, but we could certainly go to the mall and dent my credit card."

"Great."

"You know, it sounds like fun."

"It does, doesn't it."

"Will you be able to be here? I mean how do you just appear and disappear the way you do?"

Maggie thought, then answered, "I don't know how." She told Barbara about the revolving door. "I seem to be able to set some kind of clock, so I just come out of the door here at the right time."

"Do you have powers? Like moving stuff with your mind or walking through walls?"

"I don't think so, but Lucy and Angela seem to be in charge of that. They said I'd have what I needed when I needed it, so I'll just have to trust them." She stood up. "I've got to be going now." She cocked her head to one side. "I don't know how I know that, but I do." She walked toward the bedroom door, then turned. "Tomorrow. Ninish."

Barbara raised her hand and waved as Maggie walked through the bedroom door and vanished.

Barbara's dreams were troubled for the first part of the night. She was in the car with Walt and Carl, but the car was really the gaping jaws of a giant mythical beast and, as the two men jumped out, the jaws began to close on her naked, immobile body. Then she was walking down the aisle in church dressed in a bridal gown, with her mother holding her arm, ready to give her away to the man who stood beside the priest, his back turned to her. When she reached his side, he turned, but he had no face. She looked down and saw that he was a tuxedoed store mannequin with two poles holding him up where his legs should have been.

The following morning, Barbara called her office and told the woman who answered the phone that she had urgent personal business and wouldn't be in the office until the following day.

She dressed in a man-tailored shirt and jeans, white socks and sneakers, grabbed a denim jacket and bounced down to the kitchen. Bounced, she thought, was a good word for the way she felt. Light. Elastic. Good!

She made a pot of strong coffee and toasted a bagel. She sat at the table munching and thinking about the day's activities. "Good morning," Maggie said from the doorway.

"Hi. Maggie," Barbara responded. "Coffee?"

"I guess. This time warp thing I'm in is still very confusing. It seems like only a moment ago I left you last evening."

"Nice outfit," Barbara said.

Maggie looked down, puzzled. "I didn't change clothes," she whispered. Last evening she had had on an outfit similar to the clothes Barbara was wearing this morning. But now Maggie was wearing a pair of wide-legged black rayon pants and a soft gray silk blouse. "Very disconcerting," she mumbled.

Barbara poured Maggie a mug of coffee and set it down beside a pitcher of milk and the sugar bowl. "Maggie," she asked as her friend dropped into a chair. "How did you become a . . . I mean . . . ?"

"Hooker?"

"Yeah. Well . . ."

"You mean how did a nice girl like me end up entertaining men for money."

"You can't blame me for being curious."

Maggie grinned. "Of course not. And let's get this settled right now. I've said it before. I am proud of what I do, er . . . did. I had my own rules and I stuck by them at all times. My customers and I had fun. We were careful and honest."

"It's just difficult for me to believe in the hooker with the heart of gold. It's so clichéd."

"Heart of gold. I like that. I like that a lot. Anyway, you asked how I got started in my business. It began with my first divorce."

"You were married?" Barbara said, her eyes wide.

"Twice, but this is my story to tell. Anyway, Chuck and I married right out of high school in 1955 and stayed together for six years. The split was amicable. We just had nothing in common anymore. No kids, we both worked, our sex life was dull, dull, dull. He married again by the way, to a nice, mousey woman who seemed to make him happy. But that's another story.

"As a divorcee, I slept around. That was a very loose time, before AIDS, very into me first. I found that I loved sex. I enjoyed pleasing the men I was with and I had fun learning how to do it. I was still just beginning to learn about fantasy when I met Bob. He had a wonderfully creative mind and taught me about all sorts of new things in the bedroom. When he suggested we get married, I thought I'd found my ultimate sex partner and in order to keep us together, I said yes."

"He sounds like a wonderful lover."

"He was and he taught me to be a giving, creative partner."

"But . . ."

"But I couldn't stand him outside of the bedroom. He and I were exact opposites. He was a neat freak, I'm a bit of a slob. He liked his meals at specific times, all organized, I like to scrounge for myself. You get it. So, after two fantastic years in the bedroom and two awful years everywhere else, we split, too. That was 1974, and it seems like forever ago. I was intensely glad when he left, but I was horny as hell. All the time. The one good thing about marriage is that you can usually have all the sex you want."

"That sounds terrible."

"It was for me. I still worked, of course. I was manager of the computer input department at a regional bank. I had very good people skills, as my boss called them, but I was bored. Bored, lonely and horny at home and bored, stressed, and frustrated at work. Not much of a life."

Barbara patted the back of Maggie's hand, well able to sympathize with the older woman.

"One evening I just couldn't bear to go home to that empty apartment so I stopped at a bar near work. I'd been sitting at the bar for about an hour, feeling sorry for myself, when a cute-looking guy sat down on the stool next to mine." Maggie closed her eyes and a smile changed her expression from despair to enjoyment as she remembered that evening. "I remember. I called myself Margaret at that time."

"Hi," the man said. "My name's Frank."

Maggie looked up, ready to brush the man off with a clever remark. But as she took in his charming smile, she changed her mind. "Hi. I'm Margaret."

"Glad to meet you, Margaret. I come in here whenever I'm in town but I've never seen you before."

"I've never been in here before," Maggie said.

Frank placed his elbow on the bar and leaned his chin on his hand, studying Maggie's face. "You know," he said after a moment, "you don't look like a Margaret."

Maggie sipped her white wine, unwilling to make any overt gestures of friendliness toward this stranger who was in the process of picking her up in a bar. "And how would a Margaret look?"

"Oh, let's see. Margaret is very serious. Tight bun. Thick glasses. Sensible shoes."

Maggie thought about that and realized that, in the months since she and Bob had gone their separate ways, she had become just what Frank pictured. No, she thought, I won't be that person. I'm only thirty-three. She took a large swallow of her wine and sat up a bit straighter. "Okay. I guess I can't be that kind of Margaret. What would you call me?"

"Well, Margie is young, pert, and too cute to be believed, so that's not you. And Peggy is an Irish lass with red hair and freckles."

"Okay. Neither of those sound like me. So who am I?"

"You look like a Maggie. Nice-looking. Interesting and interested. Open to new experiences."

"What a line you've got," Maggie said, realizing that, whether it was a line or not, this man had made her feel younger than she had in years. She lowered her chin and looked up at Frank through her lashes. "And I must say I like it."

Frank grinned. "Me too. And it usually works."

Maggie laughed. "You admit that it's a line? How original."

"The line's original, too," he said. "And you're the first woman who's picked up on it so quickly." He tried and almost succeeded in looking like a small boy with his hand in the cookie jar. It helped that he had medium brown hair naturally streaked with blond, wide blue eyes, and a fantastic mouth.

They talked for an hour, then went to a nearby French restaurant and shared a sumptuous meal which included a bottle of fine Chardonnay and a glass of sweet, golden dessert wine. She learned that Frank was divorced, in town from Dallas for a week for his firm's quarterly department meetings and that he was charming and sexy and determined to get her into his bed. As he dropped his credit card onto the check, he took Maggie's hand. As he held it across the table, his index finger scratched little patterns in her palm. "We could be good together," he purred.

She had to admit to herself that she was turned on. But this was a man who had picked her up, not someone she worked with or who had been introduced to her by friends. He was only in town for a short time. She couldn't even delude herself into thinking this was the beginning of a long-term relationship. But she wanted to go to bed with him nonetheless. "How can you be so sure?" she said.

"I can be very sure. I can see it in your eyes, your body, the way you smile, the way you can't quite sit still. You want this as much as I do. How do you like your sex?"

"Excuse me?"

"You heard me. How do you like your sex? Long and slow, with lots of kissing and stroking? Hard and fast, like the pair of animals we are? Standing up with your back pressed against the wall and your legs locked around my waist? In the shower under torrents of hot water? Tell me and I'll make it that way for you."

Maggie shrugged. She couldn't tell him how she liked her sex because she loved it all ways. "You tell me," she hedged. "How do you like it?"

"Oh, Maggie, I think I'd like it every way with you." He lifted her hand and nipped at her fingertips.

"No," she said, more seriously. "Tell me. How would you like to make love with me? Create the fantasy and let's see how we mesh."

"You're serious. You want me to tell you." When Maggie merely nodded, Frank said, "I see you slowly removing your clothes while I watch. I watch you reveal your body to me, one small piece at a time."

Silently Maggie reached up and unbuttoned the top two buttons on her blouse and parted the sides so the valley between her breasts was visible.

"Shit, baby. I'm hard as stone already."

Maggie raised an eyebrow but remained silent.

"Okay. I see you in your bra and panties." He looked around the tablecloth at Maggie's shoes. "Yes. Black high heels. I like that. You're not wearing pantyhose, are you?"

"I won't be," she said, contemplating a quick trip to the ladies' room. She watched the flush rise on Frank's face. She was turning him on. What a trip.

"You're walking toward me, then unzipping my pants."

Maggie was very turned on and more than a little drunk. Without changing her expression, she slipped one foot out of her shoe and stretched her foot across the space between them and rested her stocking-covered toes against the swelling in his crotch.

His startled look, followed by a shift of position to place her foot more firmly against his zipper, told Maggie exactly what she was doing to him. "Shit, baby, let's get out of here," he moaned.

"The waiter hasn't brought your credit card back," Maggie said, feigning an innocent expression. She wiggled her toes in his lap. "As I remember, I was unzipping your pants. Tell me more. I want to know exactly how you see this evening we're going to have."

She watched Frank take a deep breath. "I can't think when you do that."

Again she silently raised an eyebrow. She was in charge now, quite deliberately turning Frank on, a man she had met only three hours before.

His voice uneven, he continued. "You were unzipping my pants and taking out my cock. It's so hard it sticks up like a flagpole. You're wrapping your hand around it and licking your lips."

Maggie slowly ran the tip of her tongue across her upper lip. "Like this?"

At that moment, the waiter returned with Frank's charge slip, which he signed with an obviously shaking hand. As he wrote, Maggie moved her toes in his lap. As the waiter took the restaurant copy, Maggie asked, "Could I have just a bit more coffee?"

"Certainly, madame."

"But, Maggie, I thought we were going to my room." He was almost whining.

"We will. But I need just a bit more coffee and you haven't finished your story. I was holding your cock, as I recall. Squeezing it as it sticks up through the opening in your pants. Let's see, I'm wearing a black lace bra, bikini panties, and my high black shoes. Right?" Bob had taught her about the power of a well-set erotic scene and he had marveled at her ability to use words to turn him on. Now she was using all her skill to turn Frank on. And it was working better than she could have imagined.

Frank was again lost in his fantasy. "Right," he whispered.

"And I'll bet you want me to take your cock into my mouth and suck you."

"Oh, yes," he groaned as the waiter refilled Maggie's coffee cup. Without removing her hand from his, or her foot from his lap, she poured cream into her cup and stirred.

When he didn't continue, she said, "You want me to touch the tip of your cock with my lips, kiss it, lick it, make it wet." She deliberately slowed the cadence of her speech. "Then I can slowly suck it into my mouth. Very slowly. Pulling it deeper and deeper into that hot, wet cave."

Frank's eyes closed, obviously lost in the fantasy.

"Now I pull back, but I keep sucking so your cock pulls out so slowly. Down and up, my mouth is driving you crazy." She remembered a trick Bob had taught her. "But I wrap my fingers around the base of your cock so you can't come as I keep on sucking. I don't want you to come yet, baby."

"But I want to come."

"Not until we're both ready. So now I pull my panties off and rub myself. I'm very wet, you know. I let you lick my finger so you can taste me. Do I taste good?"

"Oh, yes."

"Good. Now I pull off your pants, but I leave your shirt on. It's very sexy for me to see you all dressed in your business shirt and tie while I slowly put a cold, lubricated condom over your cock. It feels tight, like it's hugging you. Now I push you down onto the bed, straddle your waist and use the tip of your slippery cock to play with myself." She looked at his closed eyes. "Can you see me?"

"Yes," he said, his voice harsh and almost inaudible.

"Let me take off my bra so you can watch my breasts as I play with your cock. I'm rubbing my clit now. It's hard and you can even feel it against your cock. And I'm so wet. Your hips are moving, trying to push your cock inside. Shall I let you?"

"Please."

"Yes, I will. I lower myself onto you, pulling you deep inside. You fill me up so well, baby. I raise up and drop, over and over, fucking you so good. Do you want to come now? I'm almost ready." With his eyes closed, Frank groaned. Maggie rubbed her foot along the length of his cock under the tablecloth.

"I'm almost ready. Almost. Wait for me, baby." Maggie was so turned on by her description of Frank's fantasy that if she reached under the table and touched herself, she would come. But she didn't.

"Yes, baby," she said. "I'm coming now. You can feel my pussy squeezing your cock. Come with me."

"Yes," Frank groaned. Then his eyes flew open. "No." He pushed Maggie's foot from his lap. "Not here."

"No. Not here," Maggie said. "But I need a trip to the ladies' room first." To remove her pantyhose. When she returned, Frank was waiting for her with her coat in his hands. "My hotel is just around the corner."

Maggie slipped her arms into the sleeves. "Good," she said. "I find I'm in a bit of a hurry."

"Are you sure you're not a professional at this? No offense."

"No offense taken. And no, I'm not a pro."

"Well, you should be. I've been with my share of professional entertainers and no one holds a candle to you."

As they walked out of the restaurant, Maggie asked, "You've been with call girls?"

"Sure. Sometimes the company provides entertainment for the out-of-town reps. And not one of them could come close to the way you turn me on. That little story back there . . ." He wrapped his arm around her shoulder. "Holy shit."

"I enjoy turning men on. I dated a lot before I met Bob, and then he taught me about fantasy and lots of variations on straight sex. I love it all."

"You should get paid for it."

"How much do call girls make?"

"The classy ones like you make hundreds a night."

"Hundreds of dollars?" Maggie gasped.

They turned the corner and approached Frank's hotel. "Sure. I know a few people and I could introduce you."

"Hmmm."

Maggie looked at Barbara. "The evening went exactly like the fantasy we had created." She took a drink from her coffee cup. "And he introduced me to someone who introduced me to someone else and, as they say, the rest is history."

"Wow."

"Yes. Wow. And I entertained men for twenty years."

"Did you ever have any bad experiences? You read about hookers getting beaten up and stuff."

"I had one or two men who didn't get the message when I told them to knock it off, but I know how to defend myself and I seldom take chances. All the men I entertain, er . . . entertained—it's so hard for me to think of myself in the past tense. The men I entertained were all recommended, lonely business types who just wanted someone to have some fun with. You know, do the things they wouldn't do with their wives."

"Like?"

"Mostly oral sex and anal sex. Some were into power fantasies, both giving and receiving and a few were into pain."

"You mean like whips?"

"I slapped a few men on the ass, but I never did whips because I can't get pleasure out of that. Heavy pain is such a turn-off for me that I made it clear I wouldn't play those games. But most other things were as exciting for me as they were for the men I was with."

"That's amazing."

Maggie looked at her watch. "It's getting late. Get your pocketbook and your credit cards and we're off to shop."

Barbara stood up. "I can't wait."

Chapter 4

"Now this doesn't mean I'm going to jump into someone's bed so fast," Barbara said under her breath as they walked into the Galleria Mall in White Plains. "You can't make a silk purse and all that."

"Let's first get you dressed and looking like the attractive woman you are," Maggie said. As they walked, the few shoppers they saw walked around Barbara but seemed unaware that Maggie was there. "You know," Maggie said, turning to stare at a woman with a stroller who had just missed bumping into her, "I don't think anyone can see me."

"But I can see you just fine," Barbara said.

They walked passed a large clothing store and paused in front of a mirrored section of wall. "I can see us both," Barbara said as Maggie dodged to avoid a mother pushing a blue-and-white stroller.

"It's really weird," Maggie said. "I'm here. I can see me." She rubbed her arms. "I can feel me, hear me. You can, too. But to judge by the people walking by, I don't exist."

"But you do exist," Barbara said.

"Mommy," a little girl said as she passed, "why is that woman talking to herself?"

"Let's go, darling," the mother said, hustling the tot off. "It's not nice to talk about . . ."

As the woman's voice faded, Maggie said, "We better be careful. People will think you're nuts."

As they strolled around the mall, getting the lay of the land, Barbara was careful not to speak to Maggie where anyone might overhear. Together the two women stopped periodically so Maggie could show Barbara outfits and shoes that would fit her new image. With Maggie steering, the two walked toward a hair salon called Expert Tresses. "We really should start with your hair."

"I like my hair," Barbara said, reflexively tucking a strand behind her ear. "It's easy and comfortable."

Maggie raised an eyebrow. "Easy and comfortable. Two of the most awful adjectives I can think of." She stopped and turned Barbara to face her. She peered at a section of hair just above her right temple. "What's this? The roots are white here."

"I was hoping we could overlook that. It's a white streak. My mother used to call it a witch's mark."

"You dye it?"

"My mother started doing that for me when I was a kid. It's just dyed to match the rest of my hair."

"It's sexy as hell. I want you to get someone to style this mop," Maggie said, staring at Barbara's soft, medium-brown hair. "And get the dye out of that section."

"But it's unlucky and creepy. I won't."

"Barbara, baby. It's unique and beautiful and it looks great. Your mother was a wonderful lady, but in this one instance, she was wrong. Please. Cooperate. Try this."

"No."

"Look," Maggie said, guiding Barbara into a small alcove. "Do this for me and for this project. Let someone do your hair. My way. Then give it one week. If you don't like it, you can dye it back. Okay? Please. I have a job to do here."

When Barbara hesitated, Maggie continued. "And get your nails done, too."

"But . . ."

Maggie put a hand in the small of Barbara's back and pushed, aiming her toward Expert Tresses. Since the salon was almost empty, three women walked toward her as she walked in. "May we help you?"

"I need a haircut," Barbara said.

"You want it styled," Maggie said, knowing that no one else could hear.

"I want it styled."

One of the women looked her over. "My name's Candy and I think you're mine this morning. Come on over here." The pink-smocked woman led Barbara to a chair at one side of the studio.

"I have a streak right here," Barbara said, fingering a section of hair as Candy covered Barbara's clothes with a plastic apron.

"Yes, I see," Candy said. "Why do you dye it?"

"It's a witch's mark."

"And it's so kinky." Candy lifted a strand of her long blond hair from her temple. "It wouldn't look as good on me, she said. She returned her attention to Barbara. "But on you . . ."

"Well . . ."

As they started to talk about styles, Maggie said, "She sounds like she knows what she's talking about, so let her do whatever she wants. I'll be back." Over her shoulder, she called, "And don't forget the nails."

Maggie left the salon and walked purposefully back to the mirrored section of wall. With people unable to see her, Maggie stood staring at herself. Since no one could hear her, she talked aloud to herself. "It's been six months since I, whatever, and my hair hasn't grown nor does it need to be colored." She looked down. "My nails are perfect and I don't look any older." She walked close to the mirror and stared at her skin. "No new lines. No signs of age. Nothing."

"And you won't age," a voice she recognized as Angela's said. "You'll just continue as you were on the day you died. That's one of the advantages of an assignment like this."

"Have you done this kind of thing often?" Maggie asked.

"Not really, but it does happen occasionally," Lucy said. "How's it going?"

"Don't you know?"

"Not really," Angela said. "We don't have the time to watch what's happening. We just drop in from time to time."

"Could Barbara hear you if she were here?"

"No," Angela continued. "Only you can hear us, and see us if it becomes necessary. But creating corporeal images on earth is very energy inefficient and in most cases unnecessary."

"How do you like Barbara?" Lucy asked.

"Actually, she's really nice. But mousy. She's got zero self-confidence. Even with a good hairstyle and attractive clothes, she's not going to be a beauty."

"You're not a Miss America candidate yourself," Lucy said.

"Oh now, Lucy," Angela said, "that's unkind."

"Look you two," Maggie said, "I know I'm not gorgeous, but I'm attractive. I use what I've got and I've never wanted for companions, paid and unpaid."

"That's the first lesson your friend Barbara has to learn," Angela said. "It's the gleam in the eye not the meat on the bones that makes a woman sexy."

"Listen, we've got other fish to fry, as it were," Lucy said. "Go pick Barbara up. She's waiting for you."

"But it's only been about five minutes," Maggie protested.

"You already know that time has little meaning in your existence, Angela said. "Go pick her up."

Her head now empty of voices, Maggie walked back to Expert Tresses and, sure enough, Barbara had just finished signing the charge slip. Maggie looked her friend over. The white streak was now prominent in Barbara's slightly darkened, carefully cut brown hair. Styled so it fell just at her shoulders, her hair curled up at the ends and moved gracefully as Barbara moved. She looked at Maggie and shrugged.

"You look just great," Maggie said. "What an improvement. And you've got makeup on."

Barbara stuffed the charge-card receipt into her wallet and

walked out of the salon. "It's hard remembering not to talk to you where anyone might hear."

"Sorry."

"Candy gave me a few tips about foundation and eye makeup so I bought a few things and she and another woman helped me put this stuff on. Does it look okay?"

Maggie studied Barbara's light taupe shadow, soft brown liner, blush, and lipstick. "You really look nice. You'll need more for evenings, of course, but for day wear, it's just great."

Barbara stopped at the same mirrored section of the wall. "You really think so? It's so obvious. I look made up."

"You look like you took some time to enhance your looks. That's great. You don't always have to look like you got up late for work."

"I don't . . ."

"You do most of the time. There's nothing wrong with taking a little time to look good."

"It's vain."

"It's just good sense. Vanity in large doses is bad. Feeling good about the way you look is good. Let's see what we can do now about your wardrobe."

"After lunch. I'm starving."

"We just had breakfast."

Barbara looked at her watch. "That was almost five hours ago and I, for one, am famished."

In the food court, Barbara bought a corned beef sandwich with fries and a pickle. With her plate in one hand and a 7Up in the other, she found a small table off to one side of the seating area. She sat with her back to the other shoppers so she could talk to Maggie without everyone thinking she was nuts. As they talked, Maggie occasionally picked up a french fry and nibbled on it. Barbara wondered what others would see if they looked. Would a french fry just lift up into the air, then disappear?

The two women then spent the afternoon doing serious damage to Barbara's credit card. They bought several soft bright-colored silk blouses and two skirts, considerably shorter than Barbara had been used to. "You have great legs," Maggie said several times. "Show them off. You want to catch the eye of that boss of yours, don't you?"

Unable to argue without seeming like a nut, Barbara went along. In a shoe boutique, Maggie bullied Barbara into purchasing a pair of black, two-and-a-half-inch high opera pumps and a pair of knee-high brown butter-soft suede boots with stiletto heels.

As they started for the parking lot of the mall, Maggie spotted a Victoria's Secret store. "Let's go in," she said.

"I have underwear," Barbara said.

"I'll bet not the right kind."

Barbara had just about given up arguing so together the two women entered the store. Maggie all but dragged her friend to a display of lacy bra and panty sets. Both the bra and the panty were mostly net with flowers embroidered in strategic places. "Get the black one, the white one, and the light blue."

"But, Maggie," Barbara said, "they're so slutty."

A saleswoman whirled around. "Yes," she said, "can I help you? I'm sorry I didn't hear your last question."

"I wasn't talking to you."

The saleswoman looked around, then shrugged. "Those lace sets are on sale, she said. "It's buy two and get the third for a dollar."

"The black, the white, and the light blue," Maggie said, knowing she couldn't be heard by anyone but Barbara. "And don't argue. You know you want them and you don't ever have to wear them. just indulge me."

"Okay," Barbara said, looking at the pleasant saleswoman. "I'll take the light blue and the white."

"A third set will only cost a dollar more."

Maggie tapped her foot and arched an eyebrow.

"Okay," Barbara agreed. "I guess I'll take the black as well."

"Good choice," the woman said. "And the size?"

"It's been a long time since I bought undies. Maybe I better try them on." She selected bras in three different sizes.

"Certainly," the woman said and showed Barbara to the fitting room.

In the tiny room, Barbara pulled off her shirt and bra and put the new white one on. Maggie appeared in the corner of the mirrored room and let out a low whistle. "You've got a great body, you know."

Barbara turned sideways, raised her rib cage and sucked in her tummy. "I could have if I never breathed again." When she relaxed, her belly bulged a bit and her diaphragm protruded.

"You've got a very nice figure," Maggie said. "And those bits of stuff you're wearing do wonders."

Barbara looked at the white lace bra she wore. She really didn't look half bad, she had to admit. The flowers woven into the fabric were designed so that leaves and blossoms covered her nipples but the rest was almost transparent.

"Very sexy," Maggie said. "Yes, very nice. I think your boss would approve."

Barbara blushed. "He will never see me like this," she said, replacing the silk with her serviceable cotton undies.

"He will if you want him to. He'll notice you and he'd be a fool not to be impressed. You will go into the office tomorrow a different woman."

Barbara smiled.

The following morning, Barbara showered and, when she returned to her bedroom, Maggie was sitting on her bed. "Wear that new cornflower blue blouse with the black skirt. And the light-blue bra and panties."

As Barbara reached for her traditional underwear, she asked, "What difference does it make what I wear underneath?"

"If you feet sexy under your clothes, it affects the way you behave. I want you to spend the day knowing that your breasts are being held by that wonderful erotic fabric."

"But . . ."

"Do what I ask, Barbara," Maggie said. "Trust me. You want him to notice you, don't you?"

"Well, yes."

"Good. So do it my way, just this once."

Barbara sighed and dressed as Maggie had suggested. After a quick breakfast, Barbara put on her coat. "Will you be at work with me today?"

"No," Maggie answered. "I'll see you here tonight and you can tell me all about it."

Barbara arrived at work at two minutes before eight, got her coffee and settled down to work. Her boss was in court that morning and wasn't due in until after lunch. Except for a quick trip to the ladies' room, Barbara stayed huddled at her desk all morning. The people who passed by noticed her new hairstyle and makeup and several commented cheerfully on how lovely she looked. One woman complimented her on the silver streak in her hair and a young male associate actually winked at her, something that had never happened before.

Throughout her almost solitary morning, she occasionally forgot her makeover, but then she would look down at her hands typing or dialing the phone and her nicely shaped nails, polished in a medium pink, reminded her again. Maybe Steve would notice her, like in one of those romantic movies. "Oh my goodness, Barbara," he would say, "I never realized." She smiled at the thought, then shook her head and got back to work.

As she usually did, Barbara ate lunch at her desk, then returned to work, her eyes glued on the screen of her word processor. At one-thirty, she jumped as her intercom buzzer sounded. She picked up the phone and her boss said, without preamble, "Barbara, I hope you finished the Sanderson documents. Mr. and Mrs. Sanderson are due here at two for the closing." Barbara realized that she had been so engrossed in hiding her new look that she hadn't even heard Steve come in.

She prided herself on her efficiency and always had documents completed long before they were needed. "Of course, Mr. Gordon, I've got them whenever you're ready."

"I wondered with that day off you took yesterday. Bring them in here, will you?"

"Certainly, Mr. Gordon." Barbara stood up, carefully arranged her black wool skirt and straightened the collar on her periwinkle blouse. As she walked into her boss's office, he was bent over, rifling through his briefcase which lay open on the floor beside his desk. "Damn," he swore, "I can't find a thing in here. Barbara, help me, will you?"

"What are you looking for?" Barbara asked, putting the documents she held on his desk.

"The Norton file. I had it just before lunch."

Barbara crouched, exposing a long expanse of thigh and began to systematically go through the contents of Mr. Gordon's briefcase. "It's right here," she said, quickly locating the missing file. As she looked up, she saw Mr. Gordon staring at her.

"What have you done with yourself?" he asked.

"I just got a few new things."

"And had your hair done, and got new makeup. Stand up."

Barbara stood, trying not to back up under his intense scrutiny. She watched his eyes travel from her hair to her heels and back up, several times. Then he released a long, low wolf whistle. "Not bad."

"Thank you, sit," Barbara said, straightening her shoulders. "I just felt I could use a lift."

"Well, you certainly got a lift." He stared for another full minute, then cleared his throat. "Okay. I see you have the Sanderson closing documents. I think everything should be in order. I have some notes from court this morning that need to be typed up."

Barbara sat in the small chair across from Steve Gordon's desk, smoothed her skirt and crossed her legs. As she arranged her computer on her lap, she caught Mr. Gordon staring at her knees. She sat, waiting for him to begin. "Mr. Gordon, I'm ready whenever you are."

"You know we've been together for how long? Almost two years?"

"Actually, it's almost six years."

"Well, don't you think it's about time you started calling me Steve?"

Totally taken aback, Barbara said, "I guess so, Mr. Gordon. I mean Steve."

"Good." He hesitated, then opened the folder in his hand. "I had a call from Mrs. Norton this morning. Take this down . . ."

At four-thirty, Barbara cleared the top of her desk, locked her laptop in her drawer and got her coat. As she was about to leave, Steve came out of his office. "Good night, Barbara," he said cheerfully. "And by the way, that silver patch of hair is very, well, very attractive. Have a nice evening. Got a date?"

"No. sir, I mean Steve. No date."

Steve put his arm around her waist and guided her toward the elevator. "Well then, maybe there will be time for me some evening."

Unable to breathe, Barbara merely nodded as the elevator doors opened.

"Well, have a nice evening."

"And he suggested that we might have dinner sometime," Barbara told Maggie several hours later. It was all Maggie could do not to swear when Barbara mentioned the whistle. He reminds me more and more of Arnie Becker, she thought.

"He looked at me, Barbara continued, unaware of Maggie's reaction. "I mean, really looked. He thought I looked good."

"Well, you do look good. Did work go well, too?"

"Sure. We did the Sanderson closing. I had caught a few minor errors and fixed them before they became problems. I also checked on the title insurance for him."

"What would he do without you?" Maggie said dryly.

"You're not happy for me, Maggie," Barbara said. "I don't understand."

"Sorry. I'm the one who helped you with the makeover and all and I'm glad you're pleased. It's just I have a basic dislike for men who only notice women when they're attractive."

"Oh, Maggie," Barbara said, sipping a glass of Chardonnay while she sautéed chicken and vegetables. Since Maggie's arrival, she was beginning to develop a taste for wine with dinner. "That's not really true. He always knew I was there. He just, well, you know. He's got other things on his mind."

Maggie patted Barbara on the shoulder. "I do know, baby. And maybe he'll ask you out. Is that what you want?"

"Oh, that would be wonderful. Dinner, maybe a little dancing."

"Ah, yes. Slow dancing. A wonderful way to make love standing up."

"You know, I never thought of it that way, but you're right. Making love standing up." Barbara placed the chicken mixture on two plates and sat across from her friend. In only two days it had become comfortable to have Maggie around. She had a friend.

"Do you like making love?" Maggie asked, anxious to move Barbara along to phase two of her makeover.

"It's not like it is in the novels I like to read, but the few times I did it it was tolerable."

"Tolerable. What a terrible way to think about making love. No bells? No stars? The earth didn't move?"

"That doesn't happen to people like me. That's for glitzy novels and X-rated movies."

"It can happen, and it does, and it should."

Barbara sipped her wine, her curiosity aroused. "Did the earth move for you?"

"You mean did I climax?"

Blushing slightly, Barbara nodded.

"No, not every time I made love. It takes a bit of effort and consideration on the part of both partners for orgasm to occur. But I did more often than not. I found that my men friends liked it when I came even though they were paying me to be sure *they* climaxed."

"But you only discovered good sex after your divorce."

"That's true and a bit sad. I regret that Chuck and I never found out what good sex was all about."

"Do you and he still see each other? I mean, did you? Does he know what you do, er . . . did?"

"Boy, tenses are a problem, aren't they. Anyway, no, I don't see Chuck anymore. He and his new wife moved to the West Coast many years ago. We had no kids, no ties, not much in common except a lot of history, and reminiscing wears thin very quickly."

"Can I ask you a question?"

"Sure." Maggie watched Barbara sip her wine as if searching for the right words. "Look, Barbara," Maggie said, "you can ask anything you want. I may choose not to answer, but please, we're friends and this is a really strange situation."

"As a, . . . let's say woman of the evening, you had to do all kinds of things with your customers. Is all that kinky stuff really fun?"

"You mean like oral sex and bondage?"

Barbara merely nodded.

"There are a thousand things people enjoy in the bedroom. Some enjoy plain straight sex, missionary position. Some enjoy telling stories in the dark, tying a partner up, spanking, anal sex. There are probably as many variations as you can dream of. Most I enjoy, a few I don't. But that's true with all things. I love almost all foods, but I hate liver and lima beans."

Barbara laughed. "What sex-type things don't you enjoy?"

"I already told you that I don't find pain pleasurable." Maggie thought a minute, then continued. "That's about all."

"Pain? That's sick."

"No, it's not. Listen, I hate to sound preachy, but I think this is very important. Anything that two consenting adults get pleasure from is none of anyone else's business and isn't sick. As long as both partners know it's important to say no if anything feels the least bit wrong, anything else is okay."

"I guess. How did you discover which things you enjoyed and which you didn't?"

"Trial and error. Lots of trial," Maggie grinned, "and a few errors."

"Errors?"

"Sure. I got myself into a few situations where I had to give someone his money back."

"Were they mad?"

"Not really. There was one guy from the Midwest. I won't go into details, but he wanted me to hurt him. Knowing that it would please him, I tried to do what he wanted, but I couldn't. However, I had a friend who was more into the pain side of pleasure than I was so I called her. He put on his clothes and hustled over to her house. He was so grateful that he called me the next day. He told me it had been everything he had ever fantasized about."

"No accounting for taste, is there?"

"No. And you may find as time passes that there are things you enjoy that you never dreamed of."

Barbara looked startled. "I'm not interested in kinky stuff. I don't mean to put you down, it's just that I'm not that type of person."

"You have no idea what type of person you are. I'll bet you have no real idea of what gives you pleasure."

"Of course I do." Barbara got a dreamy look in her eyes.

"You want romance, slow dancing, kissing and hugging. Long, slow sex with gentle penetration and a long rest period afterward."

"Sure. Why not?"

"No reason. But there's much more to good fucking than that."

"Fucking. Such a terrible word. It's so animal."

"That's what we are, animals. And human beings enjoy a good fucking as much as the average animal does. You know when you think of it, sex is a really awkward and embarrassing thing to do. It violates any feelings of personal space you might have, you get into lots of not-too-comfortable positions, and it's really messy."

"I never thought about it that way."

"So in order to create offspring, God, or Mother Nature, or evolution had to give the animals some reward for doing this ridiculous stuff. So that's where the pleasure comes in. I read somewhere that animals will go through much more maze-running and the like for sexual gratification than for any other reward."

"It's really pleasurable, isn't it?"

"It really is. I doubt you've ever experienced an orgasm."

"Of course I have."

Maggie raised an eyebrow and Barbara looked down and sipped her wine. "There's no shame in not having climaxed. It takes time and an understanding of your own body. You're not born knowing, you have to learn. Do you know where you like to be touched? What makes you hungry for more?"

Barbara continued to stare into her wineglass.

Maggie reached into her pocket and found the audiotape she had somehow known would be there. She pulled it out and stared at the label. "I don't understand how this got into my pocket, but there's a lot about my assignment I don't quite get yet. This is one tape in a series that a friend of mine made. He creates sensational erotica and has a soft, sexy voice, so he found this unique way to package his stories." She put the tape into Barbara's hand. "I'm going to give you an assignment."

Barbara looked up and giggled. "Homework?"

"Sort of. You must have a tape player." When Barbara nodded, Maggie continued. "I want you to fill the bathtub with nice warm water and play this tape. Just play it. If you're tempted to follow the instructions you'll be given, do it. No one will be watching, no one judging. Just you. Will you do that for me?" When her friend hesitated, Maggie said, "Please?"

"If it's important to you and your assignment."

"It is."

"Okay."

"Good." Maggie patted the back of Barbara's hand. "And find a new bar of soap, one you've never used of a different brand than your usual. You'll understand eventually. And I'll see you tomorrow evening."

Before Barbara could react, Maggie strode through the kitchen door and was gone.

An hour later, Barbara tidied up the kitchen and ran herself a bath. She had always loved the huge tub in the master bathroom. It was deep enough to fully cover her body almost to her shoulders. "This is pretty silly," Barbara said out loud as she plugged in an old cassette player she had recovered from the back of her closet. But if it was important to Maggie, it was important to her, she realized. In two short days she had gone from incredulity and scorn to friendship. She rummaged in the back of the bathroom closet and found a new bar of soap, then pressed the cassette machine's play button and stepped into the steamy water.

Music filled the bathroom, music with a quiet yet pulsing beat and a soft, slightly mournful clarinet and a baritone saxophone. The sounds that filled the room felt like soft summer nights with the sky filled with stars. Barbara thought of couples in open-topped cars staring down at city lights from darkened lover's overlooks. She rolled a small towel and placed it at the back of her neck and stretched out. She sighed deeply and relaxed.

> *"Are you all relaxed?" a soft, sensuous man's voice asked as the music faded slightly. "That's very good." Barbara started to sit up. "No, don't move," the voice said. "Just lie back and relax. Let the music fill you, create dreams, fantasies. Let it evoke pictures of teenagers in parked cars."*

How did that man know what she was thinking? Barbara wondered. The music swelled again, and for several minutes the voice was silent. Then the music faded slightly and the voice returned.

> *"I hope you're naked, lying in a tub of warm water. The naked female body is such a wonder. It's so beautiful."*

Yeah, right, Barbara thought. For all he knows, I'm a dog, a hundred pounds overweight with droopy boobs and three stomachs.

"Don't think like that. All female bodies are beautiful regardless of the way they actually look. Breasts are soft, firm, large or small. Nipples are chocolate brown or dark pink. Skin is deep ebony or almost transparent white. God, I love a woman's breasts. And your bellies are concave, with prominent hipbones, or full and round. I love to feel the pulse in a woman's throat and know how it speeds up when she listens to me tell her how beautiful she is. Can you feel your pulse? Find it by stroking your throat. Go ahead. No one's watching."

Without really thinking, Barbara slid a wet finger up her neck and felt her pulsebeat.

"That's your life flowing throughout your body. You can feel it all over, in your wrist, in your foot, at your temple, in your groin. If I tell you that I want you to imagine me touching your breasts, does your pulse speed up? I love that I can do that for you."

Barbara felt her pulse. No silly man's voice was going to make her pulse beat faster. But it did.

"I want you to make your hands all soapy. Please, for me. Feel the soap, so smooth and slippery. Rub your hands over the bar, touching its contours. Close your eyes and just feel the soap as your hands caress it."

Barbara took the soap from the holder and rubbed it. She was strangely aware of the slick surface.

"Take the soap and make a rich lather, then slowly rub it on your throat. Feel the difference between the hard surface of the cake of soap and the soft, warm skin of your body. Move your hands

around. Feel your jaw, the back of your neck. Now caress your cheeks. How smooth and soft they are through the lather. Keep your eyes closed and just feel. Feel rough and smooth spots, places that are warm and those that are cool. If you have fingernails, use them to scratch your shoulders, just lightly."

Barbara did, her eyes closed, her head resting against the towel on the rim of the tub.

"You need more lather, so rub the soap again. Can you smell the perfume? Does your soap smell like flowers or spice? Can you picture a field of summer blossoms or an Oriental harem? Maybe lemons or blackberries. Inhale deeply. Fill your lungs with the scent and imagine.

As the music filled the room, Barbara breathed deeply and saw a Parisian boudoir with perfume bottles on a mirrored vanity. She vaguely remembered her mother buying her this soap many years before. She lay there seeing the boudoir. A woman sat at the vanity putting on makeup. She was dressed in a filmy negligee, waiting for her lover. Barbara opened her eyes. Now why had she created that scene? Waiting for her lover, indeed.

"I hope your eyes are still closed," the voice said softly. Barbara snapped her eyes shut. "I want you to feel other places on your body. Start with your breasts. Your soapy hands will feel so good on your soft flesh. I want you to use the pads of your fingers to stroke the flesh of your breasts, just around the outside. Press a bit and feel. Are your breasts full, or small and tight? As I told you, I like them all. Can you feel your ribs or is there deep softness? Please. I can't be there to feel your skin so you must do it for me."

Tentatively Barbara sat up slightly so the tops of her breasts were above the waterline. She slid her soapy fingers over the crests, then pressed her fingertips into the flesh. Deeply soft and pillowy, she thought.

"Find the areolas, just where the color changes, darkens. Open your eyes if you must, then close them again. Run one fingertip over the slight ridge there, all around. Keep swirling around that line. Can you feel your nipples tighten? No, not with your fingers, but feel it inside. Don't look, feel. Can you feel your nipples contract? Yes, I know they will."

They did.

"I wish I were there to touch your nipples. I would first swirl my fingers around the outside the way you are doing it. Then I wouldn't be able to resist sliding toward the tightened buds. I want to feel them but I can't, so you will have to do it for me. Touch. Squeeze. That's what I would do. I would squeeze those tight nipples. It's hard to feel it when you touch lightly so make yourself feel it. Do what you have to so that you know the touch of your fingers. Pinch, use your nails."

Barbara used her newly manicured nails to tweak the tips of her breasts. She felt it, tight, slightly painful yet very stimulating.

"I know you think this is strange and maybe you feel a bit guilty, but it's your body and you are entitled to touch it. It's God's creation and so beautiful. I know also that you're noticing that you're not just feeling your fingers touching your breasts. You are also starting to become aware of the flesh between your legs. You're feeling full, maybe getting wet, not from your bath but from your excitement."

Barbara was aware of her groin. This is ridiculous, she thought, yanking herself from her dreamy state. It's dirty.

"I know you feel that what you're doing isn't what nice girls are supposed to do, but that's nonsense. Feeling sexual and sensual is wonderful. It is what I would want you to be experiencing if I were there. Relax. You and I are alone. No one will know, or care, what

you're doing. You are just making your body feel good. What is wrong with that?"

Nothing, Barbara thought, taking a deep breath. Nothing at all. He's right. It is my body and I can touch it. That's why it was designed to feel good.

"I know you want to touch the flesh between your legs and that's so good. I get so much pleasure out of knowing I excite you. I know the water covers the parts of you that you want to touch, but you must make your hands soapy and slippery anyway. Do it for me since I can't caress you myself. Rub the soap while I tell you what I'd like to be doing if I were there."

Barbara picked up the soap and rubbed, closing her eyes as she did so.

"If I were there with you I would cup your beautiful breasts in my hands and lick the water off the tips with my rough tongue. I would suckle and lick, and maybe nip the erect tip from time to time with my sharp teeth. Can you feel me? I hope so. Don't touch yourself, just rub the soap and imagine my teeth and lips and tongue. Imagine what they are doing and how they make you feel. Are you getting tight between your legs? Do you want to touch? That hunger is what I want you to feel. Think of how my fingers would feel touching your ribs, your sides, your belly. If you're ticklish, I can touch you so it feels good, yet not make you laugh. I don't want you to giggle right now, although laughter is wonderful. Do you want me to touch you?"

The erotic music and the man's voice filled Barbara's ears, penetrating to her soul. Yes, she admitted, she did want him to touch her.

"I can't touch you, you know, and that makes me so sad. But you can touch all those places I cannot. Rub your palm over your

belly. Scratch the skin on your sides. Now the insides of your thighs. Rub, caress, stroke. It's your skin and it feels so good."

Barbara had never touched herself like this before and it was a bit embarrassing. But it felt good and she didn't really consider stopping.

"Move your fingers closer to the center of all that you need. You want to touch. Do you know how? Do you know what would feel good? Well, I do. It would feel good if you rubbed the wet, slippery place. Find that place and know the difference between the water and your own slippery juices. Feel that slick, slithery substance? Your body is making that to make it easier for me to penetrate you, but, of course, I cannot. But you can.

"Have you ever wondered what you feel like inside? Under the water, make sure your fingers have no soap left on them. Then slide one into your passage. Touch the slick walls, rub all the places you can and find out which feels the best. I would learn that if I were there. I would know when you moan or purr, when your hips move to take me in more deeply, when you become wetter and more slippery. I would know the secrets of your pleasure, and you know them now, too. Run your fingers over the outside folds. Use the other hand if you like the feel of that finger inside you."

Barbara did have one finger inside her channel, in a place she had never touched before. It felt very good and she wanted more. She used the middle finger of her other hand to rub the deep crevices, moving from side to side, enjoying her own flesh.

"Have you found your clit? I would have by now. I would have rubbed up and down both sides, feeling the tight nub swell and reach for me. I would have put one finger on either side and rubbed. Oh, that does feel good, doesn't it. I can almost see your back arch, your eyes close, and your mouth open. Put a second finger inside your body to fill it up, and a third if that feels good. Rub your clit and all the places that feel as good."

Barbara was stroking her body, marveling at all the spots that gave her pleasure.

"If I were there, I would use my mouth now. No, it's not a bad thing. It's a beautiful experience. I would lick your clit, flick my tongue over the end, then wrap my lips around it and draw it into my mouth. Just a slight vacuum to suck it in and hold it while my tongue rubs the surface. Just don't stop what you're doing while I lick you."

Barbara filled her pussy with her fingers and rubbed her clit, feeling the pressure in her belly. This was dirty, but so good. She didn't want to stop, and she didn't. The words and the music and the rubbing and the fullness inside all drove her higher. She felt something build deep in her belly, then suddenly waves of ecstatic pleasure spasmed through her.

"Oh, yes, my wonderful girl," the voice said. "Make it feel so good."

Barbara continued as the clenching subsided.

"I will not talk anymore, but leave you to the music and to your pleasure," the voice said. "Until the next time."

"Oh," Barbara said, panting. "Oh."

Chapter 5

For the next several days, the tape was never far from Barbara's mind. She thought about that night in the tub and, with guilty pleasure, repeated the experience several times, twice while listening to the tape and, more recently, once while picturing Steve Gordon. That had happened at almost three in the morning when Barbara awakened from an erotic dream, a dream she couldn't remember but one that left her so excited that she had to reach beneath her nightgown and touch herself to relieve the tension. As she touched her body, now able to find the places that gave her pleasure, she thought about her boss, his slender hands with their long fingers and carefully trimmed nails. She could almost feel those hands on her body as she climaxed.

Maggie showed up at dinner time every two or three days and they talked about inconsequentials. Barbara was dying to ask questions about Maggie's life as a prostitute but never seemed to be able to work up the nerve.

One evening almost two weeks after Maggie's first visit, Barbara said, "There's an office party tomorrow night. It's a celebration for a big case the firm won, and they've invited all of their clients, all of the staff and who knows who else. Steve, Mr. Gordon, told me that he's looking forward to seeing me there. I think he might be ready to ask me to dinner."

"That's great. Will you go if he asks you?"

"Sure. It makes my palms sweat just thinking about it."

"I'm sure it does." Maggie grinned and arched an eyebrow. "So. He makes you hot, does he?"

"Maggie!" Barbara said. "That's not it at all. He's a very nice man and I'd like to get to know him better. That's all." The thought of her middle-of-the-night fantasies made her blush slightly.

"Okay. I won't tease. But being hot, horny, and hungry isn't a crime. As a matter of fact, it's delightful. It's a high, frustrating but delicious." Maggie hesitated. "I've been meaning to ask, did you like that tape?"

Barbara blushed several shades darker. "I'll get it for you. I'm sorry. I forgot to return it and now I'm not too sure where I put it."

Maggie reached out and covered Barbara's hand with her own, calming the nervous fingers. "Don't. Just don't. You and I both know you're lying. That tape is meant to do exactly what it did. It woke you up to things about your body you didn't know. That's why I gave it to you and that's why you can keep it. Sensuality is a joy and, once awakened, well, let's just say that it's very difficult to get the genie back into the bottle."

Barbara sighed. She couldn't hide anything from Maggie. The woman was too perceptive. And anyway, there was so much that Barbara didn't know. "Maggie, you're right. This is silly. But it's very difficult, after thirty-one years on this earth to admit that I'm such a dunce about sex."

"How are you supposed to learn?" Maggie said. "All those articles in *Cosmo?* How to have an orgasm any hour of the day or night. How to lure the man of your dreams into your camper. The things about men that women don't want men to know they know. Oh, please. Give me a break."

Barbara laughed. "I read those," she said.

"And many of them have good information. But many others are pure crap. How to climax seven times in three hours. Everyone in those articles is a stud, male and female. Let's hear it for people who like to make love, climax once or twice and cuddle. Sex is so much more than how many times a man ejaculates or a woman has an orgasm."

"It is?"

"Oh, Lord, darling," Maggie said. "Sex isn't the destination, it's the journey. It's how you get to that wonderful level of excitement that allows both partners to soar together, then relax. Did you even think that if it weren't for orgasm and the calm afterward, we'd be chasing each other all the time and we'd never get anything else done. Orgasm is the final chord in the symphony, but it's the music before that counts."

"Oh" was all that Barbara could say.

"I don't mean to preach, but I just love making love."

"But isn't there one right man, one person, who knocks your socks off? One man with whom you'd like to climb into bed for the next hundred years? What about your husband?"

"When Chuck and I were married I thought it was forever and I settled down, worked, fucked, and enjoyed. But even then I used to imagine handsome men adoring me, licking and touching me. I wasn't quite clear on exactly what they would be doing, just doing kinky things to my quivering body."

"Really?" Barbara said, grinning.

"Sure. Chuck and I had a good relationship, but it wasn't enough for either of us. He found his SueAnn. She's probably a lovely girl, and because of her I was pushed out of the plain-vanilla nest I had been in, into the world of Heavenly Hash." Maggie grinned. "And let's hear it for all twenty-eight flavors."

"There's no one special? No one man who you ever wished would take you away to a deserted cabin and keep you there forever?"

"Not really. I love the deserted cabin idea for a weekend, but one man? For life? I don't think so. Someone once said that if the plural of louse is lice, then the plural of spouse should be spice. I just happen to like lots of spice."

"Well, I'm not like you," Barbara said, somehow wondering

whether what she was saying was entirely true. "I just want one man to love me and make a life with me."

"That's wonderful. Everyone should try to figure out what his or her dream is, then go for it. If that's what you want, then let's see what we can do to make it come true. Steve Gordon?"

Barbara's grin widened. "He could be the one."

"Why?" Maggie asked.

"Why?"

"Yes. What about him that makes him the right one. I don't know him much at all. Tell me. Does he have a great sense of humor? Do you two share many common interests? Is he moody or more placid? Is he easy to be with?"

"Actually, I don't really know. I haven't spent much time with him. He's not too bad to work for. He understood about my mom and let me take time off when I needed it. And he depends on me to keep him going. I'm valuable to him."

"That's not a reason to make a life with someone. He has to be valuable to you as well."

"Of course he is," Barbara said. "He's wonderful."

"Okay, great." Maggie stood up. "What about this party? How dressed up is it?"

"It's cocktail dress."

"So. What are you going to wear? You want him to notice you, don't you?"

"I do. I mean, he does." Actually, he had noticed her the first few days after her dramatic makeover, but since then it had been business as usual. Several of the other men in the office seemed to pay more attention to her new persona than Steve did. One man had actually asked her to dinner, but she had politely refused, preferring to meet with Maggie and concentrate on Steve.

"All right then, let's decide what you should wear. I saw a dress in the back of your closet the first night I was here."

The two women went upstairs and Maggie quickly pulled out the dress. "How about this?"

"Oh, Maggie. I bought that as a favor to my mom. It was one of the last shopping trips we took together before she became bedridden. I've never even worn it."

"Why not?"

"It's so, I don't know, obvious." She took the hanger from Maggie. The halter shaped chiffon bodice was soft blue with a full skirt that shaded from the pale blue of the top to a deep royal at the hem. She pointed to the low-cut back. "You can't even wear a bra. I couldn't wear this."

"Try it on for me," Maggie asked. "Come on, what will it hurt. Only I will see you."

With a deep sigh, Barbara stripped off her clothes and slipped into the dress. She adjusted the wide medium-blue belt and fastened the rhinestone buckle. While she was doing that, Maggie was rummaging around on the floor of Barbara's closet. Suddenly there was a triumphant "Taa Daa" and Maggie tossed out a pair of strappy black patent-leather sandals. "Put those on."

Barbara did, then the two women looked at Barbara in the full-length mirror. Maggie stood behind her and pulled her hair into an upswept mass, with a few strands artfully caressing her neck and the white streak prominently displayed. "God, I wish I had hair like this," Maggie sighed. "Mine's so tight and curly, I had to keep it short all the time."

"That's not me," Barbara said, looking at the striking brunette who looked back at her. "That dress and hairstyle are meant for a beautiful woman. And I'm certainly not beautiful."

"Not classically beautiful, no," Maggie said. "But a woman who looks comfortable in her skin, and particularly one who has that gleam of sensuality that you will have if I have anything to say about it, is attractive. And you are."

"Oh, Maggie. I couldn't." Could I?

"You can if you want to."

"Do you really think so? Could I knock 'em dead? Could I really get Steve to notice me?"

Maggie grinned. "I know so and I think maybe you're beginning to also."

Barbara suddenly realized things about herself she hadn't understood until that moment. She wanted to be that woman she saw in the mirror. Like Cinderella. No, not like Cinderella, she corrected herself. I don't want to be someone else for just one night. She thought about her new hairstyle and her new clothes. She realized, as she looked at herself, that in this dress she stood up straighter, looked herself in the eye. And she glowed.

"Maybe just a little," Barbara said.

"Good. That's all I ask. Enjoy the party, and don't dance only with Prince Charming. Cindy missed a lot of other really great folks at that ball."

The party was being held in the King's Room of a local hotel. Almost two hundred people were expected. When Barbara arrived, there was a four-piece dance combo playing innocuous music. Uniformed waiters and waitresses circulated with hot and cold hors d'oeuvres, glasses of red and white wine, and flutes of champagne. There was also an open bar for those who enjoyed soft drinks or hard liquor.

Barbara stood off to one side trying to figure out how to join one of the groups of laughing people. She searched the crowd for Steve, but could not find his familiar tall, slender shape. I wonder whether he's bringing someone, she thought. She looked down at the yards of bright blue skirt and thought about the hour it had taken for Maggie to fix her makeup and choose her accessories. As she moved her head, Barbara felt the large rhinestone earrings brush against her neck. Why had she allowed Maggie to talk her into those chandeliers? Why the wide bracelet? Why not her plain gold chain around her neck and her gold studs in her ears? She'd certainly feel more comfortable.

For want of something to do, she took a glass of white wine from one waiter's tray and a salmon puff from another.

"You've changed your hair," a voice said behind her. "I like it."

She turned and recognized Jay Preston, an investigator whom the firm employed for divorce work and other secret projects. "Thank you, Mr. Preston. I'm surprised you noticed." I never noticed how cute he is, she thought, still scanning the room for her boss.

"I have noticed a lot about you in the past few weeks. And it's Jay."

"I don't know what to say," Barbara said. God, he was sexy. Not handsome, Barbara thought, but the gleam in his deep gray eyes was directed entirely at her. His hair was almost black with just the beginnings of silver at the temples. Because Barbara wore two-inch heels she was only an inch shorter than he was, but he seemed to tower over her, making her think of some desert chieftain holding a sweet young woman captive. Now where had that thought come from? Barbara wondered.

"Don't say anything," Jay said. "Just tell me, are you alone tonight?"

"If you mean did I bring a date, the answer is no."

"Bring a date. You don't have to be a detective to know that that phrase means you're not married or engaged. This must be my lucky night." He took her elbow, his fingers on her naked skin causing shivers up her spine.

"You are a bit too fast for me," she said.

"I'm sorry. I just don't believe in wasting time when I see something I want."

Barbara took a step back. "It feels like you're using up all the air in here," she said honestly, sipping her wine.

Jay didn't try to close the distance between them. "Tell me about you. What do you do when you're not being Steve Gordon's Ms. Everything?"

They stood and talked for about half an hour, and found out they shared an interest in old TV comedies and cooking and abhorred partisan politics and snow. "I tried skiing once," Jay said, "and, well, I guess it's not macho to admit that after I fell more times than I could count, I took off my skis and walked down the baby slope."

Barbara laughed. "I never even tried. I had a few friends who invited me to go with them several years ago. I got there, put on boots that hurt my feet, took off the boots and spent the day in the lodge drinking hot chocolate and eating chili."

"Not together, I hope," Jay said.

"Not together, but I think I gained two pounds that day. So much for exercise."

Jay gave her an appraising look from her hair to her feet. "Not a problem," he said. "You look just right to me."

"Barbara," a familiar voice said, "there you are. I've been looking for you."

"Hello, Steve," Barbara said. "You know Jay Preston."

Steve nodded. "Preston." He turned to Barbara and put a friendly arm around her waist. "I wanted you to meet Lisa." He reached out and draped his other arm around the shoulders of a strikingly gorgeous woman. "Lisa, this is Barbara."

The woman smiled warmly and reached out a hand. "It's so nice to meet you. Steve talks about you so much."

Weakly, Barbara extended a hand. "It's nice to meet you, too." He didn't tell me much about you, she thought, and there was obviously a lot to tell. Lisa was a knockout in a long silver sequined gown.

"This is so great," Steve said. "My two girls." He hugged them both. "Dinner will be served soon. Will you sit with us?"

Jay put his arm around Barbara's shoulders. "I think Barbara intended to eat with me." He looked at Barbara and smiled.

"Yes, Steve," she said quickly. "Jay and I were just in the middle of something, if you don't mind."

"Of course not," Steve said. "Come on, Lisa. I see some people I want you to meet." The two walked away. As Barbara gazed after them, she felt a glass thrust into her hand.

"Have some champagne," Jay said. "It's good for what ails you."

"Does it show that much?" Barbara said, unable to pretend.

"Only to someone as perceptive as I am. And don't worry. I'm very good at cheering people up. I do limericks, bad jokes, and I promise not to sing while we dance."

"There's nothing between Steve and me, you know."

"I know. I do understand. And I'll leave you alone if you like. That business of sitting together at dinner was just for his benefit. Unless you'd like to."

Barbara turned from watching Steve and Lisa talk to one of the other partners and said, "I'd like that." She grinned and felt her shoulders relaxed. "This feels like a bad movie. Shunned by her boss, the heroine," she tapped her chest, "that's me, finally notices the handsome hero." She patted the lapel of Jay's tuxedo. "That's you. Then they fall madly in love and live happily ever after."

"Not *ever after*," Jay said, covering her palm with his. "I'm not that type of guy. I live for the now, not for next year. But, my love, I could definitely fall in lust with you."

"Excuse me?"

"Let me lay my cards on the table. I find you very attractive and you fit one of my favorite fantasies."

"Oh I do, do I?"

"Yes. I know more about you than you might wish. You're in love with your boss, or at least you think you are. You're an innocent, inexperienced woman who hasn't learned her own power yet. And you do have power. You radiate with it. But you don't understand it. I want to teach you so you can have anything you want."

"What power are you talking about? You're confusing me. This is some kind of line you use with people like me and I don't think I like it."

"It's not strictly speaking a line, because it's entirely honest. And you say you don't like it, but I have my fingers on your pulse and it's pounding right now. This whole thing excites you and you don't quite know what to do about it. I won't press you for the moment."

The doors to the dining room opened and Jay took Barbara's glass and put it down on a nearby table. "Will you sit with me?"

Barbara thought about how much this man was like Maggie. He was a free thinker, dangerous, charming, and totally unsuitable with goals that were completely different from hers. But she *was* terribly excited. She hesitated only a moment, gazed at Steve and the knockout, then back at Jay. It's time, she told herself. As a matter of fact, I'm long overdue. "I'd like that," Barbara said, taking Jay's arm as they joined the stream of people walking toward the dining room.

During the almost three-hour dinner, Jay was a perfect gentleman. They talked, laughed, and argued, with each other and with the other couples at their table. Between courses, they danced to the music of the combo, but Jay kept a discreet distance between them. After coffee was served, the place began to empty out. Steve and Lisa stopped at their table to say good night and Barbara smiled and wished them a good evening. The pain of seeing her boss with Ms. Knockout on his arm had diminished considerably.

As the band began a slow song, Jay took her hand and once again led her to the small wooden dance floor, now crowded with the few other couples still left. Jay took her in his arms and held her against him and their feet moved reflexively to the music. His mouth beside her ear, Jay said, "I've tried to give you some time to think about me as a real person, not as a lecherous private eye, but now the evening is almost over and I might not see you again, except in the office. I want to tell you again that I'm in lust with you and I want you in my bed. I want to lay you out on the sheets and touch you and lick you. I want to make you want me so badly you beg me to take you. I want to want you so badly that I do." He pressed his hand in the small of her back, leaning the bulge in his trousers against her belly.

Barbara couldn't speak. She was barely able to think.

"I want to do strange, unusual, extremely pleasurable things with you, things that will make you blush and scream and cry out in joy. But nothing long term. I live for now. Nothing exclusive. I love women and I love making love to them."

"Again I'm speechless."

"Let's dance for a few more minutes, then I'll take you to your car. I want you to think about everything I've said and I will call you tomorrow night. I want you to say yes, but on realistic terms. Will you think about it?"

"Will I think about anything else?"

Jay's warm chuckle tickled her ear. "Good."

Half an hour later, Jay dropped Barbara at her car. "I'll call you tomorrow, but if you haven't decided, I'll call you the following evening. Take as much time as you like. And understand that I do take no for an answer and I won't pressure you, except to promise you that it will be wonderful."

It was fortunate that, since the hotel was only two blocks from the office, Barbara had driven this route every day for many years, for she drove in a total fog. She knew what Jay was asking. He wanted to have an affair with her. A "no commitment, no tomorrow" affair. No, she told herself, It was impossible.

But God, how she was turned on. She didn't know what strange, unusual things he had in mind, but she was so curious. She wasn't stupid. She knew about oral sex, bondage, all the kinky things she had read about in novels, and she was fascinated. Isn't that how the cobra entices its victims? Doesn't he fascinate them until he can bite?

But what is the downside to all this? That nice girls don't? Is that a realistic reason not to do something that might be so good? She was so confused.

She wasn't at all surprised to see Maggie sitting in her kitchen when she arrived home. "How was it?" she asked, then hesitated. "Something happened. Did you spend the evening with Steve? Did he ask you out? Tell me everything."

Barbara did, with little comment from Maggie. "And Jay wants me to go to bed with him. No strings. No nothing. Just making love."

Momentarily Maggie thought about Angela's desires. "Get her married to that cute lawyer. Home, kids. . . ." If Maggie wanted to get to heaven, the best way was to do what Angela wanted, wasn't it? She should tell Barbara to reject Jay out of hand and concentrate on Steve. But she couldn't. Jay was right for Barbara now and what she wanted what was good for Barbara. "You have to do what you think is best," Maggie said. "But that's sometimes hard to sort out. I guess my philosophy would be, If it feels good and doesn't hurt anyone, do it."

"I keep thinking that going to bed with a man just for sex makes me a bad girl. What would my mother say?"

"From what I heard about your mother, both from you and from the girls . . ." She gazed at the ceiling, "I think she'd tell you to do what you want with none of the *good* and *bad* labels."

"I'm so confused."

"Sleep on it," Maggie said. "You don't have to decide tonight." As usual, to end the discussion, Maggie walked out the kitchen door and disappeared. Barbara went up to bed and, for the first time in her life, slept naked.

"I need to be honest with you, Jay," Barbara said into the phone the following evening. "I'm intrigued, but I'm scared to death, too. I don't know whether I want to have an affair with you that has no future. I wasn't brought up that way."

"Oh Barbara, you're wonderful. I completely understand. Look, how about this? Let me take you to dinner next Saturday. Just dinner. No commitment to do anything except enjoy each other's company."

"Well . . ." Barbara sat on the edge of her bed, playing with the hem of the pillowcase.

"We had fun together last evening and I'm not willing to let that go. Do you like Italian food? Not spaghetti, but real zuppe de peche, good osso buco with orzo. And they make the best tiramisu."

"Actually, I love Italian food." He's such a sweet man, she thought. And he seems to understand how I feel.

"As I remember, you told me you're a great cook, but let's let someone else do the cooking and we can get to know each other better. Please."

Barbara vacillated. She liked Jay a lot, but she wasn't ready for what he wanted, and she knew that hadn't changed. She didn't want a sleazy affair. Did she? "I did enjoy last evening a great deal." She took a deep breath. "All right. Just dinner."

"Great."

They made arrangements for Jay to pick Barbara up at her house the following Saturday evening.

"Maggie," Barbara said the following evening, "I'm really nervous about this dinner date."

"What are you afraid of exactly?"

Barbara sat at the dinner table, dirty dinner dishes spread around her, a cup of coffee cooling in her hand. "I've been trying to sort that out. I think I'm afraid that I'll be tempted to jump into bed with the guy. He's nice, warm, honest, and sexy as hell."

"And what if you do jump into bed with him?"

"I guess I'm afraid that I'll hate myself the next morning."

"You're right, that is a risk. So the question becomes, Is the risk worth the reward?"

"I never thought of it that way."

"Well, let's think of it that way now. If you do get involved with Jay, what's the reward?"

Barbara grinned. "He's a very sexy man and, to be perfectly honest, he turns me on. My insides get all squishy, my knees get weak, and well, I think it would be great."

"Okay, what's the reward if you tell him no."

Barbara considered for a few minutes. "I won't have any regrets the next morning."

"You won't?"

Barbara sipped at her cold coffee. "I will have regrets. I will regret all the things I didn't do."

"I think my job is to make you see all sides of this problem. You know what side I'm on. I think good sex is the best thing going. You're a big girl, and perfectly able to understand what you're getting yourself into, and you're no virgin. You understand, as I'm sure Jay does, about safe sex, condoms all that. You know how I feel, but it must be your decision."

Barbara pictured the scene, Jay stroking her hand at dinner, kissing her fingers. She'd read enough novels to know that once the hormones kicked in, resistance was futile. Then it wouldn't be her responsibility. "He'll convince me. I know he will and I'll do it."

But Jay didn't pressure her. Villa Josephina turned out to be a small Italian restaurant in Tuckahoe, with a round hostess who obviously knew Jay from frequent visits. They were seated at a table off to one side. Barbara took one look at the extensive menu and, her mouth dry and her appetite gone, she let Jay order for both of them. At first, Barbara was quite nervous and unable to do justice to a wonderful shrimp appetizer, but as the meal progressed she relaxed. Through the courses they talked. About everything but sex. Barbara began to feel like she was having dinner with an old friend, not a would-be lover. And, although he was a sensual man, he wasn't turning her on. As a matter of fact, she thought he was making an effort not to even indirectly refer to anything sexual. He had even dressed in a dark green flannel sport shirt and shaker sweater, muting any sensuality.

"I would offer you a brandy," Jay said to Barbara as the waiter brought small cups of strong espresso, "but I don't want alcohol to cloud your mind. Or mine, for that matter."

"Is that why you didn't order any wine?"

"I know what's going through your head. I know that this is a difficult decision for you, and I want you to be clear-headed." It was his first reference to the topic that had been so much on Barbara's mind. He took her hand across the soft blue tablecloth. "Whatever you decide is fine with me, but it must be your decision."

Barbara lowered her gaze.

"Okay," Jay said. "I understand."

He hadn't convinced her, pressured her or made her decision any easier. And without a push, she didn't think she could go through with it. She sipped her coffee. "Thanks. I think I'd like you to take me home," Barbara said.

Quickly Jay paid the check and drove Barbara back to her house in Fleetwood. He walked her to her door and said, "Do you think we might just have dinner together once in a while? I haven't enjoyed an evening this much in a long time." A boyish grin lit his face. "And maybe you'll change your mind."

"Kiss me," Barbara said, uncertain as to where the words had come from.

Jay looked startled, then put his hands on her shoulders. Drawing her close, he brushed his mouth across hers. He touched the tip of his tongue to the joining of her lips, then cupped her face with his hands.

Barbara placed her palms against Jay's chest and relaxed into the kiss. He was an expert, softly taking her mouth and possessing it. He explored and tasted until she parted her lips and allowed his tongue free access. Slowly she slid her hands up his chest to the back of his neck, holding him close. His fingers slowly slid up the sides of her neck and tunneled through her thick hair, caressing her scalp.

Finally he leaned back, his eyes caressing her face. "You kiss like an expert," he said. "I thought of you as being so innocent."

"I don't know where that came from. It must be that you do that to me," Barbara admitted.

Jay ran his fingers through her hair. "You know this silver stripe is incredibly sexy. Are you a witch?"

"No, of course not."

"What would you do if you were? Right now."

"That's an interesting question," Barbara said, smiling ruefully. "I think I'd make it tomorrow morning."

Jay cocked his head to one side. "Why?"

"Because tonight is causing me so much confusion. By tomorrow morning decisions would have been made."

"Do you want me to make the decision for you?"

"Yes." She paused. "No."

"What do you want?"

She looked into Jay's eyes and a slow smile spread across her face. "I want you to come inside with me."

Barbara watched Jay's eyes light up. "Are you sure?"

Barbara let go of Jay long enough to find her keys and unlock the front door. "Yes, I'm sure."

They walked into the house and Barbara put their coats in the living room. Then she slid back into Jay's arms and raised her face to his. He accepted the invitation readily. He brushed soft kisses on her eyes, her cheeks, her mouth, all the time keeping his hands on her back.

Barbara realized what she wanted. Her body was alive, impatient, unsatisfied. She ran her hands over the back of Jay's deep green sweater, then slid under it to touch his soft flannel shirt and the hard flesh beneath. She wanted, needed, him to make the next move. Push me, she cried. Seduce me. "Please."

"Oh, how I want you," he moaned, kissing her deeply again. When he pulled away, he looked around. "You know, living rooms are nice, but how about a nice horizontal surface? I want to make long, slow love to you, not paw and pet like teenagers."

Barbara motioned toward the stairs and together they walked up.

A small light was burning in the corner of the cozy room. Her bed was covered with a patchwork comforter, one pattern of which matched the curtains. Another of the patchwork fabrics covered the armchair on one side of the room, and the polished wood floor was covered with a multicolored braided rug.

This room is cleaner than it has been in weeks, Barbara realized as they entered. Maggie must have tidied up after I left for dinner. She glanced at the bed. Maggie had even changed the sheets. She had planned for this. She had known or hoped that Barbara would be here, like this, with Jay. Thanks, Barbara almost said aloud. She smiled silently as she watched Jay pull off his sweater. "Can I take that?" For want of something to do, she folded it and put it on a chair.

Jay came up behind her and slid his hands around her waist. "I know this is awkward for you," he said, his lips against the tender skin beneath her ear. "Let me lead. I promise you will like where we go together." He held her back against his hard chest and Barbara could feel the heat of his body against hers. He nuzzled her neck, planting small soft kisses on the skin he could reach. Then he turned her in his arms and again pressed his mouth against hers. She smelled his after-shave, spicy and mixed with the natural male smell of him.

Slowly the heat began to build. He kissed her over and over until all she was aware of was his mouth. She felt him press his lower body against hers so she could get used to his arousal. When he pressed, she found herself pressing back.

Jay stepped back and untied her scarf, then slowly unbuttoned her soft pink blouse. He pulled the blouse's tails from her burgundy skirt and slid the garment off her shoulders.

Barbara stood in a haze, wondering how Jay would see her, glad she had allowed Maggie to talk her into wearing her new, more daring, white lace underwear. She started to raise her arms to cover herself, but she heard Jay's voice. "Oh, my," Jay said, his eyes roaming over her body. "I expected you to have a nice figure, but you're really beautiful."

Barbara knew she weighed more than she should, but the look in Jay's eyes said he thought she was desirable. Her arms fell limply to her sides. Jay placed his hands on her ribs, then slowly slid them upward toward her breasts. "Your skin is so soft, like warm satin." His fingers reached Barbara's full breasts, still encased in the silk-and-lace bra. She felt him stroke her flesh softly, the touch muffled through the fabric. Go faster, she screamed in her mind. Push me onto the bed and fuck me. Get this waiting over with.

"No rushing," Jay purred as if reading her mind. "It's hard for me to wait, but this first time for us this night will live in my mind for a long time. I want it to be perfect. I want you to want me, not to get it over with just because your body feels empty, hollow, needy."

"But . . ."

He covered her protest with his lips, his thumbs now stroking her nipples through the cloth. Barbara knew how tight her nubs had become, and she felt the wet swelling between her legs. Jay kissed and rubbed, then held her tight while he found and opened the clasp of her bra. He let the garment drop to the floor and admired Barbara's firm breasts. He bent, touching the tip of his tongue to each crest in turn, until Barbara's knees threatened to buckle. She heard a low moan and realized that it came from her.

Jay knelt in front of her, unfastened her skirt and pulled it down. "Oh, honey," he said, seeing the matching panties and garter belt Maggie had insisted upon. "This is so sexy. I want to go slowly but you are making it very difficult." She wore the panties over the garters, so Jay lowered the tiny wisp of fabric until she could step out of it. Then he guided her to the bed with the stockings and garter belt still in place. "I think making love to a woman with stockings on like this is one of the sexiest things," he purred.

She stretched out on the bed, rubbing the sole of her nylon-covered foot over the quilt. She watched as Jay removed his shirt, then she looked at the body now revealed. He was tanned, but looked like he hadn't worked out in years. No perfect athletic body. just a man's chest covered with tightly curled hair. Not intimidating, she thought. She saw that Jay had already removed his shoes and socks and was unzipping his pants. I wish I were brave enough, Barbara thought with the part of her brain still capable of thought. I would sit up and help him pull off his shorts. Maybe, she thought. Maybe.

Jay, now naked, stretched out beside Barbara on the wide double bed. He kissed her again, then bent down and licked a swollen nipple. "Oh, yes," Barbara purred. "Yes." Hesitantly she cupped the back of his head and held him as he suckled. Shivers echoed through her body, centering now deep in her belly. She felt herself getting wetter and wanted him to touch her. Soon, she thought. Soon I'll be brave, able to touch what I want. Able to ask, show, guide.

Jay placed the palm of his hand on her belly and, over the lace of the garter belt, lowered it to the thatch of springy hair below. "So hot," he purred. "So hungry." His fingers probed, finding her hard clit, her swollen lips, her wet center. "I want you to come for me, baby. I want to watch you as you take your pleasure." He rubbed, using all his senses to discover exactly what she liked, what sent her higher. "Oh," he said, "you like to be touched right here."

"Oh, yes," she moaned, now incapable of any thought. "Yes."

"Open your eyes and took at me. I want to see your eyes when you come."

It was difficult, but Barbara opened her eyes and looked at Jay. His concentration was complete. He was stroking, rubbing, probing, all the while not taking his smoky eyes from hers. Barbara spread her legs still more, making it easier for him to reach all the places she had learned about in the past week. She couldn't speak, so she tried to tell him everything with her body and he learned quickly. Slowly he insinuated one finger into her wet channel. "That feels good, doesn't it?" he said as she gasped.

"Oh, yes," Barbara said, her eyes closing.

"No baby," he said. "Don't close your eyes. Look at me."

Barbara forced her eyes open. "It's hard," she said.

"I know, but it makes you think about something other than my hand. I want my face to fill over your mind while I fill your body." Slowly a second finger joined the first, then his thumb began flicking over her clit. "Yes, I can watch your eyes glaze with the pleasure I'm giving you. You're so hot, so hungry. I like it that I can do that to you. I can fill you, stroke you." He leaned over and licked her nipple. "Even bite you." He lightly closed his teeth on her tender flesh, causing small shards of pain to knife through her breast. "But the slight pain is exciting, isn't it?"

It was, she realized. The combination of sensations was electric. "Yes. It's good."

"I knew it would be."

He dipped his head and, as his fingers drove in and out of her pussy, he spread her legs wide and flicked his tongue over her clit. "Oh, God, she cried, her voice hoarse, all but unable to drag air into her lungs. She came as only her own fingers had been able to make her come before. He kept pulling her along, bringing waves of pleasure to her entire body. As she continued to spasm, she felt his hand withdraw. With his mouth sucking at her clit, she felt him awkwardly move around the bed, then heard the tear of paper. Briefly he sat up and, as Barbara's body throbbed with continued pleasure, unrolled a condom over his erection. He crouched over her for just a moment, then drove his hard cock deep into her. "Honey," he cried as she twisted her stocking-covered legs around his waist. "Honey, now! Yes!"

His back arched and he groaned as he pistoned into Barbara's wet body. Harder and harder he pumped until, with a roar, he came deep inside her. Her legs held him tightly against her as the waves of orgasm claimed them both.

It took several minutes for their bodies to calm and for their breathing to slow. "Oh, honey," Jay said. "That was sensational. I didn't expect you to be so responsive. You are a very sexy lady."

Barbara preened. She was feeling like a sexy lady, and she wanted to be a sexy lady. She wanted to be able to do to a man what Jay had just done to her. She had never even considered anything like that before. Conservative, mousy Barbara. Not anymore.

Chapter 6

"It was like a revelation. I understood things. I want to be a sexually free woman. Not necessarily like you, Maggie," Barbara said the next morning as she devoured a piece of toast, "but I want to feel free to do anything sexually I want."

"That's quite a change from the frightened and uncertain woman who left here last evening."

Barbara's eyes sparkled, her skin glowed. "I know, and I have no idea where it came from. But as Jay and I were making love, I just knew. I want to learn. I want to experiment. I want to do things that I never even knew existed." She giggled. "I don't even know what those things are, I just know there's more to sex than I've ever imagined."

"What about Jay? Won't he teach you?"

"Of course and I want to learn with him, but now I want to know everything, taste everything. Taste everyone." She looked down, then laughed. "You know what I mean. I guess the genie's out of the bottle and I don't want her to go back inside."

Maggie's grin spread from ear to ear. "I'm so happy for you, Barbara. I just knew that once you discovered good sex, you'd be unstoppable." She'd known no such thing, but what the hell. She was winning and, although Angela wanted marriage and a home for Barbara, it was, after all, Barbara's decision. And it seemed she had made it. "So you and Jay had it good last evening."

"Oh Lord, it was cosmic. We made love, then talked for a while, then made love again." She smiled, remembering the second time.

"God Barbara it's such a turn-on to watch someone like you open up."

It was about midnight and they lay side by side on Barbara's bed, the quilt thrown over them. It had only been an hour since her last orgasm, and already she was excited again. "I don't know how to express all the things I'm feeling."

"I can imagine," Jay said, his hand holding hers. "Your excitement is contagious. I'm not usually so quick to recover, but feel." He placed her hand on his again-erect cock. "Feel what you do to me."

"I like that. But I'm not responsible for your excitement."

"And who else is in this bed with me." He reached over and inserted one finger between her legs. She was wet. "And you are as excited as I am."

"It's just that we made love only an hour ago."

"And . . . ?"

"I should be lying here in some kind of afterglow, not lusting like an animal."

"I guess we're both animals then. And what are you lusting for?"

Barbara giggled. "I guess I have to admit that I want you again."

"I'm glad you do. What would you like?"

"You know."

"You want me to make love to you again." Jay raised himself up on one elbow and looked down at Barbara. She nodded almost imperceptibly. "Tell me," Jay urged. "Say yes."

"Yes."

"What would you like me to do? What gave you pleasure?"

Barbara pictured Jay's hands on her breast. And his mouth. That was what she wanted. But she couldn't say the words. "Everything you did gave me pleasure."

"Cop-out. Not an answer. What did you like best? When I nibbled your ear? When I stroked your tits? When I rubbed your cunt?"

Barbara's face went red. "Everything. Just love me."

"Maybe you need a lesson in words. Saying the words is very erotic. It's difficult and embarrassing, but it's also very exciting. Dirty words. Words your mother told you never to say. Words like 'fuck' and 'pussy' and 'dick.' Maybe you need a lesson on how to say those dirty words and ask for what you want." He placed his free hand flat on her belly and leaned his mouth against her ear. "What would you like this hand to do?"

Barbara was silent.

"Do you want it on your tits?"

She nodded slightly.

"Say it. Say, 'I want your hand on my tits.' "

"I can't say that," Barbara said, trying to contain the nervous giggle that threatened to erupt.

"Yes, you can and you will." He moved his hand upward until his fingers surrounded her breast. He moved his fingertips slightly, rubbing her ribs, nowhere near where she wanted his hands. "Say, 'Touch my tits.' "

"Touch me."

Jay shook his head. "Not good enough. Say 'tits.' Say it or I won't touch you."

His fingers were making her crazy. Her nipples were hard little buds aching for his hands and his mouth. She knew how good it had been just an hour before and she wanted it again. But could she say those words? She formed the word "tit" in her mind, then almost strangled on it. She couldn't get it out.

Jay's tongue was in her ear, licking and probing. Then he whispered, "Touch my tits. That's all you have to say."

His mouth was driving her wild. "Touch my . . . tits." There, she had said it.

"Such a good girl," Jay purred, his fingers squeezing her breasts and playing with her nipples. He pinched hard enough to make her gasp, but there was a stab of pleasure, too. "Now you probably want me to suck them, too. Tell me."

"Yes, please," she moaned.

"Say, 'Suck my tits.' "

"Suck my . . . tits." It was easier this time. "Please. I need your mouth."

"Oh, honey," Jay said, his mouth descending. He licked and sucked, and bit her. It was all ecstasy. For several minutes Jay played with her breasts, stroking, kneading, suckling. "God, you taste good," he purred. "But now it's time for more. You're hungry for me. You want my hands in your pussy. Say 'pussy.' "

Hearing the word made her back arch, the need almost overwhelming. "Jay, please touch me. I want you so much."

"I know you do. I know you want me enough to say the words. 'Touch my pussy.' "

"Touch my pussy. Jay, please."

"Oh, yes," Jay said, his fingers now busy driving her higher and higher. "Now I want something from you," Jay said. "Open your eyes." She did and saw his hand around his cock. "I want you to suck me the way I did it to you."

"I don't know how, Barbara said, suddenly cold and frightened. She had heard of women who "gave good head." There must be a knack to it. She couldn't, didn't know how.

"That's all right, I'll teach you." His hands still in her crotch, Jay turned, then knelt on the bed, his cock now only inches from her mouth. "Open your mouth. Just let me rub my cock over your lips so you get the feel of it." He stroked her lips with the velvety tip of his hard erection. "I'll teach you the best way. Do you want me to lick your pussy?"

"Yes."

He lay beside her, his head near her cunt, his cock only an inch from her mouth. His fingers continued to work their erotic magic. "Say 'pussy.' I know that as much as you deny it, saying those words makes you hot. Say it."

"Pussy," Barbara whispered.

"Such a good girt. Now I'm going to lick you. Try to duplicate what you feel with your tongue and my cock. If I lick slowly . . ." He gently licked the length of her slit. ". . . I want you to lick me slowly. Do it for me."

She used her fingertips to guide his cock close to her mouth. "Like this?" she whispered. She started about half-way down his shaft and licked to the tip as if it was a lollypop.

"Oh, God," he groaned. "Oh, honey."

Barbara was amazed at her ability to give him pleasure. She licked again and felt his sharp intake of breath.

Jay licked Barbara's clit lightly and she licked the tip of his cock the same way. Jay breathed hot air on Barbara's pussy and she breathed hot air onto his wet flesh. When Jay sucked her clit into his mouth, she was almost unable to think clearly enough to suck his cock, but when she did, she was rewarded with his moan. "Lady, you're a quick study."

Barbara could feel the vibrations of his voice against her hot flesh. "I hope so," she purred, hoping he could feel the same thing.

"You are a witch," he said, getting to his knees. He turned, put on a condom, crouched over her and plunged into her body. When his cock was deeply embedded in her cunt, he lifted and turned them both until she was straddling him. He held her hips and alternately lifted her and plunged her down onto his shaft. Harder and harder he drove into her, drove her onto him. "Say 'Fuck me good,' " he cried.

"Oh, Jay, fuck me good," she cried as she climaxed.

"Yessss," he hissed as he, too, came.

Barbara had been spending most of her weekends with Jay for more than a month before she saw Maggie again. One evening at the beginning of May, while Barbara was pouring herself a beer to go with the just-delivered pizza, Maggie walked into the kitchen.

"How have you been?" Maggie asked, dropping into a chair.

"Great. I've missed you." Barbara crossed to Maggie's chair and gave her a great bear hug.

"I haven't missed you, because, for me, I just saw you yesterday. How long has it been, and how is Jay?"

"It's the eighth of May and my dates have been great. We fuck like bunnies."

"Fuck. Such language." She tsk-tsked. "The Barbara I knew would never have used a word like that."

"I know, and I do keep it to a minimum except with you and Jay. But that's what it is, really. Wild, animal fornication, and it feels wonderful."

"That's terrific," Maggie said, taking a slice of pizza. She had discovered that she could eat what she wanted and food tasted great, although she had no concept of what happened after she swallowed. "I'm happy for you. Are you and Jay permanent? You know, forever?"

"Oh, Maggie," Barbara said, sitting across from her friend and taking a few large swallows of her beer. "I don't understand all this."

Maggie chewed, then said, "What's to understand? You said you guys were great together."

"I know, but it's not enough, somehow. I don't know. I've probably made love more in the past few weeks than I did in the previous thirty-one years. And I like Jay." As Maggie raised an eyebrow, Barbara continued. "I do. Really. It's just . . . Oh, forget it. I can't explain it."

"You know, I have no idea who decides when I appear, but whoever it is and however it's done, it seems you need someone to talk to right now. Try to explain."

Barbara took another long swallow of her beer and considered her words while Maggie devoured a slice of pizza. "Okay, let me put it this way. Jay's a real nice guy, but he's, how can I put this, predictable. We go to one of three restaurants for dinner. When I suggest somewhere else, he's willing but not anxious, so I don't pursue it. After dinner we go back to his place. We both love old movies, so we watch one of the tapes he has, usually an old John

Wayne flick. We share some wine, get hot and make love. All fine, but . . ."

"Dull?"

Barbara sighed. "Yeah. Dull. After that first explosive night, when we made love twice, it's once, we doze, then he takes me home. That once is fantastic, don't get me wrong. But I thought that great sex like that first night was the answer to some question I didn't know I had."

"Great sex is just that, great, but it's also not life."

"I don't understand," Barbara said, startled. "Didn't you say that marriage was too predictable? That variation and hot sex was the answer for you?"

"I did, and I believe that. But from what you've told me, your sex life has become predictable. Dull."

"Yes, but . . ."

"There's lots of good stuff out there. Maybe it's time for you to spread your newly acquired wings and look around. See what's out there. There are lots of fish in the sea, my love."

"You mean men."

"I do. Look around. I'll bet there are guys who you see every day, and who you don't give a second look to who would be fun to fool around with."

"Fool around with?"

"Yeah. Get some experience. Steak is nice, but pizza is good sometimes, too." She lifted her slice in a mock salute. "You didn't cook tonight, I see."

Barbara laughed. "I've been spending more time thinking about life and less time cooking. There is more to life than gourmet meals that I prepare myself, for myself." She picked up a slice of pizza and took a large bite. Then she got up, crossed to her spice rack and returned with a jar of crushed red pepper. "Just a little spice to give my slice some pep."

"That's what your life needs, too," Maggie said. "There are as many pleasures as there are creative couples in the world."

"You're right. I want to experiment. I want to do everything."

"And what about Jay. Does he think you're exclusive?"

"Not at all. He's seeing at least one other woman. You know, when he told me, I thought I'd be jealous, but I'm not. We're having fun and he's having fun with Joyce. I keep waiting for misery, possessiveness, but I just don't feel that. I'm happy he's happy."

"Sounds healthy to me," Maggie said. "And what about Steve. Has he asked you out yet? Have you asked him?"

"He hasn't asked me and I haven't asked him."

"Why not? You want to be with him, don't you?"

"Yes. But I want to play for the moment and I don't want to complicate things with what might turn into something permanent." She sprinkled red pepper on another slice of pizza. "And anyway, he's still seeing that knockout. That Lisa person."

"Do I hear jealousy?"

"Maybe a little. It's not like with Jay. Jay's a game. I want Steve to be serious. But not just yet. I have things to do and learn first, so we can be great together."

"I really do understand." Maggie remembered her first experiences after she and Chuck split. She had discovered that she loved sex. Good, rolling-in-the-hay, giggling, having-fun sex. "Remember the tape I gave you, the one that started all this?"

"Mmmm," she purred, "how could I forget?"

"Well, there are more in the series."

Barbara sat up, here eyes round. "There are?"

Maggie reached into her pocket and withdrew an audiotape. "This is another tape by the man who made that first one. These are erotic stories, published in an unusual way, using his bedroom voice. He's got a store in the city and sells them there and through the mail. Maybe you'll meet him sometime. He's a wild guy with a fantastic imagination." She placed the tape on the table between them. "That first one is unusual. Each of the remaining tapes is a story of people making love in new and exciting ways. Some you'll find exciting, some not. But the tapes will allow you to vicariously experience many of the things that couples do together. You can play them and see what turns you on, then go out and try to experience it."

Barbara took the tape.

"I'll be going, and you can play the tape at your leisure." Maggie stood up and walked toward the door. "How are they going to keep them down on the farm . . ." she said as she left through the kitchen door.

"How indeed," Angela said to Lucy as they flipped off the computer screen. "What did you get us into?"

"Be real, Angela," Lucy said. "You knew this might happen, and I'm glad it did. All that stuff about marriage. It's not right for Barbara, at least not yet. She's got some wild oats to sow."

"And this sudden need for her to get into kinky sex." Angela fixed Lucy with an icy stare. "Do you mean to tell me you had nothing to do with that?"

"It didn't take much." She grinned. "I guess the devil made me do it"'

"Listen, I thought we had a deal here. There's a lot riding on how Barbara's life goes from here. We agreed that there would be no meddling."

Lucy looked only a bit chagrined. "I know. I couldn't help it. I just goosed her a little. I want to see her fly. I want to see her learn about good, hot sex. A good roll in the sheets beats anything going, including marriage and fidelity."

"What you want isn't the issue here. It's what she wants. Free will is everything. If humans lose that, decisions like Barbara's become meaningless."

Lucy sighed. "I know. I'm sorry. I just couldn't help myself."

Angela patted her friend's hand. "Okay. I guess I understand. It's hard to have any resistance to temptation where you come from. But promise me. No more."

"Okay. No more."

Barbara turned on the tap to run a tub full of hot water, sprinkled a handful of bath salts beneath the water stream, then undressed. All the while her gaze kept returning to the cassette player which already contained the tape Maggie had given her. When the tub was full, she turned off the water and stepped in. Before settling into the water, she pushed the play button. The familiar sensual wail of the saxophone filled the room. She rested her head against the rim of the large tub and closed her eyes.

As they walked, Jason and Carolyn felt the cool water wash over their burning feet. The sand was white and had soaked in the sun all day. Now, as the golden disk set, the sand radiated heat into the soles of their feet, up their legs and into their bodies. Gulls wheeled and dove into the surf hunting for their evening meal and crying their brief song over and over.

The narrator's voice was sensual, soft, warm, like listening to warm heavy cream, Barbara thought as she listened. She let the voice and the story wash over her, as though she were there, seeing it, feeling it. It played like a movie in her head.

As they walked slowly along, Jason draped his arm over Carolyn's shoulder and slid his fingers down the edges of the top of her brief bikini. He allowed his fingertips to brush the swell of her lush breasts.

Carolyn loved the look and feel of Jason's lean body. As she looked over at him, it seemed that the pink and orange light of the setting sun made Jason's skin glow as though lit from within. She wrapped her arm around his waist and felt his muscles move beneath his warm flesh as they walked along the deserted beach.

"How did we get so lucky?" Jason said.

"Fifteen raffle tickets and someone's lucky fingers," Carolyn answered.

Surreptitiously Jason slid his fingers under one of the two tiny pieces of green fabric that made up the top of his wife's bikini and touched Carolyn's nipple. "Someone's fingers are still lucky."

Playfully Carolyn batted Jason's fingers away. "Stop that, silly."

"Why? This entire stretch of beach is deserted. All ours. 'Each cottage has its own deserted beach for lovers to share,' the brochure said."

"I know, but it feels so public."

Jason grinned. "I know. That's what's so erotic. Even though I know there's no one who can watch, it's like we're in public." With a gleam in his eye, Jason quickly untied the two knots that held Carolyn's top on and threw the fabric onto the sand. "Your breasts are so beautiful in the light of the setting sun."

Carolyn was surprised at how sensuous and exciting it felt to be half naked with the evening breeze making her nipples tighten. With a brazenness she hadn't felt before, she turned to Jason and swayed from one foot to the other, rubbing her erect breasts against his chest.

Jason pulled the rubber band from the single braid that held Carolyn's long red hair and buried his hands in the luxuriant silken strands. He cradled her head, bent down and pressed his lips against hers, filling her mouth with his tongue. Her tongue joined his and they touched and explored.

"Ummm," he purred, "you taste salty. Are you salty all over?" He leaned down and licked the valley between her breasts.

"Oh, Jason, you get me so excited. But it's so exposed here."

"That makes me hotter." He licked first one breast, then the other. "You skin is so warm." He bent and filled his palm with the water that lapped around their feet. Slowly he trickled the cool liquid over Carolyn's chest, and before she could react to the cold, he licked the salty drops from her nipples.

Carolyn was getting very hungry and, somehow, the idea of making love in the open added to the appeal. What the heck, she thought. It's a deserted beach. "Two can play at that," she said, filling one hand with water and dribbling it over Jason's hot shoulders. She touched her tongue to a rivulet and followed the water's path through the downy hair on his chest and down his flat stomach. The water trickled to his navel, just above his tight elastic bathing suit and she dipped her tongue into the indentation.

Jason's head fell back as Carolyn swirled her tongue just above his throbbing erection. He reached down and pulled off the bottom of her bikini and his trunks. "I want to love you right here, with the calling of the gulls and the foaming water and the setting sun shining on your body."

Jason laid Carolyn on the sand and stretched out beside her, the waves lapping to their knees. He tangled his fingers in her pubic hair, feeling a wetness that had nothing to do with the ocean. "You're as anxious for me as I am for you," he murmured in her ear. "Open for me and let me love you." He felt her legs part.

Carolyn couldn't have kept her legs together had she wanted to, and she didn't want to. She needed Jason inside her so she pulled at his shoulder until he covered her body with his.

He filled her and let her slippery body engulf him. He moved in and out, feeling both her body and the play of the waves against his legs. He wanted her to climax, needed it so he could come as well. He slid his fingers between their bodies and found her swollen clit. "Yes," she purred, "rub it. Touch me while you're inside me." His sentences were punctuated with sharp intakes of breath. "Baby, yes." She reached between them and placed her fingers over his, guiding them to the places she needed to feel him. "Right there."

It took only a few strokes more until he felt the clenching of her body around him and he could let his orgasm happen. And as it did, he held his hips perfectly still letting the semen spurt from his body into hers, experiencing her spasms of pleasure on his cock.

"Oh, darling," he whispered, feeling the water swirl around them. "That was unbelievable."

"Ummm, it was," Carolyn said. "And we still have three days here. Let's go inside and take a shower together. I understand that water can be very invigorating."

Barbara was breathless, her fingers relaxing after a frantic orgasm. As the music swelled, she thought about what she had heard. The woman asked for what she wanted. And it seemed natural and right for her. And it's right for me as well, Barbara realized.

The following Saturday, she and Jay had dinner at Villa

Josephina and, at Barbara's suggestion, had an after-dinner drink at a small club around the corner. They danced on the tiny dance floor and, loose and ready for something new, Barbara thought about the evening to come. Yes, she thought, it was her turn to lead. "How about a bubble bath later?" she murmured into Jay's ear as they danced.

"That's an interesting idea," Jay said. "But my tub isn't really big enough for that."

"Mine is," Barbara said.

"You want to go to your house after?"

"That's what I had in mind."

"Ummm. I guess you've got a few ideas of your own. Sounds sensational."

Back at her house a while later, Barbara tuned her radio to an all-light music station and, while Jay opened a bottle of champagne, she filled the tub with hot water and placed several candles around the bathroom. As she lit a match, she thought about all the wonderful things she had learned in that tub. Tonight? More new experiences, this time with Jay.

"May I come in?" Jay said, standing in the bedroom doorway.

Quickly Barbara lit the candles and turned off the water. "Sure. I'm in here."

Jay walked into the bathroom with two flutes of champagne. "I love the atmosphere," he said, handing Barbara one of the glasses. He touched the rim of his glass to hers. "Here's to new adventures."

"New adventures," Barbara said. They undressed slowly, watching in the candlelight as each part of the other's body was exposed but not touching each other. "You're gorgeous," she said as she looked at Jay's naked body. She remembered the evening when, at the instructions of the man on the tape, she had discovered her own body in that tub. She wanted to get to know Jay's body as well. "I would like to touch you," Barbara said.

Jay stretched his arms out at shoulder level. "I would like that, he purred.

Barbara used her fingertips to touch places on Jay's body she had never explored before. She discovered that he was ticklish beneath his arms and down his sides. She found the almost downy texture of his chest hair a contrast to the wiry hair in his groin. She flicked his male nipples with a fingernail and watched them tighten. She turned him around and stroked his back with her palms, then scratched a thin line down his spine to a small patch of hair in the small of his back.

She had never taken the time to know his skin and what lay beneath, from his forehead to the soles of his feet. "You are a wonder," Jay said. "You make me feel sexy, yet soft and dreamy all at once. Strong and masculine, yet weak and almost submissive."

"I like that," Barbara said. "I like making you feel all different kinds of things." She took his hand and guided him to the tub. Together, holding hands, they stepped into the still-steamy water.

The tub was large enough that they could sink beneath the surface until only the tops of their shoulders and their heads were not submerged. "How do you feel under that water, I wonder?" she said, rubbing soap on her hands. Then she rubbed his chest, arms, and legs, again wondering at all the different textures. When she was content that she had touched all of Jay's body, she handed him the soap. "Touch me now," she said.

Smiling, Jay took the soap and used lathered hands to caress all of Barbara's skin, from her underarms to the back of her knees. He washed her fingers, sucking each into his mouth, then lathering and rinsing each. Then he did the same with her toes.

She giggled when he rubbed the sole of her foot and found that, rather than spoiling the mood, Jay shared the laughter. Then the laughter turned into a splashing contest and finally, when the bathroom was soaked, they got out of the tub and bundled each other in big fluffy towels.

"This wasn't what I expected," Barbara said as she rubbed her hair dry.

"What did you expect?"

"In the movies, the people always get very passionate in the tub. This was just sensual and fun."

"Hot water makes me less than passionate," Jay said. "I get the ideas in my mind, but my cock refuses to cooperate." He took the towel from Barbara and rubbed her hair. "Have you got a hairbrush?"

In the bedroom, Jay sat Barbara on the chair at her vanity then, from behind her, began to slowly brush her hair. Barbara closed her eyes and allowed the sensuous moment to engulf her. The mesmerizing strokes of the brush lulled her almost to sleep. "Open your eyes, sleepyhead," Jay said. "No nodding off here."

"Ummm. But it feels so good." She opened her eyes and looked in the vanity mirror. Jay stood behind her, his skin still glowing from the warm water, a towel fastened around his loins. Slowly she watched Jay remove the towel from around her shoulders. Then he took the brush and scratched the bristles along her collarbone.

"Hey," she said. "That hurts."

"No, it doesn't," Jay said. "It feels like it should hurt, but it doesn't. Watch what I'm going to do." He scraped the bristles across the flesh of her breast, then scratched the tip of one nipple. He repeated the action on her other breast, then down the center of her belly.

It didn't hurt. Quite the contrary. She felt her clit swell and her lips part and moisten. Two could play at that game, she thought. She took the brush from Jay's hand, then turned and rubbed the bristles through Jay's chest hair and down past his waist. She considered, then did it. She scratched Jay's semi-erect cock with the sharp spikes. Rather than being a turn-off, as she had feared, his cock jumped, getting harder while she watched.

She turned the brush in her hand so she could brush it up the inside of one of Jay's thighs, then scratch it over his testicles. Groaning, Jay grabbed her wrist and pulled her to a standing position. He took the brush, threw it into the corner, then dragged her to the bed.

"Not so fast," she said, laughing.

"Yes, so fast." He pushed her down on her back and, with one quick motion, unrolled a condom over his cock. Then he grabbed his erection in one hand. "You did this, now let me put it where it belongs." He crouched over her and with one thrust buried himself deep in her pussy.

Barbara wanted to feel him from a different angle, so she pushed at him until he was on his knees, her pussy still impaled on his cock. He supported her buttocks in his hands as she twined her legs around his waist. "Now, baby," she said. "Fuck me."

Her request was more than granted as he withdrew, then plunged in full length. She wanted, needed, stimulation for her breasts, but, rather than wait for Jay to touch them, she cupped her flesh and pinched her nipples. Because of their unusual position, Barbara's clit was completely exposed. She wanted Jay to touch it. "Rub my clit," she said, and Jay's fingers found her immediately. He rubbed and, as she pinched her hard nipples and Jay's long strokes filled her cunt, she came, hard, with a long, loud moan.

"Oh, Barbara," Jay said. "So good. So good." And with a scream, he came, too.

They lay silently side by side while their breathing returned to normal. "I can't believe how far you've come from that timid woman I first made love with," Jay said.

"I can't believe it either," Barbara said, pulling the quilt over them. "Thank you."

"Don't thank me," Jay said. "You are a wonderful partner. We fit so well together, in all ways."

Barbara giggled. "I love the way we fit together."

An hour later, as Barbara listened to Jay's car pull out of the driveway, she thought about what Jay had said. She was a different person and she liked the person she had become.

The following evening, Barbara was back in her tub with another of CJ's wonderful tapes. She settled back in the water, now confident that the tape was going to bring her at least one orgasm. The voice filled her head.

It was warmer than usual that evening in the health club so Jack removed his T-shirt and continued to lift. Twice twenty reps with a thirty-pound weight in each hand ought to finish it off. He glanced at the clock. Almost nine-thirty, he saw. He had had a business meeting so he had begun his workout later than usual. "I thought the club closed at nine," he muttered.

Jack was well built with a smooth, muscular chest, well-developed arms and legs and an angular face. His short sandy beard covered a hard, granitelike chin. Long hair, slightly darker than his beard, was caught in a rubber band at the nape of his neck. His eyes were deep blue and a sheen of sweat covered his body as he lay on his back on the bench, lifting the barbell rhythmically. "Fifteen . . . sixteen," he counted.

"It's way past closing time," a woman's voice said.

"Seventeen, eighteen. Can I just finish?" he asked.

"Sure," the voice said, and as he continued to lift, he thought little more about it. When he finished the first thirty, he rested for a few moments, then began on the second series. "You're taking advantage of my good nature," the voice said.

"I didn't realize you were still there," Jack said, almost dropping the weights. "I'm sorry if I'm inconveniencing you."

"You're the last one here," the voice said. "I'm waiting to close up."

As Jack started to sit up to return the weights to the rack, he looked behind him. She sat on another weight bench, wearing bicycle pants, a sports bra and a tight tee top with the name of the club across the front. He had never seen her here before. "I'm really sorry."

"How sorry?"

"I beg your pardon?"

The woman stared at Jack, her eyes never leaving his. "How sorry are you? I think you should make it up to me."

Was that an invitation? Jack thought. Is this beautifully built woman making a pass at me? He was certainly willing. "What did you have in mind?" he asked, looking over the woman's body. She was small, with tight breasts, slender, well-muscled thighs, and good definition in her upper arms. Her hair was cut very short, with tight red. curls, and her eyes were green. She wore no makeup on her ivory skin and freckles dusted the bridge of her nose.

The woman stood up and walked over to the bench. She pushed her hand against Jack's chest until he was pressed back down onto his back. She put the weight Jack had been using on the floor beside his right hand. "Hold that and don't let go," she said. Jack wrapped his hand around the cold bar while the woman took the second hand weight and placed his left hand on it. "Don't let go or everything's over," she said.

Jack lay on his back on the narrow bench, his hands stretched toward the floor, his hard cock pressing upward against his shorts. God, he thought, is this really happening?

"My name's Nan," the woman said, "and I've been watching you. I think you'll be easy."

"Easy?"

"I think you will do anything I say, when I say it, and nothing more. I think you will do it all willingly because I'm going to do things to you and with you that we will both like. A lot. And you want me to do that, don't you?"

Jack could hardly catch his breath. "Yes," he whispered.

"Good. Here are the rules. You will keep your eyes on me at all times. Look nowhere else unless I tell you to. And keep those weights in your hands. If you let go, I will stop and leave at once. Do you understand the rules?"

Jack swallowed hard. "Yes," he whispered.

"Good. Let's see how hard you are already." She reached down and grabbed Jack's hard cock through the silky fabric of his work-out shorts. "I knew you'd be easy. So hard." She grasped his cock and squeezed, moving her hand slightly up and down. "Too hard, I'm afraid. I don't know whether you will have enough self-control for me. Do you have self-control?"

"Yes," Jack said, barely able to breathe.

"We'll see. You are not to come. Period. If you do before I tell you to, I will leave. Immediately. Your cock is mine to control. Do you understand that?"

"Yes," Jack whispered, staring into the woman's deep green eyes. "Yes."

"All right. Let's test that control you say you have." Nan pulled off her tee top and bra and cupped her small tight tit with her hand. "I'm going to put my nipple into your mouth. You're not to suck, lick, or anything. Just keep your mouth open."

Jack opened his mouth and felt her large nipple between his lips. He wanted to suck, to caress the warm flesh with his tongue, but he thought of her warning and her challenge to his ability to master his desires. More intense than the urge to suck was his need for the woman not to leave. He kept his lips parted, her engorged nipple brushing his tongue. She moved, rubbing the nub against his lips, his cheeks, his chin. "Stick your tongue out, but don't move it."

He stuck his tongue out and she rubbed her nipple over the rough surface. He wanted to suckle, but he used all his concentration to keep his mouth still.

"Such a good boy," Nan said, and she straightened. "You might have more promise than I expected." She stepped out of her shorts, leaving herself dressed in only her sneakers and white socks. She straddled the bench with her back to him, and lowered her wet pussy to Jack's mouth. "The rules haven't changed. Do nothing." She wiggled her hips, and the aroma of her hot cunt filled Jack's nostrils. He licked his lips, but valiantly kept his tongue from caressing the swollen flesh so close.

She lay down along his body, her cunt still less than an inch from his mouth, her mouth close to his cock. Quickly she shifted one leg of his shorts and pulled his cock free. It stood straight up from his groin. "You can't see me too well from there," she said. "Look in the mirror."

Jack had forgotten that one wall of the free-weight area was mirrored. He turned slightly to his right so he could just see around Nan's thigh. The sight was incredible. A naked woman was lying along his body, her breasts caressing his belly, her mouth just above his straining cock, her warm breath making him quiver. Her smell filled him. Her weight pressed him down. His hands gripped the weights until his knuckles went white, his muscles strained to push his cock into this woman's waiting mouth.

"You'll wait until I'm ready," she said. "Make me ready. Lick me."

He did gladly, sliding his tongue over the length of her sopping slit. He tried every trick he knew to give her pleasure, sucking her clit into his mouth, flicking the tip of his tongue across her then slowly laving the entire area. He pointed and stiffened his tongue until his mouth ached, then stabbed it as far into her pussy as it would go.

"My, my," Nan said, her breathing rapid, "you do good work. I think you deserve a reward."

Jack felt her hot mouth draw his aching cock deep inside. It would only take a moment of that level of intense pleasure for him to come. "You'll make me come," he groaned.

"You better not come," Nan said. "You've got a job to do. If you make me come first, then, and only then, will you be allowed to climax. Do you understand that?"

Jack moaned and clenched his muscles tightly. "Yes," he whispered, trying to concentrate on cold showers and snow-covered mountains. He licked and sucked, his mind divided between giving pleasure and trying to control his need to climax. Slowly he felt Nan's thigh muscles tighten. He tried to concentrate on which of the things his tongue was doing would make her come. When he rubbed his lips over her clit, she quivered. When he blew a stream of cold air over her swollen lips, her thighs clenched around his head. Yes, he told himself, I can do it for her. As he felt the ripples through her belly and the spasms of her vaginal muscles, he knew he could hold back no longer. He filled her mouth with his semen, coming for what seemed to him like hours.

It was several minutes before either of them moved. As Nan stood up, she said, "Damn, you're good. That was wonderful." She moved behind him.

Jack took a deep breath and let go of the weights. He flexed his aching fingers and picked up a small towel that lay on the floor.

"Terrific." He sat up slowly, wiped his face, drying the sweat and enjoying the lingering smell of Nan's juices. "How about going back to my place? We can pick up a pizza and continue this when we recover." He took the towel away from his face and looked around in amazement. The gym was empty. Although he looked throughout the large facility, Nan seemed to have vanished.

Jack worked out late every night for several weeks, but eventually he had to admit that he would never see her again. But he had the memory of that one incredible night, a night he would never forget.

As the story ended, the room filled with the mellow tones of the saxophone, Barbara lay in the tub and rubbed her fingers furiously between her legs. When she came it was swirls of all colors, bright and silent.

As she relaxed, she lay in the cooling water thinking about the story she had just heard. There was so much out there, so much sexual fun for people to share. Next weekend she was seeing Jay again. Could she wait? She wanted to experience everything now. Right now.

Chapter 7

The following morning, Barbara showed up at work dressed in a soft rose knit suit. Although the line of the suit itself was quite conservative, the way it clung to her body as she moved was enough to ignite fantasies in a few of her office mates. And, for the first time, as she looked at the men she passed in elevators and hallways, she noticed the appreciative glances she received. Branch out, she thought. Date. Make love because it's fun and easy.

Midmorning she went to the ladies' room and looked at herself carefully in the full-length mirror. Not a raving beauty, not even conventionally pretty, she realized shaking her head, but there was a spark there now. She smoothed her skirt over her hips and adjusted the jacket's neckline slightly to reveal just a bit of cleavage. Not bad, she told herself. Not bad at all.

"Hi," a voice said as she walked back to her desk. "I don't think we've met. I'm Alex Fernandez. I'm from Gordon-Watson's West Coast affiliate."

"Nice to meet you," Barbara said, watching the man's eyes coolly appraise her. "I'm Barbara Enright."

"Well, Barbara Enright, I'm only here till tomorrow afternoon. I know I should take my time, but when I see something as delectable as you, I can't see beating around the bush. How about a drink after work?"

"You don't waste any time," Barbara said, grinning at the man's audacity. But he was gorgeous, medium height, with deep brown eyes and brown curly hair that looked like combing it was useless. He was wearing the office costume, dark suit and white shirt, but his tie was a wild print of orange and purple. Feeling bold, she reached over and touched his tie, pressing just hard enough so she knew he felt the slight pressure of her fingers. "Nice tie."

"Thanks. So how about that drink?"

She thought about it for only a moment. "I'd like that. Tonight?"

"If you're free," Alex said, his eyes holding hers. "Since I'm going back tomorrow, we don't have too much time. Listen, I have lots of work to do, but I can probably be out of here by seven."

"Let's see how the time works out as the day progresses," Barbara said.

About four-thirty Barbara found Alex in the law library. He had his head buried in a three-inch-thick tome and several others littered the table around him. "I have a few things to do. Why don't I stop back here around seven and we can see about that drink?"

Alex looked up and smiled slightly. "That'll be great," he said, looking at his watch. "Better make it about seven-thirty."

When Barbara got home, Maggie was waiting for her. As Barbara made coffee, she told Maggie about Alex. "I'm tingling all over," she said finally. "And I initiated it."

"Don't get carried away," Maggie said, then giggled. "Hey, listen to me. Which side of this am I on?"

"Oh, Maggie, I won't get carried away. It's just that this is so much fun. Flirting. Picturing every man I see without clothes. Wondering how he would be in bed."

Maggie patted the back of Barbara's hand. "I know, and I'm

with you. Just be careful. Condoms and like that. And never do something that you don't want to do just because someone else wants you to."

Maggie looked at Barbara's watch. She had stopped wearing one because it never told the right time anyway. Whenever she went through the revolving room in the computer building, time got all shifted around. "It's getting late and you need to shower and make yourself gorgeous. Why don't you go meet Alex and let things flow from there." Maggie made a few suggestions about how to make the evening progress the way Barbara wanted it to, and Barbara listened carefully. Then she stood up. "I think I will do just what you suggested," she said. "And let the devil take the hindmost."

In the computer room, Lucy raised her arms in the air. "Yes," she hissed. "Right on, Barbara."

"Shut up," Angela growled.

It was almost eight when Barbara locked the office's heavy outer door behind her and dropped the keys back into her purse. She put her coat on her desk, then picked up the shopping bag she had brought with her and walked toward the library. About halfway down the hall she stopped. Could she do this? It had sounded like a fantastic idea when she and Maggie had talked about it, but now, in reality, she felt like she was about to make a fool out of herself. Alex probably wanted to talk to her about office politics or something.

Suddenly the door to the library opened. "Barbara," Alex said, seeing her standing in the hall. "I was beginning to think you'd stood me up." A grin lit his face.

"I'm sorry I'm late. I got held up." No, she wouldn't do it. She couldn't.

Alex walked toward her, then glanced down at the shopping bag. He peeked in the top, looked at her and smiled. "Champagne," he said, a slight catch in his voice. "Do some shopping on the way here? Is that a gift for someone?"

Now or never. "Actually, I thought you might be getting thirsty. All those books and all."

"What a great idea," Alex said, his eyes widening. "I was just going to get a soda, but this will go down much more easily. Got glasses?"

"I certainly do," Barbara said. As she slowly followed Alex back into the law library, she wondered whether he might have misunderstood. But what was there to misunderstand? An empty office. Champagne.

As Barbara closed the door behind her, Alex pulled the champagne bottle and two flutes from the bag. "What's this?" he asked, pulling out the tape player Maggie had placed there. She had included a tape Maggie had given her that contained just the erotic background music from the tapes Barbara had become so intrigued with. He put the tape in the player and pushed the play button. As he opened the bottle, the soft-summer-night wail of a saxophone filled the room.

"Great music," Alex said as he filled the two glasses. He handed one to Barbara and, with the music filling their ears, they clinked glasses. "Wonderful," he whispered, swallowing some of the bubbly liquid.

Nervously Barbara emptied the glass and Alex quickly refilled it. She sipped a bit more and looked at him standing in front of her. From the look in his eyes it was obvious that he wanted what Barbara wanted. But how to begin? As the hesitation lengthened, she decided she could make the first move. She could. Then she squared her shoulders, took a deep breath and said, "Dance with me?"

"Ummm, yeah," Alex said, putting his glass on the large oak table. "Good idea."

Barbara held on to her glass like some kind of security blanket as Alex took her in his arms. Their feet barely moved and his body pressed against hers. "I love slow dancing," she whispered into Alex's ear, alternately confident and terrified. "It's like making love standing up."

"I do too," Alex said, shaking his head. "But I don't believe this is happening. Things like this only happen in movies. And never to guys like me."

"Do you want it to happen?" Barbara asked.

"Oh, yes."

Barbara leaned back and gazed into Alex's eyes. "So?"

After a moment's hesitation, Alex's face softened and his mouth pressed against hers. The kiss was at first tentative, then deeper until Barbara felt her entire body fuse with his. When he took her in his arms, she could feel the drumming of his heart, and hers. She placed her mouth beside his ear and hummed a bit of familiar music.

Hungrily Alex placed a line of kisses from Barbara's ear, along her jawline, to her mouth. As his mouth covered hers, he took her glass and put it on the table. Then he laced his fingers with hers and held her hands against her thighs. They stood, their feet moving slightly to the deep rhythm of the music, their mouths fused, her nostrils filled with the smell of his aftershave.

Barbara was soaring. The music, which she had come to associate with erotic experiences, filled her soul, Alex's mouth teased, his tongue probing and filling, his hands holding hers immobile.

Alex slid their joined hands to the small of Barbara's back and pressed so her belly and mound were pressed intimately against his obviously hard cock. Barbara moved her hips slightly and heard Alex groan. She changed the position of the kiss slightly and tangled her tongue with his. He shuddered.

They danced until the backs of Barbara's thighs touched the edge of the large conference table. She boosted herself slightly until she slid onto the table, knees spread. Now she understood why Maggie had insisted that she change into a short denim skirt that zipped up the front. She wore a light green scoop-necked T-shirt and a denim vest that barely closed.

As Alex stepped between her knees, Barbara wrapped her legs around Alex's thighs and linked the high heels of her leather boots behind him. Between the effect of the music, the champagne, and the intensely hot look in Alex's eyes, she felt bold and daring. Her legs still around Alex's, she pushed books and papers aside until she could lie back on the cool wood.

With a groan, Alex pulled her shirt up so he could cover her lace-covered breasts with his hands. "Oh, sweet," he said, his voice hoarse. He found the clasp at the center front of her bra and deftly opened it.

"I knew you'd be gorgeous, but I had no idea . . ." he said as her breasts spilled out and filled his hands. He bent over and kissed her chest and ribs, finally covering her aching nipples with his wet mouth.

As he pulled and nipped, shafts of pure pleasure stabbed through her body. Unable to wait much longer, he grabbed the bottom of the skirt zipper and pulled it upward until the skirt was only held around her waist by a single button. "Oh, shit," he groaned when he discovered she wore lace garters to hold up her stockings but no panties. "Oh, shit." His eyes glazed as he stared at her naked pussy. "Oh, shit."

Quickly he pulled down his slacks and underwear. "Protection," Barbara said.

Alex pulled a condom from his wallet and opened the package. "Let me do that," Barbara said, standing up. She pushed Alex into a chair and unrolled the latex over the hard cock that stood straight up in his lap. When he started to rise, she said, "Let me do that, too." She straddled his thighs and slowly impaled herself on his erection.

"Oh, shit," Alex said again. "Yes, yes, yes."

When the length of him was inside her, she planted her feet firmly on the floor and levered herself up, almost off his cock, then allowed her body to drop again. Up and down, in and out, she established a carnal rhythm.

She allowed her head to fall back and surrendered herself to the music, the champagne, the heat of her desire. She reached between their bodies and rubbed her clit and the base of his cock. It took only another minute until Alex climaxed, and soon after Barbara reached her peak as well.

Panting, Barbara collapsed against Alex's chest, still covered with his white shirt and tie. "Making love half dressed is very erotic," he said. "I still have my shirt on and you're still almost wearing most of your clothes."

"God," Barbara said. "That was great." She rose and Alex quickly removed the condom with a wad of tissues. When he went to toss it into the wastebasket, she added, "Drop it into the bag. Why let anyone suspect what we've been doing?"

Alex tossed the tissues into the shopping bag as Barbara rose. She collected the champagne bottle and put it, the glasses, and the tape player into the bag.

"Leaving so soon?" Alex asked, picking up a few books and papers that had landed on the floor. "I'm running late, but we could have dinner in about half an hour."

As Alex pulled on his clothes, Barbara rezipped and tidied herself up. "I find that I'm not too hungry anymore," she said with a suggestive wink. "You satisfied my hungers just fine."

"Ummm," Alex purred, holding her and nibbling on her ear. "You aren't bad yourself."

"I'm going to catch a cab home and collapse from the pleasure of what we just did."

"I hope I'll see you before I leave."

"You might. And when you do, think about how good this was. And maybe next time you're on this coast we can do it again." Barbara picked up the shopping bag and looked around the library. "This room will never feel quite the same again," she said.

"I'll bet not," Alex said. "Sleep tight." He kissed her hard.

"Ummm, Barbara said. "Don't work too hard." As she opened the door, she looked back and marveled at the expression of pure satisfaction on Alex's face. She had put that there. Life was wonderful.

"Maggie, it was a trip," Barbara said the following morning as she poured coffee for herself and her friend. "It was sport fucking, it was no-strings lusting, it was more fun than I've had in years. And it was meaningless." Unable to sit still, Barbara paced the length of the kitchen, her cup in her hand.

"I know just how it makes you feel. Desirable, attractive, sexy."

"Yeah. All of that. No one has ever made me feel that way before. No, that's not really true. Alex didn't make me feel that way, *I* did. It's all inside me. Somehow I think it's always been there, that spark, that glow. It took you to make me see it." She walked up to Maggie, pulled her to her feet and gave her a giant bear hug. "I'm a sexy woman."

"That you are, yet you're also the same person you were three months ago, before we met."

"I feel like going to bars and picking up guys just to prove that I can do it. Then fucking their brains out, and mine, too, of course, just for fun."

"That's what sex is for. Fun. Sex with Chuck was never fun. It was okay, just not fun with a capital F. I never had fun like that until after my divorce."

Barbara sat down at the table and thought a moment. "Do you really mean that your marriage to Chuck was all bad?"

"Not bad, just boring."

"There wasn't anything good about it?"

"Marriage is for fools who are willing to settle for monotony and security."

"My parents had a good marriage, I think, until my father died. I think they were truly happy. I can remember that they used to disappear into the bedroom to 'go over finances.' They would close the door and giggle. Giggle. My mom and dad. They were truly happy."

"Maybe they were the one in a thousand," Maggie said.

"What about Bob? Wasn't that good?"

"Funny, it was the exact opposite of my marriage to Chuck. Hot sex but nothing else. It's impossible to have both hot sex and a good friendship in the same relationship."

"I hope you're wrong . . . Anyway, back to last night. Did I tell you about the tape? It was wonderful, so dreamy and erotic."

"Did you do some slow dancing? I always like to start an evening with a little concentrated body rubbing."

"Yeah, we did. And you're right about that. It is a great way to start things."

"But Alex is history?"

"He'll be in the office this morning, but I have several errands to run for Steve so I'll probably get to the office after he leaves to go back to the Coast. Anyway, seeing him the morning after would probably be a letdown." She took a swallow of her coffee.

"And Jay?" Maggie asked.

"Oh, no, he's still very much around. He's a nice man and I enjoy sex with him, even if it is a bit predictable."

"Why don't you initiate something new? Something that turns you on more than what you're doing."

Barbara looked surprised. "You know, old habits die hard. I guess I thought I could do new things with others, but I never thought of taking the initiative with Jay. Maybe I could. But I'm still such a dunce when it comes to creative stuff. I wouldn't know what to try." She raised her eyebrow a bit.

"Are you manipulating me?" When Barbara smiled, Maggie continued. "You want another of my tapes, don't you? You know you could buy some books of good erotica. They will be full of new ideas."

"I know, but those tapes turn me on. And I love both the music and the voice of the sexy man who reads the stories."

"That's my friend, the one who gave me the tapes in the first place. I think I told you that he runs an erotic boutique in the city. You should go there and meet him sometime."

"I think he'd intimidate me. He's sort of a professional at sex, and I'm such an amateur."

"He's a wonderful, creative lover with a marvelously devious mind. You shouldn't be afraid of him. You and he would make beautiful music together. I'll see whether I can get the two of you together. In the meantime . . ." Maggie reached into her pocket and pulled out another audiotape. "I want you to save this one for twenty-four hours. Put it on your dresser so you'll see it tonight when you get home from work. Think about it, but don't play it until tomorrow."

"Why?"

"It's a bit heavier than the ones you've listened to before and I want you to be really excited. So no touching, no sneaking, just let the excitement build till tomorrow. Okay?"

"If you want, Maggie. You haven't steered me wrong up to now."

Maggie looked at Barbara's watch. "Aren't you getting late for work?"

Barbara looked down. "Oh, damn," she said. "It's almost eight. I'm going to be late for the first time in years."

Since Maggie had given her the tape, Barbara had been intrigued. A bit heavier, she had said. The next night Barbara put the tape in the player and pushed play. There was music and that wonderful voice. She became wet just hearing it. I'm getting like Pavlov's dogs, Barbara thought. That man doesn't have to say anything dirty. He could read the telephone directory and I'd probably come. She stretched out on the bed, closed her eyes and listened.

His name was William Singleton and he had been working on the plan for months. First, he combed the city for just the right women, prostitutes to be sure, but women of beauty and refinement. Women who entertained men and didn't just fuck them. He paid them well and, telling them exactly what he intended, he invited the three he selected to his home.

Over the following weeks, using exotic drugs and hypnosis, he trained the girls for many hours each day. Now he could show off his creations to his friends at a small exotic party he was throwing that evening.

He checked the living room and the dining room. "Yes," he muttered as he rearranged a flower here and a napkin there, "everything's ready."

He walked down the hall and opened the door to each of three special bedrooms. In each room, a girl lay sleeping, resting for the evening ahead. Reclosing the three doors, William went downstairs to await his guests. It would be a long evening.

At eight o'clock, the doorbell rang for the first time, and by eight-fifteen there were four men in formal dress, including William, seated in the living room. Each held a drink in his hand; each talked nervously, anticipating the evening to come. Sir William Singletree was known for his erotic and highly unusual parties and his three best friends were anticipating a creative evening.

At eight-thirty, the doorbell rang again. The butler, dressed in tailcoat and patent-leather shoes opened the door. The woman who swirled through the opening was beautiful. She shrugged out of her floor-length royal-blue velvet coat and left it with the butler. She was dressed in an ice-blue satin evening dress which was draped dramatically over her left shoulder. Her right arm and shoulder were bare, which showed off the wide diamond cuff bracelet that was her only piece of jewelry. Her meticulously arranged chestnut-brown hair swept up from her long, graceful neck.

She crossed the living room and offered a perfectly manicured hand to each of the gentlemen, greeting William last.

"My dear," he said as he took Sylvia's hand and kissed her cheek, "I think everything is ready for dinner now."

Without another word, she gracefully crossed the room and disappeared down the long hallway.

"Sylvia is looking magnificent as usual," Marshall said. He was in his midthirties and the star of a successful TV series. Tall, with dark and brooding good looks, his life was a continual battle to keep women from throwing themselves at him. But willing women bored him.

"Absolutely gorgeous," Samuel agreed. At almost fifty, he was the oldest man in the group. Gray hair and matching steel-gray eyes made him look the epitome of a business tycoon, which was exactly what he was.

"Yes," William said, taking obvious pride in the looks that his dinner companion got. "Sylvia is a beautiful and surprisingly resourceful woman."

Resourceful was a strange word to use for a woman, Paul, the third invited guest, thought. But leave it to William to use words in their most unusual connotations. Paul was about the same age and height as his friend Marshall but that was where the resemblance ended. Paul was a blue-eyed blond with hair slightly longer than was fashionable. A successful writer with three best sellers to his credit, he usually managed to look just a bit individual, and his sexual tastes were unusual as well.

William looked around at his three friends. Three totally different types, each with exotic sexual appetites like his own, but each with entirely different tastes. It would be interesting to watch how each one reacted to the evening's "entertainment."

Small talk continued to fill the living room until, about five minutes later, Sylvia returned, followed by three spectacularly beautiful women. Each was about twenty-five, one a blonde, one a brunette, and one a redhead. The women were dressed in identical evening dresses, strapless and unadorned, sweeping to the floor in a waterfall of silk. The only difference was that the blonde's dress was gold, the brunette's black, and the redhead's silver. Each was perfectly made up with an elaborate hairstyle that piled obviously long hair high on each woman's head.

The three guests stared. The women were all of medium height and well proportioned. "Good evening," they said, almost in unison.

"These are your dinner companions," William said. "Sylvia, introduce our guests."

Sylvia took the hand of the blonde in the golden dress and walked her over to where Marshall was standing. "Marshall, darling," she said, "I'd like you to meet Kitt. I think you and she will get along wonderfully."

Marshall took Kitt's hand as she murmured, "It's so good to meet you."

Sylvia then walked the brunette toward Samuel. "Samuel, you and Ginny have a lot in common, as I'm sure you'll find out."

"I've heard a lot about you," Ginny said, "and I've been looking forward to meeting you."

Paul walked over to the girl with the incredibly red hair. "I've always loved redheads," he said to the girl. "My name is Paul."

"This is Cynthia, " Sylvia said. "She's to be your companion for the evening."

Almost immediately, William said, "Dinner is ready. Shall we eat?"

As dinner proceeded uneventfully, perfectly prepared dishes arrived one after another, accompanied by perfectly selected wines. The eight diners discussed politics, books, sports, any subject that anyone was interested in. Each man marveled at how perfectly the woman he was with fit his tastes, both in looks and in interests.

When coffee and brandy arrived at the table, William stood. Raising his brandy snifter, he said, "A toast to a splendid evening to come."

They all raised their glasses, then drank.

"Shall we go downstairs?" William asked.

They crossed the living room and walked down the great curved staircase to the large well-carpeted area below. The three male guests had been in William's house many times before. His parties were legendary, and the best entertainment always took place downstairs.

The three couples settled themselves on large overstuffed sofas to wait for whatever entertainment William and Sylvia had planned.

The host and hostess crossed the room and, while Sylvia gracefully took her seat, William stood beside a table on which a line of glass bells of different sizes was arranged. With great ceremony, he took a small glass rod and tapped the bell at the near end of the row. A single clear note filled the room.

William looked at each of the three women. As he gazed, each man turned and looked at his companion. Each of the three identically dressed women stared into space, seemingly out of contact with the others in the room.

"Gentlemen," William said. "The ladies are unable to hear or see what's going on right now. They have been conditioned to the sound of these bells. When I ring this one, they all respond by going

into a trance. When I tap the one on the other end," he tapped the bell, "they all return to us."

He looked at the three women. "Don't you, ladies?"

The women smiled and looked a bit confused, so Sylvia said, "You're feeling fine, aren't you, ladies?"

"Certainly, Sylvia," Kitt said. "We all feel wonderful."

William tapped the first bell and the three women again stared into space, their eyes distant and clouded over.

"Each one of these women has volunteered for a most amusing training program. Sylvia and I have spent weeks perfecting their behavior. We have done it as a present to each of you to thank you for your years of friendship and loyalty."

"You know you don't have to thank us," Samuel said. "We've always been there for each other."

"Well, I wanted to do this," William said, "so let's get on with it. Marshall, you get to go first."

Marshall looked a bit puzzled. "First for what?" he asked.

"I'll show you." William tapped a bell in the center of the row and said, "Kitt, take off your dress and show Marshall what is his for the evening."

Slowly Kitt rose. She looked into Marshall's eyes as she reached behind her and slowly unzipped her dress and gradually allowed it to inch down her body. Proudly she displayed a sensational body, covered with a golden corselet that cinched in her waist and cupped her breasts but left the nipples bare. Gold-colored garters held up matching stockings. Her shoes were also golden with high spike heels. She wore no panties and Marshall could see her blond hair between the garters.

"What do you think, Marshall?" Sylvia asked.

"She's magnificent, Sylvia." He sounded hesitant.

"Say what you wish," Sylvia said. "She won't remember anything we don't want her to."

"Well, you all know I don't like willing women. I like my women to fight me."

Sylvia chuckled. "We know that, dear. We know all your tastes. In our conversations with Kitt, we discovered that she has a match-

ing fantasy, one that she's been reluctant to discuss with anyone. But we've used that desire to train her to fulfill your fantasy, while fulfilling hers at the same time." She looked around the room, catching Samuel's eyes, then Paul's. "The same is true of your dinner companions, gentlemen. Your tastes match perfectly. Now, I hope you two don't mind waiting? We'd like to play, one couple at a time."

The two others shook their heads. If William and Sylvia did know all their tastes, it was going to be an evening worth waiting for.

"Now, Kitt," William said, "listen to me. Marshall wants to fuck you. Do you want him to?"

Kitt smiled and allowed her gaze to roam over Marshall's body. "Yes. He's very sexy and I'm very hungry."

Sylvia said, softly, "The girls are all very hungry. Their bodies have been conditioned to become physically aroused at the sound of the bells." She looked at William, then at the three men. "We have found that sexual excitement, like anything else, can be conditioned. We have trained these girls to react in specific ways to different sounds." She looked at Kitt, standing proudly and displaying her shapely body. "How much do you want him? Tell him."

A slow, erotic smile spread over her face. "I want you to make love to me. I want you to fuck me now. Please fuck me."

Marshall looked disappointed. It was too easy.

"Don't worry," William said, "we understand." William tapped Kitt's bell twice. Instantly, Kitt grabbed her dress and held it in front of her as she backed away from Marshall. "I know who you are and what you want. You want to rape me." She licked her lips. "I've seen you looking at me all evening and I'm not going to give in. Don't you come near me," she snarled.

William looked at the smile that spread over Marshall's face. "Is this more to your liking?"

"Most certainly," Marshall said. "I've always had rape fantasies, but I would never actually commit rape, hurt anyone, you know. Are you sure that she really wants this?"

"You'll have to trust me. Each of these women has been selected

for her sexual tastes and appetites. Don't worry. All of you," he looked around the room, "will get tremendous pleasure from what happens."

"If you're sure."

"I am. Now, she's all yours," William said.

Marshall stood and carefully removed his jacket and loosened his tie. He dropped the jacket on the sofa next to him but kept the tie in his hand. As he walked toward Kitt, he glanced around the room. Yes, he thought, there was everything he might need. He slowly stalked Kitt as she backed away from him. "Come here, Kitt, I won't hurt you."

"Stay away," she said.

"It will be easier for you if you hold still. I don't want to hurt you."

"I know exactly what you want, Marshall, and you won't get it from me without a fight." She continued to back away from him staying just out of arm's reach.

With sudden speed, Marshall took three steps, reached out and snatched the dress from Kitt's hands. Then, as she tried to scamper away, he snagged her wrist and pulled her to him. He twisted her arm behind her and tangled the fingers of his free hand in her hair.

Hairpins flew everywhere as long strands pulled free. Soon, still holding her squirming body, he wrapped a hank of long flaxen hair around his hand. He gently pulled her head back and pressed his lips against hers. She tried to twist away from his kiss, but his hand in her hair prevented her head from moving.

As he felt her press her lips together to keep his tongue out of her mouth, he said, "You aren't strong enough to resist me, you know."

Silently she glared at him, her lips sealed.

"Let me find out just how reluctant you really are," he said. He picked her up and dropped her on the nearest sofa. As she tried to twist away, he stretched his body on top of hers and reached his hand between her legs. He touched her pubic hair and slid a finger through her folds. He smiled. "You're soaking wet. You really do want me."

"Keep your hands off me!" she shouted.

Marshall hesitated.

"Marshall," William said, "just in case you need reassurance . . ." He tapped Kitt's bell. Instantly she was quiet. Looking puzzled about how she ended up on the sofa with her date's body stretched over hers, she gazed into Marshall's eyes and said, "Mmmm. You feel good against me. Are you going to make love to me?"

"Yes, darling, I am." Marshall nodded to William who tapped Kitt's bell twice. At the sound, she was a tiger again, squirming to get free of his hold. "God, I like it like this," Marshall said. He looked at Samuel and Paul. "Gentlemen, I could use a little help at this moment."

The two men got up and each held one of Kitt's arms. Marshall held both her legs and together they carried her over to a low table. Samuel and Paul each pulled off his tie. They stretched Kitt across the table, face up, her head hanging off the end. Using their ties and a soft rope that William provided, they tied her arms and legs to the table legs. Then they stood up and surveyed the scene. Kitt was still dressed in the corselet and stockings, but her cunt and nipples were exposed, offered to the men for their use.

"Yes," Marshall said, "that's very good. " He paused, looking at her squirming body. "William," he said, "you said that she'd be enjoying this. I want you to release her so we can both enjoy."

William tapped her bell again. "Kitt," he said, "listen to me." Kitt's body went limp. "Marshall wants you to relax and be yourself. Do you understand?"

"Yes," Kitt said, testing her bonds, "I understand. But I can't move."

"No, you can't. Does that upset you?" When she hesitated, he asked again, his voice soft, "Does it?"

Kitt looked at Marshall. "No. I find it very exciting, being tied up like this. But it's hard for me to admit it."

"I understand. Do whatever you like. If you say stop, you can be sure that I will."

Kitt smiled and again pulled against the ties that held her. "I really am at your mercy. What are you going to do?"

"Pleasure us both, I hope," Marshall said. Then he walked

around the table stroking and scratching Kitt's belly, thighs, nipples. "You're so beautiful."

Quickly he undressed and knelt at the head of the table so his hard, erect cock was level with her mouth. "I want you to suck it," he said.

Kitt opened her mouth, then paused. With a gleam in her eyes, she turned her head away, her lips firmly pressed together. "Oh, yes, baby, get into the game. Fight me."

Marshall twisted his hand in her hair and pulled her face around. "Open your mouth, bitch, and suck my cock!"

As she did as he said, he pressed his penis into her mouth. Suddenly Marshall knew she was enjoying what she was doing. He felt her lips tighten on his cock and her tongue slide over his skin. As he pulled back, he felt her create a vacuum in her mouth as she sucked. Still holding her head, he fucked her mouth until he came. Spurts of semen filled her throat and she swallowed, licking him clean.

As Marshall settled back on his haunches, he said, "What about her? She's so hot."

"What's your pleasure, gentlemen?" William asked.

"I'd like to watch one of the other girls get her off," Samuel said.

"Is that all right with you, Kitt?" Marshall asked.

"Would you like to watch?" she asked him.

"Oh, yes," he admitted.

Kitt smiled and nodded.

"That's a splendid idea," Sylvia said. "We haven't trained anyone specifically for that, so it will interesting to see how it works."

As William reached for another bell, Sylvia said, "Let me tell her. I think I'd enjoy doing that."

"Certainly," William said, tapping a different bell. A clear note, higher than any they had heard previously, sounded through the room. Ginny raised her dark-brown eyes and looked at William. "Ginny, you will listen to Sylvia like a good girl. You will hear only her voice and do whatever she says," William said.

Ginny turned toward Sylvia who said, "Dear, Kitt is so excited and she needs to come. I want you to pleasure her with your mouth."

William explained to the three men. "Ginny is our most adventurous woman. You must understand that I never ask any woman to do anything that is outside her nature."

During William's explanation, Ginny had sat quietly, not yet obeying Sylvia's instructions.

"Has she ever had any lesbian experiences?" Samuel asked.

"Several, according to her, and she enjoys it tremendously, " Sylvia said, turning to the girl. "Ginny, I told you to do something."

"Tell me exactly what you want me to do," Ginny whispered. "I want to hear the words."

"All right, my dear. I want you to do whatever I tell you." Sylvia smiled. "Now, get up and go over to the table."

Marshall was holding Kitt's head in his hands, stroking her face. "We'll both enjoy what's going to happen," he whispered to her.

Ginny approached and, at Sylvia's instruction, knelt beside Kitt. "Now suck her nipples," Sylvia said. "Take one into your mouth and suck it, hard. Tug at it with your teeth."

Ginny bent over Kitt's body and began to suck her breasts, exposed above the corselet.

"Use your hands. Pull her tits out and caress them with your hands."

Marshall could hear slurping sounds as Ginny sucked.

"Now the other one," Sylvia said. Obediently Ginny switched to the other breast.

Kitt's hips thrust upward, reaching for something, a cock, a tongue. "She needs you, Ginny. She needs your mouth on her pussy to make her come. Lick and suck her pussy, Ginny, like a good girl."

Ginny moved around the table and tentatively touched the tip of her tongue to Kitt's cunt lips. "Lick the whole length of her slit," Sylvia said, "then flick your tongue over her clit. Good. Now stick your tongue inside and pull it out. Lick. Nibble at her clit."

Sylvia walked over and placed her hand on Kitt's belly, just above her pubic hair. "I can feel her hips moving," she said. "Lick faster. Flick your tongue over her clit, then pull it into your mouth. Yes. Make her come. I can feel it coming. Don't stop. " There was a moment's pause, then Sylvia yelled, "Now! Suck hard now."

Marshall reached down and felt the tiny, compulsive movements of Kitt's hips. As she came, he pressed his mouth against hers and probed with his tongue. He thrust his tongue in and out of her mouth in the rhythm he could feel with his hand. Her climax seemed to go on for hours. When she calmed, Marshall untied her and cradled her in his lap.

As Ginny finished licking Kitt's body, Samuel stood up, unzipped his pants and pulled out his erect cock. He had to have her now. On a side table there was a jar of lubricant and he spread a handful on his cock. "Tell her to let me fuck her my way."

"She already knows," Sylvia said, "and she loves it that way. Offer Samuel what he wants, Ginny."

Ginny flipped her dress up over her back, raised her ass in the air and, still licking Kitt's pussy, parted her ass cheeks with her hands. All anyone could see were the same garters and stockings that Kitt was wearing, except Ginny's were black to match her dress.

Samuel found his cock getting even harder at her eagerness to give and take pleasure. God, he wanted her tight ass. He rubbed his lubricated fingers over her entire rear, then pressed the tip of one finger against her hole.

"Oh, yes, darling," Ginny said, holding very still. Samuel's finger pressed and released. Slowly, the pushing became a bit harder and the tip of his finger penetrated. Deeper and deeper his thrusting finger went, rhythmically forcing itself into her.

As the finger continued its assault, her hips began to thrust backward. "That feels good, doesn't it, Ginny. It's tight, but it makes your pussy hot." He reached around and fingered her sopping cunt with his other hand. "So wet. You're so wet."

Samuel stroked her pussy with one hand and fucked her ass with the other. When he felt she was ready and he could wait no longer, he lubricated his hard cock and pressed the tip against her puckered bole, then thrust deep into her.

"It feels so good, darling. Do it harder," she screamed.

Samuel kept massaging her cunt and soon felt her rear muscles relax and her hips begin to buck. "Yes," he said, establishing his own rhythm, "move your hips while I fuck your ass and finger your cunt. Move with me.

"Oh, God," she screamed, "I'm going to come."

"We're both going to come, Ginny."

He fucked her ass and rubbed her pussy until they both came and collapsed on the floor.

Barbara stopped the tape and, panting from her orgasm, she went into the bathroom and got a glass of water. That I could get so hot from just a story . . . she thought. No wonder people buy dirty books and magazines. Then she stopped herself. Not dirty. Erotic. Delicious. She made a mental note to find a bookstore or newsstand and do a little shopping. When she was calmer, she lay back on the bed and pressed play again and the story resumed. She was instantly back in the basement with William and Sylvia.

William crossed to the bar and poured Sylvia and the three men a drink. They untied Kitt and put robes on the two spent girls. Then they sat them on the sofa and put them back into their trance.

William looked at Paul. "Yours is yet to come. I just want everyone a bit rested to watch the show."

Paul smiled and rearranged his clothing over his hard cock. After what he had already witnessed, whatever William and Sylvia had in store for him would be worth any amount of inconvenience.

After they had rested for a short while, William said, "Your treat is a bit different, Paul. Cynthia has been trained for a new experience. When she hears her bell she will listen only to my voice and she will feel exactly what I tell her to feel. " William tapped a bell with a lower, more mellow tone. Cynthia sat up.

"Cynthia," William said, "it's very warm in here, isn't it?"

"Yes," she said. "Very warm."

"So warm that you think you'll never be able to get cool."

Cynthia started fanning herself with her hand. Her face began to flush and she blew a stream of cool air on her chest.

"That air you're blowing is hot and it's making you hotter. Even though this room is full of important people and you will be very embarrassed to do so, you have to pull the top of your dress down to get cool."

Cynthia looked around at the "important people" and looked very uncomfortable. "I'm so hot," she murmured, "I have to get cool." She pulled the top of her dress down and, like the other girls, she was wearing a corselet that bared her nipples, hers in silver.

"You're still so hot," William continued. *"That's not helping. Your nipples are the center of the beat. They're so hot they're on fire. You have to cool them off. Your whole tit is so hot." Cynthia pulled her breasts out of the corselet, looked frantically around the room and spotted the ice in Paul's drink. She grabbed the glass, pulled out an ice cube and rubbed it over her breasts. "Yes, that feels better, doesn't it?"*

"Yes." The word came out like a hiss. "Better."

"The ice is getting hotter from the heat of your breast. It's not cooling anymore. You need something else."

"What?" she asked, dropping the ice cube.

"Paul's mouth. That's the only cool thing in the room. But he might not want to suck your tits and cool them. You have to ask nicely."

"Please cool my tits," she said, offering her breasts to him. "Please."

Paul blew a stream of air across her nipples. "Yes," she purred, "that's cool. But I need your mouth."

Paul smiled and said, "You'll have to force them into my mouth." This was his oldest fantasy coming true.

She climbed into his lap and forced her swollen buds into his mouth. She pulled at his hair and his ears as she tried to force her whole breast into his mouth at once. He sucked and was in heaven.

"Now the other one, Cynthia. Let Paul's mouth cool it."

Paul alternated between Cynthia's pillow-soft, white breasts, filling his mouth and his hands with her flesh.

"Your tits are getting cool now," William said, "but the beat is traveling to your mouth. It's your mouth that is hot now."

Cynthia opened her mouth and panted, trying to draw in cool air. Then she picked up Paul's drink and took an ice cube into her mouth.

"That ice is still hot, Cynthia," William said. "There's only one thing here that's cool." She looked at him, puzzled. "Paul's cock. It's the only cool thing in the room.

Frantically Cynthia pulled at Paul's zipper until she could pull his pants aside and take out his cock. It was huge. Paul loved to have it sucked, but it was too big for most women.

"It's a huge ice cube, Cynthia," William said. "If you take it into your mouth it will cool you, but only where it touches. The rest of your mouth will still be hot."

Cynthia wrapped her hand around Paul's erection and opened her mouth as wide as she could. She took Paul's entire cock into her mouth, her tongue and hands moving ceaselessly. She bobbed her head, moving the "cold" cock around to cool each part of her hot flesh.

For five minutes, everyone watched as Cynthia sucked Paul's erection until it was hard for him not to come. "Make her stop," he cried. "I want to come in her pussy."

"The heat in your mouth is subsiding now, Cynthia." Cynthia's body slowly relaxed and she sat up. "Your body is warm again all over. You'd better take off your dress."

Cynthia pulled off the dress that had been bunched around her waist.

"That's better," William said. "Now the beat is flowing back, this time in your pussy. It's like hot honey running down inside your belly and flowing out of your cunt, making it warmer and warmer."

Cynthia spread her legs as she "felt" the honey flow. "Spread your legs as the honey streams down your thighs. You need some-

thing cool. The honey is making you hot. Paul's cock is still the only cool thing in the room. Sit on it. Take it inside you."

Cynthia climbed onto Paul's lap and impaled herself on his cock. "Move it around to cool your entire cunt," William said. "Up and down so it cools the sides of your passage. There's cool juice inside that prick. Tighten your muscles to squeeze out the cool juice. Squeeze and relax, squeeze and relax. That's the best way."

Paul could take no more. With a scream he came deep inside her. "Yes, you did well," William said. "Cold juice is spurting into your pussy and putting out the fire. But you must hold Paul's cock inside you or you'll get hot again."

Paul looked at William, exhausted. He had no idea what William had in mind, but he was spent.

"Have you ever felt a woman come?" Sylvia asked Paul. "Really felt it? Well, we've always thought that we could make one come just from the sound of William's voice. The only way we'd be sure is if she came while your cock was still inside and you could feel her climax. Are you game.?"

Paul looked at Cynthia still sitting in his lap. He knew she couldn't hear him or Sylvia. "Yeah, sure. I'm game. But I don't think you can do it. Orgasm isn't trainable."

"We think it is. Let's put it to the test. I'll let the other women listen, too. You can all enjoy your date's excitement."

He tapped another bell. All the women looked at William. "Now, ladies, don't move any part of your body, just listen to my voice. You will feel exactly what I tell you to feel. Do you understand?"

Cynthia and the other women nodded. "I understand."

"You feel hands on your breasts. One hand on each breast is kneading your flesh. It feels so good. Lean forward just a bit so your breasts will press into the caressing hands. " Paul felt her strain forward. "That's good. The fingers are twisting your nipples now. It's painful, but it is also exciting. The pinches have taken on a rhythm, first one side then the other. They are pulling at your nipples, milking your breasts. Those hands are making you so excited."

Paul could feel Cynthia's body swaying with the sound of William's voice. The voice was so exciting that each of the other two men were playing with the breasts of the women now sitting on their laps.

"The fingers are creating tiny electrical charges that are sparking through your tits. Hot electrical sparks that excite you and make your pussy wetter. You can feel the sparks through your ribs and your belly. Tiny pinpoints of pain and pleasure are traveling over your skin, lower and lower through your belly and now over the insides of your thighs.

"The sparks are tiny caresses now, flicking soft touches up the insides of your thighs. Now those flickers are on your pussy, pulsing over your clit."

Almost simultaneously the other two men entered their women and began pumping in sync with William's voice.

"Your clit is pulsing with the sensation. You can feel the tightness grow in your belly as your climax approaches. That tightness is traveling to your pussy."

Paul could feel his cock swell as he tried to remain still. He could feel Cynthia's juices soaking his thighs.

"Feel those pulses all over your body, in your breasts, in your mouth, in your ass. Those pulses are your orgasm approaching. You want to resist but you can't. The pull of the pulses is too strong. The pulses are pulling your orgasm from you.

"Tell me, are you going to come?"

"Yes," each woman screamed. "I can feet it . . . right now.

"Then come now. Let the orgasm come. Let the pulses flow through your cunt."

Paul screamed as he felt Cynthia's climax suck at his cock. He couldn't keep his own orgasm back and he climaxed again.

No one was sure how much later William tapped the bell that released the women from their trances. He and Sylvia tossed blankets over the exhausted couples and turned down the light.

"Good night, everyone," William said. "Sylvia and I are going upstairs."

Chapter 8

It was several weeks before Barbara saw Maggie again. She had dated Jay frequently and had had dates, and been to bed with three other men—one from her office, one a neighbor, and one a man she had met at the supermarket. She had also played the tapes frequently and found that, thanks to the attitudes of the people in the stories, she had become accepting of sex in all forms, and was able to suggest games and activities that proved both stimulating and rewarding.

In mid-June, Barbara arrived home from work one evening to find Maggie in her kitchen, cooking. After long, almost tearful hugs, Barbara stepped back, looked at her friend and said, "It's been such a long time and I've missed you. God, things smell good in here."

"I've missed you, too," Maggie said. "And I'm making corned beef and cabbage. I couldn't resist."

"You must have shopped. How did you do that? Could people see you?"

Maggie looked shocked. "They must have been able to, but I have no clue how. I never even thought about it. I just went to the supermarket and picked up a few things." She shook her head. "People must have seen me. The woman checked me out without a blink. And I had money in my wallet."

"But in the mall, no one could see you but me."

"Things in this plane of existence work strangely to say the least. When is this?"

"It's June."

"It looked springy," Maggie said. "But I cooked this anyway. It was in my mind when I arrived at the A&P."

Barbara lifted a piece of cabbage from the pot and tasted. "Wonderful. I'm glad you did. And I'm incredibly glad to see you."

Maggie hugged Barbara again. "Me too, although I just left you a few moments before I showed up at the supermarket."

Barbara opened the refrigerator door and spied a six-pack of Sam Adams. She looked toward Maggie questioningly. "My favorite. One for you?" At Maggie's nod, she pulled out two bottles.

"Sure." She pushed a long fork into the slab of meat in the pot. "Let's give this about fifteen more minutes."

The two women sat at the kitchen table and each poured a beer. "How have you been, Barbara?" Maggie asked.

"I've been great," Barbara said. "Lots of dates, lots of good healthy sex."

"Steve?"

"No. Not him. Despite all the great clothes and keeping myself looking good, he pays almost no attention to me, except as a very useful piece of furniture."

"Have you asked him out?"

"No. We did have dinner one evening, but it was with a client and his wife. I guess Lisa, Ms. Knockout, isn't the kind you take to dinner with a guy with oodles of old money. You should have seen his wife. Her jewelry was older than I was."

"And nothing remotely date-like from Steve?"

"Not a whisper. He didn't even take me home, just put me into a hired car and told the driver to take me wherever I wanted to go."

"We really have to do something about that, don't we?"

"Yes, we do. But I have another request first. Those tapes?"

"I gave you all I had," Maggie said.

"You told me that the man who made them has a store in the city. I think, well . . ."

"Yes? Out with it."

"Well, I'd like to meet him."

"His voice really gets to you, doesn't it?"

"His voice fills my erotic dreams, which, of course, I'd never admit to having except to you. What's he like?"

"He owns an erotic toy, book, and what-have-you store in the Village. He's a free spirit with a great understanding of the secret desires everyone has. And he exploits that knowledge in his stories and the items he sells in the shop. He's wonderfully creative in everything he does. And I do mean everything."

"You've been to bed with him?"

"Beds, boats, tables, CJ makes love wherever the fancy strikes him. But yes, I've been with him many times."

"Was he a customer?"

"He doesn't ever have to pay for it. He has whatever he wants, whenever he wants it. And frequently he wanted me. And I wanted him. So we did. I met him when I first went into his shop to buy a few things."

"I don't want to make love with him, I just want to see the man who goes with that incredible voice."

"The shop is called A Private Place." Maggie wrote down the address on a piece of paper. "Take one of the tapes as sort of an introduction. And keep an open mind and be ready for anything, that is, if you're so inclined."

"Oh, Maggie," Barbara said. "That's not why I want to meet him."

"Whatever you say." She took a long drink of her beer and the conversation shifted.

The storefront was unremarkable, a large window with a display of erotic books, but nothing overt enough to offend any passers-by. The words *A Private Place* were lettered on the window in ornate gold script, and there was a small sign in the corner of the window that proclaimed *C. J. Winterman, Prop. CJ.* Yes, that voice. Hours 11:00 to 5:00 Tues., Thurs., and Sat. He certainly works only when it suits him, Barbara thought.

That Saturday afternoon, as she stood looking in the window, Barbara rubbed her sweating palms together. She was nervous as a teenager, yet she dearly wanted to meet the man who had been part of her fantasies since Maggie gave her the first tape. She took a deep breath, inhaling late spring air, then glanced at her watch. Almost five o'clock. Only a few minutes until closing, but the sign read Open. She pushed open the door and heard a small bell jingle.

The store was well lit, with racks and shelves filled with sex toys, erotic games, books, greeting cards, everything the creative lover might want. She slowly toured the shop, pausing to giggle at several get well and birthday cards, then trembled a bit in front of a display of bondage equipment. As she crossed the front sales area, she overheard a young couple discussing which vibrator they should purchase.

"Do you think that's powerful enough?" she said.

"I don't want the kind that plugs in," he responded. "You're limited by the length of the cord."

"I like this one. It has a clit tickler," she said.

"If you like it, then we'll get it." The man handed a woman behind the counter a credit card as Barbara looked over a display of whips and leather harnesses.

"These are cleverly arranged so that you can strap on a dildo leaving your hands free for other pleasures," a voice behind her said.

It was his voice, the voice from the tapes. It hummed through her, making her knees weak and her pussy wet. She swallowed and turned slowly. He was about her age, average height with very curly brown hair and a sweet, almost cherubic face. His smile was open and warm. No wonder people buy stuff here, Barbara thought. He seems so innocent, as though everything in here must be ordinary. "You must be CJ," " she said.

"Is that a guess from the sign in the window, or have you been here before?"

That voice. That incredible voice.

"Actually neither. I know your voice from some tapes I've been listening to." She withdrew a tape from her pocketbook and showed it to him.

"Oh." His face lit up as he grinned. "Yes. But these are part of the special edition, ones I made up for my friends." He pointed to the gold rim around the label. "See. This is how you tell. Where did you get this one?"

"That's a bit of a long story. Let's just say I got a few of them from a wonderful woman named Maggie."

"I haven't seen Maggie in a long time. I miss her. How is she?"

How to handle this one? Barbara wondered. "Actually, Maggie passed away last summer."

"I am so sorry. She was an amazing woman. Were you good friends?"

"Oh, yes, very good friends. But that was long ago."

"And were you and she kindred spirits?"

Barbara knew exactly what he was asking. Was she a hooker? "We weren't in the same line of work," she answered. "But we shared a lot of the same feelings." Was that an invitation? She hoped so. Much as she had denied it to Maggie, she had to admit that she wanted this man as she had never wanted anything.

"And what can I do to help you?" CJ asked.

"CJ," a voice called, postponing her answer. "It's after five and my husband's waiting outside. Unless you need me, I'm leaving."

"Have a nice evening, Alice," CJ called. "And turn the sign as you leave."

"I guess you're closing now," Barbara said, unable now to ask for what she wanted. The moment was gone. "I'll be leaving, too."

"Since you're a friend of Maggie's, you're welcome to wander as long as you like. Were you looking for anything special?" He placed his hands on her shoulders and turned her toward the display of leather-and-metal harnesses. "These are usually bought by dominants, for training sessions with their subs. Do they interest you?" He spoke with his mouth close to her ear, his breath warm, his hands on her shoulders.

"Yes," she whispered.

"You're trembling. Tell me what has you so excited. The idea of wearing one of those and doing deliciously evil things to someone?" When she remained silent, he continued. "Or maybe having someone wear a harness like that and overpower you."

Barbara couldn't move, couldn't speak. She was unable to control any parts of her body. All her thoughts were concentrated on his hands, his mouth, and her aching pussy.

"Did you want to buy one for your lover? Male or female?"

"Not for a lover," she croaked.

"For yourself?"

"For you." The words slipped out, but she was glad she had said them.

"Ah." His breath was warm against her ear. "You have a fantasy about me. Maybe in the fantasy I am wearing something made from heavy leather straps with metal rings and buckles, holding you down while I violate your body." Barbara couldn't answer. "You are helpless, unable to prevent me from doing whatever I want to you. Is that what you want?" Silence. His mouth remained against her ear, his tongue licking the edge. His arm slipped across her upper chest and pressed her back tightly against his chest. "Is it?"

"Yes," she whispered.

"Good girl," he putted. "Don't move." He nipped at her ear with his teeth, then left her. She heard him pull down the shades and put the chain on the door. He returned to stand behind her. "Now no one can come in and disturb us. Come with me."

Barbara moved like an automaton, following his slender frame through a curtain and into the back of the shop. They passed through a storage area and into another room. CJ closed the door and slid a bolt home. "Now we are truly alone. You are here of your own free will, are you not?"

"Yes," she whispered.

"Do you understand about safe words?"

Barbara remembered that Maggie had explained that if anyone used the pre-agreed safe word during any bondage session, everything stopped. She nodded.

"I use a slightly different system." He placed a Ping-Pong ball in Barbara's hand. "If you drop this, I will stop anything and everything, no questions asked. Do you understand?"

Barbara looked down at the small white ball in her hand. "Yes," she said, unable to say anything more even if she wanted to. The inside of her mouth felt like cotton, her knees were jelly, and her insides were trembling so hard it was difficult to concentrate on anything else. But she was so turned on, she felt as if she could come on command.

"And do you promise me you will drop that if anything, and I do mean anything, bothers you? It's most important that I have your word on that."

"You have my word," she said.

"Good." CJ flipped a switch and the room filled with the music that formed the background on the tapes. Then he opened a small closet in the corner of the room, grabbed some clothes and stepped behind a shoulder-height screen. "Get undressed," he said, his head above the top of the screen. "I want you completely naked." When she hesitated, he snapped, "Now!"

Barbara put the ball down, quickly removed her clothes, put them on a chair and picked up the ball again.

"Let me see you," CJ said, still behind the screen. "Stand up straight, stretch your arms up over your head and spread your legs."

Barbara separated her feet slightly and raised her arms.

"Wider," he snapped.

Barbara spread her feet wider and stared at CJ's face, the only part of him she could see.

"Nice," he said, obviously fumbling with clothes behind the screen. "Good legs, nice hips. Show me your tits."

"What?" Barbara said.

"Put the ball down and hold those tits for me so I can see how full they are." When her hands remained in the air, he said, "Do it now or leave."

Barbara put the ball on the small chair at her side, then cupped her breasts. The room was warm but she was shivering, from need, from lust, and from a sliver of fear. What had she gotten herself into?

"Pinch the nipples and make them hard. Show them to me."

Embarrassed bur so aroused, she pinched her nipples until they swelled.

"Nice titties," CJ said. "Big and soft. You'll do nicely." When she went to put her feet together, he said, "Not in my presence. Your feet will always be apart, your body ready for me. Do you understand? Get the ball, then come here."

He stepped from behind the screen, now dressed in a deep brown harness. Wide straps of what appeared to be hard, unyielding leather crossed his bare chest and a leather pouch cupped his penis and testicles. He wore leather sandals that laced up his slender, yet muscular legs. He wore wide silver cuffs around his biceps and a leather collar around his neck. Whatever led me to see him as an angel? Barbara wondered. In this outfit, he was all power and control.

Holding the Ping-Pong ball, Barbara crossed the room and stood before CJ. He stared at her legs and glared. She looked down, then separated her feet.

"Stand with your chest against the wall."

She moved so she stood facing a bare wall, then felt his hand on her back, pressing her tightly against the cold surface. He raised her arms above her head, spread about as far apart as her feet. "How much of this do you want?" he asked. "I can make you cry or beg, I can hurt you or just control you. What do you want? This is the last decision you will make."

Barbara thought. She wanted to try everything. She didn't know whether pain would be a turn-on, but she had the ball in her hand and she trusted CJ completely. "Everything," she whispered. "I want to try it all."

"Good girl," he said. Then she felt the snap as cold metal cuffs were locked onto her wrists and ankles, then CJ attached the cuffs to the wall. She couldn't move. Then CJ placed cotton balls against her eyes, and covered them with a blindfold. She could see nothing.

"Now," he said, "we begin." He inserted his finger in her slit. "Such a hot slut, he said. "So wet. Let's cool you down a little."

Barbara heard noises, then jumped as something very cold pressed against her heated lips. The frozen object was inserted into her channel. "Some ice should cool you off a bit. You're much too excited." He rubbed another ice cube over her slit, numbing her flesh, yet heating her belly.

"God, that's too cold," she said.

"You will say nothing, or I'll gag you, too." When she shuddered, she felt a wad of cloth stuffed into her mouth, then another cloth stretched between her teeth and tied behind her head. Then he rubbed her clit and laughed. "You want this. Your body tells me everything."

She did want it. She wanted to give everything over to this man with the magic voice. He could do everything to her, all the things she had only dreamed about. Cold water trickled down her inner thigh but she couldn't move to wipe it off. Her mind traveled to the ball in her hand. She wouldn't drop it. Not yet. Maybe not at all.

"Now, let's see how you like this part." Suddenly she felt a hard slap on her right buttock. Then one on her left.

She groaned, making strange strangled sounds around the gag in her mouth. Again and again, his hand landed on her heated flesh. She burned. She throbbed, yet she was also incredibly turned on. The music filled her mind and the pleasure/pain filled her body. She could control her body no longer and she climaxed. Without anyone touching her pussy, without being filled with anything but an ice cube.

"No self-control," he said, laughing again. "I like that, but you're much too easy. Maybe now that you've come once, you'll be more of a challenge." Barbara felt CJ rub some lotion on her hot buttocks, kneading and caressing her skin from the small of her back to her cheeks. Some of the liquid trickled into her slit, oozing over her asshole and joining with the water still running from her icy cunt.

When her flaming ass was a bit cooler, CJ unclipped her cuffs from the wall and led her across the room. He placed her hands on a table of some kind, then pushed her so she was bent over the soft leather cover, her feet on the floor, her upper body cradled in the soft fabric, her arms hanging down. Still holding the Ping-Pong ball, her hands were cuffed to the front legs of the table and her ankles to the rear two. There were openings in the table so her breasts hung freely.

She felt fingers pulling on her nipples, then lightweight clips attached to the hard, erect flesh. "Just so you won't forget your tits," the wonderful voice said. Then he continued. "I know you can't talk, but shake your head. Have you ever been taken in the ass?"

Barbara shook her head.

"Oh, a virgin. That's wonderful."

He left her lying across the table, unable to move, her blindfold and gag in place, tits hanging, with the clips attached. Although it was difficult, Barbara used the moment to catch her breath and come down from the earth-moving climax that had ripped through her while he was spanking her. But although she had come once, hard, she knew she was close to coming again.

Then she felt his mouth beside her ear. "I have a dildo in my hand. It's quite slender, but wide enough to fill your ass. Remember the ball in your hand. I will know if it falls."

Barbara felt him stroke her back, then press his hand against her waist. "I'm going to rub some lubricant on now." The sound of his voice, telling her what he was going to do was unbelievably erotic. "Your ass will feel so filled, so fucked. It will feel strange, but wonderful." He rubbed cold, slippery gel over her ass, sliding his finger in just a tiny amount. Then he slowly inserted a slender plastic rod into her previously unviolated rear.

'No," she tried to say around the gag. "Don't." But she didn't drop the ball from her hand. "No."

"Oh, yes," he purred, slowly driving the rod deeper into her body. When it was lodged inside her, he stopped and left it there.

"Oh, God," she mumbled. Then his finger was rubbing her clit and she came again. She couldn't help it. The orgasm ripped through her, making her entire body pulse.

"Such a good slut, but again too easy. But it's my turn now." A moment later, he said, "I just want to assure you that I'm using a condom, so you don't have to worry." His cock rubbed against her cunt, moving the dildo that still filled her ass. His hips and groin pressed against her burning ass, forcing the dildo still deeper into her ass. He plunged his cock into her pussy and she came yet again, her spasms clutching at him. It took only a few thrusts for him to bellow his release.

A while later, CJ released Barbara's wrists and ankles, then removed the blindfold and gag. "You're so receptive. It makes me crazy when you come like that."

"So good for me, too," Barbara said, her breathing still ragged. "It's never been any better."

The silence broken only by the music, they dressed. There was no talk of dinner. She realized they had never even kissed. "Please come to my store again," CJ said as he opened the outer door. "There are several more things I can show you and some I'm sure you could show me."

"Maybe," she said, not being coy, just unsure whether she would repeat the experience. "I don't really know."

"That's fine," he said. Then he placed two tapes in her hand. "For another time," he said. "I just made these recently and they both focus on performing for an audience. If you're ever interested in living out this type of fantasy, let me know." With the tapes she saw that he had handed her his business card. "CJ Winterman. A Private Place. Unusual Items and Entertainments of All Sorts." It contained the store's address and a phone number. "The number rings here in the store and in my apartment upstairs."

Barbara put the tapes and the card in her pocket. "Thank you," she said, walking toward the door. "For everything."

That night Barbara lay in bed and put the tape into the player. The expected music filled the room and CJ's voice, a voice she could now put a face and a body to, began to spin his latest tale. She let herself drift into the story.

The club was warm and the lights low as the music began for the last show of the evening. Marianne stood at the side of the small stage, ready for her first effort at entertaining the patrons at the Exotica Club, a totally nude review club a few miles from her home. She had practiced her act and thought she could give them a good show. After all, she had watched the performances often enough.

It had all begun a year earlier when the club first opened. Her husband, Matt, had frequented a similar club in the city before their marriage and had often told her about the wild dancing at the storefront club be had gone to. When the Exotica Club opened, she and Matt had been among its first patrons. A bit raw at first, the club's entertainment bad improved. The comedians had become increasingly talented, the singers more professional, and the dancers more skillful in their movements. Now, a year later, shows were sold out weeks in advance and lines formed early in the evening to get the few tables or spots at the bar that might become available.

Thursday night had evolved into Talent Night, when anyone could sign up for a spot on the program and, after much urging from Matt, Marianne had finally listed herself among the performers. As she stood in the wings watching the first woman take her turn, she looked into the audience. Matt sat at a table right in front and Marianne watched him gazing at the slender, small-bosomed woman who strutted around the stage to "The Stripper." She removed her clothing slowly but a bit awkwardly, Marianne thought. The next act was a new, young comedian whose routine was filled with expletives and was quite funny. He was followed by a male dancer and a woman in a slinky dress who sang several erotic songs.

Finally, as a couple performed a tango, almost copulating right on the stage, Marianne realized that she was next, and last, on the program. The couple's performance was followed by cheers from the audience. As she looked past the lights, she could see several couples engaged in sexual play, hands in crotches rubbing, caressing. She took a deep breath and squared her shoulders. You ain't seen nothin' yet, she thought.

The lights dimmed and a stagehand pushed a large washtub onto the center of the stage and set a short stool beside it. Marianne picked up a basket of old clothes and, as the lights brightened and some soft music began, she walked slowly to the center of the stage. She was wearing a small pinafore that barely concealed her breasts and covered the front of a short skirt that came only to midthigh. She was barefoot, her long blond hair was braided, and she wore almost no make up.

As background music played, she put her basket down, sat on the stool, her knees widely spread so the audience could see the crotch of her white panties, and took a pair of men's briefs from the basket. She glanced at Matt and saw him grinning from ear to ear. She knew how much he loved watching her and, although there were probably almost a hundred people watching, Marianne performed for him alone.

She took an old-fashioned wash board and started to scrub the pants, sloshing water everywhere, including all over herself. After a moment, she stood up and tried to sluice the water from the top of her pinafore. All she succeeded in doing was wetting the entire front so her breasts were easily visible. "Oh, my," she said, looking innocently into the audience. "Oh, my." She covered her breasts and giggled, then looked into the laundry basket. She found a white T-shirt she had put there because not only was it too tight but it had been washed so many times it was almost transparent.

She turned her back to the audience, took off the pinafore and put the T-shirt on. "Better?" she asked softly as she turned back to the gathering. Her breasts were clearly visible and her dark nipples were pressing against the front.

"Yeah," some yelled.

"Take it all off," yelled others.

"I couldn't do that," she said sweetly, batting her eyelashes. "I'm not that kind of girl."

There were whistles and groans, cheers and calls of, "Yeah, right."

"I have to get back to work," she said and sat back on the stool, giving the audience another clear view of her crotch. Again she washed an item and again sloshed water everywhere. By now, whatever had been partially hidden by the T-shirt was fully revealed and her skirt was soaked as well. "Oh, my," she said again, holding her skirtfront and squeezing water from the fabric. "Oh, my."

The watchers silenced, waiting for her to remove more clothing. She turned her back to the audience and unbuttoned her skirt, letting it fall around her feet. All the while, soft music played in the background. Finally she turned back to the sea of eyes watching her, now wearing only the soaked T-shirt and a pair of tiny white panties.

"Oh, yeah, lady. Right on."

Again she sat and washed another garment, now soaking herself. "Oh, my," she said as she stood up and watched water run from her body. "Oh, my." She slowly ran her hands over her skin, ostensibly scraping the water from her legs and belly. Then she wrung out the front of her T-shirt, smiled sweetly to the audience and shrugged. With agonizing deliberation, she pulled the soaked shirt off, eventually revealing her white skin, her breasts, and dark, dusky nipples. She appeared to try to cover herself, then shrugged and apparently gave up. Then she slowly she removed the ribbons that held her hair and fluffed it free. It fell almost to the small of her back and she slowly ran her fingers through it, arranging it so it flowed down her chest, and almost, but not quite, covered her breasts.

Now, as she sat on the stool, she was only clad in her panties and her hair. She picked up another piece of wash and sloshed it around in the tub. Now her panties were almost transparent, allowing the audience only a partially screened view of her blond bush. "Oh, my," she said, standing again and looking at her panties. The audience roared and screamed, then silenced as she looked at them. They could see that this was more than just a strip show. She was letting them peek at an embarrassed girl, making them delighted voyeurs.

She slowly slid the panties down her legs, bending so those in the audience couldn't see her crotch. She remained crouched and looked at the faces of the crowd. Then she looked at Matt, who was quite obviously rubbing the bulge in the front of his trousers. She could feel an answering tingle in her pussy. "Oh, my, " she said again, then stood up, allowing the people to see her nude body. "Oh, my," she said again as she looked around. The audience was strangely silent, as if not wanting to disturb the sweet young girl and her laundry. Although several couples were making love and one woman knelt with her partner's cock in her mouth, all eyes were on the show. Wow, Marianne thought. This is great. I can turn people on. I love this and it makes me so hot.

Giving the audience a good view of her bush, she once more sat down and dropped the another piece of laundry into the water. Water flew everywhere until she was dripping. She stood up and rubbed her body to remove the water. Then she rubbed her crotch as if to remove the last of the water. "Oh, my," she said, rubbing her flesh. "Oh, my."

As she had planned, water had splashed on several people in the front of the audience, including her husband. As faces peered up at her, she walked to the edge of the stage, then slowly made her way down to the level of the tables, a small towel from the laundry basket dangling from one hand.

Several large men stood around the periphery of the room watching to see that everyone followed the club's rules. A performer could do anything to anyone in the audience. Those watching could do nothing to or with a performer without being invited.

She and Matt had discussed things that might happen and they had agreed that Marianne could do anything the mood compelled her to. Matt would enjoy watching her antics. He knew that she loved to play and that she would end the evening with him. He also knew that she loved him totally. That was enough reassurance for him. She could play to her heart's content.

She made her way to Matt and sat on his lap. "Oh, my," she said, wiping water from the front of his shirt. Then she wiped the front of his slacks, pressing all the places she knew would delight him. Under her breath, she asked, "Still all right with this?"

"Oh, yes, baby. Have fun."

Marianne stood up and moved to another man, who stared at her in rapt attention. "Oh, my," she repeated, wiping the man's face and shirt. As she rubbed his pants, she felt his hard cock. Slowly she crouched between his spread knees and unzipped his fly. With little urging, his cock sprung forth. "Oh, my," she said, clear appreciation in her voice. She curled her fingers around his large erection and rubbed, watching small drops of fluid ooze from the tip. "Mmmm," she purred, and she continued to caress his staff.

"You don't know what you're doing to me," he groaned.

"I certainly do," she said as semen erupted into her hand. "Oh, my." Minutes later, she wiped her hand and moved away. Two women were stretched out on a double lounge chair at one side of the room. As Marianne watched, they rubbed breast to breast, their hands working in each other's pussy. She walked over and tweaked two nipples, then inserted fingers of both hands into two wet pussies.

For several more minutes she wandered around the room, touching, rubbing, caressing, then she walked back up on the stage. She splashed water onto her face and allowed some to dribble onto her breasts. Her right hand rubbed her clit while her left palm slid over her nipples. She sat on the stool, her legs spread, her head back, so everyone could watch her stroke herself. And she did, she watched Matt out of the corner of her eye. He was really excited, she realized, and so was she. It had stopped being just a show. If she rubbed in just the right place . . . She stroked and caressed and then inserted two fingers into her pussy. Men and women were watching while sucking and fucking each other and Matt had his naked cock in his hand. All eyes were on her.

She moaned. "Oh, God," she yelled. "Oh, now."

As she came, a small part of her still watched Matt and the others, all approaching or just past orgasm. "Yes," she groaned as she climaxed, her juice running down her fingers. She sat for long moments as the audience remained almost completely silent. Then it erupted in applause and calls of "Way to go, baby" and "Lemme have some." Several husky men surrounded the stage to prevent anyone from getting too close.

Slowly the lights dimmed and Marianne left the stage, her breath slowly returning to normal, her knees still weak. Matt found her in the dressing room, tossed her onto the floor and drove his cock into her, unable to stop until he erupted inside her slippery pussy.

"Oh, my, baby," he said later, as he lay beside her. "Oh, my."

Barbara lay on her bed as the music filled the room. She had just climaxed for the third time during the story, glad she had learned to masturbate for lengthy pleasure and multiple orgasms, not just to scratch her itch. She thought back on what had excited her the most about the story. Performing? Giving a stranger a hand job? No. What had driven her quickly over the edge was the picture that formed in her mind of the two women.

The following evening, Maggie and Barbara sat in the living room sipping wine. "I know I sound like a commercial, but I have to say it. You've come a long way," Maggie said.

"Yes, I'm a very different person that I was when we first met."

"Are you happy?" Maggie asked. "Or at least happier?"

"I'm having so much fun, but I don't know whether it's a life."

"I don't quite understand."

"Neither do I right now, but I do know that this is an interlude, a time of change. I'm not the person I was, but this isn't the person I will be eventually either." When Maggie looked at her questioningly, Barbara continued. "Sport fucking is wonderful for right now. I'm learning about sexuality and sensuality, but not really about relationships. I don't love any of these men I'm with. I lust for them and it's exciting to be together, but none of them are people with whom I could spend a life. There's not a lot outside of the bedroom."

"I had love. It isn't much either," Maggie said, a bit of bitterness in her voice.

"What did you have exactly? With your husband, I mean. Weren't there any good times? What did you two have in common?"

"Sure there were good times. We played golf together, and tennis. We liked pizza and Kentucky Fried. We were both rather nonpolitical, but once a guy ran for the state assembly we really believed in. We campaigned, went door to door." Maggie gazed into space. "Yeah, there were good times."

"The sex was always bad?"

"It was nothing."

"Even at first? You told me yourself that first times are the best. Wasn't that true with your husband? Do you remember the first time you and he ever made love?"

Maggie smiled. "Yeah, I do. It was in my living room. I still lived at home and my parents were out. Chuck and I sat on the sofa supposedly watching TV. He touched me and kissed me until we were both crazy."

"Were you a virgin?"

"I was, believe it or not. I was almost eighteen and still untouched."

"And Chuck?"

"Ohl he had been with a few girls. But he didn't know very much."

"So it was lousy?"

Maggie considered Barbara's question for a long time. "No, actually it was cosmic. It's been so long that I guess I had forgotten. If I must be honest, it was pretty good for the first few years. Then along came," she deepened her voice like a radio announcer, "*the other woman*. I was really angry."

"And why not? He didn't tell you anything about it."

"Actually, he did. He felt so guilty that he confessed all. They had been friends for several months at work, then he got snowed in at the office. She lived nearby and offered to let him stay on her sofa. One thing led to another and that was that for my marriage."

"Did he want to leave you or did you throw him out?"

"A bit of both. We were both bored and, if I have to be brutally honest, we were both ready to move on."

"So it wasn't as one-sided as you led me to believe."

"Maybe not. I'm not ready to admit all that just yet."

In the computer room, Lucy snapped off the computer screen. "You goosed her, didn't you. You helped her to remember how it really was in her marriage. That's cheating."

"It is not," Angela snapped. "I just prodded some actual memories. I didn't create anything that wasn't already there. I wouldn't cheat. After all, took at who I represent."

"You cheated."

"And you didn't, goosing Barbara into believing free sex is fun just for itself."

"Well, it is."

"That's neither here nor there. We still have a bet, and Maggie's future will depend on the next few weeks."

A lanky, angular man walked into the computer room. "Hey. What is this place?" he asked.

"Well that's a change from 'Where am I?' " Lucy said, returning to her seat and changing the focus of her computer to the life of the newcomer. "And this place is a little hard to explain."

Chapter 9

It was several days before Barbara had the time and sexual energy to play the second of the two tapes CJ had given her. The story was, if anything, more erotic for her than any of the ones she had heard so far.

It was to be an initiation of sorts, several men to be accepted as full members of the exclusive Hathaway Group, a collection of wealthy men in their twenties and thirties who spent one evening a month at a retreat, devoting themselves to pleasures of the flesh. The annual initiation ceremony was eagerly anticipated by both the initiates and the existing members of the Group. Although several of the women at the meeting were hired, many were volunteers who had enjoyed the hedonistic activities of the Group at previous gatherings. In all, there were almost thirty men and more than a dozen women.

Although all the women would have their share of sexual fun, Scott Hathaway, the leader of the group, had selected one to take the central part in the initiation ritual. The Carnal Sacrifice she was called. As all the men stood around the raised platform, Scott extended his hand and led the honored woman to the stage.

Alyssa walked forward and took Scott's hand, her diaphanous white gown flowing around her long, shapely legs. Her breasts, barely covered by the sheer fabric, were high and full and her almost white hair flowed down her back like a pale curtain. Her face was carefully made up and she had applied perfume to all the erogenous zones of her body. She climbed the two steps to the platform and turned to face the audience. Men dressed in flowing black robes with crimson cowls stood with arms draped over the shoulders of bare-breasted women. Four men were bareheaded, and would receive their ceremonial cowls when they had completed the ritual. Everyone stared at the dais with lust-clouded eyes.

On the stage was a velvet bench, specially designed for the men's pleasure. And, after bowing to the crowd, Alyssa allowed Scott to remove her gown, leaving her gloriously naked. She stretched out on the bench on her back, her arms at her sides, her legs spread. Scott slowly rotated the table so the audience could see every aspect of the woman spread invitingly before them. Mirrors reflected from above and around the dais, and several video cameras projected images on large screens around the room. The room lights dimmed and spotlights brightened to illuminate the body on the stage. Alyssa was surprised at the heat that raced through her as one spotlight was adjusted to shine directly on her open pussy lips.

As the group watched, Scott tied Alyssa's wrists and ankles to rings in the bench with soft velvet strips. Then he released a section of the table so her head fell back, and adjusted the bottom of the bench so her legs were still more widely spread.

"Let the initiates come forward," Scott said, and the four would-be group members climbed the two steps. "Disrobe," Scott said and the men removed their robes. They were nude beneath and all had hard erections. "Take your places."

Each man moved to a different spot, one to her head, one to each side, and one between her thighs. Each man unrolled a condom over his cock. "Each of you will have the advantage of the condom, which mutes the sensation. The one who comes first will have to spend another year as an initiate, as Barry has had to do this year." He patted the shoulder of the man who stood at the woman's head. "Actually, Barry, I don't think you minded at all going through all the training for a second time. As a matter of fact,

I think you might have lost on purpose." Everyone, including Barry, laughed.

"Now, you all know the rules. First you will rub oil onto Alyssa's skin, all over her body. Then each of you will slowly take Alyssa, one in her mouth, one in each hand, and one in her pussy. Then you will remain unmoving while Alyssa does whatever she can to make you climax." He looked down at the men and women in the crowd below. "Those of you who want to copulate while you watch what is happening may certainly do so. 'Whatever gives pleasure' is our motto. And, gentlemen," he said, speaking to the four initiates, "if you can make our Carnal Sacrifice come, without coming yourself, then you all pass the initiation test automatically. But once you are inside her, you cannot touch her."

Alyssa lay on the bench, listening to the leader give his speech. Last year she had watched from the audience. The man she had been with had pointed out each man and how he was pleasing the woman on the stage and how he was being pleased as well. As they watched, she had become hungrier and hungrier until she begged the man to take her right there on the floor. Now she was on the stage ready for the ultimate pleasure.

"Gentlemen," Scott said, giving each man a bottle of oil, "you may begin."

Alyssa closed her eyes as eight hands rubbed warm oil on her belly, her breasts, her thighs. Hands kneaded, stroked, fondled, and pinched. Several fingers invaded her pussy, opening her, readying her for what was to come.

"Enough," Scott said. "Enter her."

And she was filled. One cock slowly thrust into her mouth, the latex not diminishing her pleasure. One cock was pressed into each waiting hand and she closed her fist around each. And finally one slowly filled her pussy. Then each man stood completely still and Scott said, "The job of the Carnal Sacrifice is to make them come."

Alyssa smiled inwardly and licked the cock in her mouth. Since she couldn't move her hands because of the bonds, she squeezed her fingers, one after another, to pump those two cocks, and she clamped her vaginal muscles to squeeze the cock so deep in her pussy. She was so excited it was hard to concentrate on making the men come, without coming herself. She wanted to lie there and revel in the sensation of being so full. So many men were part of her at one time.

She opened her eyes and saw that Scott was moving around the table with a video camera in his hand, taking close-up shots of the cocks. She discovered that she could see the TV screen on which the images were projected in the mirror on the ceiling above her.

It was so erotic, the vision of her body invaded by so many men. She watched the men in the mirror, their eyes closed, concentrating on not allowing their body the freedom to come. As she sucked, she heard the man whose cock had penetrated her mouth hiss. Yes, she realized, he was close. But so was she. Although the excitement was almost unbearable, she couldn't come yet, not until one of the men came first.

She increased the movements of her hands, her mouth, her pussy muscles. She hummed softly so the buzzing was echoed in the cock in her mouth. Then the man between her legs blew on her clit. That was enough. Her back arched and she came. Almost simultaneously, both the cock in her mouth and the one in her right hand erupted as well. Only moments later, while the spasms still filled her belly, the other two men came, their groans and howls filling the room.

Now that the contest was over, the cock in her cunt pumped hard, hips slamming into her groin. The men at her sides bent over and each took a nipple in his mouth. The man at her head cupped her head in his hands, holding her still and pumped into her throat. Several people in the audience moaned as they came as well. The room smelled of sex and sweat and animal lust.

Alyssa came and came and came, unwilling to allow the pulses that throbbed through her body to end. Over and over cocks invaded her, men moving around the table taking additional pleasure from her mouth, her hands, and her cunt. It was an orgy of sensation she prayed would never end.

When the men were spent, they withdrew and Scott said, "Since it was impossible to tell who came first, I will declare all the men members of the Group. And I will take my turn with our carnal sacrifice." He pulled off his robe and, unrolling a condom over his large cock, he moved between Alyssa's legs. She watched as he adjusted the leg sections of the table until her legs were in the air, her bottom exposed.

"You know what happens now."

"Yes, my lord," she said, her body throbbing with both echos of her climax and her need for more.

"Only one part of you remained uninvaded. That part is mine. Do you agree?"

"Yes, my lord."

He covered his cock with lubricant and touched his finger tip to her anus. "Are you a virgin there?" he asked, rubbing lubricant on her hole.

"Yes, my lord."

"Yet you are willing?"

"Oh, yes, my lord."

Someone else held the camera so Alyssa could see the tip of Scott's finger slowly enter her tight bole. The feeling of fullness was both unpleasant and wildly erotic. Part of her wanted to expel the invading finger, part wanted to drive it deeper. Slowly, as she watched the monitor in the mirror, the finger went deeper and deeper, stretching and oiling her for the eventual penetration. Scott withdrew the finger, then used his thick thumb to open her still further.

She had been anxious to try this type of sexual fun, yet had been a bit unsure as well. She was no longer doubtful. It was magnificent. "My lord, I am ready for you" she cried.

As he held the tip of his cock against her puckered opening, he rubbed her clit with his other hand. Then in a single, slow stroke, he filled her. She came with the first stroke, screaming her pleasure for all to hear. Scott pulled back, then thrust into her again. Over and over he filled and emptied her ass until he, too, succumbed to the pleasure of the fucking.

As he left her body, someone announced that anyone who wanted any part of the carnal sacrifice's body could take it. Many did, in her mouth, in her hands, her pussy, her ass. She lost track of the number of times she came or the number of men she pleasured.

Later, she was released from the bench and given a cooling drink. Then two women lovingly massaged her body to relax and refresh her. Finally, when she was ready, she rose and walked through the room to the applause and cheers of all assembled. She had given and taken the ultimate pleasure, and that, of course, was what the group was all about. "Alyssa," Scott said as he handed her a glass of champagne, "you were wonderful. I don't know when we've had a better initiation ritual."

"Thank you," Alyssa said.

"Would you consider being the Carnal Sacrifice again next year?"

Alyssa smiled. "It would be my ultimate pleasure."

Barbara thought about the most recent tapes for the next few days, imagining herself on stage like Marianne, performing for a bunch of strangers. Could she do that? It was an intriguing possibility. And, of course, she did want to see CJ again. And this was, after all, no-holds-barred sex. A week after she left the store, she called CJ.

"Well, hello, hot woman," CJ said. "I have been hoping all week that I'd hear from you."

"I just thought I'd call and thank you for the tape. I really liked that club scene."

"Do you think you could dance like that?"

"I don't know. It's an intriguing thought, but I think I'd chicken out at the last minute."

"You're an honest woman, Babs."

Barbara reacted automatically to hearing the name that Walt and Carl had called her all those years ago. The humiliation of the situation, the flash of Walt's camera. She could almost smell Carl's All Spice aftershave. But this was CJ's voice, a voice that had come to mean hot, erotic sex, and the sound of it made her wet. Should that experience have felt all that terrible or was it just that she didn't have a life then? She didn't have any idea what good sex was all about. But then neither did Carl or Walt. All these thoughts flashed through her mind in an instant. "I like to think so," she said into the phone.

"I have a group of friends who get together once a month, sort of like the Hathaway Group in the story. Women are invited to participate in the various activities. There's a party next weekend and I wondered whether you'd like to come."

Barbara hesitated. What CJ was describing sounded like an orgy. Was this what her sexuality was leading her to? Was this the culmination of her months of learning about herself? Voices filled her head. Do it, it will be fun. It's a sin. Enjoy. You'll be punished.

"If I can chicken out at any time, I think I'd like to."

"I promise you that any time you say so, I will take you home. Instantly. No questions asked, no recriminations."

"It sounds very interesting."

As arranged, Barbara arrived at CJ's shop at five the following Saturday afternoon, prepared for anything. CJ had promised her that nothing would happen without her permission, but, if she were willing, all kinds of new experiences awaited her. As she walked into A Private Place, his assistant was just leaving and CJ was finishing with his last customer. She stood, gazing at the bondage equipment while the customer debated whether to buy a green or a red dildo.

"Barbara, come over here and help us," CJ said loudly. When she approached the counter, he asked, "Which do you like better?"

Barbara looked at the two dildos on the counter, then at the display beneath the glass. "Actually, just to confuse you, I like that black one. It looks dangerous and erotic, and makes me think of black lace underwear and high heels."

The man who stood beside her looked at her, then said, "I'll take the one the lady likes. If my girlfriend glows like this lovely woman does at the thought of that black dildo, I'll be a lucky man."

Barbara grinned as CJ wrapped the dildo in red lace gift paper. With a thank-you, the man put the package into his pocket and left. As the customer closed the shop door behind him, CJ locked it. He walked to Barbara, placed his hand on the back of her neck and kissed her softly. "Welcome. This is going to be one wonderful night." He placed her hand against the crotch of his black jeans, cupping his hard cock. "I'm looking forward to it."

His voice turned her on like few things in the world. Without hesitation, Barbara placed CJ's hand against the crotch of her jeans. "Feel the heat? I'm looking forward to tonight, too."

CJ laughed. "You're quite a brazen bitch," he said. "Come into the back." He led her into a room she hadn't been in the last time, invited her to sit down and poured her a glass of white wine. Then he deftly opened a dozen oysters for each of them, and served them with lemon and a cocktail sauce spiced with lots of horseradish. "They say wonderful things about oysters, but I don't believe that nonsense. I just like them. We'll be eating quite a bit later, but I thought this would hold us for now."

Barbara picked up a shell and, with loud slurping noises, slid an oyster into her mouth. "I love them, too," Barbara said. She licked her lips with exaggerated movements of her slender tongue.

"The way you eat those makes me want to fuck you right here, right now. But there's a long evening ahead of us and anticipation makes it that much better."

They chatted amiably, ate and drank and, by the time they had finished, Barbara was no longer turned on. She merely felt warm and comfortable.

"As I told you, I would like to dress you up for the evening," CJ said finally. "But first, I have a question for you. Have you ever thought about shaving your pussy?"

Barbara thought for a moment. "I haven't, but I wouldn't mind, if you'd like me to."

"I'd like to shave you myself. It's very sexy for a man to look at a shaved pussy. It's so brazen somehow, so inviting and obvious. It would be perfect for this evening. If you don't ever want to do it again, you can let it grow. I will warn you, it might he a bit itchy as it grows out."

"I'll risk it. It sounds kinky."

CJ beamed. "Great. Take your jeans and panties off and sit here," he said, indicating a leather director's chair.

Slightly embarrassed at casually undressing before a man that, despite their previous activities, she hardly knew, Barbara removed her jeans, panties, shoes, and socks. She sat in the chair and CJ draped her legs over the arms so her pussy was exposed and vulnerable. Then CJ brought a pair of scissors, pan of warm water, soap, a razor, and a handful of towels.

While Barbara watched, he cut her pubic hair very short, then rubbed the short stubble and 'accidentally' brushed her now-exposed clit. From not turned-on to ravenous in only a moment, she thought. Barbara swallowed hard but tried to look as casual as CJ. Then he made lots of soapy lather and rubbed it over her pubis. Slowly and with infinite care, he shaved off all the hair, his probing fingers and the gentle rub of the razor making Barbara tremble with need.

He washed the area with a soft cloth, then smoothed on some antiseptic lotion. Then he rose and returned with a large mirror that stood on a wooden stand. "Look at your wonderful pussy," he said, adjusting the mirror so Barbara could see her hairless mound. CJ was right. It was obvious and erotic, like an opening begging to he filled. CJ stroked one finger along her naked slit. "It makes you hot looking at yourself, doesn't it?"

"Yes," she breathed, her voice barely audible.

"Then you need to he filled." CJ disappeared, then returned with a dildo like the one she had recommended to the customer. "Remember how Alyssa could watch the men as they fucked her? Now, watch in the mirror while I fuck you with this." He held the dildo against her opening, then slowly, while Barbara watched, fascinated, slid it into her body.

Barbara was shaking from the intensity of the twin sensations, watching herself being fucked with the dildo and the feel of the large member penetrating her. "May this be the first of many tonight," CJ said, kneeling between her legs and tonguing her clit until she came, her juices trickling over her now-exposed skin. "You are the most responsive woman," CJ said, rubbing her clit and thrusting the dildo in and out as tremors shook her. "And you are so beautiful when you come."

Unable to speak, Barbara just moaned.

A while later, CJ stood up and said, "If you're calmer now, we can get you dressed for the party." He looked at his watch. "It starts in an hour."

Barbara took a deep breath and took her legs from the arms of the chair. Smiling, she said, "What would you like me to wear?"

CJ reached for a box on a table and handed it to her. "The idea of presenting you to my friends wearing this makes me hot, but it will only work if it turns you on as well." Barbara opened the box. Inside was a black latex body suit with long legs, long sleeves, and openings where her breasts and pussy would be. "Picture yourself in that," CJ purred. "You would look amazing. Are you game?"

Barbara gazed at the garment. Her large breasts and now-hairless crotch would be exposed, but the rest of her body would be tightly encased in the stretchy fabric. It sounded delicious. She nodded and CJ smiled. "You delight me," he crooned, handing her the suit. "I need to change, too."

While CJ was in another room changing for the party, Barbara slowly wiggled the tight suit on over her skin. Zippers tightened the sleeves and legs until, when it was in place, it fit like her skin, with only her breasts and pussy exposed. She looked at herself in the mirror and was amazed at the wanton woman who looked back at her. "Oh, Lord," she said to her reflection. "Barbara, what have you done to yourself?"

"Made yourself into the most desirable woman I've ever seen," CJ said from behind her. She turned and saw that he was dressed in a similar black latex outfit, only his had short sleeves, thigh-length pants, and a full crotch. His swollen shaft beneath was hard to miss. "The feet of the latex hugging my cock keeps me erect all night." When he placed her hand between his legs, she felt something around the base of his cock. To her puzzled expression, he said, "I wear a cock ring to keep me from coming before I'm ready."

"Oh," Barbara said.

"Now, sit back here," CJ said, motioning her to the leather chair. "I want to do your finger and toenails."

With great care, CJ polished her now-long fingernails and her toenails with polish that was almost black. Then he asked her to close her eyes while he applied additional makeup and arranged her hair over her shoulders. She could feel him stroke the silver streak.

When he was done, he angled the mirror so she could look at herself. She opened her eyes and stared. He had used deep green shadow, heavy mascara, and deep, almost-black lipstick. She looked like an animal on the prowl. Where's the woman who Maggie met that first night? she wondered. Gone for now, she answered herself.

"Do you approve?"

"Very much," she said.

He handed her a pair of calf-high, black patent-leather boots, with spike heels. "I think these should be about your size, he said, and she slipped them on and stood up.

"Oh, yes," he said, slowly lowering himself until he was crouched at her feet. "Mistress."

Mistress. He was inviting her into his fantasy, she realized. He wanted her to control him. Did she know how? Her confusion must have shown on her face. "You'll learn how, if you're willing," he said. "There will be many there willing and able to teach you. And I will serve you." He got a cloak from the closet and draped it around Barbara's shoulders, carefully arranging her hair over the collar. "If you will allow me to lead," he said.

"Yes," Barbara said, standing up straight, now taller than he was in her high heels. "Do that."

In silence, they took a taxi across town to an old loft building in Soho. Although the taxi driver gave them a few odd looks, the trip was uneventful. CJ paid the driver and opened the door for her. They entered an old elevator and ascended two floors. When the doors opened, Barbara looked around, her eyes widening.

The room took up more than half of the loft and was furnished with tables and chairs, single and double lounges, and soft sofas. There were benches with straps and rings attached, stocks, and items that Barbara could only imagine uses for.

There were about two dozen couples, a few dancing, several sitting around tables, others in various stages of copulation. Music played in the background, similar to the music on CJ's tapes, with deep, pulsing rhythms that echoed in Barbara's soul.

As CJ removed Barbara's cloak, two men got up and walked over to them. "Who is this goddess?" one asked.

"My mistress," CJ said.

"And she allows you to speak on your own?"

"Occasionally," CJ said. "When I have pleased her sufficiently. Her name is Barbara."

"Good evening," she said, slowly getting acclimated to her surroundings and trying to figure out exactly how to behave.

"Good evening, Mistress Barbara," the two men said.

"CJ. It's good to see you," a woman called, motioning them over. The men led CJ and Barbara to a small table. "My name's Pam," the woman said as Barbara sat down. "And this is Tisha," she said, indicating the other woman at the table. "You're new to our little group."

"Yes, I am," Barbara said.

"My mistress is new to everything about this," CJ said. "But she wants to learn."

"Wonderful," Tisha said. A tiny blonde, she wore a genuine-looking policeman's uniform, with a pair of handcuffs dangling from a clip on her wide leather belt. "Let me show you what wonderful things my pet can do." She snapped her fingers and spread her legs. Barbara saw then that, like her outfit, the crotch of Pam's navy-blue pants was missing. "I like my men to be able to service me whenever I like." One of the men who had greeted her now knelt between Tisha's legs and began to lick her pussy. Tisha picked up her glass and sipped, trying unsuccessfully to look unaffected. "He's gotten too good at this," she said, panting. "Shit," she yelled, and Barbara watched as waves of orgasm overtook her.

Pam laughed. "He seems to be able to bring her off with almost no effort. I don't know whether she's that hot all the time, or he's that good." It was all Barbara could do not to stare at the woman speaking. She wore a kelly-green lace teddy that barely covered any of her athletic, ebony body, with thigh-high, green lace stockings and green satin heels. She also wore dark-green, elbow-length fingerless gloves. Even sitting down, Barbara could tell that she had to be over six feet tall. And gorgeous.

"She certainly seems to enjoy it," Barbara said.

"And why not," Pam said. "It's the best. I understand you're new to this type of fun and games."

"Yes," Barbara said, not sure what she was supposed to do.

"Watch what goes on around you and do what you think will give you and CJ pleasure."

"God, that was good," Tisha said, rejoining the conversation. "Get me something to eat," she said to the man who was now sitting on the floor at her feet.

"Yes, Mistress," he said, rising and moving to the buffet table. Pam looked at the man beside her and he quickly got up and followed.

Barbara looked at CJ. "I'm hungry, too," she said in what she hoped was a sufficiently authoritative tone. "Get me something."

CJ tried not to smile. "Oh, yes, Mistress," he said, and left the table.

"CJ's never brought a mistress here before," Pam said. "Usually he's the dominant one."

"How can someone be dominant one time and like that another?" Barbara asked.

"Many people enjoy both sides of dominant/submissive behavior. Others only enjoy being in charge, or surrendering." She smiled, encouraging Barbara to trust her. "What do you usually enjoy?"

"I don't really know. I've been tied up and I loved that. I've also listened to a lot of CJ's tapes and all the stories really turn me on. But I've never actually been in anything like this before, on either side."

"How wonderful to explore," Pam said. "To try it all out for the first time. I envy you. First times are so hot."

"I like to run the show, Tisha said. "I can't get into letting someone else tell me what to do."

"And I love it when someone tells me what to do," Pam said. "It's so liberating. I don't have to think about anything. Just do as I'm told."

Tisha gazed at Pam, her eyes wandering over the other woman's lush body. "Maybe I'll take you up on that offer before the evening is done," she said. She looked at Barbara, and the heat in her gaze made Barbara look down. "You, too, love."

The three men returned with plates of food and, as Barbara watched, Tisha held out a bit of meat and the man at her feet ate it from her hand. "Oh, this is Pet. That's what I call him since that's what he is."

"Hello," Barbara said.

Pet inclined his head, but said nothing.

"And this is Mack, Pam said, patting the man at her side on the head. "He's such a good boy."

"Thank you, ma'am," the man whispered, obviously pleased at the compliment.

Barbara took a shrimp and offered it to CJ. He stared at her, the heat in his gaze almost stinging her naked nipples. Then he took the shrimp from her fingers with his teeth.

Together, the three couples ate and talked. Actually, the women talked, the men remained silent, eating only when a morsel of food was handed to them.

Despite the thoroughly bizarre situation, Barbara was surprised at how much she liked the two women. They were honest, sexually open, and easy to talk and listen to.

When they finished, a man in a tuxedo walked to the center of the dance floor and announced the entertainment for the evening. Several men danced Chippendale-style, and a woman did amazing things with two thick candles. There was a Don't Come contest during which three men were teased until finally one erupted onto the floor. After he cleaned up the mess, he was escorted into another room by his mistress for what Barbara was told would be suitable punishment for his lack of self-control.

Then a naked man was led to the stage and his arms and neck were locked in a set of wooden stocks. Women from the audience used hands, paddles, and a hairbrush to spank his ass until it was bright red.

When the lights rose again, several couples moved toward a door at the far end of the room. "They are going to have ceremonial whippings and other heavy pain games. Some people like that sort of thing, but since many do not, whippings and things like that are held in another, soundproof room. Not my thing," Pam said.

Barbara didn't think she would enjoy watching or participating in pain for pleasure games. "Me neither," she said, glad she wouldn't lose her new-found companions.

"Barbara," Tisha said, "I can see that CJ is enjoying being the bottom, the submissive, but you don't seem comfortable with the role of top."

Barbara sighed. "I guess I'm not. I'm just not used to giving orders." She turned to CJ. "I'm really sorry. I know that having me control you would turn you on, but, well . . ."

"Don't apologize," CJ said. "Something that doesn't turn you on, no matter how much the thought of it might excite me, won't make me happy."

"Would you like to be the one controlled?" Tisha asked.

Barbara felt heat rise and thought she might actually be blushing. "I don't know."

"Yes, you do," Tisha said. Then she quickly changed the subject. While they sipped club sodas, the women made small talk. Barbara felt the heat of Tisha's stare frequently over the next half hour. At one point Tisha spent several minutes staring at her nipples. Barbara felt her nipples tighten and her pussy get wet from the heat of Tisha's gaze. "Excuse me, she said, disappearing to the ladies' room.

When she returned, she saw CJ whispering in Tisha's ear. "Barbara, CJ tells me that he would love to watch you make love to Pam. Under my orders, of course. I think you want that." Tisha stared at Barbara. "Sit down!" she snapped. Barbara sank into a chair.

"Spread your legs!" Seemingly without any control from her brain, her knees parted. "Wider." She spread her knees farther.

"Good," Tisha said, smiling. "And, if I'm so inclined, I might even let the men join you later. If they are very good, that is."

Oh God, what had she gotten herself into? Barbara wondered. But she flashed back to the scene in on of CJ's tapes. The dancer who had been able to make two women so hot that they made love in public. She shivered.

Tisha leaned toward Barbara. "The safe word is Cease. Do you understand?"

Barbara remembered the ball she had held when she and CJ had played the last time. She nodded.

Tisha took a police whistle from around her neck and blew into it. "I think we need an audience." Several other couples brought chairs and surrounded the table. "Now, Pam, kiss her."

Obediently Pam turned and cupped Barbara's face in her hands. Softly she brushed her lips across Barbara's, her tongue teasing and probing. Barbara sighed, closed her eyes and relaxed. This was very strange, but arousing. She allowed herself to be pulled into the situation. She touched Pam's cheeks with her fingertips, just brushing the soft skin. She moved her mouth and pressed it more firmly against the other woman's. The smell of Pam's musky perfume filled her nostrils.

Pam leaned forward and rubbed her lace-covered breasts against Barbara's naked nipples. Tit against tit, the two women slowly stood up, their bodies intertwined.

"Massage each other's tits," Tisha said. "Tweak those titties."

As Barbara's hands rose to touch Pam's breasts, she felt Pam's large hands on her bare flesh. "Barbara, pull out Pam's tits." Barbara pulled the cups of Pam's teddy aside and filled her hands with warm flesh. She had never felt anything like this before. Soft hands on soft breasts. Hers. Pam's. White fingers on black skin. Black fingers on white skin. Her knees almost buckled from the heat of it all.

She heard movement around her and opened her eyes to find a lounge chair now beside her. "Barbara, sit there," Tisha said, and Barbara gladly collapsed into the chair. With a few snaps of her fingers, Tisha moved Pet to one side of Barbara and Mack to the other. "Suck," she said, and suddenly two mouths suckled at Barbara's breasts.

"Do her, Pam, Tisha said, and Pam laid her chest on the bottom of the lounge chair, her mouth on Barbara's clit. "Look, Barbara. See what's happening." When Barbara's eyes remained closed, Tisha said, "I said, open your eyes!"

Barbara opened her eyes.

"That's better. But don't come," Tisha said. "Don't you dare!"

Barbara looked down. She was still tightly encased in the latex suit, the black rubber shining under the lights. Sweat pooled beneath her arms and on her belly, but the feeling was sensual, not uncomfortable. Two men suckled at her breasts, their fingers kneading her flesh. She could see Pam's face, turned up to her, her tongue dancing over Barbara's naked pussy.

Tisha didn't want her to come. But how could she keep the orgasm from building in her belly? She gritted her teeth and tried to fight the myriad of sensations trying to control her body.

"Stop!" Tisha's order could not be disobeyed.

Barbara took a deep breath as the mouths left her. Tisha looked at her. "Get up." When she did, Tisha ordered, "Pam, you sit there." Once Pam was stretched out in the lounge chair, her thighs spread wide, one leg on either side of the chair, Tisha leaned over and removed the crotch of Pam's teddy. "So wet," she said, then snapped her fingers, and the men resumed their places, now sucking Pam's nipples.

"Now, Barbara, lick her the way she licked you. Do it while we all watch."

Could she lick a woman's pussy? Ordinarily, Barbara thought in a small, conscious place in her mind, no. But she was so hot that anything was possible. She knelt at the foot of the lounge chair, lay on the bottom section and pressed her aching breasts against the rough fabric. She rubbed like a cat, trying the relieve the itching hunger in her swollen nipples. As her face neared Pam's steamy pussy, the odor of the woman's excitement surrounded her. She looked at Pam's shaved mound and saw the swollen outer lips, parted to reveal the hard clit between. She pointed her tongue and licked, marveling at the shudder that ran through Pam's body. She tasted Pam's juices. So this is what I taste like, she thought, filling her mouth with the salty tang.

Feeling increasingly brave, she explored every fold, each hollow. Using the things she understood about her own body, she quested the spots that would give Pam the most pleasure. "Fingerfuck her, Barbara. Make her come." She inserted one finger into Pam's sopping pussy, smiling at the moans and animal cries that Pam couldn't control. A second finger joined the first and, knowing what she herself enjoyed, Barbara spread the two fingers, stretching Pam's channel.

Suddenly something was behind her and there was a hand in the small of her back pressing her against the chair. She felt something slippery being spread on her ass and cunt.

"Is she hot?" Tisha asked.

Someone at her back rubbed her opening. "Soaked. Hot enough to fire."

"Do it."

As Barbara fingered Pam's pussy, she felt something rammed into her ass. A dildo? A cock? She couldn't tell. Then there was a mouth on her cunt. Whose mouth, whose cock? She had no idea. Nor did she care.

"Don't you dare come until Pam does." Tisha said, swatting

her ass hard, once. "And Pam, don't you come until Barbara does."

Barbara needed to come. She was trying to concentrate on making Pam climax and not on her own needs screaming inside her. Not yet, she told herself as her mouth worked on Pam's clit and her fingers fucked her cunt. Just a little more. She used the index finger of her other hand to rim Pam's asshole. As she slowly circled, she could feel the tiny spasms that heralded the woman's climax. But she felt her own orgasm building as well.

"Ah!" Pam screamed as she came, and Barbara's orgasm erupted seconds later. Wave upon wave of electric pleasure washed over her. She put her head on Pam's belly and allowed her fingers to softly caress Pam's calming body. Now her cunt and ass were empty, but she felt someone press against her from behind.

She turned and watched CJ rub his latex-covered cock between her spread ass cheeks, his head thrown back, his hips bucking. Tisha reached down the front of his tight bicycle pants and quickly removed the cock ring CJ had put on earlier. It took only a moment until, rubbing against Barbara's ass, he screamed loudly and he came, his cock still inside the latex shorts.

Barbara rested, then, through a haze, she felt herself guided to her feet and her cloak replaced around her shoulders. She vaguely realized that she was being told how much everyone enjoyed her presence and she numbly said good night to the people she had met.

CJ directed the taxi to her car, and then, while Barbara dozed, he drove her home to Bronxville, Tisha and Pet following in their car. He kissed her firmly at her door. "They are waiting for me. I'll call you."

"Mmmm," Barbara said, opening her door. "It was amazing. I've never experienced anything like this."

"I'm glad. It was great for me, too. I never know where these parties will lead, but it's always wonderful. Tonight was particularly terrific because I know how much you enjoyed it, too."

"You weren't disappointed because I couldn't . . . you know."

"Whatever you enjoy is great, and the things you find you don't, we won't do. It's really quite simple."

"Thank you," Barbara said, kissing him again.

"Good night." CJ climbed into the waiting car and Barbara closed the door behind her and went to bed.

Chapter 10

"I think I reached the ultimate of something last evening," Barbara said the following morning as she and Maggie sat over coffee. "It's the best time I've had in maybe forever, but after I got home I thought a lot about it, and about me."

"Thinking's always dangerous," Maggie said dryly, "but tell me about it."

"I think that I understand myself a lot better than I did a few months ago. Last evening was wonderful, but that was outside of the real world. It's not life."

"And what is life."

"For me, life is having mad, wild sex with one person, someone I know and like. Someone who pleases me inside and outside of the bedroom. CJ is a wonderfully creative lover, but that's all. He's sort of out of context." Barbara slumped. "This is really hard to explain."

"I think I understand."

"But your life with Chuck wasn't life either. What I need is equal parts friend and lover. What's depressing me is that I'm not sure something like that really exists."

"I'm not sure either," Maggie said, lacing her fingers. "But all you can do is try."

"Which do you think comes first, the friendship or the sex?"

"I think for there to be really good sex, there has to be a level of trust and friendship, a desire to please the other person. It can develop over a period of months or just in a day. Take you and Jay. From what you told me, you started the relationship for sport fucking, but it was a lot more than that from the start."

Barbara looked puzzled. "But I wasn't in love with him nor he with me. And we weren't and aren't exclusive by any means."

"All that is true, but there was a lot of genuine caring and concern, each for the other. No one was taking anything at the expense of the other. Right?"

Barbara cocked her head to one side. "Right."

"That's not love, but it's the kind of caring necessary for really good sex."

"I never thought about it that way."

"Actually, neither did I until now," Maggie admitted. "But as I think back to my good and bad bed partners, it's true."

"I guess Jay and I did have a lot of mutual respect and caring. Just not enough to build a life on. So then, what is love?"

"You think I know? I haven't a clue. To be completely honest, I think I have been in love a few times. Not just in lust, but really in love. Caring about someone else's happiness more than my own. Maybe it was that way when Chuck and I were first married." Then she thought about Paul and their last phone conversation the night of her heart attack. "And there was a guy who wanted to run away with me. He was a banker type and twenty years my junior. It never would have worked, but I did love him, in my own way."

"I've never felt that, and I want it. I guess I'll just have to keep looking."

"What about Steve."

Barbara smiled. "Maybe it's time I found out what Steve is really like. I've been in love with him from a distance, whatever that means, for a long time. But, what I understand now is that from a distance is easy. It's the up-close-and-personal stuff that's hard."

"And it's more difficult with someone who you're going to see every day, whether it works out or not."

"I know. I keep wondering whether it's worth it. It doesn't seem so important or intense now."

"Do you want to find out?" Maggie asked.

"I think I do."

Later that morning, Maggie left the kitchen and, as she had dozens of times before, found herself in the revolving door. Instead of pushing to see when she would emerge, she stopped in the dark and said aloud, "Lucy, Angela, I think we need to talk."

"Push the door," a voice said and, when she did, she found herself in the computer room. "Yes?" Angela said.

"I was wondering what there is left for me to do. Barbara has discovered herself and I think she's a happier, more complete woman. She's going to ask Steve to dinner and maybe they will end up together, just like you wanted. So what more is there?"

Lucy looked at her. "Do you think Steve is right for her?"

"How should I know?" Maggie snapped. "I'm trying to do what you asked me to do when you gave me this assignment."

"I still think Steve is perfect for Barbara," Angela said.

"Not a chance," Lucy said. "And Maggie, there are still one or two things left that Barbara will need your help with."

"If you say so," Maggie said, turning toward the door. "I just want to do the best job I can, you know."

"Of course. Just a few last loose ends. We'll send for you when we know the outcome."

"Hers or mine?" Maggie said.

"Both," the two women said in unison.

Barbara arrived at Gordon-Watson at her usual time the following Monday morning. She had taken particular care with her wardrobe, selecting a sheer white blouse and short tan linen skirt. She topped the blouse with a brown linen vest so that the sheerness of the blouse and the lacy bra she wore beneath were only evident when she unbuttoned or removed the vest. She wore sheer stockings and brown suede pumps. She took care that her makeup was sexy yet understated, then applied a new, musky perfume behind her ears and in her cleavage.

She settled at her desk and by nine-thirty was deep into a will she was assembling from a set of stock paragraphs. "Good morning, Barbara," Steve said as he approached her desk.

She looked up and held his gaze just a bit longer than usual. "Good morning, Mr. Gordon."

"What's on my calendar for today?" he said, breezing past her desk.

Barbara picked up her laptop, then followed him into his office. She settled into a soft leather chair, crossed her legs and slipped one shoe off then lifted it with her toe. Then she clicked a few keys on her computer. "You've got the Harris deposition at ten-thirty, lunch with Jack Forrester at twelve-thirty, and, if the deposition doesn't go too late, you can go over Mr. Carruthers's will and the McManister closing documents for tomorrow. And, whenever you have time, I have a list of phone calls you need to make." As she looked up, she saw Steve gazing at her swinging foot. She smothered a smile as she shifted in her chair, moving so her skirt rode up to midthigh. "Do you have anything for me?" she asked with mock innocence. When he didn't answer immediately, his eyes following her foot and the dangling shoe, she said, "Mr. Gordon?"

"Yes?"

"Did you hear me?" Barbara asked.

Obviously snapping back to reality, Steve said, "Of course." He picked up a pencil from his desk and tapped it on the arm of his chair. "Barbara, I've been meaning to talk to you. You've seemed different recently."

"Different?" She slowly unbuttoned her vest and allowed the sides to part.

"More . . ." He looked her over from head to toe, his gaze lingering on her breasts. "More, I don't know. Just more."

She lowered her head so she looked up at him through her lashes. "I hope I can take that as a compliment."

"You can." He looked her over again. "Listen, maybe we can have dinner sometime."

"Are you asking me out on a date?"

Steve hesitated, then said, "I guess I am."

"Well, I'd love to have dinner with you, Mr. Gordon." Barbara giggled. "I guess I should call you Steve now."

"I guess you should." He stood up and walked around and positioned himself behind Barbara's chair. She could feel him touch her hair. "You know," he said, "you're quite something. I'm surprised at myself for not really noticing before now."

Delighted that they were finally going to get to spend some time together, Barbara said, "Shall we say Saturday?"

She could feel Steve playing with the silver streak in her hair. "Saturday sounds great. How about Indian?"

Afraid she would spoil the mood but unwilling to eat very hot food, Barbara said, "I'm not a big fan of curry. How about sushi?"

"Raw fish?" He made a face. "I know a great steak place."

Barbara grinned. "That sounds wonderful." She was glad they had found common ground.

"And Saturday I have tickets for the City Center Ballet. I was going to ask my mother to join me, but I'd much rather have you by my side."

Barbara remembered several trips to the ballet with her mother years before. She had found it stultifying. "The ballet might be nice, and if you already have the tickets . . ." She wondered whether the gorgeous Lisa enjoyed the ballet.

"I try to get there every week or so during the season, but I can tell from your voice it isn't your idea of an enjoyable evening. I'll just give the tickets to my mother and we can go wherever you like." He sat down on the chair beside her and placed a hand on her knee. "Where would you like to go?" He gazed deeply into her eyes. "I mean, if you could go anywhere."

Barbara thought. She had read the entertainment section of *The New York Times* just yesterday. "There's a Woody Allen film festival."

"Oh," Steve said, taking a deep breath. "That would be fine."

Barbara could tell he viewed Woody Allen the way she viewed the ballet. "Maybe just a small, intimate place where we could talk," she said quickly. "We could take some time and get to know each other. And maybe do some slow dancing."

Steve's face brightened. "That sounds wonderful. But I have to warn you, I don't dance."

Barbara stared at Steve. She had been in love with him for so long. But in love with what? He was handsome, well dressed, and very intelligent. But what did they really have in common? "What do you enjoy doing? Tennis? Golf?"

"Actually, I love swimming and I lift weights. And, of course, I really like sports. But you already know that."

She had gotten enough last-minute tickets for sporting events over the years for him that she should. But she had never made the connection. "That's right. Of course. You particularly like boxing."

"I love a good heavyweight match," Steve said, taking her hand. "I guess you probably don't like that sort of thing, but you could learn. It's an acquired taste, like anchovies."

"I hate anchovies, and I think the idea of watching two men beat each other's brains out for money is barbaric." She pulled her hand back.

"We don't have to like the same things, do we?" He cupped her chin and pulled her face toward him. He kissed her softly on the lips. "I'm sure there are some things we will enjoy doing together very much."

She closed her eyes and leaned into the kiss. His lips were warm and moist and his tongue slipped between her teeth to caress her. Suddenly she felt his hand on her breast, squeezing and kneading her tender flesh like bread dough. His other hand began to unbutton her blouse. "No," she said, leaning back. "I don't think this will work."

"But, baby . . ." Steve said, reaching behind her neck to cradle her head. He kissed her harder, forcing her head back.

She placed her palms against his chest and pushed him back. "Steve, Mr. Gordon, I don't think this will work at all. I'm really sorry. It was a mistake." She stood up, put the laptop onto Steve's desk and rebuttoned both her blouse and vest. "This was really a big mistake."

"Oh, baby, don't say that. I'm sorry. This shouldn't have started in the office. Not here where there's no privacy. I understand. Let's talk about it Saturday."

"No, Mr. Gordon, let's not. Let's not see each other Saturday. This isn't going to work. I'm really sorry."

"But . . ."

"Look. We've worked well together for all these years. This is just going to spoil it. Let's just keep this as a business relationship. I like working here and I do the work well. Let's just leave it at that."

Steve stood up and heaved a deep sigh. "I think you're underestimating how good we could be."

She floundered for the right words to tell him to go away without losing her job. "Maybe I am, Mr. Gordon, but I'd rather keep a good relationship here in the office than spoil it with a extracurricular fling, no matter how good it might be." Or how awful.

"I'm disappointed."

"So am I, but I think it's for the best." She retrieved her laptop. "Did you have anything more for me or should I begin placing those phone calls? We can probably get a few things done before the deposition."

Steve looked Barbara over from head to toe. "Well, maybe you're right." Slowly Barbara left the office and walked toward her desk. Then she turned, looked at the sign beside the door. Steven Gordon. She shrugged, then grinned.

"Babs," a voice cried from the end of the soup-and-canned-vegetable aisle in the supermarket a few weeks later. Barbara had stopped in after work to pick up something for dinner. "Babs," the voice said again. "Imagine running into you here."

She looked around for the source of the slightly louder than necessary voice. Striding toward her was a person she hadn't been able to forget. "Hello, Walt," she said softly.

"Babs, you look terrific," Walt said, leaning forward and grasping Barbara by the shoulders. He looked her over from left and right, then from head to toe. "I haven't seen you in a long time. You've changed." He reached over and fingered the streak of white hair above her ear. "And this is very sexy."

Barbara gritted her teeth and tried not to glower at the man whose face she had last seen in the glare of a camera's flash bulb. I certainly have changed, she said, trying not to let all the humiliation rush back. "I haven't seen *you* in a long time."

"What have you been doing with yourself?" he asked, his smarmy smile trying to give the impression that they were old friends.

In as few words as possible, Barbara told him that she was still working at the same place and that her mother had died more than a year ago. "Nothing much else has changed." At least nothing she wanted to discuss with him.

He flashed his most charming smile. "Well, I think you look wonderful. Why don't we have dinner some evening and catch up on old times?"

"I'm really quite busy these days," Barbara said, her fingernails digging into her palms.

"If you're still at the same place, I must still have your number. I'll give you a call. I'm sure we can work something out. I really want to see you."

I don't want to see you, she thought. "I don't think it will work out," she said, turning her back and pushing her shopping cart toward the front of the store.

"Good, I'll call you."

"You know, Maggie, almost every sentence began with 'I.' He's such a prick."

"I wouldn't insult wonderful erect pricks like that," Maggie said with a twinkle in her eyes.

Barbara burst out laughing. "Thanks for that," she said. When she could talk again, she said, "I needed you to put everything back into perspective. God, he's such a jerk."

"He certainly sounds like one. But he did notice how wonderful you look." She winked. "He's obviously a very perceptive guy."

Barbara giggled as she considered how far she'd come. "I don't think I look that different," she said, "but I feel so differently about myself."

"That's so much a part of how you look. Confidence, a positive image of yourself, and, don't overlook the sensuality that's so much a part of you now."

"I guess Walt saw that," Barbara said. "He looked me over like I was the blue plate special. It made me want to punch his lights out, then take a shower."

"But does it still hurt? Think before you answer."

Barbara considered, then said, Yes, I guess it does. But I'm so different now. It shouldn't hurt anymore, but when I saw him in the market, my stomach clenched and it was as though that evening happened only a day ago."

"Maybe you need to exorcize the evil spirits."

"I'd love to. But how?" Barbara asked, flexing her fingers to try to work out the sudden stiffness.

"Revenge is good for the soul occasionally," Maggie said. "Women have weapons, you know."

"I couldn't," Barbara said, her brain suddenly scrambling, searching, planning. Maggie raised an eyebrow and Barbara smiled. "Could I?"

"This has to be your decision," Maggie said.

Barbara knew that this was, indeed, her decision. Could she do it? Even the few moments she had spent with Walt had done a job on the self-confidence she had built up over the last months. She thought about the men she saw now on a regular basis, Jay, CJ, and the others. What did they see when they looked at her?

The two women were silent for a long time, then Barbara sighed and silently nodded. She was not the same person Carl and Walt had humiliated that night years ago. She was happy, and, although she had yet to find someone who gave her everything she wanted in life, she knew that finding him was possible. And in the meantime she was having fun.

She nodded more strongly, then grinned. "I want to smash the slimy son of a bitch into pulp," Barbara said. "Starting with his overactive cock." She was quiet again, then said, "And I think I have the germ of an idea. Will you help me?"

"Do you need to ask?" Maggie said, her grin widening. The two women talked for hours until they had every aspect covered. All that remained was for Barbara to pick up a few items on her next visit to CJ's store.

The following evening Walt called, as Barbara had known he would. "Babs, I have been thinking a lot about you since we ran into each other the other day."

"And I've been think about you too, Walt," Barbara said, her voice soft and mellow.

"I was wondering about dinner on Saturday. I happen to be free and I thought we could talk about old times."

Old times indeed. The bastard acted as though they had had a wonderful, but unfortunately interrupted, dating relationship. She was spending the evening with CJ on Friday, so Saturday would work fine. "That should be all right for me, " she said.

Walt sounded a bit taken aback as he said, "Sure. Great. I wasn't sure you'd be available."

"Well, you're in luck, Walt. How about the Peachtree Lounge?" she said, selecting the most expensive restaurant she could think of. She could almost picture Walt considering whether she might be worth a hundred-and-fifty-dollar dinner.

"Uh . . . okay. That's sounds fine."

He was hooked. "Can you pick me up about seven?" Barbara suggested. "You remember where I live, I'm sure. And will you make the reservation?"

"Of course. The man should make the reservations anyway. And let's make it seven-thirty on Saturday. I'll be looking forward to it."

Barbara bit the inside of her mouth to keep from laughing.

Seven-thirty. She suspected that Walt had to make a point of making the decisions. "That's fine. I'll see you then."

On Saturday afternoon, Barbara settled into the tub and pulled out one of her favorite tapes. She played it and masturbated to several satisfying orgasms. As she dried herself off, her sensual awareness was at its height. She selected a new, basic black dress with deceptively sexual lines and spread it out on the bed. Surprised that Maggie wasn't here to help her, she picked out a black satin-and-lace teddy, thigh-high black stockings, and high-heeled black shoes. Heavy silver earrings and several bangle bracelets completed her outfit. She brushed her hair, then arranged it so, although it was high on her head, it was held with only three combs that could easily be removed. She used a curling iron so that the silver streak curved against her jaw and caressed her neck as she moved.

As she looked at herself in the full-length mirror, she knew she had created exactly the image she wanted. And without any help from Maggie. "Nice work," she told herself.

Walt rang the bell right on time. She opened a second-floor front window and called down, "The door's open. Make yourself comfortable and pour a drink if you like. I'll be down in a few moments." Although she was completely ready, she sat in her bedroom for almost half an hour. As she finally walked downstairs, Walt was pacing the living room. As he turned and saw her, his expression turned from annoyance to appreciation. "My God," he whispered. "Babs, you look . . ."

"Thanks," she said as she handed Walt her light jacket so he could drape it around her shoulders. She leaned back into him just slightly so he could inhale the exotic scent she had carefully applied behind her ears.

"I never imagined you could look like that," Walt said. "It's amazing."

"I thought a lot about you after we met last week and I realized that you never got to know the real me." She walked out the front door and locked it behind her. Walt walked around and got into the driver's seat of his Ford while Barbara opened her door and got into the passenger seat. As she fastened her seat belt, she allowed her skirt to slide up her thigh. She patted Walt's leg. "I think we're going to have an interesting evening."

They drove the short distance to the restaurant in silence. At the entrance, a valet opened her door and assisted her out, with an appreciative look. They entered the large room with a soft blue, nineteenth-century southern decor and were seated side by side on a blue-and-white patterned banquette. As they settled, Barbara reached over and grasped Walt's thigh, just above his knee. "I'm glad this evening is finally here."

Walt blinked his eyes several times and leered at her as the waiter arrived to take drink orders. "We would like a bottle of wine," he said without consulting Barbara. "White."

"I'd like to see the wine list," Barbara said.

"Of course, madam," the waiter said. "I'll send the sommelier over."

"I didn't know you knew anything about wine," Walt said.

Barbara thought about the financial analyst who had taught her to appreciate fine wine. And a few other things as well. "There's a lot about me you don't know," she purred, wondering whether Walt would be sickened by the incredibly predictable dialogue.

He leaned forward, hanging on her every word. Beneath the tablecloth, he reached over and placed his hand on her stockinged knee. Rubbing her index finger up and down his inner thigh, she glared at him until he removed his hand. It had become clear that she could do what she wanted, but he had to keep his hands to himself. Slowly, she allowed herself a slow smile. "Later."

When Walt placed both his hands on the table, Barbara saw they were shaking.

"The wine list," the sommelier said, handing her a leather-covered tome.

"Goodness, this is quite a list," she said. She leaned forward so

Walt could get a good view of her cleavage. "Walt, are you having beef, fish, chicken, what?"

She could see his gaze reluctantly rise from the shadowed valley between her breasts. "I thought I'd have a steak," he stammered.

"Good." Still caressing his thigh with one hand and holding the wine list with the other, she discussed the wine selection with the sommelier for almost five minutes.

"You have wonderful taste, madam," the sommelier said as she finally selected a 1984 California Cabernet from an obscure vineyard. "I'll get that right away."

As he disappeared, Barbara returned her attention to Walt. She licked her lips and watched his eyes follow the path of her tongue. "I hope you don't mind, but I found a wonderful wine at a ridiculous price. I'm sure it was a mistake on the list. Only thirty-five dollars. It should have been at least fifty."

Walt was in a daze and seemed not to hear anything Barbara said. Barbara talked and Walt listened through the pouring of the wine. Since Walt seemed incapable of concentrating, Barbara ordered the meal: a creamy carrot soup, sirloin steaks medium-rare with baked potatoes and sour cream, broccoli, and green salads with the house vinaigrette dressing.

During the meal, Walt spoke very little, totally distracted by the frequent presence of Barbara's hand on his leg. Her hands, her looks, her very posture were designed to keep him off-balance. Sensual, inviting, yet taking charge at every opportunity, she was creating exactly the atmosphere she wanted.

As the plates were cleared and the last of the wine poured, Walt said, "How about we go back to my place after? We could continue this wonderful evening there. I even put clean sheets on the bed."

Barbara bit her lip to keep from laughing. He still thinks he's choreographing this evening. "I have a better idea," she said. "I have some wonderful things to play with at my house."

"Oh" was all Walt could say.

"But let's have coffee first." Barbara let the tension build for another half an hour before she signaled for the check. Moments later, Walt signed the credit card slip.

They waited only a moment outside the restaurant as the valet got Walt's car. As the valet started to hand Barbara into the passenger side, she walked around to the driver's seat. "I think I'll drive. Okay, Walt?"

"Sure," Walt said hesitantly.

Barbara got behind the wheel and saw that Walt hadn't fastened his seat belt. "Here, let me help you." She leaned across Walt's body and, as Walt gazed down the front of her dress, she grasped the seat belt and pulled it across his chest and snapped it into place. "There," she said, patting his chest.

"But I'm caught," he said, realizing that his arms were trapped.

"I know," Barbara said, and tapped him on the chest again, "and I like it that way." She pressed her lips against his, licking the surprised '0' his lips formed. He stopped trying to free his arms from beneath the belt, the tent in his slacks growing each minute.

Again in silence, they drove to Barbara's house and she let them in the front door. She remembered the first evening she had had a man in her house, her first evening with Jay. So much had changed. "Come upstairs with me," she said, "and let's have some fun."

Eagerly Walt followed her up the stairs and into her room. "Now," Barbara said, "I really like to play. And I think you do, too."

"Oh, I do," Walt said, unbuckling his belt.

"Not so fast," Barbara said, slapping his hands hard. "In here we do things my way." She watched Walt consider the situation. Would he go along? To increase his incentive, she licked her lips slowly, then reached out and squeezed the hard ridge in his pants. "It will be wonderful. I promise."

Wait dropped his hands to his sides. "I'm sure it will."

She was in control. When she had first thought up this idea, she had wondered whether she could pull it off. She had been very reluctant to assume control at CJ's party, but now it seemed comfortable. Different situations, different views, I guess. "Good boy," she said. "Now that we understand each other, strip."

"What?"

"You heard me. Strip."

"But . . ." He stared at her, obviously unsure.

Barbara met his eyes and tapped her toe on the carpet until Walt's gaze dropped to her shoes.

Awkwardly, without a word, Walt quickly pulled off all his clothes until he stood in the middle of Barbara's bedroom naked. He's actually not badly built, she thought, but she also noticed that his erection had softened. She wanted to keep him continually hard so he would do anything she wanted. She pulled the combs from her hair and shook out the dark mass, allowing it to fall around her face. She separated out the silver strands with her fingers and twisted them around her pinky.

"Let me give you a taste of what's to come," she said then. Still fully clothed, she quickly knelt at his feet and sucked his semi-erect cock into her mouth. He was hard again instantly.

After only a moment, she stood again and lifted her skirt. She motioned him to his knees and pulled the crotch of her teddy to one side. "Now lick me."

Eagerly he licked at the hot, wet places between Barbara's legs. Although he seemed to pay no attention to what pleased her, he did lick many of the places she enjoyed. She'd get hers this evening, she vowed, in more ways than one. "Use your hands, too," she said and felt his fingers probe her pussy. As she wiggled, his fingers slipped toward her anus. "Umm," she said, "I like it back there, too."

As she took her pleasure, she looked down and saw that Walt had one fist around his erection. She leaned over and slapped first his hand, then his cock. "Mine," she snapped. "And don't forget again."

"But . . ."

"No buts. Your hands and your cock are mine. Unless you want to leave, of course."

Walt groaned "No," and his shoulders sagged. He was hers.

"Good. Get on all fours. I'd like the feel of my pussy on your back."

Reluctantly Walt knelt on his hands and knees and Barbara stepped over him and rubbed her wet pussy on his spine. "It's like horseback riding," she said as she settled her weight on his bark. "It always gets me hot." She had never been on a horse in her life, but it sounded good. "Move underneath me," she said. He moved a bit and she purred, "Mmmm, that's good." Slowly he seemed to get into the game and began to arch his back and wiggle his hips so his spine rubbed against Barbara's wet lips.

"You are very good at this," she said. She dismounted, reached beneath him and squeezed his cock. "And you certainly seem to enjoy it." She left for a moment, and returned with a tube of lubricant. "I love hard cocks," she said, rubbing the cold gel all over his erection and balls. "You feel so hot, so hard. I've never known anyone so hard."

She watched him preen, the oily bastard. Still rubbing his cock with one hand, she slid one finger of the other to the sensitive area behind his balls and stroked. Gradually, her caresses worked her fingers closer to his anus. "So hot, baby," she purred as she rubbed his puckered hole. She had no idea whether he'd ever done anything like this before, but whether or not he was experienced, he seemed to be enjoying her ministrations. She lightened her touch on his cock so he wouldn't come just yet.

"A horse needs a tail," she said, "and I have just the thing." She quickly found an anal plug with a slender neck just below the flange and a dozen strands of leather attached to the base. She imagined that some used the dildo end as a handle for the whip, but she knew what she wanted to do with the device.

Still on all fours, Walt looked at the item in Barbara's hand. "You're not going to hurt me with that, are you?" he said.

"No, baby," she said, rubbing her slippery hand over the flesh-colored plastic handle. "I am going to fill you as you may never have been filled before."

"I don't know," he said.

Barbara looked at his cock, now harder than ever.

"Yes, you do. It's dirty and evil, but the idea of having something invade your ass excites you." She leaned beneath his groin and rubbed his swollen cock. "You can't fool me, so don't try. Just be quiet and let me do this."

Walt shuddered but remained silent. Gently Barbara massaged Walt's rear hole with the tip of the dildo, then pushed it inch-by-inch into his rear passage. When it was deep inside, held by his tight sphincter, the leather strips made it look as though her horse indeed had a tail.

Again Barbara straddled Walt's back, undulating so her pussy rubbed against his heated flesh. "Such a good mount," she said, gazing off into the corner. She reached into her crotch and fingered her clit. "Ummm," she purred loudly. "Good horsy. Buck for me, horsy."

Walt arched his back and, with only a few more strokes, Barbara came, her wetness soaking Walt's skin.

"When does it get to be my turn?" he moaned.

Barbara caught her breath, then stood up and crossed the room. She pressed a few buttons on a small remote control, then flipped on the TV. "We'll see what you want after you've watched this hot video." She pressed the remote's rewind button then pressed play.

After a moment of snow, the image of Walt on his knees before Barbara filled the screen. Staring at the sight of his head moving against her crotch and hearing the sounds of her purrs and his pleased grunts, Walt stood up and walked, naked, toward the TV. As Walt watched himself get down in his hands and knees, he growled, "You taped the entire thing?" He reached behind him and yanked the dildo from his ass, his face turning bright red.

"The entire thing," Barbara said. She pressed fast-forward, then slowed the picture again as a clear shot of Walt, with the tail hanging from his rear, filled the screen. The camera zoomed in on the dildo in Walt's ass.

"How did you get it to zoom like that? Shit. Someone must have been holding the camera."

Maggie had been controlling the camera at that moment, but Walt would never know or understand that. Barbara let the tape play for another few moments. Then she said, "Now, go home."

Walt's breathing was raspy and his entire body shook. His eyes wildly searched the room. "How? Why?"

Barbara slowly shook her head. "You poor, stupid bastard. You don't even remember the trick you and your friend Carl played on me several years ago. The car? The camera?" She watched as recognition slowly changed his expression. "Good. I see you remember now. That was me. And you humiliated me in ways you couldn't even imagine." She smiled ruefully. "And you didn't even remember it."

"Okay. I'm sorry," Walt said as he pulled on his pants. "Really. I am. Now give me that tape." He prowled the room looking for the camera.

"I'm sure you are sorry. Now. But sorry isn't enough. Be a good boy and get out of here."

"Not without that film"

"The film is only part of it. The friend who helped me with the camera also took lots of still pictures. Like the ones you took of me that night. Those photos of you and your lovely tail are long gone." There were no such pictures, but Walt would never know that.

Walt stopped searching the room and pulled on his shirt and jacket. "What are you going to do with them?"

"Actually, nothing." She retrieved the camera from its hiding place behind some ferns on her wardrobe and pulled out the cassette. "You didn't do anything with the photos you took that night, so here . . ." She handed the cassette to Walt. "I'll hold on to the stills. Just having them is a symbol of something for me."

"You won't show them around?" Walt said, stuffing the cassette into his jacket pocket.

"No. Unless you get out of line, that is. So run along. Go home." She thought about the condition of his deflated cock and what she hoped were very uncomfortable balls. "And jerk off."

Walt stared at her for a long moment, then shook his head.

"Amazing," he said. "Just amazing." He left, and Barbara heard him pound down the stairs and slam the front door behind him.

"It's all gone," Barbara said to Maggie later that evening. "All that leftover anger and frustration are gone. I don't even hate the poor slob anymore."

"I'm glad. Did he believe you about the still pictures?"

"He did. Just like I expected him to. Thanks for aiming the camera for me. I didn't even mind it that you were watching."

"I only watched for a few minutes." She patted Barbara's hand. "You were great."

"It all felt good. And maybe Walt will think twice before he plays tricks on women again."

"I hope so. What's up for you now?"

"Just more of life, I guess," Barbara said, stretching out on the bed in her bathrobe. "I saw a T-shirt recently. It said, 'So many men and so little time.' "

Maggie laughed. "Well, babe, I've got to go."

"Okay. See you soon."

"Yeah," Maggie said, knowing it was a lie.

Maggie pushed through the revolving door and, as she thought she would, ended up in the computer room, wearing the soft white gown she had been wearing on her first visit. This was it, she knew. Up or down. And how had she done? She didn't really know.

"And we don't know either," Lucy said, as always reading her mind.

"Yes, we know you did your job," Angela said.

"And you did it well," Lucy chimed in.

"But the outcome is not quite what either of us anticipated," Angela added.

"Outcome?" Maggie said, making herself comfortable in a chair facing the women's desk.

"Oh, that's right," Angela said. "You left Barbara after her evening with Walt."

"That was seven months ago," Lucy said.

"Seven months? Oh," Maggie said. "It's funny. I miss her even though it seems only a moment ago."

"Well, once we knew you were gone permanently, we fixed it so she wouldn't miss you."

"Fixed it?"

"We erased you," Lucy said.

"You what!" Maggie yelled, jumping from her chair. "You erased me?"

Angela walked around the desk and patted Maggie's shoulder, pushing her back down into her chair. "Lucy's got the tact of a wart hog, and that's an insult to wart hogs. But try to understand." A chair appeared beside Maggie and Angela sat down, arranging her wings carefully behind her. "We couldn't let her remember you. She had come so far and missing you would have only depressed her. And she needed to remember all her changes as her own doing. It was the final step in her lessons."

"And after all," Lucy said, "how could she have explained you?"

"But . . ."

"Sweetie," Angela said, still patting Maggie's shoulder. "You really do understand."

Maggie sighed. "I guess I do. It just makes me sad." She sniffed and a lace hanky appeared in her hand.

"I know," Angela continued. "But she's doing so well now."

"Really? What's she doing?"

Lucy picked up the story. "She's got a boyfriend. Full time. They are thinking about moving in together. Barbara met him just after that evening with Walt. He's a banker and went to her boss about some legal matters. They met and hit it off immediately, both as friends and hot lovers. For a long while they dated, but continued to see other people. Now they've become exclusive and they're very happy."

"That's wonderful." Maggie wondered why she felt so empty. It was nice when Barbara needed her, looked to her for guidance, learned from her. Now her job was done and it was a letdown. She blew her nose.

"I know it's a letdown," Angela said, "but you can relish the fact that you did a super job."

"Would you like to see them, her and her boyfriend?" Lucy asked. "I can tune you in if you like."

"Not in the bedroom," Maggie said, curious to see the ending to Barbara's story. "I don't want to eavesdrop."

Lucy's fingers danced over the computer keyboard. "Not at all. They're out for the evening at a little place they frequent." She turned the monitor so Maggie could see.

In the picture, a couple danced, their bodies close. Barbara leaned against the man who held her, her mouth beside his ear. "I just love slow dancing," she whispered. "It's like making love standing up."

They turned so Maggie could see the man's face. "That's Paul!" she cried. "That's the guy I was on the phone with that last night. That's my Paul."

"That's her Paul now, and they're blissfully happy," Angela said.

Maggie caught her breath. Paul. She had really loved him, she realized. She gazed at him for a while, getting pleasure from the obvious joy on his face. Maggie sighed and smiled. "We could never have been happy together," she said. "He was a banker and I was a prostitute. It would never have worked." She watched the screen.

Paul spoke into Barbara's ear. "You know, every time you talk about slow dancing, I remember a woman I once knew. Her name was Maggie and it was very long ago. I loved her."

"Do you still love her?" Barbara asked.

"She's been dead for a couple of years. I just remember her fondly. She always liked slow dancing."

"I vaguely remember someone named Maggie in my past, too. I don't remember when I knew her, but I get warm feelings when I think of her."

Paul pressed his hand into the small of Barbara's back, moving his body still closer to hers. "I like warm feelings. Let's go back to your place and feel warm all over."

As Lucy turned off the image on the computer screen, Maggie brushed a tear from her face. "I'm happy for them. I really am."

"I know you are, dear," Angela said, rising and circling the desk again. "But that still leaves us with the problem of what to do with you."

"Yes," Lucy said. "We're still confused."

"We had a bet about how this would end up."

"And we can't even decide who won."

Lucy leaned over and whispered animatedly to Angela. Although Maggie couldn't hear the words, it was obvious from the body language that the two women were arguing. Hands flew through the air, Lucy's tail swished, and at one point Angela's wings flapped and she rose several feet into the air.

Finally Lucy said, "That's the only answer."

"I think so."

"Well," Maggie said, realizing that her fate for the remainder of all time was being decided, "have you figured it all out?"

"Actually, no," Angela said. "But what about you? Where do you think you belong?"

"I don't know either. Heaven sounds real nice, I guess, but maybe a bit dull."

"Well, I have no complaints," Angela said, looking offended.

"I didn't mean to be insulting," Maggie said quickly. "I'm sure it's a lot of fun once you get used to it. But I'm not accustomed to sitting around all day discussing philosophy."

"See, I told you," Lucy said. "My place is much more interesting."

"Yes, I'm sure it is, but I'm not sure I want to associate with the people who go . . ." Maggie pointed her thumb downward.

"Shows you have good taste," Angela said. "And I think Lucy and I have arrived at a solution, at least for the short run."

"How would you like to be an operative for us?" Lucy continued. "You would just do more of what you did with Barbara. Fix up people's lives."

"Like Michael Landon in *Highway to Heaven*?"

Angela nodded. "Maybe, but on a more earthy level. You know, teaching people to love making love."

"Teaching people to love to fuck," Lucy said, turning to Angela, a mischievous grin on her face.

Angela hurumphed, and looked seriously at Maggie. "Would you do that? We've got a lot of cases like Barbara's waiting for someone like you."

Maggie swallowed her tears and thought about Barbara and Paul. Then she considered the offer for only a moment. "I think I'd like that."

"Good," Angela and Lucy said simultaneously.

"Okay. And this time, how about giving me some powers. You know, like *the stuff* Michael Landon had."

"We'll see as the situation arises," Angela said.

"Now, come over here. I want to show you a woman named Pam." Lucy's fingers flew over the keyboard. "She's a tough one."

Maggie swiped a tear from her cheek. The girls were right. Barbara and Paul would be so good together. But it was hard to grasp that that part of her life was over. Maggie circled the table and stood behind Lucy. "That's her?"

"That's Pam. She's almost forty, divorced and dumpy."

"She must weight over two fifty."

"Aren't you the one who believes that sensuality is as much a product of the look in the eyes as the body behind it?"

Maggie drummed her fingers on the back of Lucy's chair. "I hate hearing my own words thrown back at me," she said, "and you're right, of course. Anyone can be sensual."

"She really needs your kind of help," Angela said.

Maggie took a deep breath. "Okay, when do I start?"

MIDNIGHT BUTTERFLY

Chapter 1

"That makes tonight's winning lotto numbers 1, 2, 11, 13, 16, and 23. Good luck. And remember that if no one wins tonight, Saturday's New York State Lottery jackpot could be more than seventy million dollars."

Ellen Harold opened one of her green eyes, yawned, and glanced at the blue digits on the front of the VCR. Seeing that it was just after eleven, she realized that she had, as usual, fallen asleep in her lounge chair, watching a rerun of *Baywatch*. She yawned again and stared at the 11:00 P.M. news anchor, not really listening to the day's headlines.

Ten minutes later, as the anchorman introduced the sports reporter, Ellen swung her short legs off the chair and stumbled into the bathroom, scratching the back of her neck. Barely awake, she brushed her teeth and gazed into the mirror. She sleepily looked at her half-closed green eyes and her shoulder-length, baby-fine brown hair and slightly sun-burned ivory skin. *Next time I mow the lawn*, she thought, *I've got to use more sun block.*

Didn't the guy say 13, 16, and 23? she thought as she entered her bedroom. *Hey, I might have at least three of the numbers.* Ellen played the local six-number lottery twice a week and always played the same numbers, 11 and 16 representing her birthday, 1 and 13, her older sister's, and 2 and 23, her late mother's. She scratched the back of her neck again, wondering whether three numbers pay off. She didn't really hear the rest but maybe she even had four. Afraid to hope, she undressed, pulled on her pajamas, and settled into bed. She closed her eyes and let herself drift, dreaming not of money but of romance.

She was tall, maybe five foot nine, slender. Men thought of her as willowy. Reed slim. She had thick auburn hair that fell in heavy waves almost to her waist. Tonight she was wearing an orange bathing suit like the women in Baywatch. She walked along a beach at sunset, the sand warm, the water cool as wavelets lapped at her dainty feet. Her blue eyes searched the strand before her, knowing the man she looked for would appear.

He looked a bit like David Hasslehoff, long, sandy hair dancing on his shoulders, tousled by the soft breeze. He had beautifully developed arms and shoulders, a hairless chest with well-defined layers of muscles. Muscles. She loved the idea of a man who could overpower her should he choose. But he wouldn't have to.

As they approached each other, he gazed at her, burning her with his stare, undressing her with his eyes. And she was more beautiful naked than she was in her suit. "You knew, didn't you?" he said when they were only a breath apart.

"I knew. When I first saw you, I knew." She reached out and flattened her palms against his warm skin. Beneath her hand she could feel the drumming of his heart.

"Now," he whispered. "Right now." He cupped her face, staring deeply into her eyes as his fingers glided past her temples to comb through her hair.

"Yes," she breathed.

His mouth descended and covered hers, his tongue playing beautiful melodies against her lips. She parted them, allowing his tongue entrance to her hidden cavern and the kiss lengthened until their universe was spinning out of control. She couldn't think, and knew she didn't want to, ever again.

Then, they were naked, lying on sand as soft as any feather bed, tiny waves playing with their toes. His hands covered her breasts, kneading her hot flesh, his mouth toying with her ears. "I want you," he murmured, "as I've never wanted anyone."

"Then take me," she replied, slipping her hands around his waist. Then he was inside her, his manhood large, filling every inch of her. His thrusts, his movements perfectly timed with her need, his huge body driving her upward, making her crave. His mouth covered her erect nipple, licking and sucking as his hips pressed his flesh more deeply into her.

"Oh, Lord," she said, "make me yours."

"You are mine," the man said, "always." And with one final push, warm fluid filled her and her pleasure was complete.

And in her bed, Ellen reached down and touched herself sleepily between her legs, enjoying the small spasms that completed her. Afterward, the transition from fantasy to sleep was smooth and she slept dreamlessly through the night.

The following morning, without getting out of bed, she pressed the button on top of her radio, hoping the local news would mention last evening's numbers. She had awakened thinking about the lottery and, from what she remembered from the previous evening, she probably had at least three of the numbers. The announcer's voice droned on. Suddenly, Ellen sat bolt upright and stared at the radio. "Last night's winning numbers were 1, 2, 11, 13, 16, and 23." *Those are my numbers*, she thought, pressing her hand against her breastbone, feeling the sudden pounding of her heart. *Those are my numbers. It can't be. Things like that just don't happen to people like me. I must have heard wrong.*

She threw on a pair of many-times-washed jeans and yanked on a navy T-shirt. Slipping her feet into sneakers without socks she ran out her door into the warm July morning. Without conscious thought she dashed around the corner to the little convenience store where she bought her ticket early every Wednesday and Saturday afternoon. Panting, she pushed through the front door. "Hi, Ellen," the counterman called in lightly accented English. "What brings you out this early?" Hispanic with deeply pigmented skin and heavy five o'clock shadow despite the early hour, his smile of obvious pleasure at seeing her exposed large white teeth.

"Hernando, do you have last night's winning lottery numbers?"

"Sure, they fax them to me so I can post them. Lemme see now." He shuffled some papers on the counter. "Yeah. Here they are: 1, 2, 11, 13, 16, and 23. You the big winner?" he asked with a grin. "Fifty million big ones. Cut me in, will ya?"

"Hey, Hernando," a voice called from the back room. "We just got another fax from the lottery administration. Seems the only winning ticket for last night's jackpot was sold here."

Hernando turned to stare at Ellen but she barely noticed. She was in shock. Those were her numbers. Really. Hers. She fumbled in her jacket pocket and found her wallet. Inside was her ticket. She had to check that she had really bought the right numbers. But she had. Right? Her breathing sped up and her pulse raced and she could hear nothing but a buzzing in her ears.

She clutched the wallet as she became aware that Hernando was standing, staring at her. From the back room, the voice yelled, "I wonder who won all those bucks. Do we get to know?"

"I think we just might," Hernando yelled. "Are those really your numbers?" he asked Ellen. "I remember you told me once that you always play the same ones. Your family's birthdays. Right?"

Ellen stood with her wallet in her trembling hand, unwilling to open it and pull out the ticket. Maybe she had made a mistake and played the wrong numbers, but she always played the same ones. She should just look. "I can't," she whispered.

"Want me to look at your ticket for you?" Hernando asked.

Ellen nodded numbly and held out her wallet. Slowly Hernando took it in his huge hands, reached inside the bill compartment and withdrew the ticket. "Right date," he said as he studied the small slip of paper. He looked back and forth between the list and the ticket. "One, 2, 11, 13, 16, and 23. Holy shit. Those really are the numbers." He raised his eyes and again just stared at Ellen. "Holy shit, Ellen. Fifty million. Take it in a lump and you get maybe thirty-five. Pay half to the president, and some to the governor and you get to keep maybe fifteen or twenty. Holy shit. Twenty million smackers clear. Wanna buy this place? I can let you have it for only five million." His laugh was warm as he pounded Ellen on the back. "Wow!"

Unable to move, Ellen raked her numb fingers through her hair, reflexively tucking strands behind each ear, then scrubbed her eyes with her fists. She couldn't seem to keep from shaking. "You okay?" Hernando asked. "You want some water? Only ten bucks a glass." His booming voice filled the empty store.

She shook her head. She didn't want any water and she was definitely not okay. What was she? "I don't know," she mumbled. She took the ticket and her wallet from Hernando's hand. "What do I do now?"

"I can let lottery headquarters know but you might want to talk to a lawyer or an accountant first. What are you going to do with all that money?"

"I don't know," Ellen said, concentrating on putting the ticket back into her wallet. "I haven't a clue what I'm going to do," she muttered as she walked out of the store.

"I haven't a clue," Ellen said to her older sister on the phone a week later.

"Well, love," Micki said, "you don't need to make any decisions for a while." Micki, full-time mother of three school-aged daughters, had been talking to Ellen almost daily since Ellen had called and told her about the winning ticket. "As you know, my only advice is to be good to yourself."

"I know, but I don't know what that means." With advice from a local accountant she had claimed her prize the day after winning. She had enjoyed all the attention, the whirlwind ceremonies and TV appearances. She even had the picture of her with the giant check stuck in the corner of her bedroom mirror.

She had already put chunks of money in accounts for each of Micki's children and a sizable sum in a money-market fund for her sister and brother-in-law, over their loud objections. The accountant had introduced her to a broker who invested the rest of her money in certificates of deposit and conservative mutual funds. She now had an income of more than half a million dollars a year, but she hadn't any idea of what to do next. She was still getting tapes from the medical group she worked for doing data coding and typing up the required reports on her computer. She was still eating peanut butter sandwiches and Kraft macaroni and cheese and going out to the local Italian restaurant for spaghetti with meat sauce once or twice a week.

Nothing much had changed yet everything had changed. All the people in the neighborhood knew about her winnings. People she barely knew stopped her on the street with business propositions and she was constantly asked for contributions to aid the homeless, the needy, sick children, art museums, endangered species. Representatives of charities of all types wrote, called, and even rang her doorbell, anxious to help her spend her winnings. Several people named Harold had contacted her, sure they were long-lost relatives. "Micki, my sudden fame is driving me crazy. I got another dozen letters today from people and places I don't know, all wanting money. Yesterday Mrs. Cumberland, that wonderful grandmotherly type next door came over with a plate of fudge."

"That was nice of her." Micki hesitated. "Wasn't it?"

"I thought so, too, until she spent an hour telling me about her grandson who is the brightest mind since Einstein but can't afford college. You remember Randy Cumberland."

"Sure. He was a year after you in school. A bit dorky but sweet. College? He barely graduated from high school."

"Right. He's working at Ernie's gas station rebuilding engines, and he's perfectly content, right where he belongs, but his grandmother doesn't see it that way. When I talked to her about it, she insisted that the only reason he's not Phi Beta Kappa is money. My money."

"Oh shit."

"Everyone. Even Dr. Okamura went completely over the edge yesterday."

"Over the edge?"

"I went in to pick up my tapes and he came out of the back, all smarmy. Oily. He was all over me, smiling a big sticky-sweet smile. 'How's my favorite girl today?'

"How's my favorite girl? He's never said three words to me before. So I told him I was just fine and he leaned over, trapped me against his receptionist's desk and asked me out to dinner."

"He didn't," the voice through the phone gasped. "He's married, isn't he?"

Ellen tucked several strands of hair behind her ear and shifted the phone to the other side. "He did, and he's very married. Suddenly I'm the winner of the most-likely-to-make-a-man-cheat-on-his-wife contest. Yuck. I gently removed his arm from beside me and told him that I wasn't available."

"Do you think he knows about the money?"

"Why else? Come on, Micki. Be real. I'm not particularly attractive and he's never paid the least bit of attention to me before. It's all making me crazy. Everyone's changed."

"So get away. Move somewhere where no one knows you, and no one cares. You can go anywhere, you know."

"Yeah right. Take a cruise around the world. Live a frivolous life clipping coupons."

"Why not? You can certainly afford it."

Ellen propped the receiver between her ear and shoulder and paced the length of her bedroom. "I couldn't do that. I couldn't just loll around. I'd have to do something."

"Okay. Go to medical school."

Ellen smiled. "Right."

"Listen, you can do anything you want to do. Run for mayor, open a florist shop, launch a singing career. Anything."

Ellen's loud sigh filled the room. "I know, and maybe that's the problem. I've got several million in the bank, earning more money than I can spend. It's mind-boggling and really difficult to wrap my mind around, even after all the publicity. I know I can do anything and I can't get my mind to settle on any one thing."

"Move to New York City and become a stripper."

Ellen's laugh was genuine. "There isn't enough silicone in the world to make this body worth looking at."

Micki's laugh joined Ellen's. "Okay, okay. Stripping's probably not for you but New York might be just the thing." Micki was still laughing as she continued. "I think you need to get away from here. It's too limiting for you."

Ellen contemplated. "I suppose I could have Dr. Okamura's office send me tapes once a week. The computer system doesn't care about where I am when I log in."

"You have all the creativity of a bowl of oatmeal. You've got all that money. Live! Quit your job. Let loose. I've been telling you for years but you just don't listen. You're too restricted here. It's time to move on. Bust out. Live for a change."

"I couldn't just quit my job. I'm the only one who can understand Dr. Okamura's accent, and I love doing it."

"Okay, okay. Keep the job if you must, but it's really time to get out of this one-horse town and find out what the real world's like."

Ellen dropped back onto the edge of her bed. "I didn't know you were so down on Fairmont. You and Milt seem to like it here and it's really not such a bad place."

"It's not bad for those of us who've found our paths. I've got Milt and the kids, PTA, scouts, lots of thing I love to do. You, however, are stagnating here and you'll never bloom. You don't date, you never do anything that's fun. You know just about every eligible man in town and you've rejected them all at one time or another. What kind of a future does that give you?"

Ellen paused, her sister's words slowly weighing her down. As always, Micki was right. Ellen had gone to school with just about everyone her age in town. She'd had a yearlong relationship with Gerry Swinburn, but that had ended when he got hired by a national brokerage firm and decided to move to New York City. "I've got to get out," he had said. "There's nothing here for me."

"What about me?" Ellen had said.

"I care for you," Gerry had answered, "but that's just not enough." He had begged her to come to New York with him, but at that time it had been out of the question. Now?

"I've got to give it a little thought," she said to her sister, "but maybe you've got a point."

After hanging up, Ellen sat on the edge of the bed in her tiny house, deep in thought. What did she have to look forward to, money or no money? What kind of future was there here for her? She worked at her computer and did little else. She was such a good customer at the local video store that they kept giving her special deals. She knew all the clerks at the local library by their first names. She owned enough romance novels to fill a wide bookshelf, and her sister teased that if she were snowed in for three years, she couldn't read them all.

What did she do all week? She saw her sister and family several times, she went out for dinner, alone, and she went to the movies once or twice a month. She had a few friends, acquaintances actually, and she went to their houses occasionally. Sometimes she had people over. It was all routine. Predictable. Boring.

She wandered around her small, comfortable house, deep in thought. It had been her parents' house, the house she grew up in. It had two bedrooms and she still slept in the one she had shared with Micki all their growing-up years. Nothing had changed since the elder Harolds' death in a car accident four years before. Her parents' bedroom was neat and the bed made as it always had been. A rag rug covered their floor, like the one that covered hers. Ellen remembered her mother making them from scraps of faded fabric, many cut from clothes Ellen had outgrown. Hand-me-downs. She remembered the few times when she had gotten something new, something her sister hadn't already worn and could even pick out a couple of swatches.

Yet she wasn't sad about her simple upbringing. Sure her parents hadn't been wealthy, but they had been happy. The house had always smelled of something baking and there was always laughter. Her father played piano for their weekly musical evenings and, although her singing voice was abominable, she would sing along with her sister's lovely alto and her mother's lilting soprano. To make up for her lack of musical talent, she had had her watercolors, which she had used to create beautifully painted covers for the sheet music her father was always acquiring.

Ellen wandered into the living room and lifted the seat of the old piano bench. There were several of her covers still inside and she picked up one and gazed at it, a simple scene of a country meadow surrounded by apple trees. That was such a long time ago, she thought. She ran her hand over the scratched upright piano, missing the old times.

In those years, the TV was seldom on, the family preferring books and conversation to the incessant babble of the tube. When she had friends home from school they were always amazed at not being able to watch soap operas and talk shows but soon learned to enjoy the activities and the companionship of the Harold family.

Now, as Ellen wandered through the living room, the house felt lonely, empty, devoid of the joy that had always been part of her life here. Until now she hadn't even noticed how little remained, but still she was at home here, comfortable. Did she want to be just comfortable all her life? Her footsteps took her into the kitchen. Before she was born it had housed an icebox and an old kerosene stove. Now there was a ten-year-old refrigerator and a stove that was even older. But what did she cook? TV dinners, cans of ravioli, and her favorite, Kraft macaroni and cheese dinners.

She plopped herself down on a plastic-covered kitchen chair and rested her elbows on the Formica table. Where was she going in her life? She had enough money to do anything she wanted. She could redo the entire house, but it would still be a small house in a small town.

New York City. It formed the backdrop for many of the novels she enjoyed. Life pulsed there. People were busy, going from exciting place to exciting place. Fine restaurants, museums, giant bookstores, and galleries. There were so many things to do, places to see, and she certainly had the wherewithal to do it all. She didn't have to actually move there, she could stay someplace for a while and see the sights. Why not? She could put her laptop computer under her arm and visit for a month or two, find a place to stay where no one knew about her or her money. Her work would only take a few hours a day and she could explore in her free time. At least then she'd know what was out there, and if she got lonely for Micki's family, she could come back.

Over the next few days she vacillated. One minute she was hot for a trip to the big city, and the next she was terrified. How would she act? What would she do? Where would she go?

"Listen, Ellie," her sister said about three weeks after her lottery windfall, "I looked into New York City. Remember Ashley Richardson from school? Actually it's McAllister now. She was a year behind me, two ahead of you."

"Wasn't she the tall redhead with the braces? She used to come home with you at least once a week." Ellen thought. "She had a great singing voice as I remember."

"Right. Well she moved to New York City, met a guy, and got married a few years ago. We've kept in touch, so I called and asked her to do some discreet investigation. She found a small residence hotel in midtown. The east fifties, I think. It's a converted brownstone with only six apartments, not luxurious, just clean and comfortable. The building's totally secure and in a great neighborhood."

"You went behind my back?"

"Not at all. I just asked so you'd have your options open."

"Micki! How could you!" she snapped.

"Don't bite my head off because you're afraid to take the big step. If I left it up to you you'd be here until hell froze over. I'm just asking you to consider getting away, maybe for just a few weeks. We both know it would be so good for you."

"But . . ."

"I'm your sister. I've always been more of a small-town girl than you have. You've always been more of a dreamer, an adventurer."

"Me? An adventurer? Are you sure you haven't forgotten me already?"

"Not at all. You've always sold yourself short, but before, since there wasn't anything you could do about it, I shut up. Anyway, it's really none of my business. But . . ."

Ellen raked her fingers through her hair. Some things never

change. "You always say it's none of your business, then follow it up with a but."

Ellen could hear her sister's chuckle. "Right," Micki said. "You know me so well. But I know you too, Ellie. You need this. You can do this. Get a pencil and let me give you the information Ash gave me."

If only to shut Micki up, Ellen got a pencil and paper and took down the details about the hotel. "It's something between a hotel and a condo. They cater mostly to high-end one- and two-month vacationers and they supply kitchen stuff, sheets, towels, and a maid once a week. They are pretty booked, but you can call and find out when they will have a room. Ash says that it's really moderately priced for the city." Micki mentioned a monthly rent that would have choked her before the lottery winnings. "When she called, the woman said she thought they would have something for you within a month or so."

Ellen sighed, something she'd been doing a lot lately. "Maybe you're right. I'll think about it."

Later that afternoon she opened her mailbox and could barely get her mail out. She stopped at her garbage can and flipped a huge handful of solicitations. Save the Whales, MADD, cancer, kidneys, muscular dystrophy. "They never stop," she muttered.

"Hi, Ellen," her next-door neighbor said. "Nice to see you this afternoon."

Ellen looked up and saw Mrs. Cumberland bustling toward her. She had the feeling that the older woman had been watching for her. "I'm fine, Mrs. Cumberland. How are you this lovely day?"

"Really hot. This summer had been brutal so far, and my air conditioner is on the fritz again. I just hate to have it repaired, what with saving for my grandson's college. It's so expensive."

Oh, Lord, here we go again. "I understand," Ellen said, "but do you think college is really right for Randy? He seems happy at Ernie's."

"He only thinks he's happy."

Ellen shrugged. It might be easier to just write the woman a check for ten thousand dollars, but there would always be someone else wanting more. "I've got to go in. I'll see you soon."

"Of course, dear." Ellen was sure she heard the woman murmur, "Thanks for nothing."

That was it. She'd do it. She'd spend some time in New York City where no one knew her. She'd call that hotel right away and see when they could have an apartment for her. She'd really give it all a chance. She'd stay a month, maybe more and, if she wanted to come home, she always could. This wasn't an irrevocable step, just a temporary way to see a bit of the world.

She walked from her train into the main rotunda of Grand Central Station. Actually it was what she thought Grand Central Station would look like, with marble walls and a mosaic of signs of the zodiac on the ceiling as she had seen in an article about the restoration of the old landmark. She stood in the center with streams of people flowing around her. A man bumped into her causing her to drop her pocketbook. He was tall, well-muscled, dressed in a three-piece suit fitted to his nicely proportioned body.

His hair was dark, with a small mustache and a closely trimmed beard. Wings of silver hair accented his handsome face. "I'm so sorry I jostled you," he said.

"Oh, no problem."

"Ah, but there is." He bent over to help her pick up her purse and its scattered contents. "You look a bit lost."

"Just a little."

He straightened and handed her her purse. "Are you new to the city?"

"This is my first time here."

"Well let me help you. My limo is outside and I can take you wherever you want to go."

"I couldn't let you do that," she said.

"Of course you could. My name's Paul Broderick." He extended his hand.

"And mine's Ellen. Ellen Harold." As he took her hand she felt a jolt of electricity. God, *she thought*, he's a sexy man. *She allowed*

him to lead her through the great doors and, as he had said, a stretch limousine waited at the curb. He handed her in while the chauffeur placed her suitcase in the trunk.

The interior of the limo was comfortably cool and smelled of leather and Paul's aftershave. She gave him the address of her apartment and, as they drove, he told her about himself, holding her hand throughout the journey. It was a long drive and, as they talked, he rummaged in a small cabinet and retrieved a bottle of Dom Perignon. As she sipped from a tall, slender champagne flute he stroked the back of her neck and it seemed only natural for him to take the glass from her, set it down, and touch his lips to hers.

The kiss was deep and long, their tongues gently seeking each other's deepest pleasures. His lips still in contact with hers, he pressed a button and an opaque partition slowly closed, separating them from the driver. Now they were cocooned in a world all their own.

"Paul, this is too fast," she whispered.

"Not if people know as quickly as we did how much we mean to each other." He held her shoulders. "Please. It's so right."

"Yes," she sighed, "it is."

Soon they were naked, and he stretched her out on the smooth, soft leather seat. He stroked her skin, swirling his fingers over her breasts, nuzzling her neck, his naked body against hers. "You know I won't be able to let you go," he purred in her ear. "We'll have to make our relationship more official."

"I know." Then she felt his manhood pressing against her flesh. Magically he was inside, stretching and completing her. The movements of his body gave her wonderful pleasures until he finally arched his back then collapsed.

In her bed, Ellen fell asleep.

"Oh, lord," Lucy said, sliding her palms down the thighs of her tight black leather pants. "She has the dullest, most uncreative fantasies I've ever participated in. They sound just like those romance novels she's always reading."

"Well then," Angela replied, rubbing the back of her neck beneath her flowing blond hair, "stay out of them."

"I would love to, but I checked back and her dreams have always been like scenes from bad novels. I figured that once she won the lottery she would begin having fantasies worthy of a thirty-two-year-old woman. These are puerile, suitable for a fourteen-year-old." Her fathomless black eyes flashed.

"So why don't you just let her alone? What's she to you anyway?"

"You know I'm always interested in lottery winners. I get some of my best recruits there. And you know her numbers? They add up to 66. That's close enough to our number, mine and the boss's." She aimed her thumb downward and jabbed at her desk.

"Leave the poor woman alone, Lucy."

"But shit, Angie, she has to get a life."

"She will, and please don't call me Angie."

"Angie, Angela, Angel, what difference does it make."

"I prefer the name I selected. Angela. It's not quite so obvious."

"In order not to be obvious, Lucy snapped, tapping her long, perfect nails on the desktop, "you'd have to remove the wings."

"I wouldn't talk, lady. What about that tail of yours?"

Suddenly identical messages, in huge letters, flashed across their matching computer screens. LADIES. CEASE!

Each woman, looking chastened, tapped in a quick, YES, SIR, although the sir each referred to resided in totally different areas of the firmament.

"Well," Angela said, "anything we choose to do about Ellen will just have to wait until her future is a bit clearer."

"I guess. I just wish she'd . . ."

"Wish all you want, but let's get back to work." Each woman picked up a long printed list and began pounding on her computer keyboard. "#123,492,478, hell, #123,498,293 heaven, #123,498,012 heaven, #124,493,121 hell."

"Hold it," Angela said. "Number 121 goes to heaven."

"Not if I have anything to do with it."

"We'll just see about that."

Chapter 2

It took almost three weeks before the arrangements were complete. Micki had agreed to come over once a week and water her sister's plants and do whatever else needed to be done in the tiny house. She'd park Ellen's eight-year-old Toyota in her driveway and move it occasionally to keep it going, and sort the mail and send along anything important. The doctors in the medical group would send their tapes to Ellen's address in the city once a week and Ellen would update all the appropriate computer records. Since her new apartment was already furnished, she had to bring very little so she put just a few things into a box and shipped them to her new address. Ellen was delighted that the hotel was content to go month to month, so she hadn't had to sign any kind of a lease. That way she could play things by ear and move back to Fairmont whenever she pleased.

On a hot, late-August morning, Micki drove her sister to the train station in Schenectady. As the train prepared to leave, the two women hugged and shed a few final tears. "Please tell the kids I love them and I'll miss them. I'm afraid they'll forget me."

"Of course they won't. You're not going to Siberia. You'll come back and visit or move back whenever the fancy strikes you."

"I'll miss you and Milt so very much."

"I know that, he knows that, and the girls know that." Micki playfully swatted her sister on the behind. "Now get on that train and get the hell out of here."

"I love you, sis."

"I love you too, babe." Micki gave her sister a gentle shove and pushed her toward a passenger car. "Move. Now!"

Her eyes still swimming, Ellen grinned. "Yes, ma'am. I'll call you tonight." She dragged her suitcase through the train-car door just as the loud bell reminded passengers that the train was leaving. She slid into a seat and scootched over to the window, dragging her suitcase with her. As the train began to move, her eyes locked on her sister's and the two women waved. "I'm going to love being in the city," she told herself aloud. "I am doing the right thing." She wiped her tearstained cheek with the back of her hand. "And if I hate it I can always come back."

When the train was fully underway, Ellen stood and adjusted her lightweight jeans and Mickey Mouse T-shirt. Since the car wasn't crowded, she settled her suitcase more permanently on the seat beside her and gazed out the window as New York State passed beside the tracks.

She changed trains in Albany so it was late afternoon when the train crossed a river and she was suddenly surrounded by tenements spray-painted with graffiti. The train slowed and stopped at 125th Street, then plunged underground.

"Grand Central, last and final stop," the conductor's voice boomed over the loudspeaker. "Please check around you for your personal belongings." Surrounded by bored travelers, Ellen settled her pocketbook on her shoulder, grabbed her suitcase and, as the doors opened, stepped onto a dingy platform, following the crowd into the main area of Grand Central Station. Like a tourist, which, of course, she was, she stopped in the middle of the huge main hall and looked around.

It looked exactly as she had imagined it, huge and cavernous, filled with tens of thousands of people. Since it was rush hour, hurrying commuters streamed on either side of her, hustling toward openings in the sides of the rotunda. For several minutes she just stood, staring. Most of the commuters looked hot and wrinkled in suits with jackets slung over their arms, dresses that looked limp and damp. Many of the women wore sneakers and socks and carried fancy leather attaché cases. A good percentage of the people were talking on cell phones while they walked, often skipping to one side suddenly to avoid more of the onrushing horde.

Shaking her head, and with no idea where she was going, Ellen walked toward an exit, dragging her wheeled suitcase behind her. Suddenly a man who looked remarkably like the man in her fantasy plowed headlong into her. He brushed off his three-piece-suit and snapped, "Hey, watch it, lady. Don't just stand there and gawk."

"Excuse me," Ellen said, wobbling a bit before regaining her footing. Okay, so much for fantasies. Now needing air, she picked up her pace and aimed for a wide doorway to the outside. Avoiding two more collisions, she finally gained the street and, pulling her suitcase, she walked to a corner. One sign said Forty-second Street the other said Vanderbilt Avenue.

Her contact at the hotel had suggested that she take a taxi to the building but Ellen had thought that was really extravagant. Now, however, not sure of which way to walk, and totally flustered by the crowds of people, she spotted a taxi discharging a passenger right in front of her so, as a business-suited man got out, she got in. The interior of the cab smelled strongly of pine deodorant but it was cool and much quieter than the outside.

"I can put that suitcase in the trunk," the driver said with a strong Jamaican accent.

"No, thank you, I'm all right."

"Your first time in New York, Miss?" he asked as he turned down the flag on the taximeter.

"I'm from upstate," Ellen said. "It's a bit overwhelming."

"I'm sure it is at first." He sighed, looking at her in his rearview mirror. "Where to?"

When she had given him the address the driver took off with a jerk strong enough to slam her back against the seat. Fortunately Ellen was too busy staring out the windows to care about the start-stop ride. No wonder they call them the canyons of New York, she thought, gawking as she craned her neck, leaning down to try to see the tops of the buildings. She soon realized that it was impossible so she settled for looking down the side streets as the taxi moved uptown.

Finally the cab stopped in front of a beautiful building made of dark red-brown stone with a deep red door with carriage lights on either side. Ellen looked at the taximeter and almost gasped in shock. "Seventeen dollars?" she said.

"Without tip," the driver said.

"Right." She gave him a twenty-dollar bill and told him to keep the change, hoping that was enough. When he didn't offer to help her out, she opened the door and scrambled onto the sidewalk, dragging her pocketbook and suitcase behind her.

She looked up and down the side street. It was a warm evening so the street was filled with people. There was a small restaurant on the corner with a few outdoor tables, all filled now with *New Yorkers.* It amused her that she thought of Manhattan-ites in italics, like *them,* not us. Maybe eventually she'd feel part of it all. And if not . . .

She climbed the few steps to the front door and turned the knob. The building manager had told her about the security so she wasn't surprised that the building was locked. In Fairmont, no one locked their doors, but this was the big city so she rang the bell marked MANAGER and almost immediately an attractive woman with gray hair and deep blue eyes swung the door wide. "You must be Ellen Harold," she said, "and I've been expecting you. I'm Pam Thomas. We spoke several times on the phone. I'm here to help you with anything I can." Taking the handle of Ellen's suitcase, the woman said, "Let me show you to your apartment. You're on the second floor, number 21."

As Ellen climbed the single flight of wide, carpeted stairs, Pam prattled on about how the building had been converted into six apartments, each with a bedroom, a living room, a small eat-in kitchen, and a bath. "Everything you need can be provided, from linens to daily or weekly maid service. Just decide what you need and let me know." She took a key from her pocket and opened the door of the apartment on the right. "Home, sweet home," she said cheerily, handing Ellen two keys. "This is for your apartment and this is for the front door."

Pam swung the door wide and Ellen walked into a large airy room with a view of the street behind heavy security bars. The furnishings were somewhere between a motel and a regular living room: functional chairs in a navy tweed, an oatmeal sofa, and matching oatmeal drapes. The tables and small hutch were dark wood, the paintings on the wall institutional florals in muted shades of pink, blue, and beige. Ellen wondered whether the paintings had been bought to be decorative or to merely blend into the motif. Even the carpet was a tight weave of blue and beige designed, she supposed, to wear well and not show dirt. Although there were lamps and two vases filled with flowers, the room had a coldness about it.

"We just had this room completely cleaned when the previous tenant moved out so please feel free to move the furniture and add whatever little homey touches you might want." She crossed the room and opened a door. "This is the bedroom."

Ellen gazed through the door at a similarly functional room done in southwestern shades of dusty blue, soft desert pink, and beige. "And this," Pam said, pulling open a pair of beige painted louvered doors, "is your kitchen. Do you cook?"

Ellen gazed into a small room with barely enough room to change your mind. It had the requisite appliances, with a tiny table and diminutive chairs. "I do, but I imagine I'll be eating out most of the time."

Pam spent the next fifteen minutes filling Ellen in on the building regulations, the maid service, and the location of the nearest laundry, dry cleaners and such. Finally she said, "Well, I'm sure you want to get settled, so I'll leave you. I live in 11, just below you, so if you need anything, just ring my bell. Tomorrow perhaps we can sit together and get to know each other. Once you've been here a few days, I'll be glad to answer any questions about the neighborhood, where to eat, where to shop, and things like that."

"That would be wonderful. I'll just ring your bell."

For several weeks Ellen prowled Manhattan. She visited museums, enjoyed some and was bored by others. She went to seven Broadway shows, enjoyed most and was bored to tears by two. And she walked. She window-shopped along almost every street and avenue, ending up on a few occasions in less-than-desirable neighborhoods.

She ate at fancy restaurants and felt a bit embarrassed at being frequently asked, "Will someone be joining you?" She found she was much more comfortable at a tiny luncheonette around the corner from her apartment where she read while she ate or just listened to the counterman yelling, "Scramble two, whiskey down, bacon and burn it."

She received the packet of tapes each Tuesday and by Friday she had entered the information into the computer and modemed it back to the office in Fairmont.

Almost a month after moving to the city she was on the phone with her sister for their weekly chat. "I've been thinking about coming back home."

"Ellen, why? We've discussed and discussed it. There's nothing here for you right now."

"There's nothing here for me either. I tried it, and I've enjoyed parts of my visit but it's over now and I'm coming home."

"Ridiculous. You've only just tasted the tip of the New York City iceberg. Jump into the pool. Swim around. Indulge."

"In what? I'm bored. I have nothing much to do and I can't just wander around like a gypsy." Ellen propped her feet on the small wooden coffee table and crossed her ankles. *I want to go home,* she confessed to herself. *I feel like a fish out of water here. Am I slinking home like a coward? Not giving it a chance? Do I really have to give it a chance?*

"Haven't you met anyone to pal around with?"

"Not really. I've spent some time with Pam, the gal who runs this place, but she's got her own friends and she goes out every night. She's friendly enough, but it's just not my style."

"I had hoped you'd meet some men there, date, you know."

"Yeah, right. No such luck."

"Have you made any efforts to be social?"

Ellen sat up and shifted the phone to her other ear. "You mean like go to a bar and sit around waiting for some man to ask me what my sign is?"

"Not that, but, well you know."

"Actually no, I don't know. I have no idea how to meet people of either sex."

"So why don't you do something. Take a course, volunteer somewhere where there are people."

Ellen settled back. She'd indulge her sister, listen to her suggestions as she always had, then go home. She'd had enough.

"I can't do all your thinking for you but maybe it's time you did something you always wanted to do. Take an art course for instance. You were always the talented one. Remember those watercolors you did for Dad's music? Since it's getting into fall, how about volunteering for a political candidate or at a local hospital?"

Art course. That was an idea, something she hadn't thought of. "Hmm," she said after a moment. "That's not a bad idea. Actually that's two good ideas you just had."

"Which ones?" Micki asked, her voice brightening.

"I could take an art course. I've always thought I had a little talent. There's a gallery a few blocks from here and according to the sign in the window the owner runs classes on the mornings when the gallery is closed."

"You said two ideas."

Ellen's eyes brightened. She might just do that. "The hospital volunteering isn't bad either. There are so many hospitals in the city, I could maybe read to patients or volunteer in the gift shop." Giggling, she said, "You know I just caught myself. I was thinking that I couldn't do something without getting paid, you know like a real job. But hell, I don't need the money, do I? I could just do it because I want to."

Micki's warm voice narrowed the distance between Fairmont and New York City. "You sure could. I think that sounds wonderful. Go for it, girl."

Later that afternoon Ellen pulled on a pair of well-worn jeans and a faded T-shirt and, since with the beginning of fall it was getting a bit cooler, she added a light windbreaker. She walked the few blocks to a storefront with a large gold-lettered sign announcing The Templeton Gallery. In the corner of the window sat a small carefully printed card stating that art classes were available. She strolled inside and looked around. The walls were painted stark white, one scattered with landscapes, several of windblown rocky coasts, some of pastoral forest glens. Another wall was covered with still lifes of fruit baskets, flowers, china, and crystal while two other walls were hung with portraits. As she peered at the signatures she saw that each wall featured a different artist. She sighed and stared at a particularly dramatic seascape, muttering, "I wish I could paint like that."

"Do you paint?" a male voice behind her asked.

Startled, she turned and gazed into a pair of sexy deep-blue eyes. "Just a little."

"Many people have undiscovered talent, just waiting for the right situation to unleash it. Maybe you're one of those."

Ellen tore her gaze from the man's eyes and took in the whole man. He was tall, and towered over her five-foot-three-inch frame. He had coal-black hair that flopped over his forehead and a tightly cropped beard and mustache that gave his handsome face a distinguished look. She guessed that he was around her age.

"Are you?" he asked again, his words musical with a slight Irish brogue.

"Am I what?" Ellen said, dragging her mind back to the present.

"Are you a vessel of undiscovered talent?"

Ellen snorted at the absurdity of the comment. "I doubt that, but I have been thinking of taking an art class. I used to paint watercolors back when I was younger, before my parents died. My sister always said I had talent." She slammed her mouth shut when she realized that she was rambling.

"I'm sure you do and maybe a class is just the thing." He extended his right hand and Ellen noticed the heavy coat of black hair that covered his wrist, below the turned-up sleeves of his light blue shirt. "I'm Kevin Duffy and I run this gallery. I also give classes upstairs Monday, Wednesday, and Friday mornings. I have one specifically on watercolors each Wednesday although we're pretty flexible around here and the classes usually focus on techniques necessary to any artist, regardless of the medium."

Since it seemed rude not to shake his hand, Ellen took it and marveled at the warmth and strength of his grasp. He held her hand just a moment longer than was necessary, gazing into her eyes with almost hypnotic intensity. Then they separated and he strode to a desk and returned with his card and several flyers. "This is me," he said, handing her his card, and this is the schedule of classes. There's no strict regimen so once we get you settled, you can come any time, attend one class or several. It would be entirely up to you." He pulled a pen from his pocket and ticked off the classes on Wednesdays. "As I said, this is a class in basic watercolor techniques." He looked into her eyes again. "The classes are a bit pricey, but well worth it if you're thinking about getting serious about your work. I suggest that you take a class, free of charge of course, so you can taste what we do. Then you can decide whether the cost would be justified."

Ellen could barely get her breath. "Oh, I think I can manage the cost." She took the paper. "You know, I might just try it."

Still gazing into her eyes, Kevin handed her another sheet of paper. "This is a list of some of the basic supplies. You probably have some of the items, but there's a lot of stuff you need if you really want to paint seriously. Of course, the items with the stars next to them are the only ones really necessary, the rest are just nice to have. The right paper's important, of course, and the quality of the colors."

"Oh yes, I'm sure they are."

"There's an art supply store I can recommend on Twenty-seventh Street. Ben Kellogg, the owner, really knows his stuff. If you ask for him and tell him you're a friend of mine taking a course, he can steer you toward the right equipment." Kevin took one of the sheets from her and wrote the address and the owner's name on the back.

At that moment, the phone rang and Kevin, seeming reluctant, turned to answer it. "Maybe I'll see you at the class next Wednesday."

"Oh yes," she sighed as he grabbed the phone and began a lengthy conversation. "You certainly will."

She found the art store and enlisted the assistance of the owner, who was more helpful when she casually announced that she was new to serious watercolor and needed start-up supplies. She listened to the man rattle on about Kordofan gum and oxgall and the differences between pan and tube watercolors. He regaled her with the advantages of small sable brushes and wider synthetic ones and, of course, she just had to have a short, flat boar bristle one. He spent almost half an hour discussing paper—single sheets, pads, and blocks—then helped her select charcoal and graphite drawing sticks and several thicknesses of pencils. By the time she had gathered only the "most basic" supplies she had spent more than two hundred dollars.

At home, Ellen unwrapped her purchases, opened a large sketch pad and sharpened a stick of charcoal on the sandpaper pad as she had been shown. With a few quick strokes she created the shape of a face with a short beard and piercing eyes. While it didn't really look like Kevin, it was obvious that she had him in mind. Three hours passed while she made drawing after drawing of men with beards and graceful hands.

Finally empty of ideas, she made herself a pot of macaroni and cheese and, bowl in hand, stretched out on the sofa with her feet on the coffee table. When she finished, she set the bowl down and closed her eyes.

She walked into Kevin's studio to begin her classes, but as she looked around at the garret-like room she discovered that she was alone. No other students this morning? She was sure he had said Wednesday.

Kevin emerged from a back room, dressed in a pair of khaki pants and a paint-splattered shirt, both hugging his muscular body. "I knew you'd be here."

"I c-c-came for class," Ellen whispered.

"No you didn't," Kevin said, taking her paint box from her shaking fingers. "You came for me."

Ellen gazed into his deep-blue eyes, unable to tear her gaze away.

"You came because you knew we'd be here alone, aching for each other. Tell me you knew." He held her upper arms in his steely grip. When she remained silent, he whispered again, "Tell me."

His lips were against her hair and she could feel the heat of him even through their clothes. Had she known? "Yes," she said, "I knew."

Ellen leaned against him and he enfolded her within his warmth and surrounded her with the manly scent of him. She lay her cheek against his chest, listening to the accelerated beat of his heart, deep and steady. "God, I want you," he said, the sound rumbling in his chest.

Ellen raised her hands until her palms lay splayed against his shirtfront. "And I want you."

His lips met hers in a searing kiss, one that flowed through her body like molten lava.

"Okay," Lucy said in the computer room, slamming her hand on the table, "I've had enough of her girlish romantic fantasies. They sound like every mushy novel ever written. Let's get real here. Life isn't like that. Love at first sight. I've been waiting for you." She made a rude noise. "God, it's such slop."

"Don't, Luce," Angela said, looking up from her screen. "Don't get involved in Ellen's fantasies. It's not nice."

"Nice. Pooh." She ran her blood-red nails through her long,

straight, black hair. "That woman is going to fantasize herself into heartbreak. She's got that man so tangled up in her dreams that she's bound to be disappointed. She's dreaming of him like he's some kind of paragon of manhood, handsome and sexy, a man who knows all the right moves. Next she'll be thinking about how he prowls like a jungle cat. What she needs is a real man and a real fantasy. Good, hot, sweaty sex with lots of hands and mouths, cocks and pussies."

"Lucy, really. Watch your language. My boss might be listening."

"He created great sex so why shouldn't we all enjoy it. The words are just ways of accelerating the heartbeat and arousing the libido."

Angela glared, but said nothing. "Now," Lucy said, tapping a nail against her front teeth. "I'll just create a real fantasy for Ellen and see how she likes it."

Angela sighed and shook her head, knowing that once Lucy got an idea into her head she couldn't or wouldn't be talked out of it. "Okay, where was she . . ."

Ellen stood in the warm garret with Kevin's arms around her, enjoying the beat of his heart. Suddenly he picked her up in his arms and carried her to the bed in the corner of the studio, then he began to unbutton his shirt. "What . . . ?" Ellen whispered.

"You know why you came. To be with me. Now we can do it all. Let's get naked."

Back in the computer room Angela snapped, "If you make her dream like that, you'll drive her schizo. If you want to change her fantasies, you have to be gentle and gradual. 'Let's get naked' indeed. Go easy or she'll bolt."

Lucy heaved a sigh. "Okay. I guess you're right. I just like to get right to the good stuff."

"Just a little push. Okay?"

"Right. Just a little push in the right direction."

"You know why you came to me. Let me love you the way you were meant to be loved."

"I want that, but I'm afraid."

"I would never hurt you," Kevin said. Then he cupped her face in his hands and brushed his mouth across hers. "I would never do anything you didn't want."

She let out a long breath. "I know," she purred, moving her face to taste his lips. She slid her hands up his chest and held his broad shoulders. "Yes, I know."

Then his hands stroked down her ribs and slipped beneath her sweater to caress her bare skin. Heat. Her skin burned with molten fire everywhere he touched. Lava flowed through her body, to her breasts, between her legs. She could barely breathe, barely think. She wanted to remember every moment of their time together but her mind was in a whirl trying to cope with the sensations bombarding her. His mouth opened and hers opened beneath it. Their tongues dueled, their bodies blending, pressing against each other.

His palms stroked heated paths up her sides to her back where he deftly unhooked her bra. His fingers traced an erotic path to her aching breasts. He plucked at her erect nipples, drawing feelings from her that she hadn't known she possessed. Quaking with need Ellen grabbed the back of Kevin's shirt and pulled it from his pants so she could slide beneath and touch his skin. Her hands wouldn't be still, touching, scratching, urging him on. She tangled her fingers in the heavy hair on his chest, finding and caressing his small nipples.

With a single motion, he pulled her sweater over her head, then dragged her bra off and tossed it in a corner. His eyes devoured her naked skin while he tugged off his shirt and pants. When he stood, naked, in the middle of the small room his arousal was obvious.

Ellen just stared. His nude body was gorgeous with wide shoulders and narrow hips. Her eyes devoured him, avoiding only the nest of dark hair that filled his groin. "Yes, look at me," he purred. "Look your fill, but I want to look at you, too."

He quickly unbuckled her belt and dragged her jeans off until she stood wearing only tiny white lace panties. "So beautiful," he said, his eyes telling her how gorgeous he thought she looked. He closed the small distance between them and held her close so that the entire length of him pressed against the entire length of her. She could feel his hardness against her belly.

"Okay," Lucy said, "It's time for them to get it on."

With one motion he grabbed the front of her panties and ripped them from her body. He cupped her buttocks and lifted her, fitting his mouth over hers, pulling her legs around his waist. The tip of his cock pressed against her opening and with one violent thrust he was inside of her. Still standing in the center of the room, his strong arms held her, raising and lowering her body so his cock slid deep inside, then withdrew. Over and over he fucked her until she was mad with it, holding his strong shoulders, grasping his hips with her legs.

With a roar of triumph, he lifted her so he could bite her erect nipple and, with the shard of pleasure/pain, she felt her body convulse around his cock. He lowered her to the floor, never leaving his place inside her, then pounded into her, driving his cock still deeper until, with a bellow, he came.

"Phew," Angela said. "You do create a great love scene, Luce."

"Love, shmove. It's good hot sex that counts." Lucy settled behind her desk. "You know, I think she's a candidate for Margaret Mary. It's about time Ellen learned about life and men and great sex, and Margaret Mary's just the woman who can do it."

"I have to agree but you know that she hates it when you call her Margaret Mary. It's Maggie and she's perfect for this job."

In her living room Ellen awoke with a start. She remembered the dream in vivid detail and her hands shook with the memories. She had never before had such an erotic one, so detailed. It was as if she could still feet the man's . . . the man's . . . well, feel the man inside of her. She touched the crotch of her jeans and found herself hot and damp. "Phew," she said. "That was some dream. I wonder where it came from."

"Probably from your subconscious," a woman's soft voice said.

Ellen jumped so suddenly that she almost fell off the sofa. She whirled around and saw a woman standing at the window, gazing out onto Fifty-second Street. She looked about fifty, with curly black hair and deep brown eyes. "I used to live around here, you know," she said. "It's such a great neighborhood."

"H-H-How did you get in here? Who the hell are you? Get out of my apartment!" Ellen was almost shrieking. Was she losing her mind?

"Actually I can't. I've been sent here to do a job and I really have to do it. It might mean the difference between Heaven and Hell for me."

"Out! Now! I don't care who you are or what you're here for. Out!" Ellen couldn't keep her voice from quaking, afraid she would burst into tears if the woman didn't leave.

"Relax and I'll explain. You're Ellen Harold and I'm Maggie Sullivan. I'm here to help you and once you understand all that we have to do, we'll get along just fine." She sighed. "It's always hardest at the beginning but you will get used to it. I promise." She twisted a strand of hair around her index finger. "Sit down and give me a few minutes to explain. Okay?"

Ellen made a supreme effort and controlled her voice. Sounding much calmer than she felt, she said, "No. I'm sorry but no. Whatever you're selling I don't want any. Whatever you're advocating, I'm against it. Just leave and we'll forget this little incident ever happened."

"I told you, I can't leave. I'm afraid I'm here to stay." She bustled to the tiny kitchen area and opened the miniature refrigerator. "Have you got any wine around here? I think we could both use a glass."

Chapter 3

Numbly, Ellen pointed to the cabinet over the sink. "There's a bottle of cabernet in there and the glasses are in the same cabinet." Why couldn't she get this person to leave? She stared at the woman called Maggie and tried to decide who or what she was. Dressed in a calf-length flowered-print skirt and a soft gauzy rose-colored blouse, she had warm, toast-brown eyes and an open face that at any other time Ellen would have trusted. Nevertheless, Ellen decided that in one more minute she'd have to call the cops and get this loony out of her apartment.

Maggie unscrewed the top from the wine bottle, half-filled two glasses and offered one to Ellen. "Don't call the cops just yet," she said. "Give me a few moments and I promise you'll understand. Really."

Ellen accepted the wine and took a swallow of the harsh red liquid. Maggie sipped and coughed. "Blah," she said. "You'd think that with all your money you wouldn't have to drink this sheep dip. I'll drink almost anything but this is almost too awful for me."

"Sheep dip?" Ellen said softly. "It's good red wine, and what the hell do you know about my money. Is this some kind of kidnapping? You want ransom?"

Ignoring Ellen's questions, Maggie said, "This is true sheep dip. It's overly tannic, lacks any real fruit and has a finish that tastes like furniture polish. And no, this isn't a kidnapping and there's no ransom."

Ellen just shook her head. The wine tasted like all the red wines she'd ever had. Even if it were bad she wouldn't let this woman have the satisfaction of showing it. "I think it's just fine." She took another large gulp.

"'Okay. Lessons on wine. That's on the list."

"What list?"

"Let me start at the beginning so you'll understand—well at least as much as I understand. But first, what's today's date?"

"Date?"

"Today's date. What is it?"

"It's September 28."

"What year?"

With no clue as to what was going on, Ellen answered, "1999."

"I've been dead for more than four years."

"Right, and I'm the tooth fairy. You know," Ellen said, "maybe you should sit down. Is there some relative I can call to come and pick you up?" *Where has this loony escaped from and how can I get her to voluntarily go back there? Soon. Now.*

"I'm dead. I don't know any other way of explaining it to you. Your reaction is really predictable and I can certainly understand your reluctance to accept me. Actually I've met several women in the last few years and each one of them has reacted the same way." She gazed into space. "I've got to think of a better way to break the news about myself. I'll have to think about that. Maybe in the future I should just say that I'm a fairy godmother." She returned her gaze to Ellen. "Any way you slice it, however, I'm a ghost, sent here to help you with your life."

"I don't need any help with my life, and I don't care whether you think you're Napoleon or Moses. It's time for you to leave." Ellen rose from the sofa and started toward the apartment door.

Maggie shrugged. "I told you I can't leave and, for the moment, neither can you, but you can give it a try. It might help clarify a few things." She motioned toward the door so Ellen crossed the room and turned the knob. Nothing happened. The knob turned beneath her hand as it was supposed to, but the latch didn't move. She pulled at the door but it wouldn't open. "Open this door!" she shouted.

"I can't. It's not under my control. We're stuck here until we understand each other."

"Okay. I'm calling the cops."

"That won't work either, but you're welcome to try. Go for it."

Ellen picked up the phone and heard the familiar dial tone, yet when she pushed the buttons, nothing happened. The dial tone continued as though she hadn't dialed at all. "Who set this all up? Are you here to rob me? You obviously know about the money so how much do you want?"

"I told you, I don't want money. I only want to help you."

Since the apartment was only on the second floor and overlooked a busy street she could shout for help. Ellen tried the window but, like the door, it wouldn't open. Maggie gracefully settled on the far end of the long sofa, spread her skirt around her, and sipped her wine, making an ugly face as she did so. "Now, can we talk?"

Ellen looked from the door to the window to the phone, then dropped onto the far end of the couch with her hand on the telephone. As soon as this was all ironed out she was calling the cops and that was that. "Okay, talk but just make it quick. And please, no 'I'm dead' stuff. I'm not that crazy yet."

"I am dead and there's no help for that. I died in 1995 of a sudden heart attack."

Just humor her, then she'll go away. "Okay, you're dead. I believe you." *Just let her talk until she's ready to get the hell out of here.*

"I can prove that part if you'll just come with me into the bathroom." When Maggie stood and walked toward the small bath Ellen reluctantly followed. Maggie directed her to stand in front of the mirror and Maggie positioned herself behind her. Ellen gazed into the mirror and saw her reflection clearly, but in the mirror she was alone. She turned and, sure enough, the woman stood just behind her shoulder, but, as Ellen's gaze returned to the mirror she was by herself. No Maggie, no wineglass, no nothing.

"I don't reflect," Maggie said, "because I'm dead. Only you can see or hear me."

Ellen stared, then turned several times to assure herself that the woman was right. Maggie didn't reflect. What the hell was going on? Ellen rubbed her forehead, now totally confused.

Together the two women walked back into the living room. "Okay. Let's say I believe that," Ellen said. *Although I don't.*

"I know you don't but you will, eventually. Let me try to explain a bit more. Before I died, I was a very high-priced call girl—or I guess you'd say a call woman in my case." They settled onto opposite ends of the sofa.

"A hooker?" *Sure, right. Fine. That tops it all. A dead prostitute. Right.*

"You know, I've learned to hate the word *hooker. I* was a wonderful woman who just happened to have sex for money. Some women will put out for dinner and a movie, I just took the cash."

"Well, that's a unique attitude," Ellen said her voice heavy with sarcasm.

"It's not unique at all. I merely entertained lonely men. We went to dinner, had great conversations, shared lots of laughs and ended up in bed together—actually in bed and other places. They gave me money because they enjoyed what we did together and wanted to reward me, compensate me for my time. It was just that simple."

Ellen looked a bit less incredulous as she said, "You make it sound like a lark. What about love and marriage?"

"Love is wonderful, don't get me wrong." Maggie uncrossed and recrossed her legs spreading her skirt artfully around her. "I have loved several men in my time but good hot sex has little to do with love with a capital *L.* It's loving of a different sort. I cared about my clients. I wanted to make them happy and they wanted the same for me. We cared about one another. That didn't mean, however, that we wanted to spend our lives together, walking hand in hand down the yellow brick road. A great roll in the hay on occasion was enough."

What the woman was saying seemed to make sense, somehow, at least for her. "Okay, okay. You don't need to get up on your soapbox. Whatever you did, you did, but that still doesn't answer the basic question. What the heck are you doing here? I certainly have no intention of becoming a hooker—sorry, call woman—so what's this all about?" Ellen listened to what she had just said. Had she really accepted that she was talking to the ghost of a dead prostitute?

"You're my latest case. Lucy and Angela sent me to try to wake you up to the possibilities in your life."

"I don't need any help, thank you. I'm doing just fine."

"If you're so fine, then why did you just have that long conversation with your sister?"

"How the hell . . . ?" Ellen saw the small smile on Maggie's face. "Okay, but I'm fine. Tell your friends to butt out!"

"Lucy and Angela don't butt out easily. They send me on assignment and I'm stuck until they decide I've done my job. If I don't complete my mission I have no idea what happens. Maybe I end up in Hell after all."

"End up in Hell?" Ellen tucked her legs beneath her and held her wineglass in front of her, almost as protection against what she was going to hear. "Okay, explain. I'm listening."

"Where to begin? More than four years ago, I had a fatal heart attack, after which I just appeared in the computer room." As Ellen started to interrupt, Maggie held up her hand. "Let me tell this in my own way. It's difficult enough to believe any way you slice it, but it's all true." Ellen's body relaxed.

"The computer room is the place where the 'up or down' decisions are made about everyone who dies. You understand, Heaven or Hell. Most cases are easy, I gather. Either Angela, she's an angel you understand, or Lucy, she's a representative of Lucifer, gets the poor slob and it's off to transportation. Then what? I've no idea.

"Anyway, they had a problem with me. I was a prostitute so by rights should have gone . . ." Maggie made a thumbs-down gesture. "However, I was a really good person, helping people sexually and other ways. I was kind to children and animals, well you get the idea. So Angela argued on my behalf as I sat there about as confused as you are now. Finally the two women decided on a test for me. They sent me down to earth to help a woman named Barbara to learn about her sexuality. Barbara blossomed, with my help of course, but in the end that didn't really make the decision for them. So Lucy and Angela decided to keep me on for a while as a consultant. They send me to earth from time to time to help someone." Maggie took a swallow of wine, and grimaced. "We really have to improve your taste in wine." She set the glass on the coffee table. "You are my latest assignment."

"Why me? What did I do to warrant this attention? Whatever it was, I want to undo it."

"Actually Lucy frequently plays the lottery, or plays with it, and she's particularly interested in winning numbers that add up to 66 like yours did."

"I'll bite. Why 66?"

"Second cousin to 666, the devil's number. When you won, she brought you up on her computer and thought you and I would get along well."

"She thought that I needed someone to tinker with my life? You can tell her that my life is just fine, thank you." Ellen cupped her hands around her mouth and faced the ceiling. "Listen, Lucy, Angela, take your minion and go," she called loudly. "Vamoose, scram. Find someone else to play with. I'm just fine."

"You're really not as fine as you could be. Your sex life is a mess and that's what I'm here to correct. Lucy told me about your fantasies."

Ellen bolted from the sofa. "They know my fantasies?"

"They know just about everything, and Lucy isn't a great fan of your dreams. She tweaked your last one, you know."

Ellen remembered the dream she was having right before Maggie's appearance. It had been different from her usual. Vastly different. Shit. "Shit!" She swallowed hard. "Sorry."

"Don't be. I've heard all those words before and sometimes they can add spice to your language."

"Assuming I believe all this, which I'm still not sure I do, I don't want you. I like my sex life the way it is. Just go away."

"You may not want me, but you need me, and I need you. I have a job to do and you're it."

"Okay, so what exactly is your job? What do I have to do to get you to go away?"

"It's really what *we* have to do. We have to help you understand about sex."

"I already understand about sex; my mother educated me just fine. I know about intercourse, condoms, the whole nine yards. What else is there?"

"Oh, my darling," Maggie said, "there's so much. As the Carpenters said, 'We've only just begun.' "

Ellen sighed. "I will admit that right now my sex life is a bit on the thin side, but that's bound to change in the near future."

"Thin?" Maggie stood and began to prowl the room. "Your sex life is non-existent and if you continue the way you're going it won't improve anytime during this millennium or the next. You're stuck in a sexless rut. You have a tiny opinion of yourself so you're defeated before you start. Your fantasies are unrealistic and you're constantly disappointed that the real world isn't like the one you imagine."

"Thanks," Ellen said dryly.

"It's the truth. You sit here with all the resources of the city spread in front of you, and enough money to enjoy them to the fullest." She stopped and focused on Ellen. "Look at this room. It looks like no one lives here. No plants, no pictures, no old magazines. No old anything. It's all sterile, as if you're just waiting to run back to your small town."

"I really don't want your opinion."

"I don't care what you want. I'm going to tell you a few things you need to hear. You're like a butterfly, too afraid of the outside world to come out. You peek out of your cocoon with a little periscope and you never *experience* anything."

"Oh, please. Really."

"That's you. Miss Sexual Underachiever of the Month—of the Decade. Now, however, you have the opportunity to change all that with me to help you every step of the way." She sat back down on the sofa and took Ellen's hand. "Be honest with yourself just this once. Wouldn't you like to be a bit more interesting to men? Wouldn't you like to have a few dates, go out for dinner occasionally, climb into bed with a horny guy and let him make you seriously crazy for an entire night? Doesn't that thought curl your toes?"

As Ellen started to give the standard answer, she looked into Maggie's eyes. If she were to be completely honest, what Maggie was suggesting sounded really good. She wanted to be attractive to men. She wanted a man to look at her the way Kevin had but not, as she accepted, because she was a potential client with an open wallet. She wanted a real sex life.

When she didn't respond, Maggie continued, "I thought so. I'm grateful that, at least inside your head, you're being honest." She reached over and held Ellen's hand tightly. "Let me do what I know how to do. It won't hurt and I won't make you do anything you don't want to do. I can help, really I can, with your looks, your clothes, but most of all with your attitude. Please."

Ellen sighed. She realized that she had accepted everything this woman said. Maggie was the spirit of a dead prostitute who had been sent to help her become a sex goddess.

"Not a sex goddess, just a woman who knows her own worth, in and out of bed."

Ellen expelled a long breath, then lifted her glass. "I guess I have nothing to lose."

Maggie picked up her wineglass and the two women touched rims. "To the future, and how we can improve it together." They sipped and Maggie made a face. "And here's to better wine."

Ellen sipped. "Better wine? Isn't this the way wine is supposed to taste?"

"Not on your life. Let me give you a demonstration of what we can achieve together."

Ellen's eyes brightened. This could be really good. "Are you going to zap up a bottle of something terrific?"

"I don't zap anything. Actually I've been after Lucy and Angela to give me the power, you know, like Michael Landon in *Highway to Heaven*, but so far, nothing." She looked at Ellen seriously. "What I meant was let's go to the wine store and buy something special. Then we can have a taste comparison and you'll see what you've been missing. Let's make that a symbol of what you've been missing in the rest of your life. It's getting late but in this neighborhood there's always an open liquor store."

With a great sigh, Ellen decided to go along with Maggie, at least for the moment. As they left the apartment, Ellen noticed that the door opened without any problem. She guessed that Lucy and Angela were satisfied that she wouldn't run away and spoil Maggie's plans.

A few minutes later the two women were inside a small neighborhood store. "Let's get something a bit pricey for our first try. Later I can teach you how to get a nice wine for under twenty dollars a bottle." Maggie puttered around the racks on the wall. "For now, however," she said, returning to Ellen's side, let's splurge."

"Okay. What should I get?"

"Are you talking to me?" A small man with a potbelly strode over, his balding head sweating slightly. Puffing, he said, "Can I help you with something?"

"I'd like a bottle of nice red wine," Ellen said. She turned to Maggie. "Did you see anything you liked?"

"I like everything we stock," the man said.

"Remember that he can't see me so he has no idea you're not talking to him," Maggie said. "Just let him suggest and I'll steer you to something sensational." She paused. "Tell him you need a really nice bottle of red wine for a really fancy dinner you're attending. Maybe a cabernet sauvignon."

Ellen repeated Maggie's words, stumbling slightly over the word *sauvignon.*

"Of course," the clerk said, obviously dubious about her knowledge of wine. "How about this?" He led her to a rack on one wall. "We have some nice Australian cabs, not quite as expensive as the really fine Californias. These are nice wines with good fruit and well within the average pocketbook."

"Nope," Maggie said. "Tell him you want a good California cab."

"Cab?" Ellen whispered.

"Short for cabernet," Maggie explained.

"Excuse me?" the clerk said, totally confused by Ellen's apparent talking to herself.

"I'd like a good California cab."

"Of course." He bustled to another area of the store and pulled out another bottle. "How about this?"

Maggie leaned over and read the label. "Not bad. Ask him whether he has a 1990. That was a superb year. It might be a bit over the hill, but I loved the nineties."

"Do you have a 1990? That was a superb year."

The clerk's body straightened. "Nothing quite that old, I'm afraid but some of the more recent vintages are just wonderful. I might have something you'd enjoy over here." He walked to a corner and touched a rack of bottles reverently. "These aren't cheap, but you should like them if you're looking for a really good cab. I can, of course, take you into the cellar in the back for the really fine wines."

Maggie gazed at the rack and grinned. She pointed to one bottle, a Mount Eden Estate Bottled cabernet. "Take that one."

Ellen looked at the price. "Fifty-five dollars?" she gasped.

"I told you it would be a bit high-priced," the clerk said. "I can certainly find something else. You can have the regular estate bottled, rather than the Old Vine Reserve. It's only thirty-five."

"Take the Old Vine," Maggie said.

Ellen looked doubtful but Maggie vehemently nodded. With a shrug Ellen pointed to the more expensive bottle and said, "Okay. I'll take this one."

A bit bemused at the double conversations, the clerk lifted the bottle and took it to the cash register. "Cash or credit?"

Ellen pulled out her credit card and handed it to the clerk. "You know," Ellen said to Maggie, "I'm not sure I have a corkscrew."

"I beg your pardon?" the clerk said.

Maggie pointed to a hanging display. "That one will do fine." Ellen pulled a deep red contraption off the rack and dropped it on the counter.

As the man turned to his credit-card reader, Ellen could hear him mutter, "She buys a fifty-five dollar bottle of wine and doesn't even have a corkscrew." She watched his head shake as the machine printed her receipt. It was all Ellen could do not to giggle.

Back in the apartment, Maggie withdrew the bottle from the brown paper bag and put it on the coffee table. With new glasses from the kitchen, she showed Ellen how to use the corkscrew and how to properly pour the wine. "At least you have the right glasses," Maggie said, holding the wine-filled glass up to the light.

"All this is such silliness: right glass, right year. Wine makers put the mystery in it so folks like me will spend a lot of money on the stuff, afraid to do something wrong."

"Not really. The shape of the glass is important for holding the nose properly. You grasp it by the stem so you don't change the temperature or get finger marks on the outside of the glass. A clean, clear glass helps you see the wine and enjoy the color." Maggie held the wine up to the light. "Look at that gorgeous baby."

Ellen looked. "Nice," she said, unimpressed.

"Okay. We'll get to color later. Do this." Maggie swirled the wine around the glass and Ellen did the same. "Now stick your nose in there and inhale."

"Wow," Ellen said as she breathed in. "It smells really nice."

Maggie smiled. "You only half fill the glass so you can swirl it and let the shape of the glass capture the aroma, the nose. I'm not going to bore you with a lesson on bouquet right now, I just want you to know there's more to wine than just the taste. Now take a small amount in your mouth, and try to gently inhale at the same time. Taste is mostly smell." She watched as Ellen tried to inhale and sip at the same time.

"Holy cow," Ellen said, relishing the exploding flavors in her mouth. "That's wonderful. I love it."

"I knew you would." She handed Ellen her glass from earlier. "Taste this now."

Ellen sipped the screw-cap wine that she and Maggie had been drinking and scrunched her face. "This really shouldn't be called the same stuff." She put that glass down and picked up the glass of the California cab, taking another sip. "I have to admit it. You were right."

"I'm right about a lot of things. Sex is the same as wine. The more you learn and the more you experience, the better it gets."

"I'm starting to believe you." Ellen sipped the wine, smiling as the tastes and smells bombarded her senses. "Maybe you do have something to teach me."

Maggie grinned. "I certainly do, and I'm beginning to think that I've got something pretty nice to work with." She touched the lip of her glass to Ellen's. "To new frontiers in wine and everything else."

For the first time Ellen felt excited about her future. "This might just be fun."

"It will be a blast."

"Where do we start?"

Maggie reached into the side pocket of her skirt. "I have—sorry, had—a good friend named CJ. He writes great erotic stories and records them on CDs." She withdrew a slender CD jewel case. "You need to understand what good sex is about, to expose yourself to new and exciting realities. I know that you've got a CD player so just relax and listen to the first one of these. Open your mind and pretend the woman is you."

Ellen took the CD and looked at it, puzzled. *Just After Midnight—A Collection of Erotic Stories by CJ Winterman. Read by the author.* "Erotic stories? Me? Why?"

"I think I told you about Barbara. She was the first woman I helped and I gave her some stories on CD too. She found that they really gave her a new look at sex. She learned that whatever people do that doesn't hurt anyone is okay. From your fantasies, I gather you've had very little experience."

"I wouldn't say that?" Ellen said, thinking that she actually would say that.

"Let's just say that I'd like to broaden your mental horizons before I try to broaden your physical ones. These stories are all about the power of magic to give us the freedom to do and say what we want. Listen to one or two a night, and see how you feel. I suggested that Barbara listen in the bathtub with a glass of wine, all nice and relaxed. You might find that some of the things the people do curl your toes, some things might not be your taste. Just understand what's out there so you learn what you want and what you don't. Then we'll take steps to try and get it for you."

"Why the title *Just After Midnight*?"

"At midnight people become a little bit more adventurous. The characters in the stories use magic to create adventure but in real life we sometimes need to push ourselves out of the nest and be daring, creating our own magic. With the right outlook it can be midnight at any time of the day."

"Okay. I'll listen to a story if you want me to." Ellen was surprised that in the space of a few hours she'd accepted Maggie and decided to take her advice. This was almost as much of an upheaval as winning the lottery. "I won't promise anything."

"Of course you won't and I don't expect you to. The stories are also great for communication. One woman I worked with played them for her boyfriend. They listened together and he was just as turned on as she was. They learned a lot about each other and their desires, too."

"I guess two people could exchange ideas that way without having to talk."

"You got it." She patted the hand that held the CD. "It's getting late and I've got to be going now. I don't know when I'll be back, it just sort of happens. The next time I see you, we'll have lots to do."

"There's one thing I need for you to do when you see those

friends of yours. Tell them to butt out of my fantasies. I want what goes on inside my head to be mine, and only mine."

"Point made." Maggie stared at the ceiling. "Hear that? I couldn't agree with Ellen more. If you're listening, ladies, you'd better have gotten the message. Let us handle all this. You two keep out!"

In the computer room Lucy covered her ears with the heels of her hands. "Don't yell. We hear you."

"So you'll leave Ellen's fantasies alone? She's got to grow at her own speed, without your interference. Do I have your promise?"

Lucy sighed. "I suppose, but it's such fun pushing her a bit."

"No pushing," Maggie's voice said. "Not even a little bit."

"Just make it snappy. I want to see progress soon."

"Lucy . . ." Maggie said, her voice rising.

"Okay. No pushing."

"And no asking Angela to do it for you."

"Shit," Lucy snapped, staring at Angela with a guilty expression on her face.

Grinning, Angela said, "She knows you too well, Luce."

"All right, Maggie. I'll leave her alone." She glared at Angela. "Don't call me Luce."

Maggie sighed, then said to Ellen, "Done. They got the message, loud and clear."

"See you tomorrow?"

"Lucy's getting impatient so I'm sure you will."

Ellen watched Maggie open the apartment door, walk through it, and just sort of disappear. Fade away. Slowly the door swung shut and Ellen collapsed on the sofa. Part of her brain was spinning, trying to put all the pieces of the preceding few hours together. Part of her couldn't grasp what had happened, yet another part already missed Maggie's comforting presence. This was all moving too quickly and Maggie had said that Lucy was already impatient. She glanced down and saw the CD still in her hand. What the hell. In for a penny . . .

Chapter 4

Wineglass in hand, Ellen wandered into the bathroom and turned on the taps in the tub. She set up a small, portable CD player that she'd brought from upstate on the toilet seat, poured some bath salts that Micki had given her last Christmas under the rushing water and watched bubbles rise up the sides of the tub. When the water was as high as it could get, she stripped off her clothes, put the CD in the player, and climbed into the hot bath. With a long sigh, she settled beneath the soothing water and sipped her drink.

Why am I hesitating? she asked herself. *Play the thing.* Yet she didn't press the play button. *I'm embarrassed*, she admitted to herself. *I've never read a dirty book or an erotic story before.* Hot scenes in contemporary novels had always excited her, but that was different. She wasn't reading those just for stimulation. And listening? It seemed so personal.

She sipped again, enjoying the slight buzz the wine was causing. Maggie was right about the wine, she thought, so maybe she was right about this. She reached for the player. She could always switch it off. She pressed the button.

"Just After Midnight—A Collection of Erotic Stories by CJ Winterman. Read by the author."

The voice was deep and rich and the music in the background reminded Ellen of saxophones on warm summer evenings. She rested her head against the back of the tub and closed her eyes.

"Is there magic in the world? Skeptics doubt that magic exists, or ever did exist. Are they right? I don't know, but there are still a few people who are willing to keep an open mind, people who believe in old stories, ancient legends, and possibilities. Like the possibilities inherent in the Elixir of Lust.

"Anthony was lost. He was utterly, completely, and totally lost. He had gotten out of the cab at what he thought was an intersection around the corner from his girlfriend's apartment, but as the taxi pulled away he realized that this wasn't the place he had thought it was. He turned, prepared to hail another cab, but there was not one in sight. As a matter of fact, there were almost no cars in sight either.

" 'Okay,' Anthony said out loud, 'I'll just have to find a phone and call a cab or a limo or whatever. Anything to get me to Elaine's in time for dinner.' Elaine was not usually in the best of moods when he was late for one of her infrequent home-cooked meals. 'Shit,' he hissed.

"He looked up and down the street for a store that might have a phone, but in this rundown area, who knew what you would find behind the shabby doors. Ultimately he selected one at random, between a dilapidated clothing store and a vacant lot. He peered through the grimy front window and saw a shape moving around inside. 'At least there's someone in there,' he mumbled. He gazed at the sign, letters in Magic Marker on a piece of dingy yellowed cardboard propped in the corner of the window. HARRY'S POTIONS AND NOSTRUMS. HARRY GAINES, PROP. *Another cardboard sign proclaimed* HOURS 10:00 A.M. TO 6:00 P.M. WEEKDAYS. Well, *Anthony thought gazing at his watch and seeing that it was just five to six, it ought to be open.*

"He pushed at the door and, as it swung slowly to admit him, a bell rang. 'I'm closed,' a scratchy voice called.

" 'It's not six yet,' Anthony said, 'and anyway I just want to use your phone.'

" 'Closed is closed,' the voice wheezed as a stooped, wizened old man emerged from behind the dusty counter. 'Sorry. Come back to-morrow.'

" 'I just want to use your phone to call a cab,' Anthony re-peated, this time more loudly.

" 'Phone's only for customers,' the man said, scratching his crotch through his baggy trousers.

" 'Please. I'll pay you for the use of the phone. I've got to get a cab. If I don't get one soon my ass is toast.'

" 'Toast?' the man wheezed.

"He needed this guy to let him use his phone so Anthony took a deep, calming breath. 'Please. My girlfriend will kill me if I'm late for dinner. She's cooking for me and she gets totally pissed if I'm not there on time.'

" 'Phone's for customers only,' the man repeated.

" 'Okay I'll buy something. What do you sell?' At this point it didn't matter much what the guy was selling as long as it meant that the man would allow him to use the phone.

" 'That's better,' the man said. 'I sell potions, powders, nos-trums, all kinds of things that people need. What do you need?'

" 'Need? How about a million dollars and a cab?'

"The man's laugh was brittle and ended in a spasm of cough-ing. 'A million dollars. That's a good one. You've got a good sense of humor, young man. Now tell me. What do you really need?'

" 'Right now I need to get a cab and a good story to explain to Elaine why I'm late.'

" 'Elaine's your girlfriend, right?'

" 'Going on three months now.'

" 'Do you love her? Does she love you?'

" 'I suppose.' Anthony had had enough of conversation. He would buy whatever the old man offered, within his price range of course. 'Now listen. What can I buy so that I can use the phone?'

" 'I suppose I could sell you a love potion.'

" 'Sure. Right. A love potion. If only it were that simple.'

" 'But it is that simple. I can sell you a love potion, or a lust potion, if you prefer.'

" 'A lust potion?' The old man had certainly gotten his attention with the phrase.

" 'That's what I said. Does that interest you?'

" 'How does this lust potion work?'

" 'The Elixir of Lust is really very straightforward. You put a drop on your finger and touch your girlfriend. Then she lusts after you.' He leaned closer, a wheezy laugh escaping from between his yellowed teeth. 'If you put a drop or two on her pussy, she'll go crazy.'

" 'How much?'

" 'Only twenty dollars for a small vial. Enough for many evenings of delight. In the future, the price might be a bit higher. When you realize the potential of the elixir of course.'

"Anthony was sure that the stuff couldn't possibly work, but if buying some would get the use of the phone, he would do it. 'I'll just take the twenty-dollar vial, and a phone.'

"Several minutes later when the cab was on the way, the man handed him a small vial of yellowish liquid with an old-fashioned cork closing the opening. 'Here's my card, too, young man. Even if you use the Elixir of Lust sparingly, and you should of course, you might want to order more at some point. Just call and I'll have some ready for you to pick up.'

" 'This will be fine,' Anthony said, seeing the cab pull up in front. He stuffed the vial and the business card in his jacket pocket and scurried out.

" 'I can't believe you're late,' Elaine whined as Anthony walked into her kitchen. 'After all the time I took making this lasagna and now it's cold.'

" 'You can put it in the oven and reheat it. I'm sure it will be wonderful.' He reached out to hug her but she twisted away.

" 'It's ruined,' she moaned. 'Ruined.'

" 'Please, baby. Just try.' Anthony picked up the casserole dish and almost burned his hands. 'It's still hot. I think we can just eat

it the way it is.' He leaned over the dish and gave an exaggerated sniff 'It smells sensational.'

" 'The bread will be overdone.'

"Anthony sighed and wondered whether it was all worth it, but when he thought about being alone, no sex, no female company, he swallowed hard. It had been difficult to get Elaine to go out with him in the first place. He was twenty-six and, since he wasn't good with women, she was his first real, steady girlfriend. 'Come on, darling, I know it will be great.'

"She pouted prettily and consented to join him at the small table in her kitchen. They talked pleasantly over lasagna and bread, both wonderfully cooked despite the delay, and sipped some delicious Chianti.

"Later, as they sat on the sofa watching a video, Anthony thought about the small bottle in his jacket pocket. It had cost him twenty bucks. Maybe it would do something. He headed for the bathroom and, on the way back to the TV, got the vial and slipped it into the pocket of his jeans.

"The movie was a sad love story, and, while Anthony found himself bored, Elaine was paying close attention, dabbing her eyes with a tissue. With as little movement as possible, he withdrew and uncorked the tiny bottle, pressed his finger over the opening and tipped the vial. The yellowish oily liquid coated a small area on the pad of his index finger. He put his arm around Elaine.

" 'Come on, baby,' she said. 'This is the best part of the film.'

"He touched the oil to the side of Elaine's neck and stroked his finger down her white skin. When nothing happened immediately Anthony wasn't surprised. Chalk it all up to getting here almost on time and making Elaine happy. Twenty bucks wasn't too high a price to pay.

"For several minutes Anthony merely stared at the TV, bored to tears. "Baby,' Elaine said suddenly, 'why don't you pay attention to me instead of the movie?'

"Surprised by her sudden shift, Anthony said, 'I thought you were enjoying the film.'

"Elaine's head dropped back onto Anthony's arm. 'Not as

much as I would enjoy you,' she purred, turning her lips toward his mouth.

"Anthony leaned over to place a gentle kiss on his girlfriend's pursed lips and, as their mouths touched, Elaine reached out, cupped the back of his head and dragged him closer. She held his head tightly against hers, pressing her tongue between his lips. 'Mmm,' she purred, changing the angle of the kiss to better fit her mouth against his.

"Anthony was stunned. Elaine was usually passive, pliant, willing, but never the aggressor in matters of sex. Tonight, however, she was devouring him. She moved so she was straddling his lap, her hands tugging at his shirt. Could it be the Elixir of Lust? Anthony wondered. Could the stuff really work? What a blast!

"Anthony thought little more about it. Reveling in Elaine's newfound aggression, he tore at her clothes as she dragged his belt from its loops. Soon they were naked, Elaine climbing all over him in an effort to get closer. She pressed his hands to her breasts, then urged him to tweak her nipples. With her head thrown back and her chest pushing against his hands, she panted like an animal in heat.

"Anthony's cock reacted predictably, growing and hardening with Elaine's every movement. As she prepared to mount him he remembered what the wheezy old man had said. 'Put a drop or two on her pussy, she'll go crazy.' He found the vial in his pants pocket and put another drop of the oily liquid on his finger. Then he rubbed his finger over her swollen pussy-flesh, pushing it into her channel.

" 'More,' she screamed. 'Fill me up. Fuck me with your fingers. Do it!' Frantically she bucked against Anthony's hand as he drove two, then three fingers into her. Almost incoherent with lust, she grabbed his wrist, pulled his fingers from her pussy and plunged downward onto his erect shaft. Over and over she raised her hips, then dove onto his pole. Knowing this couldn't last, Anthony thrust upward, meeting her every movement. It was only moments until he erupted, spurting jism deep into her pussy.

"As he panted, he watched Elaine eagerly rub her clit, finally succeeding in bringing herself to a climax of earth-shattering pro-

portions. Together they collapsed onto the sofa and lay there long minutes until their breathing finally calmed. 'Holy mackerel,' Elaine said, stroking his chest, 'I have no idea what came over me, but that was incredible.'

" *'It certainly was,' Anthony said. 'Magnificent.'*

"*Later that evening, home in bed, Anthony relived the entire experience. It must have been the elixir, he realized. It was difficult to accept but the stuff must have worked, and when he put a drop on her cunt, well she nearly exploded. He found his cock getting hard just thinking about it. I wonder. . . .*

"*He climbed out of bed and fetched the small vial from his pocket. As he lay back down he uncorked the bottle and again coated his finger. Then he touched the oil to his cock, stroking it along its length.*

"*The effect was almost instantaneous. Brilliant colors filled his vision. Images of naked women playing with their breasts, tempting him with hugely erect nipples. Pussies of all sizes and shapes, some shaven, some thick with curly pussy hair, thrust toward him, dripping with juices. Fingers stroked the wetness and then coated his lips with it.*

"*He could feel hands all over his body, stroking his toes, his calves, under his arms, between his fingers. Mouths kissed and licked every inch of his body. A tongue—no, several tongues—licked the length of his erection. A hot, wet mouth enveloped his cock, taking the length of it into a dark wet world of erotic sensation.*

"*Without realizing he was doing it, Anthony wrapped his hand around his cock and stroked the length of his shaft. He cupped his balls with the other hand and closed his eyes to better enjoy all the sensations at once. In only moments he came, wads of thick come splashing onto his belly, then he felt nothing more until morning.*

"*As he slowly awoke he recalled the previous evening in detail. One drop on his cock and he had had the best orgasm of his life. Over the next few weeks, he saw Elaine several times, but the frequency diminished. Every night he used the Elixir of Lust on his own cock and found that he didn't need Elaine or anyone else. His fantasies and the yellow oil were enough.*

"Finally one evening he took out the vial and realized that it was just about empty. He stared at it, rubbing his pinky around the inside to retrieve the last remnants for that evening. Tomorrow, he reasoned, he'd call the man and order more.

"The following morning he searched for the business card the old man had handed him. He'd washed the jeans he'd been wearing that day several times since then and the card was nowhere to be found. He turned his room upside down. No card. He even called Elaine and asked her whether the small white card might have fallen out of his pocket, but she hung up on him. He tried the yellow pages and the phone company but got nowhere. He got a cab and roamed the area around Elaine's house looking for the shabby old doorway with no success.

"That was many years ago. It is said that on any given afternoon a now-aged man named Anthony can still be found asking everyone on the street whether they'd ever seen a store called Harry's Potions and Nostrums. Good luck, Anthony.

Ellen roused herself from the stupor she had fallen into and pushed the stop button on the CD player. With little hesitation she slid her hand down her belly and through the hair beyond. As she found the slippery folds of her pussy, she thought about the story she'd just heard. If she were to be as honest with herself she would have to admit that her fingers felt good rubbing her clit. Faster and faster she rubbed, circling her clit and sliding over her juicy flesh, feeling the difference between the water and the fluids that flowed from her body.

"Oh, God," she moaned as her pleasure grew. Her breathing quickened, her heart pounded and she wanted. For the first time she slipped one finger into her channel and, as her orgasm washed over her she could feel the pulses of her pussy with her inserted finger. "Oh, God."

She lay in the tub for several more minutes before climbing out, drying herself with a small white bath towel and sliding into bed. She fell into a dreamless sleep.

The following morning Ellen awoke, her mind already churning. Maggie. What did the ghost really want from her? Did Ellen want great sex? Of course she did, but what did the phrase *great sex* mean to her? She realized immediately that she had no idea. She wasn't a virgin. She and Gerry Swinburn had had a sexual relationship for almost a year before he moved to New York. It had been all right. After all it had been her first, and up to now only, sexual experience. They had gradually moved from heavy petting to each rubbing the other to climax to actual intercourse in her parents' living room while they were away. She and Gerry had never spent the night together although they had planned to move in together before his defection.

What did she know about good sex, or even mediocre sex? Did she want to know about all the variations on plain old intercourse? Ellen stretched out beneath the covers and smiled. Yes. She did. Now that she had the opportunity, she accepted that she wanted to know it all. She wanted to enjoy the company of men, in and out of bed. She wanted to feel attractive, like the well put together women she passed on the street each day. She wanted to look sophisticated, classy, like she knew the secrets of the world. She wanted to know those secrets.

Ellen wriggled against the cool sheets and realized that she was naked. The previous evening after her bath she hadn't stopped to put on pajamas, and being naked felt wonderful. Her body felt wonderful, satisfied yet hungry for more. She climbed out of bed and padded into the bathroom, closed the door, and gazed at herself in the full-length mirror. Not bad, she thought. She was a bit overweight with flesh covering her bones and softening her shape but she didn't look flabby. Face? Well, there wasn't anything there that made her cringe.

No. It wasn't her looks that were the problem. A little help with wardrobe and such and her body would pass muster. It was her mind that, as yet, wouldn't get her anywhere in the land of the sexually knowledgeable. She needed an education.

She grabbed the CD player, still sitting on the toilet seat, set it up on her bedside table and climbed back between the sheets. She pressed the play button and the familiar voice began.

"Is there magic in the world? Skeptics doubt that magic exists, or ever did exist. Are they right? I don't know, but there are still a few people who are willing to keep an open mind, people who believe in old stories, ancient legends, and possibilities. Like the possibilities inherent in the Wine of Willingness.

"The bottle was on the bottom shelf of the wine store, covered with dust. Leslie didn't know what teased at her, but she bent down and pulled the heavy bottle from its cubbyhole. 'Hey, Darryn,' she said, 'how about this one for tonight?'

"Her husband came up beside her and looked at the old bottle in her hand. 'The Wine of Willingness. What a name! I've never heard of it. It's got no year, no appellation, no nothing. What made you pick that one?'

" 'I haven't a clue,' Leslie said, 'but it seemed to draw me over.' She rubbed the grime from the back label. HE WHO DRINKS THIS WILL BE ABLE TO ENJOY PLEASURES BEYOND HIS WILDEST DREAMS, *she read. 'Wow. That's quite a promise.' She grinned at her husband. 'Let's give it a try. What have we got to lose?'*

" 'I'll tell you what we have to lose. This is obviously someone's idea of a kinky game, maybe a gimmick to sell wine. It's probably overpriced swill.' He took the bottle from Leslie's hands and walked to the counter. 'How much?'

"The clerk looked the bottle over for the bar code but found none. 'This must be private stock. Let me look the price up for you.' Moments later, after flipping through pages in a large notebook, he said, 'Wine of Willingness. Strange name and I've never seen a bottle before.' He continued to flip pages. 'Ahh. Here it is.' He stared. 'I don't get this price. The book says that any couple, and it specifies a couple, who wants a bottle of the Wine of Willingness gets it for nothing. This is really odd but if that's what it says, that's what you get.' He looked at Leslie. 'You his lady?'

" 'Yes,' she said.

" 'Well then, I guess there's no charge.'

" 'Free?' they said in unison.

"The clerk turned the book so Darryn and Leslie could read the

entry. WINE OF WILLINGNESS. ANY COUPLE WHO BRINGS YOU A BOTTLE SHALL BE TOLD THAT IT'S FREE. IT CANNOT, HOWEVER, BE SOLD TO AN UNACCOMPANIED PERSON. *'Do you want to take it?' the clerk asked.*

" 'For nothing? Sure. Why not?'

"The clerk slipped the wine into a bag and, totally confused, Darryn and Leslie took it home. As they finished preparing dinner, Darryn took out the wine opener. 'I feel like I stole this,' he said.

" 'I know. That was so weird.'

"Darryn looked over the label, then rubbed off more grime. 'Wait, it says more.' He read the words, almost obscured by the discolored paper. SIP THIS WINE TOGETHER AND THEN EXPRESS YOUR FONDEST WISH. THE WINE OF WILLINGNESS WILL DO THE REST. *This is really nuts.'*

" 'As long as the stuff's not too awful what the heck.'

"Darryn uncorked the wine and poured two glasses. The liquid was deep ruby red and almost seemed to glow from the depths of the glass. 'It looks wonderful,' Darryn said. He placed the glass near his nose and inhaled. 'Wow. It's got a bouquet that won't quit. Fruit, flowers, everything. I hope it tastes as good as the nose.'

"Leslie took her glass, appreciated the color, then breathed in the deep aroma. 'That's fantastic.' She sipped. 'This is a find, a wonderful full flavor, with so much of everything, earth, fruit, I even taste blackberries and, well, everything.'

"Darryn sipped. 'This is some of the best wine I've ever tasted.'

"Throughout dinner they drank until the bottle was almost empty. Giggling, they stacked the dishes in the sink and walked into the living room, ready to watch TV. 'You know,' Leslie said, 'the bottle said we should each tell our fondest wish.'

" 'That's silly,' Darryn said. 'My fondest wish was that the wine wasn't lousy, and it wasn't. That's that.'

" 'Don't be such a slug,' Leslie chided. 'What's your fondest wish? Really.'

"Darryn settled on the sofa and draped his arm around his wife's shoulders. 'I wish I could make mad, passionate love to you right here and now.'

" '*Why couldn't you?' Leslie had always been a bedroom person, but tonight, with a buzz from the wine, it seemed just fine to do it here in the living room. 'Would you like to make love here on the sofa?'*

"*Darryn's eyes widened. 'Oh, baby. I've always wanted to love you in every room of the house.'*

"*Leslie's mind was filled with possibilities. It all sounded so wonderful. 'I never thought about the kitchen, but why not? Sounds deliciously kinky.'*

" '*Would you take off your clothes? Right here and now?'*

" '*Sure. Would you like to watch?'*

"Shit, *Darryn thought,* this isn't happening. My prim, conservative little wife is volunteering? *'Would you strip for me?'*

" '*That sounds perfect.' She stood up, moved the coffee table out of the way, then tuned the radio to a station that specialized in music from the seventies. She started to move her hips to a disco beat, bumping and grinding to the heavy percussion. Her eyes closed, she swayed, slowly unbuttoning her shirt.*

" '*Oh, baby,' Darryn said. 'Go with it.'*

" '*Of course,' she sighed, dragging her shirttails from her jeans. She pulled it off and swung it by one sleeve, windmilling it around until it flew through the air and landed in Darryn's lap. At an agonizingly leisurely pace, she pulled off her shoes, socks, and jeans. Prancing around the living room in only her white cotton bra and panties, she danced to the rhythm. When the song ended she stopped and stared at her husband. 'Do you like me?'*

" '*Oh, God, yes,' he said, unable to believe what he was seeing. His cock was straining at the crotch of his jeans, but he sat still, not wanting to endanger his wife's mood. 'You're so sexy.'*

"*Leslie stood between his knees, bent down, and grabbed his erection through his pants. 'Hmm. You certainly do think so. Now it's your turn. You can strip for me.'*

" '*Strip? Men don't strip.'* Well, why not? *Darryn thought.* If it makes her as hot as it makes me, what the heck. *As Leslie settled on the couch, Darryn slowly stood and listened to the disco beat of the new song on the radio. He had always hated dancing, but this wasn't dancing exactly; he was putting on a show like those*

Chippendale guys. He wiggled his hips and was rewarded with a heated gaze from his wife. He turned and let her watch him move his ass, bending over so he could look at her between his spread legs. While his back was to her, he opened his shirt and pulled it off.

"As he turned around, she yelled, 'Go for it, hunk.'

"Hunk. Yeah! He mimicked thrusting, driving his hips forward, watching his wife's eyes riveted on his crotch. He quickly pulled off his shoes and socks, then danced around the living room, curling his toes in the carpeting. Why hadn't he noticed before what a sensual thing carpeting was? He danced his way to the couch and pulled Leslie to her feet, pressing his crotch against her mound. Together they sinuously rubbed their bodies together, getting hotter and hotter.

"Do it in every room of the house, *Darryn thought. He danced his wife into the kitchen and, with the disco beat pounding in his head, he lifted her onto the counter, pushing canisters and small appliances out of his way. He quickly draped her legs over his shoulders until she was totally open to him with only her white panties covering her.*

"He rubbed his finger over her already damp and hot mound, listening to the small cooing noises she made. He watched her close her eyes and let her head drop backward. Darryn spied a jar of jam on the counter and unscrewed the top. Pulling one of Leslie's bra cups to one side, he coated her areola with thick strawberry preserves. As Leslie looked on in amazement, Darryn's long tongue found her, slowly lapping at her erect nipple.

"With one swift motion, Leslie removed her bra and scooped a large dollop of jam onto her finger, using it to coat her other nipple. Darryn feasted on his wife's body, spreading jam and licking until he was ready to rip her panties off and take her right on the counter.

" 'Not yet,' Leslie said, sliding down. She patted the counter and, with a lift of his hip, Darryn slid onto it. Quickly Leslie removed the rest of Darryn's clothes and coated his raging hard-on with jam. As Darryn watched she slowly drew his strawberry-flavored cock into her mouth. Darryn was in heaven, delighted and amazed at his wife's willingness to take him orally, as he'd always

wanted her to. As his mind blurred, the phrase the Wine of Willingness *whirled in his head.*

"With a motion of her head, Leslie urged Darryn from the counter. 'Every room,' she purred. She grabbed his hand, dragged him into the dining room and stretched out on her back on the dining room table. 'Here too,' she growled.

"Darryn realized that the table was just the right height for his cock so he pulled Leslie to the edge, yanked off her panties and plunged his still-sticky cock into her soaked pussy. As he slammed into her, he had to grip her hips to keep her from sliding across the table. 'Yes, yes, yes!' she screamed, louder and louder. 'More! Fuck me! Fuck me hard, now!'

"Darryn kept pounding into her, spurred on by her screams and the needs of his body. Over and over he rammed his cock into her sweet pussy until he could no longer control his body. 'I can't stop it!' he cried and, with a final plunge of his hips, he poured semen deep into his wife.

"She didn't come, *Darryn thought as his cock slowly withdrew from his wife's body. 'Do what you need,' he growled. With little hesitation his prim little wife reached between her legs and rubbed her beautiful snatch with her long fingers until, only moments later she slammed her elbows into the table, almost lifting herself off the surface. 'Yes! Oh, God, yes! Now!'*

"Later, curled beside his wife in bed, Darryn said, 'I don't know what came over us, but it was fantastic. Maybe the Wine of Willingness had something to do with it.'

" 'It's too bad we don't have anymore,' Leslie said, sleepily.

" 'If we agree to be honest with each other, and as free as we were tonight, maybe we don't need any more magic wine.'

" 'We should make a pact. Every bottle of wine will be like the Wine of Willingness.'

" 'And every glass of water, too,' Darryn said and Leslie giggled as they fell asleep."

Chapter 5

When Maggie arrived in Ellen's living room an hour later, Maggie was wearing a royal purple silk shirt and a pair of off-white leans. She had covered the shirt with a white fringed vest and she wore matching cowboy boots.

"You look great," Ellen said, gazing down at her Mickey Mouse sweatshirt, black jeans, and sneakers. "I wish I had your flair for clothes."

"Actually I'm not sure where my clothes come from. They just show up in a dressing room right before I arrive here. I've been doing this for months and I still don't have any idea of how it all works. How was your evening?"

"I listened to the first two stories on the CD and I think I understand what you've been trying to tell me." One of Maggie's dark brows lifted. "I guess I want to find out what's out there," Ellen continued. "I want to date, have some fun, enjoy what life has to offer."

Maggie's grin lit her face. "Your speech is still filled with 'I guess' and 'I think' but so far so good. You're learning that everyone has the right to good things, including great sex, and that sometimes it's necessary to go and get it."

"I think I'm ready to give it a try. Where do we start?"

Maggie gave Ellen a critical once-over. "Clothes, I think, and maybe some time at a salon I know of. Manicure, pedicure, hair, makeup, the works."

"You know, I still catch myself wondering whether I can afford something like that. I guess I'm not used to having the money to do selfish things."

"What I'm suggesting isn't selfish. It's a necessary part of becoming someone new and different. I worked with a woman who didn't have much money. Her makeover consisted of a home permanent with a little new color added, a magazine article on makeup, and a trip to Wal-Mart for cosmetics. We added a new scent, a few inexpensive clothes, and voila. You don't need money."

"I understand, and I do need to feel good about myself and about where I fit. I guess I'm ready. Let's do it."

"What time is it? I can't wear a watch since time has little significance to me." When Ellen looked puzzled, Maggie continued, "Time is a relative thing. For example, it feels to me as if I just left you moments ago, but I know I've got new clothes and, since the sun's shining, I assume that it's morning now. The time in between just seems to disappear. Actually it could be a morning several months after the evening I gave you the CD. I'd never know the difference."

"So how do you know when to arrive? Or do Lucy and Angela make those decisions."

Maggie's brown eyes gazed upward. "Oh, they're in charge all right and they make the decisions. The other women I've worked with tell me that I seem to show up just when I'm needed."

Ellen didn't know whether it was bad manners to probe too deeply, but her curiosity had gotten the better of her and Maggie seemed willing to answer questions. "Where do you go when you leave here?"

Maggie seemed confused. "I've no idea. Sort of nowhere, I guess. I don't age, my nails and hair don't grow." She ran her fingers through her dark curls. "I don't even need a touch-up. I seem to look the same and feel the same as I did when I . . . died."

Died. Ellen still had a difficult time absorbing the fact that this woman, who seemed more alive than most of the people she knew, was really dead. "When was that?"

"In July of 1995 I had a heart attack in my sleep. All very painless. I went to bed one night and woke up in the computer room with Angela and Lucy."

Ellen glanced at her watch. "It's only eight-thirty. Want coffee? I know you drink wine, but do you eat? I don't usually have breakfast but I can see what I've got if you're hungry."

"Coffee would be nice but I don't usually eat. Sometimes I get hungry or thirsty but most of the time it's sort of nothingness in my stomach."

In the kitchen, Ellen put ground coffee into the top of the maker and poured in cold water. She sat at the tiny table with Maggie across from her. "What's it like? Being dead, I mean."

Maggie propped her elbows on the table. "For me, except for some of the logistics, it's not too different from being alive. I've had some great experiences and met some wonderful people. Strangely enough I enjoy what I'm doing."

Ellen had no concept of what it would be like to be dead and to be bounced around in time the way Maggie was. "Do you mind me asking all these questions? It's just so foreign to me."

"I don't mind. I've asked a few myself and I have to tell you that Lucy and Angela aren't long on sensible answers."

Ellen couldn't suppress a grin. "I'll bet. Tell me about the others you've helped. Without violating confidences, I mean."

Maggie leaned back and stretched her legs beneath the table. "Barbara Enright was the first. She was a wonderful woman, as they all were really. Each one merely needed someone to open them up to the possibilities of good sex, to help them feel good about themselves."

"I feel good about myself," Ellen protested.

"You're a bit different. It's more your outlook. You need to learn to get out there and do things rather than peeking out at the world. You need to get your feet wet, then to soak the rest of you. Dive in. Give things a try."

"I try things," Ellen protested. "I came to the city, didn't I?"

"You came to New York City at the insistence of your sister but once you got here you did nothing to fit in."

"I did lots of things," Ellen snapped. "I've visited most of the places in the city that Micki told me are worthwhile. Museums, art galleries, the top of the World Trade Center, St. Patrick's. I've been everywhere."

"I know you think you have, but did you try anything new, just for you?" Maggie leaned forward and her eyes locked with Ellen's. "Have you been anywhere that Micki didn't suggest? Have you done anything really different, gone to the zoo, Coney Island, or the Bronx Botanical Garden? Have you considered taking a cruise? Visiting Tokyo? Have you tasted sushi? Have you had a massage? Have you bought anything to make this apartment more than a nomad camp? Have you ever done anything daring just because you were curious?"

Ellen sat up straight. "Maybe not, but I like just looking."

"Looking's fine for a while, but now it's time for tasting. Since I know about sex and men, I'm hoping that will be the vehicle to pull you from visiting to living."

"What does sex have to do with living?" When Maggie just raised an eyebrow, Ellen continued, "You know what I mean."

"I'm afraid I do. If I were going to color your world right now I'd have to use pastels. Now it's time for emerald and scarlet, indigo and marigold. Let's be honest. Even your fantasies are insipid, wimpy. What do you really want out of life? Lucy and Angela seem to think they know, but do you?"

Ellen considered. "I always thought I was satisfied with my life. When I won the lottery I thought I'd just do more of what I've always done."

"I know but there's so much more to life than what you've always had. Don't you want to at least sample some of what's out there?"

Ellen slowly settled back in her chair. "You mean like taking that art class."

"You did that at Micki's suggestion but it's a start, a small step in the right direction." Maggie grasped Ellen's hand. "You don't have to dive in, but you're thirty-two. It's time for getting your feet wet in the immense ocean of what there is."

"If you say so."

"No, not because I say so, because you're curious and because you're feeling just a little bit braver than you did yesterday."

"That little old chicken, me."

"You don't have to do everything at once, and I'll be there to hold your hand, figuratively, if not literally."

"Maybe you're right. Maybe it's time to live a little." She held her thumb and index finger about a half an inch apart. "Just a little to start."

"That's fine. We'll take it just a bit at a time and I'll help all I can."

"Thanks. Will that be enough for you? Enough to make Lucy and Angela happy?"

"Forget about all of us. This is your life, as Ralph Edwards used to say. We're just here to give it a little kick."

"That sounds okay. May I ask you a personal question?"

"Sure. Shoot."

"How did you start? Being a call girl, I mean." She gulped. "I'm sorry. I mean . . ."

Maggie's eyes held nothing but warmth. "Stop falling over your words. They're only words. I was a hooker. I had sex with men for money and I enjoyed it."

"But prostitution . . ."

"Prostitution is such a charged word with all kinds of overtones. Let's just say this. I loved good sex, and so did most of the men I was with."

"Most of the men?"

"You know it's interesting. Some wanted companionship, someone to be with and there wasn't any sex at all. Just a nice decoration for a party or dinner or someone to talk to who had no other issues."

"No sex at all?"

"There were a few times like that when some longtime client

just wanted to be with someone who didn't want anything from him." Her impish grin brought a smile to Ellen's face. "Of course there were others who wanted something unusual, something they couldn't get with anyone they didn't pay. Something fun and kinky."

"I guess you had to do all kinds of kinky stuff."

"I did, and I had a heck of a lot of fun too. If it's not fun for both parties, it's not fun for either."

"Weren't there men who just wanted to, well, fuck." Heat rose in Ellen's face at the use of such a four-letter word.

"If they just wanted to insert tab A into slot B they didn't have to pay my kind of money. A clean, hundred-dollar-an-hour call girl would do the trick."

"You charged more?" Ellen said, her eyes wide.

"Lots more. I charged between seven hundred and a thousand dollars a night."

"Phew. I never imagined. Were any of the men you were with married?"

"Of course. Many were. Most of the married men I spent time with thought their wives wouldn't want to do the things we did together. I think they were probably wrong, but after one or two protests that they should communicate their desires with their spouses, I gave up and we played."

"You think their wives would have been interested in kinky games?"

"Sure, why not? Listen, we've got to get a few things straight if we're going to have fun learning together. Your expression tells it all." Ellen became aware that her face was registering her disbelief and her distaste. Maggie squeezed her hands. "Listen and try to open your mind. There are many ways to share good sex, ones you've probably never even considered: oral sex, anal sex, toys, bondage. If two consenting adults want to do it upside down, hanging from the crossbar of the kids' swing set, what's wrong with that?"

Ellen sighed. "I guess."

Maggie stood and took two mugs from the counter and filled them with strong coffee. She inhaled. "I love the smell of freshly brewed coffee. What do you take? Milk? Sugar?"

"Black's fine."

"Me, too." Maggie brought the cups to the table and sat back down. "You're limited by the fact that you've never had mind-altering, toe-curling, fan-flippin'-tastic sex."

"Hey, now, wait."

"It's true, whether you admit it or not."

"I've had sex."

"I know. With that Gerry character. He was a nice guy but a lightweight."

"You know about Gerry?"

"I know everything about you." When Ellen started to respond, Maggie held up her hand. "Almost everything, and I'm sorry that Angela and Lucy pry. It's just their way." She sipped the hot brew. "I don't mean mediocre sex with Gerry, nice as he was. I mean climaxes when you've screamed, begged for more, literally felt like your orgasm should have registered on the Richter scale. When you've felt like it would go on forever, but it was over in an instant, then we'll talk about what's kinky."

"I'm sorry." She thought about Gerry. The sex with him had been fine. Comfortable.

"Comfortable. Right. A mediocre experience at best."

"I wish you'd stop reading my mind."

Maggie looked contrite. "My turn to be sorry. I don't really read your mind, it's just that some of your thoughts are so loud I can hear them. Think about it. Comfortable sex. Sweatshirts and old slippers are comfortable. Sex should be more than just satisfying."

"Was your sex always . . . how did you put it? Mind-altering and toe-curling?"

"Of course not. I don't mean that it has to be earth-shattering every time, but at least now and then it should make you scream. Mine? Well sometimes it was wonderful. Sometimes it was what my friends—I always liked that word better than clients or customers—wanted and I had to get my pleasure from their pleasure."

"What was the best one?"

Maggie sighed. "That's a really tough question. So many of my friends were wonderful and enjoyed our mutual pleasure. We did things that blew all of our socks off."

Ellen giggled. "Sounds wonderful. Your worst?"

"A few times I had to give a man his money back because I wouldn't do what he wanted."

"Like?"

"I'm not into pain. Whips and things."

Ellen's lip curled. "That's disgusting anyway."

"No, it's not. It's terribly exciting for many people and for them it's a sexual turn-on. It's just not one for me and I decided early on that I wouldn't do things just for money."

Ellen tried to wrap her mind around people wanting to be whipped. "You wouldn't hit someone if they wanted it?"

"Oh, the occasional slap on the ass is great. It adds a touch of a different kind of spice. I just couldn't go further. Or, rather, I didn't want to."

"You never did anything you didn't want to do?"

Maggie twirled a strand of black, curly hair around her finger as she considered. "I never needed money that badly. I guess I was pretty fortunate."

"Did you ever get into trouble with the law?"

"No, I never did. I was on my own, no partners, no pimp. I didn't need anyone else, I had great word of mouth. And I didn't get into situations I had the slightest doubts about."

"What kind of kinky things did you do?"

"Curious?"

Ellen blushed slightly. "I've read about unusual sex in novels and such, but I've never talked frankly to anyone who has done anything."

"It's fine to be curious. If I have my way, by the time I'm done with you you'll have tasted lots of 'unusual' things." Maggie's eyes became distant. "I really enjoy oral sex, both giving and getting. Anal sex took a bit of getting used to but once you get past the taboos, it's really hot. I've made love in some really strange places and I've done it with several people at the same time."

Ellen sat up straighter. "You did? You were part of an orgy?"

"Sure. Why not?" Maggie stared at Ellen. "Dying of curiosity?"

Ruefully, Ellen nodded. "Okay. I admit it."

"I remember one evening. We were all a bit tipsy, not too drunk to know what we were doing of course, but just enough to release our inhibitions and let it all hang out. That was one hell of a great evening."

"Wow. Would you tell me?"

"Sure. I've got no secrets. I'll use just first names to protect the delightfully guilty."

Ellen refilled the empty coffee cups and sat back down. "Okay. Give."

"Josh was a regular. He traveled a lot on business and usually called me when he was in town. One day he phoned and asked me if I wanted to go to a party. He made it clear that there would be lots of public sex, but that I wouldn't have to participate if I didn't want to."

"You mean he would pay you to just watch? To go to a party with him? Why?"

"He had no one special and it was a badge of honor to bring someone who's not hesitant to play. I have a feeling that several of the women, and maybe the men too, were professionals."

Ellen was shocked. "The men? Professionals?"

"Sure. There are male prostitutes who cater to the desires of sexy, horny women. Why not?"

"I guess I never thought about it that way." Ellen wondered what she would do with a male prostitute and sadly realized that she had no idea what she would ask for."

"You'll learn," Maggie said softly. "I promise."

Ellen reached out and placed her hand over Maggie's on the small kitchen table. "Thanks. Just be patient with me."

Maggie nodded. "No problem."

"Okay. Tell me about the party."

"Josh knew me pretty well. He knew that, although I wouldn't be compelled to do anything, I wouldn't have a problem making love while someone else watched and that was the idea of this party. We'd done it in public a few times.

"In public?"

"Well sort of. He liked to go out to dinner and see how hot he could get me. He knew if he got me hot, I'd do it in a hansom cab, in a restaurant with a few waiters watching, at the beach. You get the idea. So he knew that that part of it wouldn't be a problem. He also knew I was usually game for almost anything. He knew my rules. No drugs, and condoms always.

"Josh is . . . was . . . probably still is . . . I hate trying to make sense of the tenses. Josh was a very good-looking man, tall with really curly chestnut hair that I loved to run my fingers through, and deep hazel eyes. He had a nice body that had added a few pounds over the years I knew him. With the amount of traveling he did, he wasn't able to work out and control it so he always referred to our sex as exercise. 'Just for health reasons,' he'd say." She looked at Ellen and Ellen watched her face soften at the memory. "Then he'd pat his spare tire and grin."

"Was he a good lover?"

"He was a great communicator and experimenter. He loved to try new things. I have a theory. There aren't really any good lovers; there are merely people who are great together, and maybe they wouldn't be nearly as good with other partners. We were marvelous together."

"Interesting," Ellen said, not sure she believed. Could she be a good lover? Would someone ever say that they were marvelous together?

"We arrived at a small, neat, suburban-looking house in Brooklyn about nine and the party was in full swing. The music was dreamy and Josh and I did a bit of slow-dancing." Maggie closed her eyes again. "I love slow-dancing, vertical body rubbing. I could feel that the atmosphere and the delicious Long Island iced teas we were consuming were having an effect on his libido."

"What were you wearing?"

"I had an amazing blouse that I loved to wear. It was sleeveless, made of a silky red fabric that clung to my breasts and clearly showed my nipples. From the front it had a rather demure neckline, a V with just a hint of cleavage. The interesting part was the back. There wasn't one, just a few strings that tied over my shoulder blades and that was it down to the waist. From the front I was Suzie schoolteacher and from the back I was almost naked."

"Sounds fabulous."

Maggie smiled at the memory. "It was. I wore it with a very short black skirt, five-inch black heels, and thigh-high black stockings. You could just see the lacy tops below the skirt. Josh was wearing black jeans with a yellow cotton shirt."

When Maggie seemed to get lost in the obviously wonderful memories, Ellen said, "So you did some slow-dancing."

"Right. After a few dances, other men began to cut in and I danced with some really nice guys. About an hour after we got there one of the men asked me if I was interested in going in the large hot tub in the basement. It sounded great so I suggested it to Josh. Soon we were downstairs and the joint was jumping. The downstairs was decorated like a forest clearing, with lots of huge split-leaf philodendrons and ficus. Huge drooping ferns and flowering jungly plants hung from baskets all around the room and the air was wet and heavy and smelled of herbs and earth.

"The center of the room was dominated by a twelve-person hot tub with a wide ledge around it that, in addition to couples draped over one another, held pitchers of frozen drinks and trays of munchies. Two couples lay on the ledge beneath heat lamps, hands and mouths busy. At that moment the tub contained eight or nine people, all naked, as I quickly found out. 'Wanna get naked and dive in?' Josh growled in my ear, his hot breath making me shiver.

" 'Sure,' I said, kicking off my shoes. Being naked in public has never bothered me."

"I'm sure that's true," Ellen said, "but I'm sure you look great without your clothes."

"Some women look better than others nude but that doesn't make as much difference as you might think. At that party there were four women in the tub. Two had nice figures, one was about fifty pounds overweight, with pendulous breasts and tremendous thighs, and the fourth was really skinny, with almost no breasts at all, just nipples on her ribs. However, everyone had a great time and once the initial gawking subsided, we all had an equal amount of fun. It's mostly mental attitude."

Ellen reflexively looked down. "But that initial impression makes so much difference."

"Does it? And are you really interested in the kind of man to whom that matters so much?"

Ellen sat silent. She realized that what Maggie said made sense, but in her heart she vehemently disagreed. It might be okay for Maggie, who looked really good, but not for her. "So you just stripped?"

"Actually Josh knelt at my feet and slowly peeled my stockings down my legs while several people watched. He deliberately slid his fingers down the inside of my thighs. I have to tell you that that drives me wild. Then he slid off my skirt and kissed my belly over my tiny bikini panties. 'Turn around,' he said, and I did. He untied the strings that held the blouse together and it fell to the floor."

"You, of course, had nothing beneath," Ellen said, with a clear idea of what Maggie must have looked like. Maggie was obviously no kid, but she looked really good despite her age.

Maggie winked. "Of course not. I sag a bit and wish I had more natural uplift, but what the hell. Josh liked me just the way I was, which was obvious when he turned me around and nibbled my nipples. I'm a sucker for that and Josh knew it. He always knew just what made my knees weak and my pussy wet."

Ellen tried not to be startled by Maggie's choice of words.

Maggie's eyes flew open. "Sorry for my language. In my line of work I tend to be rather straightforward. Does it bother you?"

"It's a bit of a surprise coming from you."

"Remember what I did for a living."

"I know, but you look so . . . classy."

"Thanks for the compliment." Maggie closed her eyes again and returned to that night. "So anyway, Josh stripped and we climbed into the tub. The water was wonderful, hot enough to make an impression but not so hot that it muted the ability. I settled beneath the bubbles between Josh and another man. The other man was soft and paunchy, with deep blue eyes behind coke-bottle glasses, which he frequently had to slosh through the hot water to unfog. While we talked I felt hands on my breasts, both Josh's and this other guy's."

"He just touched you without permission?"

"Everyone had tacit permission to do whatever they wanted. I knew that if I had asked him to stop he would have but I didn't because it felt so good. I was getting really hot and it was getting more and more difficult to carry on a coherent conversation. The man looked at Josh who nodded, giving his permission for whatever he wanted to do. 'I'd like to do everything with you.' He was breathing heavily. 'Whatever you like,' I said and almost immediately his fingers were between my legs. God he had great hands."

As Maggie relived the experience she wondered how much Ellen was ready for. She had reached for the man's cock beneath the bubbling water. It had been soft. "Don't underestimate junior there," he had said. "All this hot water poops him out, but he recovers quickly."

"I'm glad," Maggie said. "I would hate to be the only one here getting excited."

"Oh, you're not," the two men said almost simultaneously. "Why don't you sit up here?" the man said, patting the wooden ledge. Maggie hoisted herself from the tub and seated herself on the edge. Each man touched a knee and urged her legs apart. While Josh sucked on one of Maggie's breasts, the other man crouched between her legs. "God, you're so juicy. I love a sweet pussy like yours." He slid one finger through her folds and Maggie braced her hands and allowed her head to fall back, savoring the feeling of being pleasured by the two men. Soon she felt the finger slide into her channel, almost immediately followed by another.

"Oh God, that feels good," she moaned, almost unable to catch her breath as a third finger joined the other two. Josh nipped at one engorged nipple and pinched the other hard. At her gasp, the two men laughed.

"She's a hot number," the man said to Josh. "My name's Al by the way. I guess we should at least know who we are as we play with this hot little piece."

"Her name's Maggie and she's as hot as they come." Maggie heard Josh's rough laugh. "And she does come."

"I'll bet," Al said as he thrust his fingers in and out of Maggie's dripping pussy.

Josh climbed out of the tub and Maggie stretched back onto the ledge. Josh crouched beside her and rubbed his cock against her cheek. When it became erect he growled, "Take it all, baby."

Maggie opened her mouth and it was quickly filled with Josh's erection. She always loved the feel and the taste of him and used her tongue to give him as much pleasure as she could. She soon found it difficult to concentrate, however, as Al's mouth found her clit and licked and sucked her flesh.

Too soon Maggie felt the waves of orgasm washing over her body and, as the spasms controlled her, she felt Josh's cock erupt in her mouth. She tasted his tangy come and swallowed, trying not to allow any to flow out of her mouth.

"Oh, Maggie, you're so sweet," Al said. "I want to fuck you so bad."

Her voice ragged, she said, "If you've got protection."

"I always come prepared." He obviously enjoyed sex immensely and his laugh was infectious. "And I'm always prepared to come."

Maggie heard the familiar sound of ripping foil and then her cunt was filled. "You feel so good," she said as his thrusts drove her upward toward a second orgasm.

Josh idly played with her nipples as Al drove his cock into her again and again. As Al threw his head back and rammed into her one final time, Josh pinched both her nipples and she came again.

Maggie returned to the present, opened her eyes and gazed at Ellen. "I don't think you're ready for the gory details just yet so let's just say that I got enormous pleasure from his fingers inside me and from his magnificent mouth and tongue. When Josh climbed onto the ledge I indulged in my love of fellatio while the other guy fucked me senseless. What a kick. Two men spurting at almost the same time, one in my mouth and one inside my pussy. It was great."

"Wow," Ellen said, her mind whirling. It wasn't just what Maggie had done, it was also her comfort level with it all. She made no excuses and Ellen realized that none were necessary. She obviously had delighted in it all. Listening to Maggie, Ellen was understanding more and more. "It sounds like quite an evening."

"Actually there was a lot more," Maggie said, "but I'll bet it's late enough to get going."

Ellen looked at her watch. "Holy cow. It's after ten."

Maggie grabbed the two cups and put them in the sink. "Let's do it."

"Where do we begin?"

"Let's see whether we can get you an appointment with a new stylist I found on my last assignment." She gave Ellen the phone number. "Ask for Ashley. She's a whiz with hair and makeup." When, due to a fortunate cancellation, Ellen had gotten an appointment for that afternoon, Maggie continued, "I think we should start with clothes."

"What are we buying?" Ellen asked, wondering in what way her wardrobe was insufficient.

"We're getting you a few things that make you feel like the woman I think you can become, a combination of worldly and curious."

"Worldly and curious. Can clothes say that?"

"It's the attitude that matters more than the wrapping but some new duds will certainly help." Maggie grabbed Ellen's purse and tossed it to her. "Let's do some really serious damage to your credit card."

"Okay. You're the boss."

"One thing," Maggie said, grabbing her jacket. "Remember that you're the only one who can see or hear me. Be a bit careful or you'll end up at Bellevue for observation."

Ellen laughed. "Will do."

Chapter 6

Ellen and Maggie walked out into the crisp early fall air of Manhattan. They wandered past shop windows that displayed clothes of all kinds. Each time Ellen indicated something she liked, Maggie sneered. *Wimpy* and *pastel* became her favorite words. Finally they stopped outside a small boutique in the East Sixties. "I used to shop here often when I was alive," Maggie said. "Great stuff." She pushed open the door and Ellen hurried in behind her.

"Good morning, madam," a woman said as she stepped out from behind a rack of blouses. It was all Ellen could do not to gasp. The woman looked to be in her late sixties, with marshmallow-white hair and pale blue eyes. It was obvious that she had been a startlingly beautiful woman and even now she was stunning. Her attire, on the other hand, bordered on bizarre. She was wearing a chartreuse cotton jacket with the sleeves pushed up to her elbows over a cinnamon-and-teal patterned blouse and tailored red slacks. Ellen looked down and found herself staring at a pair of iridescent green sneakers. The woman lifted one foot and wiggled it at the ankle. "Don't you just love them?" she said. "I have tennis shoes to go with almost every outfit. I think it's just too kicky."

"I guess I should have warned you about Flora," Maggie said.

"She's a character and her mode of dress certainly is bizarre, but she's got a great eye for style on other people."

"Can I show you something specific or are you just browsing?" Flora asked.

"Well, Flora, I'm just looking for now."

Flora's head snapped around. "How did you know my name?"

"Oh," Ellen said, realizing her mistake. "I had a friend who used to shop here. When I found myself in town, I thought I'd drop in."

"Oh yes? It's nice to have someone recommend my little establishment. What is your friend's name?"

"Her name's Maggie. I mean her name was Maggie."

"Oh, Maggie Sullivan. One of my best customers. What a tragedy. She was so young when she died."

Ellen gazed at Maggie whose expression was unreadable. "Yes, it was, wasn't it." It was so hard to reconcile the Maggie who stood beside her with the woman who had died four years before. Without realizing how awkward the moment was, Flora bustled to a rack of dresses. "I know you said you were just looking, but can I direct you to something more specific? Dresses, suits, blouses? You're a size twelve, aren't you?"

"Yes, a twelve." Soto voce she asked Maggie, "What am I looking for?"

"Anything that's not insipid."

"I can't tell her that."

"Just look around and I'll tell you what to try on."

To Flora, Ellen said, "I'm looking for something new and different from what I usually wear."

"And what is that, if I may ask?"

She considered only a moment. "Well, my friends tell me I'm too pastel, that I need bright colors and some bold prints."

"Bravo!" Maggie said, loudly.

"With your coloring, something bright should look really great. Let's see what I've got."

In just a few minutes, Flora and Maggie had helped Ellen select several looks, each totally different from anything Ellen had ever worn. "I don't know whether I can do this," Ellen said, walking out of the shop's dressing room in a pair of bright red slacks with a white shirt with a wide red stripe and a gold vest. The outfit was held together with a red, gold, and white scarf artfully tied around her throat. "Wonderful," Flora and Maggie said in unison.

For almost an hour, Ellen tried on dresses, pantsuits, and blouses until she had five outfits set aside. She changed back into the first pants ensemble and, in a daze, fumbled in her purse for her wallet. As she pulled out her credit card, Flora said, "If you'll pardon me for saying it, you really need at least one pair of shoes and a matching bag to go with all this."

"You need new underwear, too," Maggie said. "Enough K-mart specials."

Ellen glared at Maggie who had kept up a running conversation, making it difficult for Ellen to respond without appearing to talk to thin air. "I know," Ellen said to Flora and Maggie simultaneously. "I feel like an old house. You change one thing, recover one chair, and everything else looks shabby."

"You don't look shabby at all," Flora said. "You look bright, shiny, and new. Very chic. And remember that everything you've gotten is a classic. With different accessories, they each will last for years. Very practical."

Ellen grinned. "Thanks. It will all take a bit of getting used to."

"You think this is something," Maggie said, "just you wait until Ashley gets her hands and scissors on you."

Maggie accompanied Ellen to Michael's, an exclusive-looking salon in the theater district. The interior was all done in red-and-black patchwork, with black sinks and chairs and operators dressed in patchwork smocks and black pants. "I have an appointment with Ashley," Ellen said to the receptionist, a seemingly natural blonde with a perfect face that couldn't be re-created by any means except the right genes.

"You're Ellen, of course. Ashley will be right with you. Can I take your packages?" She put Ellen's packages in a locker, hung up her new vest, then pressed a hidden button. It was only a moment before a tall, slender woman appeared in the salon uniform.

"Look at Ashley," Maggie said as the woman in her midthirties approached. "She's not a particularly attractive woman, but she's a whiz with makeup and she's done her hair in a style that brings out her best features. That's what we want for you."

Ashley smiled and held out her hand. "Welcome. Follow me."

Ellen shook the woman's hand, then followed Ashley to an operator's station and settled into the chair. "Okay," Ashley said, "what can I do for you?"

"I'm not really sure," Ellen said, ruefully. "I just got some new clothes and I guess I want to look worthy of them."

"Okay," Ashley said studying Ellen's face in the mirror. "Do you have anything specific in mind? Cut? Curl? Color?"

"I'm honest enough with myself to admit that I'm not an attractive woman. I guess I didn't pick my parents too well. I don't know what you can do with what I've got to work with."

"Okay. Let's take a look." Ashley ran her fingers through Ellen's fine hair and rubbed a strand between her fingers. Then she lifted Ellen's chin and moved it left and right, staring critically at her face. "Good bones. I love the green eyes with your ivory skin. Difficult hair as it is now, very straight and very fine, but we can work with that. Small nose, generous, quite sexy mouth."

Ellen stared in the mirror at her mouth. It was just an ordinary mouth with ordinary lips. "Sexy mouth?"

"That slightly pouty lower lip is great. I would use a slightly lighter color lipstick in the center of your lower lip than you use on the rest of your mouth."

"Really?" Ellen asked, still staring.

Ashley seemed not to have heard. "I would do dangling earrings. Your face can't take big round ones but slender hanging ones will accentuate your cheekbones." She peered at Ellen's face and hair then crossed her arms and leaned against the counter. "How brave are you?"

"Very!" Maggie yelled from behind Ellen's chair.

"Not very I'm afraid," Ellen said.

"Ellen," Maggie warned, "you promised."

"I did not," Ellen said.

"Excuse me?" Ashley said, obviously puzzled by Ellen's comment.

"Nothing. What would you suggest?"

"If you're feeling brave, I would go darker with the hair. Deep brown to show off your skin and eyes."

"Darker?"

"Yup. I would also give it a slight body wave and cut it short so it surrounds your face, but doesn't bury it." She got a hairstyle magazine and found a picture of the style she had in mind. "It won't be a dramatic change and I promise that it won't make you uncomfortable. You'll just look like a well retouched picture of yourself."

"Really?"

"I don't think you're ready for something too ultra, if you know what I mean. Let's keep this gentle, a small step for starters. You can always get more-so the next time."

Ellen gazed at the model's picture in the magazine. She was beautiful, but she also had a look, like she understood it all. "That's the look you're after," Maggie said. "That confidence. I think Ashley's right. No drastic changes, just enhancements and a new attitude that can only come when you're happier about yourself."

Not knowing that Maggie was talking, Ashley picked up one of Ellen's hands. "One more thing. You really must get a hand-spa treatment and then have your nails done. I'd recommend wraps in this climate."

"Wraps? Claws?"

"Not at all. I would suggest what we call street-length just over the tips of your fingers. With maybe a soft mauve polish but we've got more than a hundred shades to choose from."

"Say yes, Ellen," Maggie said. "Just say yes."

"I guess," Ellen gulped.

"Hair and nails?" Ashley asked.

Maggie raised her ever-ready eyebrow and Ellen took a deep breath. "Hair and nails."

Maggie squeezed Ellen's shoulder. "Good girl. You'll be glad you did. I promise."

"Right."

"Right," Ashley said, a bit puzzled.

Maggie waved to Ellen and, as she watched, her friend faded away. Her friend. Ellen realized that, in just a few hours, Maggie had become just that. A friend. It still shocked her to see the evidence of Maggie's ghostly existence but she was rapidly getting used to it, or as used to it as she could.

Several hours later, Ellen was gazing at her new look when she saw Maggie slowly reappear. "Wow," Maggie said. "You look fantastic. Ashley was right. You look like you've just come back from a long vacation. The hair's perfect."

"Yeah," Ellen whispered. "It is, isn't it." Ellen had been staring at her reflection in the long mirror for several minutes. She wasn't beautiful. Far from it. But she was classy. Stylish. She looked put together somehow. Ashley had darkened her hair until it was the color of ranch mink and cut and shaped it until it lay sleek against her jaw. She had also used her makeup skills to highlight Ellen's cheekbones and bring out her deep green eyes. As Ellen stared she had to admit that with the way Ashley had done her lipstick she did have a sexy lower lip. "Ellen," Maggie said, "you look sensational."

"Yeah," Ellen breathed. She held up her hands, short, slender fingers tipped with comfortable-length soft mauve nails. "Yeah." For the second time that day Ellen pulled out her credit card without worrying about how much she was charging.

On the way home, Maggie and Ellen stopped at a shoe store and selected several new pairs of pumps and three new pocketbooks to match. Then, just when Ellen thought they were done and that she was juggling as many packages as she could carry, Maggie dragged her into a leather shop and over to a rack of buttery soft cream-colored leather vests with brown bone buttons.

She pointed to one. "Try that on. I think it will look great over most of what you've just bought."

Ellen had long since given up arguing, so she stacked her purchases on a bench, slipped off her yellow vest and slid her arms into the leather one. "Oh. This feels so good," Ellen purred, rubbing her hand up and down the front.

From behind her, a low-pitched male voice said softly, "Yes, it does, doesn't it. It looks like it was made for you."

Ellen blushed and said nothing, assuming the voice came from a store clerk. "I'll think about it." She looked at the price tag and blanched. She really liked the vest, but she wasn't going to get shilled by some fast-talking salesman, although, if he worked on commission, she didn't blame him for trying to talk her into buying it.

"Your choice of course," the man said, "but I think you should take it."' He moved from behind a rack of jackets. He appeared to be in his mid-thirties, with deep brown eyes, sandy, sun-streaked hair that he wore pulled back in a short tail and a long, sandy mustache. His rugged, not-really-handsome face was deeply tanned, as though he spent quite a bit of time in the sun. No, Ellen thought, not handsome, but friendly and warm, attractive in its openness. Over his tan slacks and plaid sport shirt, he was wearing a brown leather jacket with brass buttons. "Now that you've heard my opinion, I'd like yours. What do you think of this jacket?" It was cut like a sports jacket, but fashioned of deep tan leather that was as soft as fabric. "It's a bit pricey but I really like it. Should I take it?" He turned so she could see the back and sides.

Ellen was nonplussed. "You're thinking of *buying* it?"

Her confusion must have shown on her face because he said, "You don't like it." He slipped the jacket off and started toward the rack from which he had obviously taken it.

"Actually, I do like it. It's really quite becoming." She fumbled for words. "I'm sorry. I thought you worked here and were trying to talk me into purchasing something."

His sudden smile made his face even more attractive. "Oh. I get it. No. I don't work here. I have been gazing at this jacket in the window for weeks and I finally decided to come inside and try it on." He slipped it back onto his shoulders. "You really like it?"

"Yes, I do."

"At these prices, it should come with two pairs of pants. I almost dropped when I saw the cost, but what the heck. You only live once. I just got a bonus and I thought I'd treat myself." He stopped talking. "Sorry. I'm rambling."

"Not at all. And you're right. You do only live once. I'm going to buy this vest and I think you should get the jacket."

He looked at the price tag again, then shrugged. "I'm glad you're getting that vest. It suits you."

"Thanks." Ellen struggled to find something to say as the man slipped the jacket off, draped it over his arm and walked toward the cash register.

Maggie chimed in, "This is your chance to try out the new you. Keep him talking. He's really cute."

"What should I say?" she whispered.

"How about asking his name?"

Ellen trailed after the man, fumbling in her purse for her wallet. "What's your name?" Ellen blurted out, then blanched.

The man's smile was bright. "I'm Jim Lucas. And yours?"

"Ellen. Ellen Harold." She slipped the vest off. "Thanks for the advice." He pulled out a credit card and it was only moments before the transaction was completed and he had the jacket in a box under his arm. As he walked away, Ellen found her credit card and gave it to the salesclerk, then, while he was ringing up the sale, she gathered her shopping bags.

"Ellen," Jim called.

Swallowing, Ellen turned and said, "Yes?"

"Don't forget this," he said, holding the bright yellow vest she had left draped over the rack.

"Oh yeah, thanks again." She stuffed the vest he handed her in one of her shopping bags, then signed the credit-card receipt.

Leaving the store, Jim held the door for her. "I live just around the corner, so if you live in the area, maybe we'll run into each other again."

"Maybe we will," Ellen said, moving so Maggie could exit the store behind her. As Jim turned south, Ellen turned north.

"Just great," Maggie said as they approached Ellen's building, her voice dripping with sarcasm. "A cute, sexy guy tries to pick you up and what do you do? Nothing. Not a damn thing. So much for the new you."

"I couldn't let him pick me up. It's not right. It's not safe. He could have been a creep, a thief, a molester."

"Right. And he could have been a millionaire, a diplomat, who knows. You could have encouraged him a bit. You didn't have to invite him to your apartment, but you could have made conversation. Maybe he would have asked you out for a drink."

"Maggie, new me or old me, I'm not that kind of girl. I don't let men pick me up."

Maggie sighed and threw up her hands. "Okay, okay. I hear you. I'll be patient. You'll come around."

"Maybe I won't ever be the kind of woman you have in mind," Ellen said, opening the front door of her building.

"Listen, I'm sorry, love. I didn't mean to snap at you. You're right. You can only be who you are. I know there's someone really special under all that insecurity, and I'm just impatient for you to try your wings."

"Maybe there isn't," Ellen said, stopping at the foot of the stairs, her shoulders slumped. "Maybe I'm just the same old me with a new hairdo. New paint doesn't make the basic structure any different."

"I know it's been only twenty-four hours, but I think I already know you pretty well. The more adventurous you is in there somewhere. I'll relax and stop pushing."

"Thanks. I wish I were as sure of me as you are."

"I understand and on that note, I'll leave you for tonight. You look tired and the day's been full of changes and you need time to adjust, get used to the new you, at least on the outside. I'll see you, well I don't know exactly when I'll see you again, but it will be soon. I'll be around."

As Maggie faded into the stygian darkness that always preceded her periods of inactivity, she could hear voices in her mind. "She's going to be a tough case," she heard Lucy say. "You've got your work cut out for you."

"And it's not just sex, Maggie," Angela's voice added. "You've got to get her to understand about being a woman. About getting involved in the world, not just peeking out at it."

"I know, ladies," Maggie muttered. "I know."

The following morning, Ellen received her weekly package from the doctors in Fairmont and for two days she dutifully coded and entered the data into her computer. Finally she uploaded the completed information to the medical database and e-mailed the files to the doctor's office.

Saturday Ellen wore one of her new outfits as she wandered around Manhattan, trying to feel confident, assured, and classy, with limited success. She looked around her with a more open mind, aware that there were things in New York that she wanted to try that she hadn't previously thought about because Micki hadn't mentioned them. She made a mental note to find out the schedule of the ferry to the Statue of Liberty and the one to the renovated Ellis Island. They were both touristy places to visit, but she was, after all, a tourist and she was curious.

Finding herself at the Hudson River, she decided to visit the Air and Space Museum and found herself fascinated by the military hardware on display. Late in the afternoon, as she walked east, she felt her stomach rumble. As she approached her building, she spotted a small Indian restaurant. She heard Maggie's voice asking, 'Have you ever done anything daring, just because you were curious?' She had never tried Indian food, always afraid it would be too spicy, but today, she stopped and gazed at the posted menu. "I have no idea what most of this stuff is," she muttered.

"Then maybe I can help you," a familiar voice said.

She whirled around and saw the man whom she had encountered in the leather shop. Today he was wearing black jeans, a black shirt, and the tan leather jacket she remembered from the store. He wore high-heeled intricately tooled black cowboy boots so he was several inches taller than she was. "I'm sorry?" He was quite nice-looking and shouldn't have made her nervous, she thought, but he did.

"You said you know nothing about Indian food," he said. "I come here often and I was just stopping here for dinner myself. I thought that maybe, if you were alone, I could join you and help you with the menu."

"I'm afraid I'm on my way somewhere."

"Now I'm the one who's sorry. I took your advice and bought this jacket, now I thought you could take mine and enjoy Indian food. I'm Jim. Jim Lucas." He held out his hand.

"I remember," Ellen said, flustered and blushing slightly. "I'm Ellen." She shook his soft, uncallused hand. Although he looked like a cowboy, she would bet he had never done any manual labor in his life.

"I remember you, too, Ellen." He dropped her hand quickly after the handshake. "Are you sure you must run off? I can see I make you a bit nervous and I don't blame you. Here I am trying to pick you up in the middle of a dangerous city. I guess you're right to be careful, but I was hoping, since this is our second meeting . . ." His smile was charming.

Suddenly Ellen heard Maggie's voice in her head. "He's not asking you to come to his apartment. It's a public restaurant. What harm could it do?"

"It could do a lot of harm," Ellen answered.

Jim's face fell. "I understand. I had hoped I looked harmless. I am, you know. Divorced, unattached, employed, charming." He paused. "Lonely." His look managed to combine Don Juan and Lassie.

In spite of herself, Ellen started to laugh. "I guess I'm just being overly cautious. I'm sorry. You really are being quite nice." Ellen heard Maggie's applause, then the sound faded.

"Hooray," Jim said. "Does that mean you'll let me buy you

dinner? I can explain all the nuances of the menu. Have you ever had Indian food before?"

"No." Ellen was again completely flustered. "I mean, no, I've never had Indian food before but yes, I'd love to join you for dinner. And no, you can't buy me dinner but we can go dutch."

Smiling, Jim nodded. "Wonderful." He placed his hand in the small of Ellen's back and guided her down the few steps into the small dining area. The restaurant seated about three dozen, with soft beige linen tablecloths and candle-lamps on each table. Since it was still early, they had their choice of tables and Jim chose a well-lit table off to one side. Ellen was glad he hadn't chosen something dark and secluded.

When Ellen was seated, Jim said, "They don't have a liquor license so we'll have to settle for herb tea, if that's all right with you."

"Sure," Ellen said, interlacing her fingers in her lap so she'd have something to do with her hands. During the moment's silence that followed, Ellen's mind churned. What should she say? How should she act? Should she have let him pay for dinner? She reached for her water glass but her hands were shaking so hard that she was sure she'd spill something so she replaced her hands in her lap, fumbling with her napkin.

"Listen, Ellen," Jim said, "it doesn't take a genius to see that you're really nervous about this. You look like a cornered animal ready to bolt at the first wrong move. How can I help you to relax?"

"I'm relaxed," Ellen protested.

"Right. And you always shred your napkin in Indian restaurants."

Ellen looked down and saw that the paper in her lap was torn into several long strips. She had the good grace to smile, weakly. "I'm sorry. This isn't the real me, I guess. I'm not much for dating."

"So what is the real you?"

"I'm a solitary person, quite used to eating alone. And I'm certainly not used to being picked up by strange men."

Jim raised an eyebrow the same way Maggie did. "I don't think I'm that strange."

Ellen laughed nervously. "I didn't mean that. Oh, damn. I'm a wreck. I have no clue what to say, how to act, what to do." At that moment, the waiter brought two cups of steaming tea.

After the brief reprieve, Jim said, "Why don't you do what you want, say what you think, and let's see what happens? You said that you don't date often."

"I don't date at all, really."

"I can't imagine why not. Are you new to the city?"

"I'm from upstate. I came into a little money and I decided to visit here." Surprisingly, she talked for several minutes, responding to Jim's gentle, non-intimate questions. "Now that you know the basics about me how about telling me a little about you," Ellen said, more interested than she cared to admit to herself.

"I'm thirty-eight and, as I told you before, divorced. No children. My ex didn't want any."

"And you did?"

"I didn't at first, but then over the two years Carrie and I were married, I realized that, to her, children meant permanence, something she didn't really want, and I did. Slowly it dawned on me that we were looking for totally different things so we split just over a year ago."

"Was it difficult?"

"Not nearly as difficult as I thought it was going to be, but I'm still not used to Saturdays. When you're married, you always have a date for Saturday night. When you're alone, the empty Saturdays become a symbol of something, so when I don't have other plans, I eat out." He hesitated, then continued, "To be honest I lied when I said I was planning on having dinner here. I hadn't decided where to eat so when I saw you heading across town I hoped you were alone. I'll admit I was looking for an excuse to talk to you again, so when you paused in front of The Flower of India, I said I was planning to eat here. I was anxious for company and hoped you were, too."

He was a nice man, neither a molester nor a millionaire. Just a lonely guy looking for company. Ellen suddenly realized that she was lonely, too, and was glad to have someone to share a little time with. Usually she was content with her own company, but now she found she was enjoying having someone to talk to. "Actually, the company's nice for a change." When the waiter arrived, he and Jim carefully explained many of the dishes on the menu. "I don't think I like spicy food," Ellen confessed.

"Most of the dishes here can be prepared anywhere from mild to spicy," the waiter explained with a heavy Indian accent.

"Why don't we order the assorted appetizers and two main dishes? That way you can sample several different things. I'll get a few of my favorite condiments, too. Are you game?"

Am I game? she thought. "Sure. Why don't you pick two things you like and I'll sample everything?"

Jim ordered several items and the conversation flowed easily until the plate of appetizers arrived. The waiter placed it in the center of the table, then carefully wiped two small plates and placed one in front of each of them. Jim pointed to a chunk of bright-red meat. "This is tandoori chicken, an Indian specialty. A tandoor is a clay oven that bakes whatever you put inside, usually chicken, lamb, or shrimp marinated in yogurt." He leaned forward and whispered, conspiratorially, "It's frequently very dry because the chicken is cooked without the skin. It's one of my least favorite meats but in small bits it's not too bad."

Ellen grinned as he described the other things in the assortment. She tried the tandoori and had to agree with Jim, tasty, but very dry. The ground meat was delicious and the vegetable-filled pastry was unusual and wonderful.

When she grinned, Jim said, "I'm glad you're pleased," and the friendly atmosphere continued as the main course arrived. He showed her how to use her *chapati*, an Indian flat bread, to pick up delicately spiced pieces of lamb in a creamy sauce, flavored with crushed almonds.

"I'm amazed," Ellen said as she licked her fingers. "This is delicious and not spicy at all."

"Would you like to taste this one?" he asked, indicating a bowl filled with lumps of meat covered with a thick green-brown sauce. "It's a bit more . . . interesting." He spooned a small piece of meat and a bit of sauce onto her bread. "It's called *murgh saag*. It's chicken with a spinach sauce. I'll warn you, it's got a small kick so start with a small bite. If you don't like it, give it to me. It's one of my favorites."

Ellen tasted. "It's great. I've never tasted anything like this before, and I'm sorry I haven't."

"Not giving it to me?"

"Not a chance." Later, when she reached for her water glass, he intercepted her hand. "If your mouth's a little hot, take a bit of the *raita*. It's yogurt with cucumber and spices. It will cool your mouth much more quickly than water." When she smiled at the cooling effect of the raita Jim grinned. "That's my girl." Then he blushed. "I didn't mean that the way it came out. Of course you're not my girl."

"I know that, Ellen said, helping herself to some rice sprinkled with carrots and peas, and covering it with a bit of the spinach sauce. Sensing his sudden discomfort, she added, "Now it's time for you to relax. I hope we've passed the really awkward part." She handed him the lamb plate. "Have some more."

The rest of the meal passed with comfortable conversation. She learned that he was a computer programmer and worked for a company that made plumbing supplies, maintaining its Web site and order-entry system. He had been born and raised in Texas, and for the past fifteen years had lived in Manhattan several blocks south of her apartment.

After a dessert of something called *gulaab jamun*, a spherical pastry swimming in a honey sauce, they sipped tea and waited for the check. Jim made no protest when she handed him money to cover her half. Finally, they walked outside. "Can I walk you home?" he asked.

"It's a little soon for you to know where I live."

"That's fine, as long as you don't disappear. May I have your phone number at least, so maybe we can do this again some time?"

Ellen sensed that he was trying to sound casual but that this was important to him. If she were to admit it, it was important to her as well. "Sure." She wrote the number on a small piece of paper and handed it to him. "Thanks for a delightful evening. I'm sorry I'm so difficult, but I hope you'll forgive me."

"I certainly do. Someone from a small town like you are should be cautious. There are a lot of kooks and weirdos out here." He pulled a card out of his wallet. "Here's my name, address, phone number, e-mail address, pager number, and all that. Is it okay if I call you in a week or so?"

"I'll look forward to that." As Ellen watched Jim walk to the corner and turn south on Second Avenue, she realized that she was looking forward to seeing him again.

When she arrived in her apartment, she was grinning. She had had a dinner date with a man—and it felt wonderful. She undressed and, as she was about to flip on the TV she spied the CD player on her bedside table. She was in just the right mood for a story, ready to have her horizons widened. She stretched out on the bed, turned down the light, and pressed play.

Chapter 7

The narrator's voice was sexy, the background music soft and sensual. Ellen found that her body tingled all over. This story began the same way as all the others.

"Is there magic in the world? Skeptics doubt that magic exists, or ever did exist. Are they right? I don't know, but there are still a few people who are willing to keep an open mind, people who believe in old stories, ancient legends, and possibilities. Like the possibilities inherent in the Ring of Obedience.

" 'Would you like your lover to obey your every wish, lady?' the old man asked.

" 'Sure, who wouldn't,' MJ said, amused at the off-the-wall question the ancient peddler asked. Disregarding his salesman-like approach, she walked to the other side of his street-corner display of watches and rings and looked down at the usual clutter of knock-off watches.

" 'I have just the thing for you,' the man said.

" 'Actually I'm looking for a birthday gift for my husband.' She shook her head at the knock-off watches—Omaga and Rollflex—then moved around to the group of rings. She picked up a silver wolf's head, then peered at a skull. No. Not right. He wasn't the

skull type. She realized the old man was watching her so she picked up a large gold-looking signet ring with a gothic S on it. 'No. I don't think there's anything here he'd like.' She put the signet ring back on the tray and turned to leave, disappointed. Her husband Steve's birthday dinner was that night and she still hadn't found anything to give him.

" *'But what would you like?' the vendor asked. MJ glanced back at him, then looked a bit longer. He was much older than the usual run-of-the-mill sidewalk vendor, with piercing deep blue eyes that seemed to see to her soul. He looked both spooky and wise although how those two things could go together she had no idea.*

" *'What I want isn't the question. It's not my birthday, it's his.'*

" *'You said you would like your husband to obey your every wish.' The man picked up a Celtic knot ring of woven strands of gold and silver. 'This will do that for you.'*

"*MJ took the ring from the vendor's hand. As he blathered on about obedience, she tuned him out. The ring really would be perfect for Steve, she thought. He loved unusual things and he was of ancient Irish heritage. It looked like it would be the right size, too. 'How much?'*

" *'It's priceless.'*

"Yeah, right, *she thought.* Here goes the part I hate. Bargaining. *'I'm sure it is, but how much?'*

" *'He who wears it must obey she who gave it. You'll see.'*

"*Enough. Then, as MJ started to put the ring down the man said, 'Fifty dollars.'*

" *'You've got to be kidding! Fifty dollars for something from a pushcart? Not a chance.'*

" *'You have no idea what you're passing up,' he said. 'This could mean everything to you. I can let you have the Ring of Obedience for forty dollars, but that's my final offer. Pass it up at your own peril.'*

MJ was about to replace the ring on the vendor's tray when she made a rash decision. It would probably turn Steve's finger green but what the hell. It was really right for him, and the old guy seemed so sincere. 'Ring of Obedience. Forty dollars. Okay, I'll take it.'

" 'Good. Very good.' As MJ rummaged through her purse for her wallet, the man continued, 'Just place it on his finger and from then on he won't be able to resist any suggestion you give him. And he won't be able to remove the ring himself. The only way to get it off is for you to take it from his hand. Of course it will only work on the man you love, not anyone else. Do you understand?'

"No reason not to humor the guy. 'Right. Obedience. Only I can take it off his finger. Got it.' She handed him two twenties and he gave her a small blue velvet box for the ring.

" 'If he puts it on your finger, you'll be under the same power. You will be unable to resist anything he wants you to do.'

" 'Sure. Anything you say.' She tucked the ring into the box and slipped it into her pocketbook.

"That evening, she and Steve went to a fancy Italian restaurant to celebrate his twenty-eighth birthday. After a glass of wine, she pulled the small velvet box from her purse and placed it on the table between them. 'Happy birthday, sweetheart.'

"He picked up the box, opened it, and stared. 'Wow. This is fantastic.' He pulled the ring out and gazed at it beneath the light from the small candle on the table. 'It's really great. Wherever did you find it?'

" 'I hate to admit it, but I got it on a street corner. It will probably turn your finger all kinds of colors but I really liked it and thought it would look fabulous on you.

"When Steve started to put the ring on, MJ took it from him. 'Let me.' She slipped it onto his right ring finger, where it fit perfectly.

" 'Oh, baby,' Steve said, leaning forward. 'It looks just wonderful.'

"MJ leaned toward him and they kissed softly. At that moment the waiter arrived. 'May I take your order?'

" 'MJ?'

" 'Why don't you order for me?' she said.

" 'Certainly.' Without hesitation, Steve ordered veal with pasta and salads for both of them.

" 'Very good, sir,' the waiter said, striding toward the kitchen.

"During dinner Steve kept admiring the ring. 'You know, maybe it would look better on my other hand.' He pulled at the ring, but it wouldn't come off 'Hmm. It seems to be stuck. Never mind. It looks great right there.'

"MJ reached for his hand and easily slipped the ring off. 'That was easy. Are you sure it was stuck?'

" 'It was stuck fast.' Steve slipped the ring onto the index finger of his left hand. 'I wonder how you got it off so easily.' He looked at his hand, then shook his head. 'Nah. It looked better on my right hand.' Again he struggled and again the ring wouldn't budge.

"MJ remembered the peddler's words. 'He won't be able to remove the ring himself. The only way to get it off is for you to take it from his hand.' She reached over and easily slipped the ring from his left hand and replaced it on his right. 'Hmm.'

" 'It's really funny the way it seems to get stuck when I try to get it off yet you have no trouble.'

" 'Yeah. It is curious, isn't it.'

"Throughout the meal, MJ thought about the ring. A couple of times she asked Steve to do something really simple and each time he did it without question. Just coincidence, she thought. Should I give it a test? A real one? Nah. I can't really believe what some vendor says. 'Baby, how about going dancing after dinner.' Steve hated dancing and always refused.

" 'Sure. Sounds like a great idea.'

"MJ's eyes widened. Could this be? 'But it's your birthday. Shouldn't we do something you want to do?'

" 'If you want to go dancing, then dancing it shall be.'

"Did she really want to go dancing if this ring thing truly worked? Not a chance. She wanted to be home, in bed. However, the ring needed a more serious test. 'Actually, I'd like you to go into the men's room and take off your jockey shorts, then come back and hand them to me.'

"Shit, here it comes, *she thought.* He'll burst out laughing and that will be that. *She was grinning, ready to enjoy a shared joke, when Steve stood up and, without a word, headed toward the men's room. Moments later he returned, handed her his shorts and sat back down as though it was the most normal thing in the world.*

"This is too weird, but too funky not to take advantage of. 'You know how I love your cock,' MJ said, 'so I want to know it's ready for me for later. Are you hot?'

" 'You know I am always hot for you.'

" 'Is it hard?'

"Steve grinned sheepishly. 'Yes. Actually the feeling of my dick rubbing against the inside of my zipper is making me really horny.'

" 'Then unzip. I want to see.'

"Steve looked puzzled, but reached into his lap and, from what MJ could see from her side of the table, unzipped his pants. 'This is really kinky,' Steve said, 'but I seem to want to do whatever you want. Silly, isn't it?'

" 'Yes,' MJ said, 'it really is.' She slipped off her shoe and placed her stocking-covered foot in Steve's lap. Sure enough, his cock was naked, poking from the opening in the front of his pants. Naked and hard as a rock. She rubbed her foot up and down the length of him, smiling as she saw how distracted he was. 'Think about my foot,' she purred. 'Think of how good it feels, how hot you're getting, how difficult it is not to come.'

" 'Shit, baby, why are you torturing me?'

" 'Is it really such torture?'

"Steve grinned. 'Yes. Well, no. Your foot feels wonderful.'

" 'Good. Then concentrate on it.' There was utter silence at the table as MJ stroked Steve's hard cock with her stocking-clad foot. Finally she said, 'What you really want to do is to rub your cock until you come, isn't it? Right here in this restaurant.'

" 'Yes,' Steve groaned.

" 'I would never embarrass you, of course, so you can cover your hand and cock with your napkin. Then rub yourself until you come. I'll just keep stroking you with my foot since that feels so sexy.'

"Steve looked at MJ. 'It feels decadent and kinky, but I really

want to do it.' As she watched, he covered his lap with his napkin and rubbed his cock. The bemused look on his face was quickly replaced with one of rapture. Suddenly MJ could feel the spasms rock his erection and the wet stickiness on her foot. He had really done it. This was truly amazing.

"When he had cleaned himself up and they were having coffee, MJ confessed and told Steve all about the peddler and his story about the ring. 'I didn't believe it,' she said, 'but it seemed to work. You appeared to be incapable of resisting whatever I said.'

" 'Could it be?'

" 'I certainly didn't think so,' she said, 'but consider what just happened. You masturbated right here in public. Would you ever have done anything like that before tonight?'

"Steve shook his head. 'No. I guess not. That's some kind of power. You could really use it for evil.'

" 'The old man swore that it would only work between us and I'd never do anything that I didn't know you'd like.' She slowly pulled the ring from his finger. 'I'll only use it when we agree that you should put it on. It does have great erotic potential, doesn't it?'

" 'Phew. It certainly does.' Steve took the ring and gazed at MJ. 'What happens if I put it on your finger?'

" 'I obey you.'

"Steve motioned to the waiter. 'Check please.' He turned to MJ. 'Let's go home. We've got to play with this thing some more.' "

Ellen took a deep breath. Her entire body had reacted to the heat in the story. *Could I ever do something like that?* she wondered. She thought about the dinner that she had shared with Jim and pictured herself in MJ's place and Jim in Steve's. Jim had his hand in his crotch, so hot and under her control that he masturbated in public. As she thought about it, her hand rubbed her mound and slid back to her clit. Her orgasm was almost too quick, crashing over her suddenly and completely.

The following day was warm and sunny so, rising quite late in the morning, she dressed in a new outfit, a vibrant green silk shirt and a pair of tailored beige slacks. She added a long, thin brown belt, slender gold earrings, and her leather vest and headed to the local diner where she often stopped for breakfast. As she walked along Fifty-second Street she saw a small restaurant advertising a champagne brunch. *Why not?* she thought. Something different.

After a leisurely meal with two glasses of orange juice and champagne, she again wandered around the city. About three, as she walked back uptown she spied a small antique clock in the window of a dusty antique store. Inside she asked the clerk the price and was flabbergasted to find out that it was more than three hundred dollars. "Sorry," she said. As she headed for the door, the woman called, "Wait. Maybe I could do something for you." She went into a back room and returned with an index card. With an exaggerated sigh, she said, "I could let it go for two seventy-five."

"Two and a quarter and not a cent more," Ellen said, wondering where the words had come from. She thought the clock was beautiful and would look just perfect in her living room but to spend that much money frivolously was silly. She hated bargaining, but still . . .

"I'm so sorry. I couldn't let it go for anything less than two fifty."

Two hundred and fifty dollars. This was ridiculous. "Okay," she heard herself say. "I'll take it."

"You've made a good decision," the woman said and took the clock and Ellen's credit card to the rear of the store. Soon Ellen was walking toward her apartment with the clock in a shopping bag. Her apartment. She was beginning to think of it that way. She stopped at the corner and added a large bunch of flowers to her purchase. *My apartment.*

The next day was Monday, the day of the art class. She considered not going, but no. The butterfly was going to venture out of her cocoon, and without Maggie's help, even if it killed her. She looked over her new purchases, but finally dressed in an old pair of jeans and a sweatshirt and added her navy windbreaker. Painting clothes, not a stylish outfit. She wasn't here to impress anyone, just learn to paint and she certainly wasn't trying to impress Kevin. One man in her life at a time was enough. So, with her art-supply box in hand, she headed for The Templeton Gallery.

She entered the gallery and followed the signs to the second-floor workshop where the classes were held. The room was almost the size of the entire gallery, with windows on two sides and several skylights. The air smelled of art, of oil and turpentine, thinner, and fixative. She saw Kevin standing at the side of the room, looking over the shoulder of a middle-aged man who held a charcoal pencil in his hand. As she looked around, Ellen saw that there were a total of six people, each standing in front of an easel with paper clipped to backing, working silently with charcoal, trying to get the right perspective on a vase of flowers on a pedestal table at the front of the room. Canvases covered with cloths were propped against the walls around the perimeter of the room. Shelves held what Ellen imagined were sculptures, also covered. Several pieces of furniture were scattered around the periphery.

She stood in the doorway for a moment until Kevin spotted her and rushed over. "It's Ellen, isn't it?" He was dressed in casual gray jeans and a soft blue V-neck sweater that brought out the blue of his eyes and showed a large amount of heavy black chest hair. He had pushed the sweater's sleeves up to reveal strong forearms covered with more thick, black hair. "You've changed your hair."

Flattered that he remembered her name, and flabbergasted that he had noticed her new look, Ellen nodded weakly. "I-I-I thought I'd try out a class and see what I can do."

"We're delighted to have you. I'd introduce you around but right now everyone is doing a five-minute exercise." He guided her to an empty easel and helped her set up a pad of textured paper. "We're playing with line today, trying to get the essence of a shape with as few lines as possible." He found a charcoal pencil in her box and helped her sharpen it. "Just relax and try to get with the flow of what's going on. I'll come back to you later." At that moment a timer that had been ticking away in the background sounded. "Okay, everyone." He put a book and a candle in a brass holder on the small table, cranked the timer and said, "Next. Go!"

Ellen took her charcoal pencil and quickly sketched the items in front of her. In what seemed only seconds, the timer sounded again. "Okay," Kevin said, as he added a bowl of fruit and a few soft brushes to the book and candle. "Here's another. Take fifteen minutes with this one and I'll come around and see how everyone's doing." He repositioned the cloth on which the items rested then said, "Okay. Go!"

As Ellen worked she noticed that Kevin wandered from easel to easel, commenting, adjusting, suggesting, all in a gentle and supportive tone. When he arrived behind her he said, "As you finish an exercise, take a new sheet and put the previous one beside you so I can look at your work without disturbing you."

Ellen flipped back a page and tore off the previous exercise. Kevin held it up and studied it as Ellen looked with him. Each object was portrayed in only a few lines, but the overall effect was not only shape but solidity. "This is quite good for a rank amateur. You've got a good hand and a good eye. It's quite obvious, however, that you've had no formal training." He looked from her work to her. "I'm sorry. That came out sounding insulting and I didn't mean it that way."

"You're right, though. I've never had a lesson. I just draw what I like, and it seems to come out okay."

Ellen saw genuine appreciation in his eyes. "It most certainly does. Your sense of line is really wonderful."

"I haven't drawn anything in more years than I care to think about. Do you think I can make something that will give me pressure?"

"That's an interesting way to put it. Most people are concerned with whether they can create something salable."

"I'm not interested in selling my work, just enjoying it." Ellen realized that this was the first time she had ever done something for pure pleasure, without an ulterior motive.

"I always rant and rave about people who are only interested in the monetary aspect of art. In my mind, if you get joy out of what you're creating, that's the object of the game. If you sell something, so much better." He glanced at the timer at the front of the room. "This arrangement has only another minute, but we'll do several more. The class lasts until twelve. Stay after and let's talk." When Ellen nodded, Kevin hustled to the front of the room. "Okay," he said, "let's do another fifteen-minute exercise."

Two hours later only Kevin and Ellen remained in the workroom. Toward the end of class, Kevin had introduced Ellen to the other students. Each was warm and open with, "Glad to meet yous," and "Welcomes." One woman suggested that one day they have lunch after class. "What a nice group you have," she said when Kevin had finished cleaning up the front of the room.

"I seem to attract the nicest and most talented people." He stood behind her and Ellen could feet the warmth of his breath on her neck as he talked. "You included, of course, but I do have a collection of very talented artists in my classes. You met Joseph Overman, the guy with the heavy eyebrows and the glasses." Ellen pictured the inept-looking man who seemed to have trouble seeing the end of his brush through his amazingly thick glasses. "He's having a one-man show at The Morris next month."

"He is? What's The Morris?"

"A very prestigious gallery in Soho. It's quite an honor for him."

"And for you, too, I'd say."

Kevin nodded, then lapsed into silence gazing at her work, finally saying, "You know, you've really got talent. I hope you'll continue to come here."

She had no idea whether she actually had talent or whether Kevin was just saying that to get her to sign up for a series of classes, but she found she didn't care. She was doing something just for the hell of it, and she hadn't had as much fun in a long time. "I have no clue whether I have talent or not, but I really enjoyed this morning. I think I'd like to come back. I've read your brochure and I think I can deal with the cost of ten lessons to start."

"Wonderful." He took her credit card and hustled downstairs, returning several minutes later with a receipt for her to sign and a handful of signed business cards. "You turn in one of these each lesson. That way I don't have to keep track of what days you come. I do classes Mondays, Wednesdays, and Fridays, and my brother, Sean, does them on Tuesdays and Thursdays. He sculpts so unless you want to play with clay, come on my days. Most classes, like this morning's, are applicable to any medium, but I have some special ones from time to time that focus on techniques for a specific medium. There will always be a schedule posted both up here and downstairs. Why watercolors, by the way?"

"I used to paint when I was a kid and I always enjoyed poster paint so I guess I just thought that made sense. Otherwise, I've no fixed ideas."

Kevin tipped his head to one side. "Let me ask you this. If you could paint anything in the world: landscapes, portraits, still lifes, animals, what would you paint?" When Ellen didn't answer immediately, he continued, "Close your eyes and see yourself in your living room, gazing up at a blank wall. Now see a frame there, filled with something you created. You're happy to look at it, pleased that it came out so well. Got that?"

"Yes," Ellen said, eyes closed.

"Okay. What's in the frame?"

"It's a landscape, I guess. Soft green trees and a lake."

From close behind her, Kevin whispered, "Tell me more."

"There are flowers and puffy white clouds. Two people are having a picnic. They are obviously laughing and enjoying the warm sun but they are small and you can't make out their faces."

"Okay," he said softly. "That's a good place to start. Just because you're thinking about landscapes doesn't mean you can overlook the basics though. It doesn't free you from work and exercises like the ones we were doing today. You need to master line and form, shape and contour. You must learn about composition and texture." He grasped her shoulders and stood close to her back. "And in your painting, were those people you and me by any chance?"

Startled, Ellen realized that she hadn't had any sexual thoughts about Kevin since she arrived, but now her mind was filled with the feel and smell of him. The hair on the back of her neck prickled from the feel of his breath. "You know, of course, that I paint. I was wondering. Would you pose for me some afternoon?"

"Me?" Ellen thought about her fantasy. Being alone with Kevin, just the two of them. *Be real, Ellen,* she told herself. *He's just a painter looking for a free model.*

"Sure," she said, trying to keep her voice light. "Why not?" Don't get carried away, she lectured herself.

"Good. That's great. Could you sit for me one afternoon this week? I'm just finishing something, but Thursday would be wonderful."

"Can you just take time from the gallery like that?"

"My brother Sean and I co-own the Templeton. He sculpts while I cover the downstairs, then I paint while he gallery-sits. Could you come on Thursday?"

Why the hell not? "Okay."

"I need to tell you something that might change your mind." She could feel Kevin's sigh. "I was considering letting you show up then telling you but I have too much respect for you to create an awkward scene. I paint nudes."

Ellen felt the heat scorch her cheeks. "Nudes? Why me?" she squeaked, unable to get anything else sensible out of her mouth.

Kevin took her shoulders and turned her around to face him. "Honestly? You have a wonderful combination of sensuality and reticence, power and modesty, curiosity and hesitancy. If I could portray that, I'd be a genius. I want to try." He brushed her lower lip with his thumb. "And you have such a sexy mouth."

Ellen couldn't get any coherent thoughts through her brain. It was as though her entire body was paralyzed and all the energy of movement flowed into her swirling thoughts.

Kevin cleared his throat. "I'm sorry. I've embarrassed you and I didn't intend it at all. Really. I'm not making a pass at you, I was just being truthful, something that often gets me into trouble. Please. Feel free to say no, but also consider saying yes. The human body is so beautiful that it's what I enjoy painting most."

Ellen realized that her hands had crept up until they were covering her breasts. She certainly didn't have a body that men wanted to paint.

"Let me show you a few of my paintings and maybe you'll understand." She didn't protest when he led her into a small side room. Paintings stood on the floor, balanced against the walls. They were all of nudes, reclining, seated, standing, posed and in natural positions.

"These are very good," Ellen said, overwhelmed by the quality of the work. "They live. They almost breathe."

Kevin's smile lit his face. "That's what I hope people will see in them."

"The women are all so lovely," Ellen said, more sure than ever that she couldn't pose for him.

"Are they? Look more closely. They are all just ordinary women."

Ellen took a better look and quickly realized that Kevin was right. There were no perfect bodies, no models' shapes yet all the women were, each in her own way, beautiful. "Why do they all look beautiful?"

"Because, when I paint them, they feel beautiful. That's all it really takes to make a woman beautiful."

"Not really," she said, but she continued to stare at the room full of nude women.

"Really. Let me prove it to you. Let me sketch you on Thursday. Come at about two. If you don't want to stay, I'll understand. If you just want to sit, fully clothed, and let me try to capture that wonderful attitude, that will be enough for me."

She could keep her clothes on, yet he could make her look beautiful? Should she do it?

"Listen, Ellen. I'll be here at two, waiting, hoping you'll show up. If you do, we will do only what makes you comfortable. If you're not comfortable I can't paint you anyway. Please come. But if you don't, I'll understand, and of course you'll still come to my classes. Okay?"

"I'll think about it."

"Bravo!" Lucy screamed. "She's going to go for it."

"Lucy, you promised not to eavesdrop," Angela snapped.

"I know, but she's such a fascinating case. You know me. I can resist anything but temptation."

"Luce, you're incorrigible. Don't promises mean anything to you? How's she ever going to feel like she has any privacy?"

"She doesn't."

"I know that, but she doesn't."

Large letters streamed across Lucy's computer screen.

"LUCY—YOU AREN'T GETTING ANY WORK DONE. PAY ATTENTION TO BUSINESS AND STAY OUT OF THINGS THAT DON'T CONCERN YOU."

"Yes, sir," Lucy said, returning to a stack of computer printouts. "But I decide what concerns me," she whispered.

Chapter 8

When Ellen wandered into the kitchen the following morning, Maggie was sitting waiting for her, a gift-wrapped box on the table in front of her. "I took the liberty of starting coffee," she said. She pushed the box toward Ellen as she settled across the table. "This is for you."

Ellen settled at the tiny table and picked up the flat box, wrapped in shiny red paper with a black ribbon and intricately tied bow. "You didn't have to get me anything. You've been so much help already."

"It's not from me. I found it in the changing room."

"Changing room?"

"The changing room is where I am just before you see me. I'm just there, and there are clothes waiting for me appropriate for what I will do that day. I dress, then open the door and I'm here, or wherever. Lord the verbiage is so difficult." She combed her fingers through her hair. "Anyway, I found this on a bench and the card's addressed to you."

Ellen took the package and pulled off the attached card. The envelope was small and black as was the business card inside. "For Thursday," it said in white ink. "Knock him dead. Love, Lucy."

"It's from Lucy," Ellen said, barely able to keep her jaw from dropping. She pulled the paper off the box and opened it. In a nest of black tissue paper lay a tiny lacy bra and matching bikini panties, both in a soft blue. As Ellen held them up she realized that, while they were totally decent, they were also decadent, with carefully selected areas of thick and thin lace. "She's got to be kidding," Ellen said, gaping at the lingerie. "I couldn't wear anything like this."

"Why not, and what's happening on Thursday? And what day is it now?"

"Actually, it's Tuesday, and quite a bit has happened since I saw you last." She told Maggie all about Jim and dinner the previous Saturday evening. Then she spent several minutes discussing Kevin's painting class. "Oh, and he asked me to pose for him next Thursday." She ducked her head. "Nude."

"Wow. Quite a step out of your safe little cocoon, I'd say."

Ellen's head snapped up abruptly. "Just a damn minute. How does Lucy know about Thursday?" she snapped. "Has she been watching me again? I thought they both promised to stay out of my life."

Maggie held her hands up, palms outward. "Hold it. I have no control over Lucy. To be honest, I doubt that anyone has, except maybe her boss." She chuckled. "And I'm not even sure about him."

"The nerve of her." Ellen almost ran into the living room and dropped onto the sofa. She jumped up again and paced. "The nerve."

Maggie followed her into the living room, a coffee mug in each hand. "I would suggest that you just don't think about her," she said with infuriating calm. "She's become more and more of a busybody lately, but she can't really affect what you do unless you let her." She handed Ellen her coffee and settled in an overstuffed chair. Changing the subject she asked, "What are you going to do about Thursday? I hope you're going to pose for him."

"I don't know," Ellen said with a long sigh, propping her feet on the coffee table. "Part of me wants to be brave and daring, to go along with my new look and all, but part of me is terrified that I'll get myself into something that I can't get out of."

"I know you don't know Kevin very well but from the feelings that you get, do you think you have to worry about him attacking you? Do you think he'd stop if you said no to something?"

Ellen thought a moment. "I think he would. I don't know why I say that. He might be a total con artist, bilking unsuspecting women out of their life savings for art lessons and midday sex." When Maggie raised her usual skeptical eyebrow, Ellen said, "Okay. He's probably not on *America's Most Wanted* and somehow I do trust him."

"So what you're saying is that it's *you* that you don't trust."

Ellen took a long time going into the kitchen and refilling her coffee cup. Maggie was right, of course. What she didn't trust were her own feelings and needs. Until recently she hadn't realized how much she had been missing in life. Sure, she had been depressed when Gerry moved to the city, but she had made a life for herself without a man in it. But was that really life? Didn't she need more? Wasn't that why, deep down beyond the obvious, she had come to the city? Ellen had never been particularly introspective but now, as she finally looked into herself, she had to admit that she was curious about men and sex and relationships. More and more, thoughts about what she'd been missing had been filtering into her consciousness.

As she returned with her coffee, Ellen picked up the conversation. "I guess what I'm scared to death of is being out of my league, of discovering that I know nothing about loving." Tears started to gather in her eyes. "I'm terrified of having someone like Kevin make a pass at me, then being so inept that he laughs at me or just gives up in frustration."

"No one's born knowing or confident," Maggie said, handing Ellen a tissue from the pocket of her jeans. "Every woman in the world has had doubts like yours from time to time. Women who've been out of the dating scene for a while wonder whether anyone will ever be interested in them again. Some women stay with men who are incredibly bad for them because they are frightened that they will never have sex again."

"You never had doubts," Ellen said with a sniff.

"Of course I did. Not as much in my later years, of course, although I was often worried that a new man would be disappointed in my body or my performance. In my early years, I was nervous almost all the time, but it's attitude that matters. If you force yourself to feel confident, then the confidence will become real very quickly. It's like 'Whistle a Happy Tune.' Make believe you're brave and all."

Ellen smiled through her tears. "I can't imagine you've ever being scared of a man and his opinion of you."

"I remember when my friend Frank's boss, Norman, called me the first time. We talked for almost an hour. I knew it was an interview of sorts, on Frank's recommendation. He was judging me, not on my sexual prowess but on my charm and intelligence. He must have found me pleasant enough because he invited me join him, his wife and a nameless, important bigwig from out of town at a political fund-raiser the following Saturday evening. I was going to entertain the client in whatever way presented itself. He didn't want me to tell the client that I was being paid and I wasn't totally comfortable with that, but at that moment I would have agreed to anything."

"A phone interview for a job as a prostitute?"

"Sounds a bit strange, but it actually made sense. He wanted to know whether I could make intelligent conversation and be entertaining outside of the bedroom. Finally he told me about the dinner. The candidate was an archconservative and I was a flaming liberal but somehow I agreed to attend anyway. And, of course, the money was a great incentive. Norman suggested some cover story and that was that.

"As the evening of the dinner approached I almost backed out. What did I know about which fork to use or how to make small talk with some guy who would know that I was a paid companion? What would he expect? Would I be able to make love with someone just for money? I was a wreck."

"I look at you and I can't imagine you not confident. How long ago was that?" Ellen asked, her attention riveted on Maggie's story.

"More years than I care to think about. I began in the business in 1974 or thereabouts."

"How did it all start, if you'll pardon me for asking?"

Maggie sipped her coffee. "I had been married. It was great sex but nothing else. After a few years, we split and I spent months lonely and horny as hell. I was in my early thirties, at my sexual peak with lots of energy and nowhere to spend it. One evening, on my way home from work, I stopped for a drink and a really nice guy picked me up. To make a long story short, Frank and I ended up in bed together, sharing a very satisfying night, and lots more after that. When he understood where I was in my life, he suggested that, if I loved sex, I should get paid for it. He mentioned me to his boss who often had to find companions for lonely businessmen. That was Norman."

"Didn't Frank mind sharing you?"

"He wasn't interested in a permanent relationship and had a very open mind. He liked it that I was happy and he knew I needed the money."

"Wow. You found a real gem right off the bat."

"He was pretty terrific, but about a year after I met him he got transferred to the West Coast and out of my life."

"You didn't go with him?"

"Sweetie, I told you. It wasn't that kind of relationship. Understand this. These men—Frank was the first of many—were fun to be with, date, and fuck, but not long-term material for either of us. I had long before decided that I wasn't a one-man woman, and I made that perfectly clear to all the men I dated more than once. I like variety, experimentation, originality. I like the thrill of a new bedroom with a new partner."

"Didn't any of the men get serious?"

"Oh, sure. There was one man, Paul, who kept proposing. I knew he wasn't really serious. We were great in bed and had lots in common but it just wasn't enough. And, of course, he was years younger than I was."

Ellen sipped her coffee. "I want someone who's interested in building a life together with me."

"Great. Go for that, but you have to kiss a lot of frogs to find one handsome prince, so if you learn to love kissing, it's all wonderful."

Laughing, Ellen almost choked on her coffee. "Boy, I've dated a few frogs in my time but not recently. Maybe that's why I want some permanence."

"What's right for me isn't necessarily right for you. If you want to find the right guy, however, you have to be brave and do some dating."

"Kevin's not a date. He's someone who wants me to pose nude. This could be sex, but it's not dating."

"Even if Kevin's not long-term material, he's experience. You know, it's easy to tell a frog from a prince, but it's much more difficult to tell Mr. Right from Mr. Almost-Right. You need to sample what's out there before you'll have any idea who's going to fit with you for the long haul."

"Brave. Right." Her sigh was loud. "Anyway, let's get back to you. You were telling me about your political dinner. Frank's boss Norman."

"Right. I decided that if I was going to be successful in the business, I had to look the part so I made myself over with hair, makeup, and nails, just as you did." She fluffed her short, curly hair. "Remember women were still going to bed in curlers so I found a cut that would still look good after a night's tumble. I spent almost a week's salary on a dress. It was black silk, bias cut, long and slender with classic lines that came straight across above my breasts with little, skinny straps. I reasoned that it wouldn't go out of style too quickly and would accessorize easily to change its look. I added a floral-print sequined jacket, black strappy sandals, and a plain gold necklace and earrings."

"Sounds gorgeous."

"You know, that dress really helped my confidence and I needed it that night. It almost became a fiasco." Maggie's thoughts drifted back to that evening.

"As planned, I arrived as the cocktail hour was ending and found a seating card with my name on it. I wended my way through crowds of black-tie-clad men and women in outrageous gowns and found my table toward the front of the room. As I approached I recognized Norman from his description of himself over the phone. To make everyone feel at ease I was to pretend that I knew him and that he had invited me to fill the final empty seat at the table, which was to be next to my date. I transferred my small black beaded handbag to my left hand and extended my right. 'Norman,' I said. 'This is such a pleasure. I can't thank you enough for calling.'

" 'Maggie, darling,' Norman said, taking my hand and putting my face close. 'It's been an age.' He bussed my cheek. 'What have you been doing with yourself?'

" 'Just this and that,' I said. 'You know how I hate talking about me. How have you been?'

"We made small talk for a few moments, then Norman introduced me around the table. 'And this is Walter O'Reilly from our Atlanta office,' he said, indicating an overweight man with an overly tight cummerbund that made him took like twenty pounds of mashed potatoes in a ten-pound sack. He had a real salesman smile, a florid complexion, and a roving eye. His gaze oscillated from my face to my cleavage.

" 'That's not Radar,' he said with a loud laugh. 'Just Walter.'

" 'Radar?' I asked, wondering whether I could go through with the evening.

" 'From *M *A *S *H*. Radar O'Reilly's real name is Walter. Don't you watch?'

" 'Of course,' I said, planting a smile on my face. 'Nice to meet you, not-Radar.' His laugh boomed so loudly that people at adjoining tables turned to look."

Ellen's nose wrinkled. "He sounds like quite a character."

"Oh, he was. I just stared, sure I was going to have to run for the hills. I thought about the money and shook his hand. *Confidence,* I told myself. *It's all in the attitude.*"

"How did you deal with the fact that you were going to spend the night with someone who you didn't like?"

"I just went along minute to minute. I couldn't insult Norman or Walter so I just let myself drift, and made sure I looked like I was enjoying every second of everything." Maggie chuckled. "I had made my bed, so to speak, and now I had to lie in it.

"So Norman finished the introductions. 'This is Barrett Olkowski, Norman said. 'He's a top chemist from our midwest research facility. He's worked on some of our most important breakthroughs and he's here for a symposium. He was going to spend the evening in his hotel room so I insisted that he get out for a few hours. I'm not sure, of course, that I did him any favors what with the boring speeches he'll be sitting through, but the food's usually good and, now that you're here, so's the company.'

"I pulled my gaze from not-Radar and considered Barrett. He was about my height, sort of owlish looking with soulful brown eyes and thinning hair. Norman guided me to a seat between Walter and Barrett."

"Were you supposed to be with Walter or Barrett?" Ellen asked.

"That's the silly part. As I sat down I realized that I didn't know which man was my date. Norman had neglected to tell me anything about the man I was being paid to entertain and he didn't pick up on my not-too-subtle hints. So I had to be nice to both of them, and in Walter's case, it wasn't easy. Barrett was a quiet guy, content to eat and let the conversation swirl around everyone else throughout the multi-course meal. Not-Radar, on the other hand, was boisterous, rude, and a general pain in the ass. He told nasty jokes, making fun of blacks, Jews, Polaks, as he called them, and anyone else he could get his mouth around. He also got his digs in on Liberals and Democrats."

"Didn't anyone complain?"

"Remember those were the days before political correctness

when it was all right to tell jokes of any kind as long as someone laughed. I smiled and frequently cringed inwardly, crossing my fingers that Barrett was mine."

"How did you manage with the silverware and all?"

"I carefully watched what everyone else did and followed their lead. It really wasn't as difficult as I had feared. What was hard was making both men feel like they were special, while personally loathing not-Radar. I think that was the moment when I decided that I was never going to get into a situation like that again. I was going to chat with each client on the phone before any date. If I didn't like him, it was no dice. I wasn't ever going to do it just for the money again. That night, however, I was hooked. A deal's a deal and I was prepared to go ahead with whatever I had to."

"You really never did it just for the money again?"

"Never. I kept working for a while and I built up a nice little nest egg. As you've found out in the past few months, kiss-off money is the best thing there ever was."

"Kiss-off money?" Ellen asked.

"Money enough to tell anyone to kiss off, to quit your job, to tell any obnoxious slob, like not-Radar, that you're not available. You get the idea."

Ellen nodded as she considered her lottery winnings. She could tell Dr. Okamura to kiss off any time she wanted. It gave her a completely different outlook on life and, as Maggie said, it was, indeed, freeing. "Was not-Radar the guy you were supposed to be with, and how did it work out?"

"During the speeches Walter was on one side of me cheering on the candidate, a conservative who made Ronald Reagan look liberal while, on the other side of me, Barrett groaned from time to time. Finally the guy finished and many of the members of the audience got up to leave. In the confusion, I finally got to talk to Norman."

"So which guy was it?"

"Norman was horrified that he had neglected to tell me that important bit of information. 'I'm so sorry, Maggie,' he whispered. 'Walter showed up Friday afternoon and asked whether I had a ticket for tonight so I invited him along. Barrett's the guy I am paying you for. I didn't realize that I'd never told you the name of the man I wanted you to entertain. Barrett's such a shy guy but he's a cracker-jack chemist and a really nice man when you get to know him. He's single and, beneath it all, very lonely. I really just wanted to show him a good time in the big city. I didn't tell him about you and I'm hoping you can get him to unwind, in spite of himself. I want him to feel attractive, good about himself.' "

"I'll bet you were relieved," Ellen said.

"Yes, and no. I was delighted that Walter wasn't my date for the evening, but I wasn't sure I could deceive Barrett either."

"So what did you do?"

"As the place was emptying out, a dance band began to play some slow music. While Walter was talking to Norman, I asked Barrett to dance with me. I love slow-dancing and I was hoping to loosen him up a bit. While we danced I asked him about himself and got little more than one-syllable answers. A bit frustrated, I asked about his work and he told me it was all secret. Finally, as we were walking back to the table, he said, 'You don't have to be nice to me, you know.'

"I tried to look puzzled, although I knew exactly what he meant. 'I know I don't have to be nice to you.'

" 'Please,' he said, whirling to glare at me, 'I own a mirror. Let's be honest here. The only reason I can think of for your being nice to me is that you're a pro who Norman hired. He's threatened to do it for some time. I don't need a professional hooker to charm me into bed. I'm perfectly capable of taking care of myself.'

"I was flabbergasted that I had been that obvious, and a bit relieved that I wouldn't have to lie about it. 'I'm sure you are and I'm not going to deny that Norman invited me to be your date for the evening.' I wanted to find a way to just spend some time with him. He seemed like a scared rabbit and I found that I was becoming fond of him. 'Listen. You're right. I'm being paid for this, but if Norman doesn't see us spending time together, I don't get paid and, to be honest, I need the money. If we just sit for a while, or dance, later you can tell Norman you were really tired or something, so he wouldn't think that you didn't find me pleasant company."

"That was very clever. You're such a sweet person," Ellen said.

"I just like people, and I saw what Norman liked in Barrett. He was a really nice guy with an attitude problem a mile wide. His attitude problem totally eliminated mine. I convinced him to take pity on me so we sat at the table and just talked for a while. Later, as we danced, I could tell he was attracted to me. His palms got sweaty and he fumbled for his words when he held me. I rubbed my body against his and enjoyed the feeling of his excitement. 'You know I'm already paid for the evening,' I said, 'and I think we could be good together: He looked dubious but I continued, 'Why don't we go up to your room and order a bottle of wine from room service? We don't have to do anything you don't want to but we can leave our options open.'

"I could see uncertainty in his eyes. 'I'm not a charity case, you know.'

"I cupped my hand over his erection. 'You don't need charity.' I took his hand, slipped it under my jacket and placed his palm over my breast. 'You may not know this but when a woman gets aroused, her nipples become erect.' I held his hand tightly. 'This isn't charity.'

"I half-expected him to pull his hand back, but his eyes locked with mine. He said nothing, but he nodded." Maggie looked at Ellen. "Do you want to hear the details? I don't usually kiss and tell, but this was twenty-five years ago. I think the statute of limitations has run out."

"Sure," Ellen said, resting her elbows on the table. "I'm fascinated. How did you get around his shyness? That must be an unusual problem."

"It's funny but it's a more prevalent problem than I would have imagined. Men would call me, then chicken out. I'd arrive and they'd tell me that they'd changed their minds. Men have performance anxieties, too, and since I'm the pro they figure that if they can't get it up then they'll be humiliated."

"Really? I never considered that a man might be afraid like that."

"Me either. Anyway, Barrett and I had a conversation in the elevator. I decided to be completely honest and, by the way, I've been that way ever since." She drifted back to that evening and replayed the scene in her mind.

"Listen, Barrett, let me be completely straight with you. I'm really new at this entertainment business. I like you and I think you're a really nice guy and, frankly, you turn me on. I really like the shy type. I'm ever so glad that you know I'm a professional because I had already decided that I couldn't go on lying. I'd love to just sit and talk with you and, if something happens, that's fine. If not, fine, too. How about that?"

"You're a really nice lady," he said, "and, I must admit, you're sexy as hell. I've been thinking lewd thoughts about you all evening but I find that the idea that you're so—well—experienced, scares the shit out of me."

Maggie was delighted that Barrett had said more in one elevator ride than he had said all evening. She grabbed his arm and pressed his elbow against the side of her breast. "Let's just see where honesty gets us."

In his room Maggie removed her jacket while Barrett called twenty-four-hour room service and ordered a bottle of wine and two glasses. "Are you hungry?" he asked, holding his palm over the receiver.

Maggie's eyes lit up. "You know, I was so nervous about the evening that I didn't eat much dinner. I'm starved."

"Burgers for two?" When Maggie eagerly nodded, Barrett added two burger specials to his order. They chatted for a while until the room-service waiter arrived and set up the table for their midnight meal. Finally able to enjoy each other's company, they gobbled their burgers.

Each plate had arrived with french fries, an assortment of

fruits and vegetables, and a large half-sour pickle. With a gleam in her eye, Maggie picked up the pickle and, gazing into Barrett's eyes, licked the end of it with her pink tongue.

"You're deliberately teasing me," Barrett said, his voice suddenly breathy and hoarse.

"What's the problem with that?" Maggie asked, still licking the pickle.

Barrett reached out and grabbed her arm. "Nothing. Absolutely nothing," he said as he took a big bite out of the end of the pickle. Maggie held out a strawberry and Barrett nibbled the end of it, while holding a slice of pineapple for her to suck on.

She drew the pineapple slice into her mouth and with it, Barrett's fingers. Her tongue danced over his fingertips and her eyes locked with his. "You are a witch, you know," he said. "I would have sworn that I couldn't feel as capable as I do right now with a prostitute." He looked shocked, then added, "I'm sorry. I didn't mean to insult you."

Maggie sat back in her chair. "You didn't. I enjoy sex and now I get paid for it. I'm glad you're feeling capable because I'm getting really hungry." She stood up, unzipped the back of her dress and let it fall to the floor and pool around her feet. She was wearing a tiny wisp of a strapless black bra, panties that were little more than a crotch panel and a few strings, a black garter belt, and stockings. "Interested in playing a bit?"

Barrett just stared as Maggie walked around to his side of the table and sat down on his lap. "I'd love to play with you," she continued, "but only if you're comfortable."

With a groan, Barrett grabbed the back of her head and pulled her down. "I'm not a bit comfortable, but I will be soon." He pressed his mouth against hers and kissed her, tangling his tongue with hers. As they kissed and he slanted his head for better contact, Maggie thought he was becoming surprisingly forceful and decisive. He completely controlled the kiss and eventually slipped his hands up her ribs to cup her bra-covered breasts. He pulled his head back and moaned, Take all this off." As they stood, he said, "Leave the stockings and belt on. They are really hot."

Quickly he dragged off his clothes as Maggie removed her underwear. He stripped the covers off the bed and they stretched out across it. "God, I never imagined the evening would end up like this," he said. Maggie just smiled as he pressed his body against hers. She slid her hands up and down his back and flanks and finally touched his erection. He was hard and ready.

With her hands she urged him over her as she spread her legs. Although she wasn't urgently hungry, she felt so good about being with Barrett that she knew she was wet and ready. As he supported his weight on one elbow, she took his other hand and together they reached between her legs and found the slippery center of her sex. "Touch me there," she whispered. She guided his fingers to her clit and positioned his middle finger on her spot. "Here," she purred. "Like this." She moved his hand as she climbed toward her own orgasm. Quickly she dropped her hand as his fingers learned her needs. He quickly found other places that made her moan and undulate her hips. "I need you inside me."

He thrust his penis into her hot, wet channel as he continued to rub her clit. Her breathing had speeded up and she knew that she was close to coming. "Feel it," she moaned. "Hold still inside me and just feel."

Following her instructions his body stilled, his cock lodged fully inside of her. As he kept rubbing she felt the pressure build, then explode. "Now, feel. Feel what it's like for me to come with your hard cock inside me." She felt the spasms of her orgasm grip his cock, contracting and squeezing him.

"Oh, God, Maggie," he moaned as, without any additional movement, he spurted inside of her. He collapsed, his hands now softly stroking her arm. Panting, he said, "I've never felt anything like that. You came. I could feel you."

"I know. I love coming like that, so I can feel every movement, too. It's almost like I'm caressing you with my body."

"You can't fake that, can you."

Maggie cupped his face and gazed into his eyes. "Not a chance. You did that for me."

"You're one hell of a woman, Maggie."

Maggie returned to the present as Ellen said, from across the kitchen table, "That was something. It must have made him feel ten feet tall that you came. I would guess that women can't fake that. You didn't fake anything, did you?"

"Nope. It was a joint experience and we had promised complete honesty after all." Maggie slumped back in her chair, almost as drained as she had been after sex. "I found in the years that followed that honesty in sex is probably the most important thing there is, even for a prostitute."

"Didn't you ever fake it or lie to make some customer feel good?"

Maggie sighed. "I guess I did, but somehow I don't consider them lies, just ego boosters. In general, I told the truth to everyone, most importantly myself."

"Telling yourself the truth is basic."

Maggie leaned forward and grasped Ellen's hands. "Have you been telling yourself the truth about Kevin?"

"I walked into that one, didn't I? Maybe not. If I were to be completely honest I would admit that he intrigues me and I'm really curious about what might be. Anyway, I'm sure he's only looking for a model. I'm probably building all this up in my mind."

Maggie's dark eyebrow arched again. "Maybe not."

Ellen took a deep breath. "Maybe not."

"So you're going to pose for him?"

At that moment, Ellen knew. "I am, and the devil take the hindmost."

Maggie's laugh was warm. "Don't let Lucy hear you say that."

Ellen joined the laughter. "Right."

Chapter 9

Later that morning Maggie noticed the new clock and the flowers sitting on an end table in a water glass. "You've moved in," she said.

"I guess I have," Ellen said with a small smile.

That afternoon they picked out a cut-glass vase and a small lamp for Ellen's dresser. Maggie also insisted that Ellen buy three pillar candles with holders for the bedroom and a CD of dance music in case a date came back to her apartment. "Not likely," Ellen had protested, but she made the purchases anyway.

Despite all her talk, Ellen changed her mind a dozen times. She couldn't possibly. She certainly could. Why should she take the risk? Why not? She hadn't gone to class on Wednesday, afraid to face Kevin, but lying in bed that night she tried to create the scene. What would it be like? Would he be tender, demanding, hesitant, forceful? Would he undress her or would she have to take off her clothes in that huge room? Would he be a good lover? She stopped herself, sure that if she built it all up in her mind she'd be disappointed with the reality. *Afterward,* she thought, *when nothing happens I can dream about what might have been.* All Thursday morning she thought about nothing but the afternoon's modeling session.

At one o'clock she stood in her bedroom, the wispy underwear that Lucy had given her on the bed. Would it seem like an invitation? Would he misunderstand? Was it a misunderstanding? Damn. She picked up the lingerie and put it on. Then, before she could change her mind, covered it with a pair of well-washed jeans and a soft, wheat-colored flannel shirt. She added socks and loafers then reached for her navy windbreaker. *Why not something new and more stylish?* she asked herself. *Because this outfit makes me feel more comfortable*, she answered, *and I need all the support I can get.*

She walked out into the cold and windy New York fall afternoon and headed for The Templeton Gallery. By the time she had walked the few blocks, her cheeks were pink and her fingers chilled. As she opened the door, a small bell sounded and a nice-looking man who appeared to be a smaller version of Kevin bustled to the front, dressed in what she now assumed was the store uniform, casual, well-washed, black jeans and a soft cranberry shirt. "Good afternoon. May I be of assistance?"

This must be Kevin's brother. "Hi. I'm here to see Kevin."

"You must be Ellen. He's upstairs. He's been pacing all morning, afraid you wouldn't come."

"Really?"

He looked chagrined. "I'm probably not supposed to tell you but he's really excited about painting you." He closed his mouth with a snap. "In my brain and out my mouth." He cupped her chin and turned her face left and right with small humming noises. "He's right, you know. You've got great bones and there's a wonderful quality about your expression." He paused and, as she frowned, he dropped his hand. "I'm sorry to be so forward, but we're really informal around here. I'm Kevin's brother, Sean, and I play with clay. I'd love for you to pose for me sometime, too."

Ellen looked down at her ordinary body. "Why me? I don't get it. I'm nothing special, no supermodel or anything."

"Supermodels have no appeal to true artists. We like women with substance." He paused. "Oops, that didn't come out the way I'd planned. I hope you'll accept my apology."

"For what?"

She saw that he was actually blushing. "I intimated that you're not so slim."

"Well, I'm not. Does that please an artist's eye?"

"For Kev and me it does. We've studied in Europe where they don't seem to have the incredible passion for bones and skin with nothing between. The old masters loved women with flesh on their bones. It's warm, soft and," he added as he took her hand, "sexy." He lifted her hand to his lips and kissed the back.

"Oh," Ellen said, not quite knowing whether he was making a pass at her. These brothers were quite a pair. "I think I'll just go upstairs and see where Kevin is."

"Right." He dropped her hand and took a step backward. "I hope you'll seriously consider posing for me sometime, too."

"I'll certainly think about it." Ellen wondered how much time the brothers spent in that upstairs studio with lonely women who took art classes to while away idle time. Was that what she was doing? Ellen shook off the negative thoughts. Who cared why she was there, she just was.

She climbed to the upper floor where Kevin was working, his back to her. He was dressed in casual black pants and a shirt the color of new grass. To her surprise he was barefoot. The studio smelled of chemicals and paint and music played somewhere in the background. She recognized the work as Mozart, but had no idea of the name or number. She walked up behind Kevin and peered over his shoulder at the sketchbook propped on his easel. "That's me!" she gasped.

Kevin jumped, placed his hand on his chest and let out a deep breath. "*Phew*, you startled me. When I get to working, I'm afraid I become a bit deaf so I didn't hear you come in." He took another breath. "It is you, sort of."

Ellen stared. The naked woman on the pad definitely had her face, captured with a few quick strokes of Kevin's pencil. The body, however, was classically lovely with soft curves and shadowed hollows. "Oh, I wish my body looked like that."

"I hope you don't mind my taking a bit of painter's license. I have no real idea what your body looks like under all those clothes, so I just let my imagination wander." He took her hands and bussed her cheek. "I'm so glad you decided to pose."

"I'm not so sure you need me. I like the way I look on your page better than the real thing." She realized that she had reflexively clutched her jacket tightly around her.

"You're embarrassed," Kevin said, "and I'm so sorry. I didn't intend to put you off." He took her hand and kissed her palm. "Please tell me you forgive me."

Ellen burst out laughing. He was so overly sincere that it became a bit saccharin. "You're quite something," she said, her lack of belief obvious.

Kevin joined her laughter. "Okay. Busted. My technique usually works. Please. Let me take your coat. Honestly, I didn't intend to offend or embarrass."

Honestly. Ellen heard Maggie's words. Be honest with yourself. "Honestly I am a bit embarrassed. I'm not used to men thinking about me without clothes." She pointed to the sketch. "I wish I looked like that."

"I'm glad you look just like you do and I'm so happy that you decided to come here this afternoon. Are you willing to disrobe or shall we begin with your face?"

Ellen took a deep breath. "Let's begin with the face and see how comfortable I can get with all this."

For almost an hour Kevin sketched while they talked. From time to time he changed her position on the old-fashioned burgundy velvet sofa that he had pulled to the center of the room. Finally he walked to where she was sitting. "Are you tired? You've been holding still for quite a while."

"I'm okay."

"You're being wonderfully patient with me." He stood, towering above her. "Could I unbutton a few of those buttons? I'd love to get an idea of your skin tone." When she didn't object, he reached down and slowly pushed three bone buttons through the buttonholes on the front of her shirt. His knuckles brushed her skin making her shiver. "Your skin is so warm," he purred, parting the sides of her blouse.

Suddenly Ellen couldn't concentrate, couldn't think at all. "You've got such beautiful, soft skin," he said, stroking his index finger down her breastbone to the valley between her breasts. Then he walked back to his sketch pad and picked up his pencil. "You know what I'd like you to do when you're comfortable?" His voice was soft and it was almost as if Ellen could feel it caress her.

"What?" she asked, breathless.

"I'd like you to finish unbuttoning your shirt and take it off. Would you do that for me?"

Almost without conscious thought, Ellen opened the lower buttons and pulled the shirt down her arms. The room was comfortably warm, yet she had goose bumps. How could she do this? Yet somehow she was and, trying to be honest with herself, she liked the way he was looking at her. She told herself that he was probably a total phoney, but right now he was concentrating on her, directing all his charisma at her like a searchlight. Did she mind? Not at all.

"You look as good as I thought you would and I love that sexy bit of lace you've got on." He made a few quick lines on his paper, then said, "Would you go further?" He approached again and slid one finger under her bra strap. "How far would you go?" He pulled the strap down over her shoulder until the fabric slipped off her breast. Slowly, his finger stroking across her skin, he found the other strap and slipped it off. "So beautiful," he putted. "I knew you'd be beautiful."

His look said she was beautiful and that was enough for Ellen. She reached behind her and unfastened the bra and dropped it behind the sofa with surprisingly steady hands.

"Yes," he said. He ran one finger down the curve of her breast. "So lovely. I wonder how you taste." He knelt beside the sofa and flicked his tongue over her erect nipple. Then he licked the other, and blew on the wet skin until her breast swelled and the nipple contracted to an almost painful nub. "Yes. Like that. Like a Venus preparing to meet her lover."

Some small part of her brain wondered how many women he had seduced on this sofa with exactly the same words, yet she didn't care. This was *her* experience. He was just window dressing. She reclined on the slightly threadbare sofa, stripped to the waist and felt sexy and desirable and who cared why. She watched as he returned to his easel and, with an almost fevered intensity, slashed his pencil across the paper. Slowly she toed off her loafers and pulled off her socks.

She felt like another person, and loved it. She slowly got to her feet and, as he gazed heatedly at her, unfastened the waist of her jeans and lowered the zipper. Kevin dropped his charcoal on the ledge of his easel and just stared as she hooked her thumbs in the waistband and pulled the jeans over her hips and down her legs. Finally she stood wearing just the tiny panties. "You have fooled me entirely," Kevin said.

"I have? How?"

"I thought you a tiny mouse but you are a chameleon, showing different faces to whomever looks at you." He closed the distance between them, causing her to take a step backward. "Yes," he purred. "You are at once timid and bold." He held her chin between his index finger and thumb. "And for now you are mine."

His lips closed over hers, his tongue invading, searching, taking. Ellen had never been kissed the way he was kissing her. It involved her entire body, not just her mouth, causing her knees to buckle, her nipples to tingle and molten heat to flow through her belly. She braced her hands against his chest and only his arms around her ribs kept her from collapsing. Then, in one quick move, he swept her up and lay her on the sofa. As she watched, he pulled off his clothes until he stood, gloriously naked.

He was gorgeous, his skin well tanned and covered with heavy, dark hair, his shoulders broad, his hips narrow. As she gazed at him, her eyes were drawn down through the whorls of hair on his chest and the narrow strip over his belly to the black nest of his rampant erection. He was huge and Ellen was sure that nothing that size could ever enter her body. Yet his smile was confident as his gaze caressed her as hers caressed him. Carefully he removed her panties and pushed her legs apart until one foot rested on the floor, and one on the sofa back. Then he crouched between her knees. "You knew this was going to happen, just as I did. Tell me you want it as much as I do."

Ellen took a deep breath. Honesty. "I do. I'm just a little scared. I've never done anything like this before."

Kevin combed his long fingers through her pubic hair. "I can take away all your fears." His fingers found her, slipping over her already sopping flesh. Then he bent over and his mouth followed his fingers. "I love the taste of a woman's body." His tongue found every fold of her, licking and stroking everywhere she hungered. She threaded her fingers through his long hair and held on tightly, keeping his head between her legs. She was being driven higher and higher by his talented mouth.

Then he did two things that drove her over the edge. Almost simultaneously he filled her with two fingers and his mouth found her clit and sucked. She screamed as an orgasm slammed through her. She realized in some still-aware place, that it was the first time she had come without her own hands touching her body.

She felt him leave her momentarily and heard the telltale ripping of a condom package. Then he was back, his giant cock driving into her, filling her body, pushing her open, more aware of him than she had been of any man.

Again she felt the waves, the convulsions of her channel against his penis. "Yes, Ellen, oh yes." Then he was incapable of speech as he bellowed and came inside of her. Yet even as his orgasm took him, he didn't stop playing with her clit. His mouth moved to a turgid nipple and he bit down lightly. Again she felt an orgasm crash over her, spasms taking her, making her claw at Kevin's shoulders.

Finally her body quieted and Kevin stretched out beside her so she could feel the pounding of his heart. "That was amazing," he said, his voice hoarse. "I've never met a more responsive woman."

Ellen had never experienced anything like making love with Kevin. Her body was exhausted, satiated, yet fresh and new. She giggled. "I'm so happy I want to laugh out loud." And when she did Kevin joined her.

"I knew when you showed up that we would end up here," Kevin said. "I've been dreaming about it all week."

"If I were being honest, I knew it, too."

Lazily he stroked along her hip, yet Ellen felt his sudden intensity. "Will you come back again soon? Tomorrow?"

"Kevin, this is all very new to me. Let's take it slowly, okay?"

"I don't want to go slowly. I want to devour you six times a day. I want to make love to you in every possible way."

Ellen held his gaze and tried to put her feelings into words. "I need to keep this all in perspective. Today was wonderful, amazing, like nothing that's ever been for me before and I don't want to spoil it. I want to go slowly. Please."

"How can I do that when every time I look at you I will see and feel what we've had this afternoon?"

More Kevin Duffy patented charisma? Did he say this to every woman he made love to on this sofa? Who cared? It would burn hot, but she'd try to tame the flame if she possibly could.

"I want to be able to attend your art classes without feeling like the blue-plate special. I don't know whether it's possible, but let's at least make an effort to keep everything in its place. I need to come to class tomorrow morning and see whether I can concentrate on painting with you in the room. I hope I can since I don't want to find another teacher . . . for anything." When he started to say something, Ellen covered his lips with her fingers. "I also want to continue what we've done here. Do you really want to paint me or was that just a convenient way to get me up here alone?"

Kevin let out a quick breath and nodded. "I actually want to paint you."

"Maybe one afternoon next week. You can paint, and then, if we both want to, we can indulge in other passions."

"You are a difficult woman, but sensible. Come to class tomorrow. I can't be with you over the weekend. That's when the gallery is busy and I've got other commitments. Can you be here with me Tuesday afternoon? You can pose, and whatever." His leer was so exaggerated that she grinned. He continued, "Having to wait until Tuesday will make the weekend go slowly, but I will know I have something to look forward to as well."

Ellen wondered whether she could juggle her feelings as well as she had just told Kevin she could. She wanted to make love with him over and over. It felt like a drug, making her crave more and more yet she wouldn't allow herself to become addicted. She was too new at all this. "Yes. Tuesday afternoon."

Ellen wandered home in a daze and, as she had half expected, found Maggie waiting for her in the kitchen, an open bottle of wine and two half-filled glasses on the table. "I know where you've been, but I didn't eavesdrop, I promise, although I will admit that, if I could have, I'd have been really tempted. Want to talk?"

Ellen dropped her jacket on the counter and sunk, exhausted and drained, onto a chair. She took several swallows of the wine. "Wow. This is sensational. Did you bring it?"

"I did. I've no idea how it is that sometimes I can walk into a store and appear just like any other person, but I brought this to celebrate or commiserate." She raised her ever-inquisitive eyebrow. "Well? Which is it?"

Ellen couldn't suppress a grin. "Celebrate. It was fantastic, toe-curling, earth-moving sex."

"I'd love to hear as many details as you want to tell," Maggie said, "but I'd be content with just the look on your face." She hesitated, then slammed her palm on the table. "Like hell I would. Tell, woman!"

Ellen told Maggie many of the details of the afternoon, omitting only those that were too personal, both to her and to Kevin. "It was astounding."

"So, you're in love."

"With Kevin? Not at all. I do think that I'm in love with good sex, however."

"You're in lust and you're a very smart woman to know the difference. Bravo!"

"Thanks. I hope I can live up to my big talk."

"I think you can," Maggie said, finishing her wine, standing up and squeezing Ellen's shoulder. "I'll leave you to your sketching and your fantasies. I'll be in touch soon, I guess. I don't think Angela and Lucy are through with us yet."

"I'm glad." Ellen stood and gave Maggie a heartfelt hug. "You've become very important to me."

Maggie returned the hug. "That goes double for me." She left the kitchen and Ellen heard the front door close behind her. She picked up her wine and sipped. Maggie had given her several lessons in wine and now she was able to appreciate the bouquet, the color, the myriad of flavors. In the kitchen, she opened the closet over the counter where she kept several bottles of wine. She pulled out all the ones with screw caps and put them in a bag beside her garbage can. "Out with the old, and in with the new."

Filled with enthusiasm for life and all parts of it, she walked into the wine store in which she and Maggie had bought her first bottle. The same clerk was standing behind the counter waiting on an older couple. She walked to the wine rack on which she had found that first special bottle and studied, now better able to understand the labels. "Yes, of course," he said, walking up behind her. "The Mount Eden Estate." He nodded and looked impressed. "Was it as good as I've heard? I've never actually tasted it."

"Yes, it was. Great nose, fabulous color, and all the ripe fruit you could want. It was a great choice, but that was for a special occasion. I'm interested in something now that won't disappoint, but that's not quite so pricey."

By the time she and the salesclerk finished she had two bottles of white and two of red, and she had held her own with the clerk. Her. Ellen Harold, girl wine enthusiast. Small-town woman in the big city. She was learning.

That evening, Ellen daydreamed, reliving her wonderful afternoon with Kevin, and did some sketching. She had been to the local branch of the library and selected several books on drawing and painting. She had read that, although she needed to get out and find places to paint, she could do some landscapes from pictures or from her imagination. In the library's extensive video section she had taken out a travel tape of Hawaii, thinking that the unusual vistas would give her inspiration. As she sat on the sofa with the remote control in her hand, the phone rang. Absently she picked it up, expecting to hear her sister Micki's voice. "Hello?"

"Hello, Ellen. It's Jim."

Ellen hit the pause button and dropped the remote on the sofa beside her. "Well, it's so nice to hear from you," she said, wondering how she could hear his voice over the pounding of her heart. After their dinner together the previous weekend, she had been enthused about seeing him again, but when he didn't call for several days she assumed she wouldn't hear from him again.

"I said I'd call you in a week or so but I must admit that I got impatient. If you're not busy this weekend, maybe we could have dinner again, this time my treat." He rushed on. "Of course if you're busy I'll understand. Maybe we could do it some other time."

"Whoa," Ellen said, stopping the onrushing words. "This weekend would be fine. How about Saturday?" Was this really her? Ellen asked herself. She was being so much more aggressive than she had ever been. Maybe it was because he was being so tentative, unsure, so sweet and shy, exactly the opposite of Kevin.

"Oh. Saturday would be great. I was thinking, well, have you ever had Japanese food?"

"You mean sushi? Raw fish? I don't think I could." She didn't think she was that brave.

"Actually there is a small, really fine restaurant called Senbazuru right around the corner from where we ate last week. It has tempura and sukiyaki as well as sushi and sashimi. You could have cooked food and I could have what I like."

Ellen heard Maggie's words. *Have you ever tasted sushi?*

"That sounds terrific. What time shall I meet you?"

"Still not comfortable with telling me where you live, I see." When she started to protest, he said quickly, "That's fine. Eventually I hope you'll decide that I'm just a lonely guy questing an attractive woman to spend time with."

Cordless phone in her hand, Ellen stood and walked into the bathroom and stared at herself in the mirror. Not so attractive, she thought, but not half bad. Maggie was right. It was the attitude. "What time?"

"How about seven," Jim said and gave her the address of the restaurant. They talked for a few more minutes, then hung up. Ellen lay back on the sofa, unable to suppress a grin. She had a date with Jim. And another date with Kevin for sex. Shit. She thought of the seventies song. She was woman, hear her roar. "*Roar!*"

The following morning was Friday and she knew that Kevin was holding class. She really wanted to attend so, taking her courage in both hands, she grabbed her paint box and headed off. Surprisingly, she took her place at an easel with little awkwardness and got to work quickly. Kevin was professional and only as attentive to her as he was to the other students. Just before the class ended he walked up behind her and whispered, "I wish we were alone."

From that moment on work became impossible. As she was leaving, he said, "I hope I didn't ruin your concentration."

Her mind had filled with images of what they had been doing in that very room the previous afternoon. She blushed. "You did, just a bit but I did manage to get some good work done."

"I'm amazed that I managed to concentrate, but I did, too. Will you be here Tuesday?"

Ellen's blush deepened. "I think so."

"I hope so."

Friday evening, after an afternoon of reading about art and working with her paints, she made herself a pot of macaroni and cheese, watched some TV, and then settled in the bathtub. She had lit a few candles and poured a capful of a new body oil beneath the spigot and placed the CD player on the counter. Now her head was filled with erotic images of Kevin and Jim, the sound of clarinets and the voice of the narrator of the sensual tales of magic and power.

Chapter 10

"Is there magic in the world? Skeptics doubt that magic exists, or ever did exist. Are they right? I don't know, but there are still a few people who are willing to keep an open mind, people who believe in old stories, ancient legends, and possibilities. Like the possibilities inherent in the Mask of Invisibility.

"Ben had lived on the same block most of his life. Several years before, when he was nineteen, an adult club called the Pleasure Parlor had set up shop several doors down from his apartment building and since then, every time Ben passed be gazed at the mysterious-looking doorway. LIVE SEX ACTS *the sign read. 'See it all happen right before your eyes.' If he only could just slip inside and see what all the fuss was about.*

"It wasn't that he didn't have girlfriends. Right now Sue was his steady and he had found himself actually thinking about marriage. Yet, they hadn't had great sex. It was good with Sue but there were no rockets, no fireworks, no earthquakes. Was it just that he hadn't found the right woman, or did that kinky stuff only exist in Playboy *and XXX-rated movies? Was there something wrong with him or with her? Would she be interested in something a bit more acrobatic? He'd probably never know.*

"One evening on his way home from an evening with Sue, he

passed the Pleasure Parlor. 'Come on in! You know you want to see what goes on inside,' the guy standing at the doorway said. 'Only ten bucks.'

" *'Not tonight,' Ben said, as he'd said at least once a week since the club opened.*

" *'Why not, buddy? Lots to see.' The guy, an over-developed, muscle beach type winked at him. 'Lots!'*

" *'Not tonight,' Ben repeated and walked on. What if one of his friends or neighbors saw him walking into that place or worse, saw him inside, utterly fascinated? He couldn't risk the embarrassment.*

"*Several strides later, he heard,* Psst. *He whirled around and saw a tiny woman bundled into a heavy brown coat and woolen scarf, signaling him from a doorway. 'I know that you really want to get inside,' she said, 'and I can help you.'*

" *'Sorry,' Ben said, turning back toward his building. 'Not interested.'*

" *'Sure you are,' the woman said, walking up beside him and placing her hand on his arm. 'Things go on in there that you might never see anywhere else.'*

"Shit, *Ben thought.* Another come-on. These places will use anything to get a guy to pay ten bucks to get inside. *'I'm really not interested but thanks anyway.'*

" *'Listen. This isn't a come-on. I just want you to see the sights. It's truly educational.'* "

"*Ben tried to remove the woman's hand from his arm, but her grip was surprisingly strong. 'Please, lady.' He tried to get a better look at the woman but the coat covered her body completely and her face was almost hidden beneath her scarf.*

"*The woman grinned. 'Lady. That's rich.' She moved in front of him and stared directly into his eyes. 'Listen, Ben, it's this way . . .'*

" *'How do you know my name?'*

" *'I just do. It's my job. Anyway, I know what you want. I know what you need.' She pulled a slender piece of black cloth from her pocket. 'This is the Mask of Invisibility. Put it on and you can go inside and experience what's there for you. No money, no embarrassment, no nothing.'*

"Ben stared at the Lone Ranger-type black domino dangling from the woman's fingers. 'Okay, what's the angle here?'

" 'No angle. I just want this for you. If you're going to think about marriage to Sue, you need to know what else there is in the world.'

" 'How did you . . . ?'

" 'Don't worry about trivialities. I am giving you the opportunity of a lifetime here. Stop arguing.'

"Ben was intrigued. 'How much?'

" 'No charge. You get to use it until tomorrow morning. After that, it becomes just a piece of cloth.'

" 'Right. Sure. You really expect me to believe this bull?'

" 'It's not bull. Take the mask and put it on. Walk up to Artie there by the door and see whether he asks you for any money.'

" 'Maybe this is some kind of sick joke the two of you cooked up.'

"The woman's shoulders rose and lowered in a long, drawn-out sigh. 'Okay. Go into the all-night drugstore, the supermarket, whatever. Pick up something and walk out without paying. You'll see that this really works.'

" 'Why me?'

" 'Let's just say I'm a guardian angel. Does that make it any easier to understand?'

"He shook his head. 'Not really.'

"The woman pressed the cloth into Ben's hand and said, 'Just use it and you'll see everything. And no one will see you.' She cackled at her little joke and disappeared. Just vanished into nothingness. One minute she was standing holding Ben's arm, and the next she was gone. A voice whispered into Ben's ear, 'One more thing. Tell Sue about what you see. You'll be very surprised.'

"Ben whirled around but the sidewalk was empty. The only reminder he had of the woman's presence was the black mask in his hand. This is all ridiculous, *he told himself as he balled the domino up in his fist and headed for a sidewalk trash can. And yet. . . .*

"With his hand suspended over the trash he looked at his fist and the cloth inside. He had always operated on the 'what's in it for me' principle and he couldn't figure out what was in this silli-

ness for the woman. Why had she given this to him? It had to be some kind of elaborate practical joke, but why?

"When he couldn't come up with an answer, he decided to play along, at least for a few minutes to see what would happen. He walked several blocks to an all-night convenience store, tied the mask on and slipped inside, afraid he'd be taken for a stickup man.

"He walked around the store, seemingly unnoticed. Several people stood on the checkout line as he picked up a six-pack and stood behind a tall, heavyset man with a magazine and a large bottle of soda. 'Thank you, sir,' the clerk said to the tall man as he finished paying for his items. Then the clerk turned away and began to rearrange the cartons of cigarettes as though there was no one else in line. Ben put his beer on the counter but there was still no reaction.

"He looked down at himself and to him there seemed to be no difference. He could see himself perfectly, but the clerk was completely ignoring him. 'Sir,' he said. 'I'd like to pay for my beer.' There was no reaction from behind the counter. 'Sir!' Nothing.

"He turned and glanced at a mirrored sign. He wasn't there. He waved his free hand at himself, or rather where he should be in the mirror, but there was nothing reflected. No Ben, no beer, no nothing. He lifted his hand from the six-pack and it suddenly appeared on the counter but he still wasn't visible. The clerk turned, looked around with a puzzled expression on his face, then picked up the six-pack and replaced it on a stack beside the counter. Then he returned to his cigarette stacking.

"Hmmm. Interesting. It seemed as if the mask worked. No one could see him. Amazing. So what are you waiting for, *he asked himself. He dashed out of the convenience store and headed toward the Pleasure Parlor. Finally he'd see what went on inside and no one would be the wiser. None of his friends or neighbors would be able to see him.*

"He walked up to Mr. Bodybuilder, still hawking the Pleasure Parlor's attractions and looked him right in the eye, his face inches from the bouncer's. Nothing. Ben shook his head in wonderment and walked through the black curtains. The air was thick with smoke and the room was so poorly lit that at first he could see very

little. It smelled of tobacco and sweat and the pungent odor of sex. The music was almost deafening, pounding drums, the rhythm unmistakable.

"He looked around and saw that the audience was entirely male. At the front of the room there was a small stage where two women, wearing only G-strings, danced to the exaggerated beat. As Ben's eyes adjusted he saw that they were not bad-looking. They had nice figures with large breasts and prominent nipples. On one side a redhead was grinding her hips, her hands rubbing her crotch suggestively. On the other, a brunette was gyrating against a brass pole, pressing her large tits against the metal.

" 'Bring on the stud,' someone in the audience yelled. The chant of 'Stud, Stud,' was picked up by others in the room.

"Finally a man in a tux walked out onto the stage. 'You want Stud?'

" 'Yeah,' screamed the men in the audience.

" 'Say it again,' Tux yelled.

" 'Stud!' the men screamed.

" 'Okay. Anyone want to leave?'

" 'No!'

"Ben wondered who Stud was, but whatever was going to happen he was ready. He walked up to the stage and perched on the edge, invisible to everyone in the room.

" 'Okay,' Tux said. 'Lock the doors!' Several men walked to the exits and, with exaggerated motions, closed and locked the doors. 'No cops in here tonight!'

" 'Stud! Stud! Stud!' There were whistles and feet stomped. The rhythmic clapping was almost deafening.

" 'All right. Let's bring on Stud.' Tux left the stage and the two women faced the opening in the burgundy curtain across the back. Suddenly the curtain parted and a man stepped out. He was dressed in black pants and black cowboy boots. A small black vest covered with silver conchos barely concealed his well-muscled, naked chest. He wore wide leather wristlets, a wide, black leather band around his forehead, and his long hair was tied with a black leather thong.

"Ben had never cared about looking at other men, but this guy was the hunkiest, sexiest guy he'd ever seen. Although Ben knew it was all just an act, it certainly appeared that the two women were staring at Stud with hunger in their eyes.

"As the man walked toward the front of the stage, Ben got a good look at his face, deep brown, piercing eyes, a wide sensual mouth, and a gold hoop earring in each ear. There was something of the pirate about him, lusty and pure male. Stud looked at the redhead and said, 'Stay there. I'll get to you later.' Then he crossed to the brunette who was standing, her back against the brass pole. Without a word, he grabbed her wrists and pulled them sharply behind her around the pole. He pulled off his headband and bound her arms. With her shoulders pulled backward, her large breasts pressed forward, her nipples hugely erect.

"Down,' Stud said and the brunette slid down the pole until she was on her knees. The man grabbed her tits and pushed them together, then rubbed the front of his pants against the cleft between them. With thrusts of his hips, he fucked her tits. 'Great boobs,' he said. 'Who wants them?'

" 'Me!' several voices from the audience said.

"Stud looked over the audience, then pointed to a man on one side of the room. As the man stood and made his way between the tightly packed tables and onto the stage, Ben could see that he was of average height and build, wearing slacks and a button-down shirt. 'She's yours,' Stud said. 'Let's see what you can do with her.' The man unzipped his pants and pulled out his already erect cock. He pressed the brunette's large tits together and rubbed his cock in her shadowy valley.

"Stud reached to a man at a front table and took his beer glass. Slowly he poured the liquid over the woman's breasts until the man threw back his head and bellowed as come spurted from his cock. Applause filled the room and Stud yelled, 'Later for the rest of you.' The sound in the room grew to deafening proportions.

"As the exhausted man left the stage to return to his seat, Stud crossed to the redhead. He pointed to her crotch. 'You were bad,' he growled. 'I saw you. You watched Tina's boobs and you touched

yourself.' The woman hung her head. 'Do it again.' The redhead rubbed her crotch with both hands, her face obviously enjoying the feel of her hands.

" 'That's very bad.' He opened the ties at the side of her G-string and pulled it off. Ben stared at her red bush, neatly trimmed to a small triangle. Stud motioned again and the redhead buried her fingers in the curly red thatch. Stud allowed her to continue for a moment, watching her obvious excitement, then slapped her hands. 'Bad!'

"The cry was taken up by the audience. 'Bad! Bad! Bad!'

"Stud looked at the men. 'What should I do?'

" 'Punish her! Punish her! Punish her!'

"A man at the front of the room grabbed his chair and hoisted it up onto the stage. Then Tux walked out with a short, brown leather crop.

" 'Do it! Do it! Do it!'

"It seemed to Ben that, although the woman tried to appear frightened, her eyes shone with lust as she stared at the crop. Ben was amazed. This was all new to him. He'd read stories and seen pictures, of course, but here he was in the middle of a real scene. This was really happening, and it seemed as if the redhead wanted it. Badly. Ben found that his palm itched and the urge to slap her was almost irresistible. As the woman draped herself over Stud's lap, Ben could almost feel the sting of his hand against her bottom. Shit. His cock was suddenly harder than he'd ever imagined. He looked over the crowd to reassure himself that no one could see him, then unzipped his pants and took out his raging hard-on.

"As Stud raised the crop, Ben wrapped his hand around his cock. The crop whistled through the air and came down across the redhead's buttocks. She bucked and screamed but from this close Ben could tell she was getting hotter and hotter. Again and again the crop landed on her buttocks, leaving red stripes across white flesh. Tears filled her eyes, and yet she didn't move, didn't try to evade the sting of the crop. It was obvious to Ben that she was enjoying it all.

" 'Eight . . . nine . . . ten!' the audience yelled.

" 'That's enough for tonight,' Stud said, 'as long as you're a good girl from now on.' He pushed her onto her haunches and unzipped his pants. His cock was huge, bigger than anything Ben had ever seen. He leered at the redhead as he rubbed his erection. 'Suck.'

"Greedily she took him in her hand, then opened her mouth and drew in about half of him. Her hand covered the rest as her head bobbed against his groin. Over and over she pulled back, then took him in. Finally, he pushed her away and, with the men watching, spurted come all over the woman's face. Grinning, she licked her lips, then scooped up the come with her fingers and licked.

"Ben was close to coming himself, but he decided to take advantage of his invisibility once more. He climbed onto the stage and approached the brunette, still on her knees, tied to the pole. Would she feel him? He lifted her magnificent breasts and buried his cock between them. He looked into her confused face. She could feel him, but she hadn't any idea what she was feeling. Suddenly her hands were free and she was holding her breasts, her head thrown back, a look of pure joy on her face. Ben pinched her nipples and thrust his cock between her slippery tits. As he pinched harder, the brunette's face contorted and she used one hand to rub her crotch.

"He came. He had wanted it to last, but it was impossible. As the come left his cock and landed on the brunette's chest, he could see it become visible. Then the woman screamed, obviously in the throes of a violent orgasm. Stud walked over and hissed, 'That's not part of the show. You're supposed to come with one of the paying customers.'

"She panted, then said, 'I don't know what came over me but it was as though someone was fucking my tits and pinching my nipples. You know how I get when anyone does that.'

" 'There's no one here,' Stud whispered.

" 'I know. It was just so real.'

"Ignoring the brunette's orgasm, Stud looked out over the sea of men's faces. 'Okay, guys.' He pointed to several men, 'Your turn.'

"Ben caught his breath and made his way to the door. He quickly unlocked it and, totally exhausted, headed home.

"The following evening, he met Sue at her apartment. As the

woman had promised, the mask had become just a piece of black cloth that morning. He had put it on and had seen himself quite clearly in the mirror, looking like a poor-man's Lone Ranger. He had spent the rest of the day reliving the previous evening. Over and over he watched the redhead and the crop. Again and again he felt his cock between the brunette's tits.

"As he settled on the sofa with his arm around Sue, he remembered the woman's words. 'Tell Sue about what you see. You'll be very surprised.'

" 'I had the most bizarre experience last evening.'

" 'Really?' Sue said, her eyes sparkling.

" 'Well, it's a bit difficult to explain. A woman gave me something.'

"Sue grinned. 'Then she found you.'

"Ben's head whipped around. 'Who found me?'

" 'Sorry. Continue your story.'

"Ben cupped Sue's face in his palm and turned her toward him. 'Something's going on here. Tell me what you know about last evening.'

He watched Sue try to lower her eyes but his hand held her fast. He could read guilt in her eyes.

" 'Okay. I've seen the Pleasure Parlor and I knew you wanted to see what went on inside. I thought it might give you some interesting ideas.'

" 'What do you know about what goes on in there?'

" 'My ex-boyfriend used to go there and he told me all about it. Did you see Stud? And did he spank one of the girls?'

" 'Yes.'

"Sue pulled Ben's hand away and stood. 'Well?'

" 'Well what?'

" 'Did it turn you on?'

"Ben cleared his throat. Although she might not like it, he wasn't about to lie about it. 'Yes.'

" 'I hoped it would.' She leaned away from him and stroked her bottom. 'Did you watch him fucking her tits?' She rubbed her breasts, pushing them together beneath her sweater.

" 'Yes, and before you ask, that turned me on as well.' He watched Sue's grin widen. 'What do you know about my guardian angel? Did you set that up somehow?'

" 'Is that what she told you? That she was your guardian angel?'

"Ben thought back. 'Actually, she said she was a guardian angel.'

" 'Right, silly, she's mine.' Sue sat back down and pressed her body against Ben's.

" 'Holy shit,' Ben said as he reached for Sue's breasts. 'Holy shit.' "

Ellen had used her fingers to satisfy her hunger during the story and now she pressed the stop button. Spanking for sexual pleasure. She never would have imagined it, but the narrator made it seem so real, so natural, just a part of good sex. She wasn't ready for experimentation to that extent. Was she?

She sighed, closing her eyes and enjoying the erotic images that whirled in her head. Kevin's studio. The feel of the velvet sofa fabric beneath her naked buttocks, the smell of turpentine and paint mixed with Kevin's aftershave, the feel of him filling her. Again her fingers slipped between her legs and rubbed her clit. The sound of Mozart in the background, almost drowned out by Kevin's harsh breathing, the taste of his lips. Would she have enjoyed it if he had gotten a bit rough? She didn't know but the idea didn't repel her as it might have earlier.

In her mind the scene shifted to her dinner date with Jim. How would he be as a lover? Her eyes flew open. Was she really thinking about Jim in those terms? If she were to be honest with herself, yes, she was. "And," she said aloud, "what's wrong with that?" How had she changed so much in just a few weeks? Before she met Maggie she had been smaller, shy, unwilling to experiment. What had Maggie done to her? She and Kevin had only been together once but, with the help of the erotic CD stories and with Maggie's encouragement Ellen was able to admit, to herself at least, that she was curious, anxious to see the variations that the sexual world held. Until now she had been peeking out of her cocoon. Now, although she wasn't a true butterfly yet, she was eager to give her new wings a real try.

Chapter 11

Over the next several weeks, Ellen's life fell into a pattern. She met with Kevin once or twice a week. He sketched and painted various views of her naked body and afterward they had great, toe-curling sex together. Neither, however, was under any delusion. This was fun and games. They cared about each other, but not in the deep, long-lasting way that would define marriage or even a semipermanent relationship.

She saw Jim every weekend. One crisp fall day they rented a car and drove through Westchester County, stopping at farm stands, drinking fresh apple cider and eating homemade doughnuts. They spent an entire day exploring the South Street Seaport area and another poking around Nyack with its quaint shops and restaurants. They took the Staten Island ferry, riding on the open deck even though the thermometer hovered close to forty degrees.

They got to know each other, too. She felt comfortable with him, relishing their time together as she used to enjoy her time with her sister. It was almost as though she had compartmentalized her life: Kevin for sex and Jim for friendship.

Between dates, Ellen did her work for the doctors in Fairmont, and sketched. She practiced the techniques she learned in Kevin's art classes and those she gleaned from books on all aspects of painting and drawing. She also watched television, went to movies, and filled her time with exploring New York. One Saturday afternoon, she and Jim saw a Saturday matinee of a smash hit musical. As they walked out of the warm theater, Jim asked, "What would you like to do now? It's a bit early for dinner."

Since they had had a large lunch, Ellen had to agree. Jim had picked her up at her apartment a few times but they had never spent any time there. The play had been a rather sensual love story and Ellen found that her sexual juices were flowing. She gazed at Jim, his soft sandy hair and thick mustache, thought about his easy smile and great sense of humor. Why was Jim always relegated to the role of friend? She looked at him as a man and found he was attractive. How would that mustache feel against her skin? she wondered.

Ellen had often considered what it would be like if Jim made a pass, but he had never stepped even the slightest bit out of line. A few good-night kisses were as far as they had gotten. Although they talked at length about their lives, no explanation had even presented itself. Was he gay? Had he been so badly burned by marriage that he wasn't interested in anything intimate? Was it her? Recently she had begun to wonder whether her newfound boldness was all an illusion. Maybe she was still the same small-town person she had been when she moved to New York. New hairdo, new clothes, new makeup, even her new sexuality didn't change the basic person she was and maybe Jim knew that. It seemed obvious that he wasn't about to make any moves, maybe it was time for her to ratchet up their relationship. "How about coming back to my apartment? We can share a bottle of wine and I think I have some cheese to nibble on. Then we can decide what to do about dinner." Ellen could see the surprise in Jim's eyes.

"I'd like that," he said.

As she let herself and Jim into her apartment, she realized that the change in it was startling. Now it was warm, with the insipid floral oils on the walls replaced with museum-quality floral prints framed in silver. The tables were covered with pots of ferns and philodendrons. Cyclamen and African violets cluttered the living room windowsill. Ellen had bought several coordinated pillows to liven up the sofa and a small Oriental rug in deep blue, cranberry, and gold lay beneath the coffee table. "Nice place," Jim said. "It's comfortable, and just right for someone like you."

"For someone like me? What does that mean?"

"I have always had the feeling that you might decide to decamp one morning and move back to Fairmont. I know you're enjoying your art classes and such, but I haven't gotten the feeling that you're here permanently. It's sort of like you have one foot here and one back home. I kind of thought that when your money ran out you'd go back to the way things were before."

"Really?"

"I've noticed that when you say the word home you always mean upstate. I've tried to protect myself from being too disappointed when you tell me you're going back. When you 'find yourself' I mean."

Interesting, Ellen thought. Although Jim didn't know about the extent of her lottery winnings, she had told him that she came into a bit of money and was staying in the city to find herself. She wasn't sure what 'find herself' meant, but it was a good enough phrase to explain where her head was at the moment. Where was she heading? Strangely she realized that she had no more idea about that than she had when she arrived in New York City. She was just gliding. Shouldn't there be more to life than just occupying time? "I never thought about it that way," she said aloud. "I guess I don't know what the future holds for me just yet."

She opened a bottle of Chablis and they sipped. As they sat, staring into space, Ellen wondered what he was thinking. Was he wondering how to get out of this situation gracefully? Didn't he find her attractive? "Why haven't you ever made a pass at me?" she blurted out. Better to know than to wonder.

She could hear Jim's startled intake of breath, then he just stared at the wineglass in his hand and sighed. "I've told you that I don't like getting into anything deeper when I know it's not going to last. I'm not sure I'd be good at a one-night stand."

"We're hardly one nighters. We've been seeing each other for two months."

"Okay. If I were being totally honest, I didn't want to rush things. Two months seems like a long time, but . . ."

"Is that all?" Ellen asked, feeling brave enough to continue the conversation. "Honest?"

With another loud sigh, Jim put his glass on the table. "Honesty's tough. I'm a pretty lonely guy," he began. "I don't have many friends, and most of the ones I have are men. I have enjoyed your company so much for the past weeks that I was scared of something messing that up. You were so reluctant to have me up to your apartment that I decided that you weren't interested in going further than just friendship so I forced myself to be content with that."

"You always seemed so confident. You picked me up in the store and again outside the restaurant that first night."

"My confidence is all an illusion. I saw you, alone and, I hoped, as lonely as I was, so I bucked up my courage and approached you. It turned out so great I've been afraid to mess it up by pushing things further."

Ellen put her glass beside Jim's. "What if I said I was interested in going further?" As she spoke she sensed Jim pulling away.

With a rueful grin, he said, "I would be scared to death."

"Scared? Of me?"

"You're an attractive woman. I'm sure you've had your share of men and, although you never talk about it, you probably have someone special right now." He hesitated, then plunged on. "I'm not good with women, except as friends. There was my wife, of course, but that was different. It took her two years to discover that she didn't want any more time with me. I guess there's something wrong with me. Women don't seem to continue a relationship with me once we've been to bed."

With the wine heating her belly, Ellen thought of Maggie's words. "You know," Ellen said, "I have a good friend, a woman by the way, who once told me that there aren't really any good lovers. There are people who are great together, but wouldn't necessarily be nearly as good with other partners. Good lovers come in pairs." As she spoke she realized that, thanks to Kevin, for the first time in her life she was being the sexual aggressor. It was a heady feeling.

"That's a nice theory," Jim said, his shoulders slumped, "but I'm not sure I buy it."

"Tell me, if you had a magic wand and could have anything you wanted with a woman in bed, what would you want?"

Jim moved slightly farther away from her. "Damn, you do ask the most uncomfortable questions."

"You don't have to answer, I'm just curious."

His deep breath was loud and prolonged. Then he grinned shyly. "Do I have to be honest again?"

"I wish you would be," Ellen said, unwilling to let him off the small hook she had put him on. She had learned a lot about sex from Kevin and from the stories on the CD Maggie had given her.

"That's an interesting question. A magic wand. I guess I would want her to want me as much as I wanted her." He smiled. "I'd want her to tell me what she liked so I wouldn't be trying to guess all the time." He stopped as if realizing that he might have said too much. "What made you come up with such a question?"

"I thought it would be a good way to learn about you." She remembered Maggie telling her about using the stories on the CD for communication. It just might work with Jim, if he had the open mind she thought he did. If not . . . "The same friend I mentioned earlier gave me a CD with a collection of highly erotic short stories. They are all about magic and having the power to have sex exactly the way you want it and the idea intrigued me. Actually there's a story on the CD about a man who wants to know what his girlfriend likes."

"A CD with erotic short stories? An interesting idea. I must confess that I'm a Web surfer and I read lots of porn."

Would the story totally embarrass Jim or would it open the path to good communication? According to Maggie, the ability to communicate was the most important thing for good sex. In for a penny . . . "I don't know the difference between pornography and erotica, but these stories are soft and loving. I could play it for you. I'm afraid it's really explicit." She laughed. "I'm not sure

I could look at you while we listen, but I think all of the stories have valuable messages."

"I'd like to hear the one you were talking about," Jim said.

Ellen retrieved her CD player from the bedroom and set it on the coffee table. She realized that it had gotten quite dark outside as the fall evening advanced so all she had to do was turn off one lamp and the room was plunged into almost complete darkness, the only illumination coming in was from the streetlights outside the window.

Jim took her hand. "It seems we've just found a mutual love for explicit tales. Okay. Play on, McDuff."

Realizing that their relationship had just passed a milestone, Ellen pressed play.

"*Is there magic in the world?*" the voice said as the music faded. "*Skeptics doubt that magic exists, or ever did exist. Are they right? I don't know, but there are still a few people who are willing to keep an open mind, people who believe in old stories, ancient legends, and possibilities. Like the possibilities inherent in the Cloak of Veracity.*

"*Zack liked to prowl antique shops. He seldom bought anything, but he had a love of anything that had once been used, touched by people who had died long before he was born. So in stores all around the city he sat in eighteenth-century chairs, rubbed his long fingers over George V tables, even wrote a note on a French desk supposedly owned by Marie Antoinette. He felt some kind of connection to all those who had touched and sat and written before him.*

"*One afternoon he was browsing in a new store in a very high-class part of town when he stumbled on a soft gray cloak with elaborate gold buttons. 'What in the world is this?' he asked the bored salesman.*

"*The man wandered over and gazed at the cloth. 'I'm told it's the Cloak of Veracity, the very one that Merlin created so Arthur could find out what Guinevere was up to.' He laughed. 'I guess he never got to use it, huh.'*

" 'Cloak of Veracity. What does it do?' Zack asked.

" 'The one who wears it is incapable of telling a lie.' As if sensing a man with money, the clerk continued, 'I'm told it's genuine.'

"Zack picked it up. 'It can't be really old,' he said. 'It's in perfect condition. No wear and tear at all.'

" 'That's one of the properties of the cloak,' the store clerk said. 'It remains in perfect condition and has throughout the ages.'

"Zack swirled the cloak around his shoulders. He started to say that he wasn't really interested in the thing, then found himself saying instead, 'How much?'

"The clerk reached up to the small collar and looked at the tag safety-pinned to it. 'It says three hundred dollars.'

" 'Okay,' Zack said, 'never mind.' He swirled the cloak like a matadore. Cloak of Veracity indeed.

" 'I could let you have it for two-fifty,' the clerk said.

"Zack let the swirling cloak land on the clerk's shoulders. 'How much?'

" 'Actually that thing has been here for more than six months and yours is the first genuine offer we've had. No one believes it's real. I'll take anything I can get over a hundred bucks.'

"Zack cocked his head to one side. 'Interesting.' He removed the cloak. This is probably some kind of scam, he thought, but it's a fun gimmick. 'A hundred dollars and not a cent more.'

" 'Well,' the salesman said, seemingly unaware of what he had said with the cloak on, 'I couldn't possibly accept such a low offer.'

"Zack started to put the cloak back across the trunk where he had found it. 'Not a cent more.'

" 'Okay. You win. You drive a hard bargain, sir.'

"As Zack left the shop with the cloak in a box under his arm, he glanced at his watch. 'Shit' he muttered. 'If I don't hustle my buns I'm going to be late.' He broke into a trot and arrived at a small neighborhood restaurant at exactly one o'clock. His girlfriend, Shelly, was waiting, looking particularly lovely in a soft blue wool dress. 'I'm sorry I'm late,' Zack said when they were seated at a small table. 'I got to browsing in that new antique store a few blocks east and I lost track of time.' He placed the box on his lap.

"Staring at it, Shelly said, 'Oh, wonderful. You did remember. I was sure you wouldn't.' Her blue eyes were bright with anticipation, her white teeth revealed by her wide grin.

"Remember? Shit, *Zack thought.* Her birthday. I forgot completely. *Zack and Shelly had been going together for more than five months and he was really fond of her. He felt the box resting on his thighs. The cloak.* You know, *he thought,* I'd rather be lucky than good any day. *'Of course I remembered,' he said, lifting the box. 'That's why I was late. I looked and looked for just the right thing. I fell in love with this and I hope you like it.' He handed her the box and she opened it and gazed at the contents.*

" 'Oh, Zack. It's beautiful,' she said, fingering the soft fabric. 'It looks like something someone would have worn hundreds of years ago.' She leaned across the table and gave him a small kiss on the lips. 'No other man would have thought to buy a woman clothing, and this is just perfect. Can I put it on right now?'

"Phew. Even if the veracity part was a gimmick, she liked the cloak. 'Sure. I'd love to see how you look.'

"Shelly stood and carefully placed the cloak over her shoulders. 'Zack, it's wonderful.' She sat back down, the cloak still around her.

" 'Would you like to order?' Zack asked.

"Shelly gazed at Zack, a glint in her eyes. 'I'd really prefer to go back to your place and celebrate my birthday privately.'

"He had never expected an answer like that. Shelly enjoyed their occasional lunches out and never made leading suggestions like the one she had just made. 'Really? Don't you have to be back at work?'

" 'Mr. McAllister is away and I really have nothing to do. I'll call them and tell them I'm taking my birthday afternoon off. Then we can spend it together.'

" 'Wow. That would be great.' He stood. 'Let's get out of here.'

"Shelly called her office and made her excuses, then they chatted on the short walk to his building and up in the elevator. Although Shelly was a bit more outspoken than usual, Zack didn't think much of it. As he closed the apartment door behind them, he asked,

'Would you like something to eat? We didn't get lunch after all. I could see what's in the kitchen.'

'I don't want to eat,' she said softly. 'I just want you.'

"Zack stood stock-still. Never had Shelly behaved as she was now. Could it be the cloak? Was she being forced to tell the absolute truth? 'You want me? For what?'

"Shelly ducked her head. 'I just love your body. It makes me hungry just looking at you but it really embarrasses me to say it.'

" 'Let's go inside,' Zack said, leading Shelly into the bedroom. 'We can talk about this.' As she sat down on the edge of the bed, her soft skirt slid up her smooth white thighs. She pulled her skirt down just a bit and clasped her hands primly in her lap.

" 'Now, tell me,' he said, 'what would you like me to do now?'

"Shelly's gaze fastened on Zack's. 'I would like you to touch me.'

"Zack crouched at her feet and placed one hand on her knee. Her stockings felt slithery beneath his palm. Slowly he slid his hand to the inside of her thigh, working his fingers slowly upward. 'Does that feel good?' he asked.

" 'Oh yes,' she purred. 'Very good.'

" 'Then spread your legs slightly so I can touch you better,' Zack said softly and was surprised when she did as he asked. He eased his fingers to the top of her stockings and found the soft, incredibly warm skin above. He kept his fingers moving, occasionally brushing the crotch of her silky panties.

" 'Maybe we should take off some of these clothes,' Shelly said.

"Not the cloak, *he thought. She stood and dropped the cloak onto the bed, then pulled her dress off over her head and stood before him wearing only her undies, garter belt, and hose. He quickly removed his clothes until he was wearing only his briefs. 'Aren't you cold?' Zack asked. 'Let me wrap this cloak around you.' Before she could get her bearings he swirled the cloak around her near-naked shoulders. 'That should keep you warm.'*

" 'I'd rather you kept me warm,' she said, moving closer, pressing her satin-covered breasts against his chest, raising her face for a kiss.

"Zack pressed his mouth against hers, softly at first. Then, encouraged by her enthusiasm, he wrapped his arms around her and,

as she opened her mouth, he pressed his tongue inside. For long minutes they played, tongue to tongue, her hands sliding up his chest to tangle in his hair.

" *'What would you like now?' he asked.*

" *'Undress the rest of me,' she said without hesitation, 'and kiss everything you uncover.'*

"Her bra went first. Zack loved her beautiful breasts and eagerly kissed and suckled their tempting, erect nipples. He drew first one bud then the other into his mouth, sucking and nipping until he could hear Shelly's rasping breath. 'More,' she groaned.

"He knelt at her feet and slowly pulled her silky panties down to her ankles, lifting each foot so she could step out. 'Spread your legs a bit,' he said hoarsely. When her legs parted, he eased his fingers through her pussy hair to her hot, wet center. She was soaking, dripping love juices and trembling. He knew she wanted to lie down, but he kept her standing, caressing all the tender places usually so carefully hidden.

"Finally, when he thought she could take no more, he lowered her to the bed, the cloak still partially around her. His erection was so large, it was almost painful, but he wanted to hear her ask for him. 'What now?'

" *'I want you inside of me. Fill me up. Please.'*

" *'Maybe this way.' He pressed first one, then two fingers inside her, pushing, then withdrawing in mock intercourse. He sucked at her white breasts while be finger-fucked her pussy.*

" *'Baby, fuck me. Please. I want to feel your cock inside of me.'*

"Never had she used such language, and it aroused him still further. 'Right now, baby,' Zack said. 'Right now.' He quickly put on a condom then touched the tip of his cock to her heat and slowly pushed inside. It obviously wasn't fast enough for her and he felt her fingernails on his buttocks, urging him deeper. Still he held back, waiting until she was thrashing and squirming. Then she wrapped her legs around his waist and drove her hips upward until he was lodged totally within her.

"He could feel small tremors in her channel, then a tight squeezing. 'Oh, baby,' he moaned, unable to resist any longer. He pulled

back, then plunged, over and over until, with a scream she came. Only moments later his orgasm mimicked hers.

"Later he rolled onto his back and Shelly snuggled against his side, her head on his shoulder. 'Wow,' she said. 'I don't know what came over me, but that was amazing.'

" 'Yes, it certainly was.' He shuddered.

" 'You're chilly. Let me just put this over you.' She draped the cloak over the two of them. 'Was this lovemaking okay?'

" 'Okay?' he said, unable and unwilling to deny anything, 'it was the best ever.'

" 'Is there any way I could make it better?'

"Zack felt his cock stir. 'Not better, just more. And there are so many ways.' He tucked the cloak around the two of them, knowing he would be incapable of telling anything but the truth about their lovemaking, and delighted at the prospect."

Ellen found the stop button on the CD player by touch in the darkened room and pressed it. She felt the distance between her body and Jim's. "I'm sorry. Did that story turn you off?" she asked as the silence dragged on.

"Oh no," Jim said. "I'm a bit overwhelmed. I never realized that others had the same doubts, the same insecurities, and the same desire to know what to do. The author of the story must have known, however, because he hit the nail right on the head."

"What if you had a cloak like that right now?" Ellen whispered. "Would you throw it around my shoulders?" Would she be brave enough to tell him what she wanted? Well, she thought, she'd gotten herself into this and she really wanted to make love with Jim. Now! Yet she wouldn't rush him.

Jim took her hand in his and she could feel the trembling. "We're not going too fast?" he asked.

"I find you very attractive and I think we'd have fun together. It just seems a natural way to go."

Jim took another deep breath and asked, "If I threw the cloak over your shoulders, what would you say?"

"I'd say that I'd like you to kiss me."

Chapter 12

In the dimly lit room, their mouths came together. Jim's lips were soft and warm, tentative yet firm. Ellen felt her body melt against him as his arms wound around her shoulders. His tongue slipped between her lips and their heads naturally moved to deepen the kiss. He threaded his fingers through her hair and she rested her palms on his shoulders. "Oh, sweet," he murmured, moving his mouth against hers.

"God," Ellen said, separating for a moment. It was obvious that the story had done more than facilitate communication. It had turned him on. "You take my breath away. You're a fantastic kisser." In one small part of her mind she thought about Kevin. He was a sensitive lover, but he wasn't particularly into kissing. Shy and a bit hesitant as Jim was, he had a terrific mouth.

"Like your friend said, maybe it's just that we're good together." His mouth again fused with hers, fueling the fire in her belly. For long minutes they kissed while his hands caressed her back and hers grasped the front of his shirt. The world faded and there was nothing but the two of them. She threw her head back as Jim's lips moved along her jaw and down the side of her neck. "You make me feel brave," he whispered. "If you were wearing that cloak now, what would you say?"

She'd gotten herself into this, she owed him honesty. She took his hand and placed it on her aching breast. Her nipple was hard, almost painfully contracted and she needed his touch. "I want you here."

"Oh, Ellen," he moaned, filling his palm with her flesh.

She fell back against the sofa and pressed against his hand, reveling in the feel of his fingers kneading her breast. "You make me so hungry." She unbuttoned her blouse and urged his hand inside.

He touched the cup of her bra and slid his fingers beneath the lace, finding her pebbled tip. "Tell me," he growled.

"Pinch it. Make me feel you." He did and it caused bolts of molten heat to stab through her. "More," she groaned.

In one motion Jim grabbed the front of her blouse and pulled it from her skirt, popping one of the buttons in his haste. He quickly dragged it from her shoulders and, in one motion unfastened her bra and yanked it off, tossing both across the room. "Now what?" he asked, more a demand for an answer than a question.

Ellen felt the cool air against her burning skin. "Your mouth," she moaned. She cupped her breast. "Here."

"I want to see you," he said, fumbling for the light and turning it on. "Oh, God, I knew you'd be beautiful." He dropped his head and his mouth found her turgid nipple, drawing it inside.

She was barely able to think, but in some far-away part of her brain she realized that she was as excited as she had been with Kevin. Different. Not better, just different. Different. As she cupped her palms against the sides of Jim's head and held him close, his lips did magical things to her breast. Then his fingers found her other nipple and she was no longer capable of thinking anything.

Without conscious thought, her fingers unbuttoned his shirt and yanked it off. "I want to feel your skin against mine."

He held her, his mouth playing music on her lips, his chest hair rubbing against her wet nipples. Textures. It was all textures. His chest hair tickled her, his fingernails scratched her back, his soft lips nibbled at her mouth. Then he sat back, his eyes glazed. “The cloak is still around your shoulders,” he said, his voice rough. “Tell me, what now?”

“I want to see all of you. I want you to undress me, too. Let’s go inside.”

She led him into her small bedroom and turned on the light. In one motion she pulled the covers off the bed and dumped them to the floor. She stood at the bottom of the bed, legs slightly spread. He knelt at her feet as he pulled off her shoes, lifting first one foot then the other. As he fumbled with her garters, he said, “I can’t get my fingers to work.”

Quickly she pulled off her skirt and unhooked the garters. She dropped her hands at her sides as he slowly peeled the nylons down her legs. He pressed his face against the tops of her thighs and kissed the soft white skin there, allowing his breath to heat her. He rubbed his long mustache over her belly and she couldn’t decide whether it tickled or just drove her crazy. As he kissed her mound through her panties, he cupped her buttocks to hold her close.

Ellen gently drew him up. “Now you,” she said. Marveling at the mat of sandy hair that covered his chest, she ran her fingers through the soft fur, then over his male nipples as he trembled beneath her palms. Unable to control her own body enough to crouch, she sat on the floor and tugged off his shoes and socks, then she slid her hands up the front of his pants, stroking the large bulge with her thumbs. She unbuttoned his slacks and lifted herself to her knees. “I’ve always wanted to do this,” she whispered, grasping the tab of the zipper in her teeth. Slowly, inexorably, the zipper opened. She remembered how good his breath had felt so, as the top of his pants parted, she blew on the opening of his shorts and smiled as she felt him shudder.

His hands lifted her and together they lay down on the bed. He moved so they were head-to-foot and his mouth found her mound through her panties. His heat and the magic of his mouth made her crazy with need, but she restrained the urge to rip off clothing and drag him inside of her. Instead she covered her teeth with her lips and bit him through his shorts.

"Damn, woman," he growled, "if you do that I won't last worth a damn."

"Who wants you to last?" she asked.

"You've still got the cloak on," he whispered.

"Fuck me, she told him. "I want you inside of me. Now!"

He yanked off his shorts and her panties and climbed off the bed. She watched as he found a condom in his pants pocket and opened the foil. "Let me do that," she said.

Taking the rolled latex, she held it against the tip of his penis and slowly—agonizingly slowly—unrolled it over him. "You said 'Now!' if I recall."

Ellen giggled. "So I lied."

"You can't lie with the cloak around your shoulders."

She held his cock in her hand as he knelt over her. Raising her hips, she said, "Yes. Now! Do it!"

He needed no help finding the center of her wet pussy and he plunged inside. Over and over he thrust, then found her clit with his fingers between their bodies. He angled his pelvis so he could piston into her while rubbing her nub with his thumb. "God, baby, so good," he gasped.

"So good," she echoed as she climbed to the ultimate heights. She grabbed his ass cheeks and held him tightly against her as he came, then she joined him, the power and rhythm of his pounding pushing her over the edge.

They lay together dozing for quite a while, until finally Ellen asked, "Is that cloak still around my shoulders?"

"Of course," Jim said.

With a wicked grin she admitted, "I'm hungry. Let's get dinner, then come back here later and see what develops."

Laughter coloring his voice, he said, "Done. I like the way you think."

"Way to go, Ellen!" Lucy cried, pumping her fist in the air. "I knew she had it in her. Seducing a man isn't an easy task. She's certainly becoming my kind of woman."

"Lucy," Maggie said, appearing on a chair in the computer room. "You promised not to watch."

"She won't know, and I only watched for a few moments."

"Lucy," Angie said, "you didn't."

Looking not the least bit contrite, Lucy said, "Let's just say the devil made me do it."

"Right," the two other women said.

"So it seems Ellen's becoming a sexual being," Maggie said. "What's left for me to do?"

"She has to become a complete woman. She has to understand her power and her responsibility," Angie said, "especially with all that money."

"Hey, who said anything about that?" Lucy argued. "All I wanted was for her to learn to fuck like a bunny."

"That's not enough, Luce," Angela said. "She's learned a little about sex, thanks to Maggie here, but there's more to real life than casual sex."

"You're not talking about marriage and all that traditional claptrap, are you, love?" Lucy's tail twitched.

"No, not really. Now that she's stuck her head out of her cocoon, she's got to figure out where she fits. She's got to leave the nest and make her place in the world."

Maggie sat forward in her chair. "That's a bit out of my league. Am I supposed to teach her that, too? Me, who spent most of her life enjoying the hell out of casual sex? I think you've got the wrong woman for this part of the job."

"Not at all," Angela protested. "You weren't married for most of your adult life but you know where you fit. You gave pleasure, taught men about themselves, and saved many a marriage with your wisdom."

"Come on, Angela," Maggie said, "I was just a hooker."

"If you had been *just* a hooker you wouldn't be here. It's the good you did that keeps you in limbo here with us."

"So what am I supposed to do now?"

"Just be there when the time comes to help her understand

where she's going. Not a specific destination, just a direction. She has none right now."

"I'm not sure I know what you mean."

"You will. Just be yourself and you'll know what to say when the need arises. It will be a while, but the moment will come."

Maggie shook her head. "If you say so, ladies."

"We do," the two women said together.

As Maggie disappeared from the computer room, Lucy looked at Angela. "We do?"

"We do." Angela's wings quivered as the two returned to their computer screens.

It was wonderful for Ellen to watch the way Jim changed over the following weeks. They dated at least twice a week and their lovemaking became freer and more creative, with Jim taking the lead as often as Ellen did. He laughed during sex and made suggestions about fantasies he'd like to act out. One evening he suggested that they listen to a random story on the CD and do whatever the characters in the tale enjoyed.

Ellen giggled. "I know all the stories by heart by now," she said, "so it would be unfair for me to pick one. They progress from the traditional to the, well let's say kinky. Why don't you pick a number from one to eight?"

The twinkle in Jim's eye was obvious. "You know, before I met you I would have picked one or two. Now, let's see what number eight has to say."

Ellen hesitated, knowing the theme of that story. "You're in for quite a surprise," she said, pressing the play button.

"Is there magic in the world? Skeptics doubt that magic exists, or ever did exist. Are they right? I don't know, but there are still a few people who are willing to keep an open mind, people who believe in old stories, ancient legends, and possibilities. Like the possibilities inherent in the Wand of Forgetfulness.

" 'Look out!' Phil, among others, shouted as the old woman

started to cross the street. A taxi, careening around the corner, was heading straight for her.

"The woman looked around, seemingly dazed by the shouting, still standing directly in the path of the speeding vehicle. 'Look out, lady!' Phil shouted again but the woman seemed frozen, unable to take the two steps that would move her out of harm's way. No way around it, *Phil thought. He leaped out into the street, grabbed the slight woman by the shoulders and dragged her onto the sidewalk just as the taxi roared past, the driver making obscene hand gestures.*

" *'Goodness, young man,' the woman said, her hand placed against the center of her chest, her breathing ragged. Trembling, she continued, 'I heard you call, and saw the car but I couldn't seem to move.' She grasped Phil's arm trying not to collapse.*

" *'It's okay now,' Phil said. 'You're safe and none worse for the wear.'*

" *'Thanks to you.' She placed her hand flat on her chest again and took several deep breaths. 'My goodness I'm all fluttery. I can't thank you enough.'*

" *'I didn't do anything special,' he said. 'I just did what had to be done. Lots of other people would have done the same.'*

" *'But they didn't and you did. You were very brave and you deserve a reward.'*

"Phil stared at the woman's unkempt appearance. She seemed one step up from a bag lady, her clothes worn, patched, and many times washed, her straggly hair caught under a faded brown bandanna. 'It's nothing. Please don't think about it anymore.' He started to move toward the bus stop.

" *'I know you're probably running late, but let me do what I want. It's not nice to argue with an old lady.' She rummaged in the large shopping bag that hung from one skinny wrist. 'Here's what I'm looking for,' she exclaimed, withdrawing a slender box about a foot long and no larger around than a quarter. Pressing it into Phil's hand, she said, 'This is the Wand of Forgetfulness. If you touch someone on the shoulder with this, he or she will forget what-*

ever you've done for the past hour or so. You could rob banks, tell your boss off, whatever. It's of no use to me now and I do so want you to have it.'

"Phil tried not to take the box but the woman persisted. 'Please. Humor an old lady,' she said, holding Phil's hand closed around the box.

"Realizing that it was easier to just take the silly thing than to argue, he shoved the package into his briefcase. 'Thanks, ma'am,' he said.

"The woman patted him on the shoulder. 'Use it wisely. Oh, and you can only use it three times. Then you have to give it away.'

" 'Sure. That's wonderful. Thanks. Really. I appreciate it. Now I've got to catch my bus.'

" 'Of course. You're my hero, young man, and thank you again for saving my life.'

"Phil thought little about the slender box in his briefcase as he rode the bus home. After a dinner of Kentucky Fried Chicken with his wife, Kate, and their two children, he played with the kids while Kate finished up some business she'd brought home. After the children were in bed, Phil and Kate sat in the living room holding hands.

"As he relaxed, Phil told Kate about the strange woman who had given him the Wand of Forgetfulness. 'That's really silly,' Kate said, looking at the box in Phil's hand. 'I can't believe she actually told you that. Do you think she believed it?'

" 'She seemed to believe every word of what she told me.' He opened the box and withdrew a slender ebony rod with silver tips on each end. 'It looks like one of those batons conductors use.' He stood up and waved the stick in the air as if leading an orchestra. 'I think it makes me look very distinguished.'

" 'You look silly,' Kate said, grinning, 'but awful cute.'

"As he sat down, Phil tapped Kate on the shoulder with the wand. Kate looked a bit confused, then said, 'What's that thing?'

" 'What thing?'

" 'That stick. It looks like the thing conductors use with orchestras.'

"Totally puzzled, Phil said, 'This is the wand the old woman gave me.'

" *'What old woman?' Kate asked.*

" *'Nothing,' Phil said, shaking his head. He dropped back onto the sofa. She bad completely forgotten what be had just told her. Could what the old woman said be true? Did the wand really work? He had to think about it then maybe test it out. But he only had three cracks at it and he'd already used one.* Stop it, *he told himself.* You're starting to sound like you believe this junk.

"Phil thought of little else for several days and finally decided to give the wand another chance. He called his secretary into his office, gave her a list of meaningless tasks, then touched her on the shoulder with the wand. She remembered nothing of what he had just said. Amazed he dismissed the baffled woman and dropped into his desk chair. It had actually worked, and he had one more opportunity to use it. What would he do?

"Rob a bank? Not a chance. He wasn't that kind of person. Tell his boss off? Why waste his final shot? No, he would have to wait and continue to ponder. There would be a right moment and he'd be ready.

"Several weeks later, Kate and Phil sent the children to Kate's parents overnight so they could attend a party with Kate's boss and several important clients. Kate chose to wear an incredibly sexy teal-blue dress that was so tiny that as they stood around a table of hors d'oeuvres Phil saw several men gaze longingly at his wife's neckline and great legs. Not that she flirted or gave them any encouragement, of course. He just had one hell of a sexy wife.

"As he gazed at her, he focused on the amazingly erotic nape of her neck. He had always found that spot an incredible turn-on and the way she was wearing her hair, pinned up in a tight twist, just accentuated it. All Phil could think about was kissing and biting that deliciously tasty spot and the one where her neck joined her shoulder. He pictured himself ripping the dress off her body, tying her to the bed then kissing and fucking her senseless. He moved to ease the pressure in his suit pants. Tying her to the bed.

"She'd never go for it, *he thought.* Not his sweet little wife, mother of his children, but hell he was hungry. He just wanted to throw her down and take her, eat her alive then fuck her brains out. He began to think about the Wand of Forgetfulness. He could do anything he wanted, then just tap her on the shoulder and she'd forget. He could really do it.

"*Suddenly the bulge in his pants grew to still more uncomfortable proportions.* I can do whatever I want, then just tap her and she'll forget. I can have the best sex ever and it would fuel fantasies forever. *He sighed and slipped a hand into his pants pocket so he could adjust his cock more comfortably in the front of his jockey shorts.* How am I going to last until we can leave? *he wondered. The evening dragged but he made it through, thinking and planning, deciding exactly what he was going to do, and how. He had it all figured out by the time they arrived back at their house.*

" *'That was a really nice evening,' Kate said, yawning. 'I'm beat.'*

" *'Let's go upstairs,' Phil said, guiding his wife up to their bedroom. When he had closed the door behind them, he ordered, 'Take that dress off.'*

"*Kate looked at him a bit startled. When she didn't move quickly enough Phil said, 'Take it off. Now! Unless you want it ripped off your body.'*

"*Kate stared, then giggled and said, 'I love you when you're masterful.' She slithered out of the dress and stood there dressed in a silk slip, a slight grin on her face.*

" *'You won't be smiling long,' Phil snapped. 'Get over here.' God it felt good, giving instructions. And when it was all over he'd just make her forget.*

"*Slowly Kate walked over looking a bit puzzled. 'Baby, what's gotten into you?'*

" *'I just want to fuck your sweet body.' He grabbed her wrists and pulled them behind her, holding both in one large hand. He grabbed the back of her head with the other and buried his face in the soft skin of her neck. He nibbled, then bit her, not strongly enough to cause real pain, just enough to make her body stiffen. He devoured her shoulders, then nipped his way up to her ear. He sucked the lobe into his mouth and used his teeth until he felt her breathing quicken. He turned her around and, still holding her wrists, he licked and bit the nape of her neck for several long minutes.*

"When he had kissed and licked and nibbled as much as he wanted, he pushed her onto the bed. He had thought it all through so without giving her a chance to react, he quickly grabbed two of his ties and fastened Kate's hands to the headboard. He watched as she squirmed, admiring what her writhing did to her breasts as they pressed against the satiny fabric of her slip. 'Baby, what's this all about?' she hissed.

" 'I want you. This way. My way. And you can't do anything about it.' He watched her start to speak, then close her mouth. 'Good girl. You have no say in this.' When she remained silent, he continued, 'Good. I see you understand. Now, I hope you're not wearing panty hose.' He yanked off her shoes and, finding stockings and garters, he unfastened one stocking and dragged it down her leg. Then he used it to tie her ankle to the footboard. He quickly did the same to her other leg.

"Now he took several minutes to admire his deliciously sexy wife, tied spread-eagle to the bed, ready for whatever he wanted to do. Where to begin? From the bathroom he got a large pair of shears. He sat beside his still-silent wife, snapping the shears loudly, then, without a word, he began to cut the slip up the front. 'I've dreamed of doing this forever.' When he reached the top, he spread the slip's sides and gazed at the tiny wisp of lace that held her breasts. 'So beautiful,' he whispered.

"He leaned over and used his teeth on her already erect nipple, biting hard so she'd feel it through the material. Then he bit the other. Back and forth he moved until the cups of her bra were wet and he could see her dark areolas and the large protruding tips. Then he cut through the front of the bra and parted the cups so he could admire his wife's naked breasts. No, *he thought,* not breasts,

tits. Creamy, white tits. *'You've got great tits,' he said, amazed that he could use such a word in front of his prim little wife. But he'd make her forget it all later.*

"Kissing her full on the mouth, he felt her tongue reach for his. God, he was hot. He snipped through shoulder straps and pulled both slip and bra out from beneath her. Then he cut the garter belt and the sides of her panties. 'You've also got a beautiful bush. I can't wait to fuck your sweet pussy.' He could say the things he'd always wanted to growl at her while they made love.

"He looked at her face momentarily and saw her wide eyes, her slightly bruised mouth. 'Sexy as hell,' he said, his voice harsh. 'You make my cock so hard I could almost come in my pants.' He reached between Kate's legs and fingered her slit, her legs unable to close, her body unable to avoid him. She was dripping wet, squirming against his hands. He stabbed his thumb into her. 'No, I'm not going to come in my pants. I'm going to come in your sweet pussy. I'm going to fuck you hard and fast, just the way I want.'

"Quickly Phil dragged off his slacks, shirt, and underwear. His cock was so hard it was almost painful. He stretched out on top of his wife, running his hands all over her now-naked body. He rubbed his scratchy cheek on her belly, pinched her nipples, scraped his nails down her sides. Then, when he couldn't wait another minute, he plunged deep inside of her, ramming his cock into her pussy over and over, not caring about her pleasure, only his own. 'Such a hot little snatch. So tight. So wet. God so good,' he moaned. 'God! Shit!' He came almost too quickly, thrusting his cock into Kate's body.

"Later, after he caught his breath, he rolled off her and untied her wrists and ankles. 'Damn. It happened too fast, and I only had one chance.'

"Kate opened her eyes and stared at her husband. 'What do you mean only one chance?'

"He got the slim ebony wand from his dresser drawer. 'You've forgotten the story, but I already told you what this is and how I got it.' He told her the story again, and included his tap on her shoulder and his secretary's forgetting his errands. 'So that's the

story. I've wanted to fuck you like that for years, but I knew you'd never go for it. So now I can tap you with this wand and you won't remember.'

" '*Why in hell would you do that?' Her eyes were wide and shining.*

" '*Excuse me?'*

" '*Why would you want me to forget the best sex I've ever had?'*

" '*You mean you enjoyed it?'*

" '*You mean you couldn't tell?'*

"*As Phil thought back he realized that she had been extraordinarily wet. She'd been thrashing around on the bed, as much as she could while tied, moaning and calling his name. He'd been so wrapped up with his own pleasure that he hadn't been aware of hers. He felt stupefied.*

" '*I probably wouldn't have gone for it if you'd given me a choice, but once you tied me up, I was incredibly excited. And those words you said, you know, the dirty ones, made me so hot. I must have climaxed a dozen times.'*

"*Phil's mind was reeling. 'Really?'*

"*Kate grinned and kissed her husband. 'I wouldn't have believed it myself. Don't you dare use that wand on me. I want to remember this until we get the chance to do it again. We can, can't we?'*

"*Phil put the wand on the bedside table. 'Oh, Kate, I never knew. I've fantasized about a night like this for years. I just never had the nerve to try it.'*

" '*You did now, and it wasn't perfect. You came too fast, after all. I guess we'll just have to practice. I wonder whether we can get my parents to take the kids next Saturday night.'*

" '*If not, I'll bet mine will. I'll see to it.' Phil snuggled against his wife. The Wand of Forgetfulness had turned out to be a godsend. Thanks, lady, he thought. Thanks a lot.*"

Chapter 13

"Phew," Jim said. "That was some pretty heavy stuff. Have you ever done anything like that? Been tied up I mean? Do you think it would turn you on?"

Ellen was trembling. She had known, of course, what the story entailed, but she had never considered listening to that story with a man, much less telling anyone how it made her feel. They had always been honest with each other, however, a quality she treasured. "I've never done it, but the idea of it makes me crazy."

Jim turned her shoulders and cupped her chin so she had to look him in the eye. "Good crazy?"

"I have always been honest with you so yes, good crazy."

"I was hoping you'd say that." As he continued, he looked a bit chagrined. "We have always been honest with each other so I have a confession to make. I've listened to all the stories on the CD before. I knew what number eight was about, and this was my way of asking whether you'd be interested. You're not the only one who thought about using the stories for communication." Ellen just stared at him as he continued, I couldn't ask you right out so I thought up this way to find out whether you'd be interested in playing."

"You planned this?"

He held his hands up, palms out. "I confess. I've been playing the CD whenever I get the chance. Last weekend, while you were in the shower, I finally listened to that last story and the picture of you, tied to your bed has been driving me nuts ever since." He draped his arm around her shoulder. "I couldn't think of how to tell you, so I . . . well."

Ellen took a deep breath. How far they had come. Two people, both unsure of their own sexuality, now able to discuss something so intimate, so scary, so kinky. With a gleam in her eye, she asked, "You wouldn't actually do something like that, would you?"

Jim stared at her for a long time. She winked. "Would you?" He smiled, nodded, then grabbed her wrist and pulled her to a standing position. "Yes, I would." He all but dragged her into the bedroom, pushed her down onto the bed, then growled, "Stay right there." He disappeared into the living room and returned a moment later.

Silent, Ellen stared at the plastic shopping bag he'd been carrying when he arrived. As she started to sit up he snapped, "Don't move."

"I'm sorry," she said, easily slipping into a submissive role.

"Good. Now, I'll bet you're curious about what's in this bag. Actually I got really daring on my way over here. We've passed that adult toy store on the next block several times and I've been tempted to go in. This afternoon, I did, and I bought a few items."

"You actually went in?" Ellen asked. "I've been tempted so many times, but I've never had the courage."

"Be still, woman," Jim said. "I'm the boss here tonight." Ellen lay back on the bed and grinned. This was so great and he was so wonderful. He had changed so much since their first evening together, confidence growing week by week. He sat beside her and asked, "You trust me, don't you?"

"Totally."

His face lit up as he stood up. "Strip."

Silently, Ellen removed all her clothes and lay back on the bed while Jim rummaged in the bag and pulled out several leather straps. "I've been dreaming about this since I first heard that story." He gazed appreciatively at Ellen's naked body, then buckled the straps around wrists. "I surfed the Net looking at pictures of women tied up and I got some great ideas. The store gave me more."

He pulled a belt with rings and chains attached all around from the bag and fastened it tightly around her waist. He snapped the ring on one wristband to the end of a short piece of chain with a small padlock, then ran the chain through a ring at the front of her belt. Another padlock connected the chain to her other wrist. "You know," he said, slipping out of character, "I never would have imagined that I'd have the nerve to do this, but with you anything's possible."

From the bag he took two more straps and fastened them to Ellen's ankles, forced her to bend her knees then clipped the ankle straps to chains on the belt so her heels almost touched her buttocks and her legs fell open. He ran his finger through her slippery pussy. "You're so wet. This makes you as excited as it makes me, doesn't it?" When she didn't answer, he raised his voice. "Doesn't it?"

Ellen couldn't think. She was helpless, forced into a most revealing position, her body displayed and wide open for him. And she was so incredibly turned on. "Yes," she said, her voice ragged. "Oh, God, yes."

"Good."

Still fully clothed, Jim put the bag on the side of the bed. "Now the fun part." He withdrew a large flesh-colored dildo from the bag and held it where Ellen could see. "I've never played with toys before, but you make me feel daring." He slid the tip of the plastic phallus through her soaked folds, then slowly pushed it into her body.

Ellen's hips bucked as she tried to fuck the dildo, but Jim held it immobile deep inside of her. "Don't be in such a hurry," he purred. "We've got all night."

"Please," Ellen begged, "you're teasing me, driving me crazy. Please."

"Please what?"

"Shit," she hissed. "Get those clothes off and fuck me."

Jim grinned. "Nope. Not just yet." He pulled the dildo out slowly, then pushed it back in. In a slow-motion imitation of thrusting, he teased and tempted, never letting her have what she so desperately needed. Finally he pulled a chain from the bag, threaded it through the ring on the base of the dildo, clipping it to the back of the belt, then to the front. Now the dildo was tightly imbedded, unmoving in Ellen's pussy.

Her muscles grasped the dildo, squeezing, trying to make still more intimate contact. She moved her hips but the phallus remained still. "Oh, baby, please," she moaned, almost incoherent.

Jim only smiled, then knelt on the floor beside the bed. He brushed his mustache over her erect nipples, then nibbled on the tips. He licked and bit the flesh on her sides, her belly, her thighs as she moaned and begged him to fuck her. Then he said, "I'll bet I can make you come with just one touch." He reached between her spread legs and tapped on her clit.

Her orgasm was explosive, the power of it almost overwhelming her. When she collapsed, replete, Jim moved the dildo inside of her and she was back as high as she had been before her climax. How was that possible? She didn't know and didn't care. Over and over he teased orgasms out of her until she was totally exhausted. Then he stripped and stood beside her, grasped a handful of her hair and forced her head back. He held his erect cock and growled, "Open your mouth."

She had performed oral sex on him several times before but this was different, more elemental, primitive. He had never come in her mouth, but tonight it was as though it was preordained that she would swallow every bit of his come. She opened her mouth and he rammed his cock inside. She sucked, licked, and nipped at him until, with a long groan, he came, spurting in her throat.

Later, they showered together in her tiny bathroom. As he washed her mound he said, softly, "Was that all right? What I did, I mean?"

"Couldn't you tell? It was wonderful, explosive. It must have registered on seismographs from here to Alaska." She took the soap from him, lathered her hands, and cupped his testicles and flaccid penis in her hands.

"I don't think I'm going to be ready for sex again for a week," he said as she massaged him.

"I wouldn't bet the farm on that," she said. As she rubbed, his cock stiffened.

"You're a witch," he said. "I want to fuck you again right here but the condoms are in the bedroom."

"Don't worry about that," she said, rubbing his cock. "I don't think I'm up to another round, so I guess you'd better just fuck my hand."

"What?"

Water pouring over her head, she snapped, "Do it. Now!"

She filled the palm of her hand with shampoo and made a tube of her fingers. Jim rammed his cock through and came quickly.

Later, stretched out on the bed together, he asked, "What are you doing for the holidays? I'd love to spend the millennium celebration with you."

"I'm leaving for Fairmont in the morning," she said. When had she decided that? she wondered, but she knew when she said it that it was the right thing to do. She wanted to see how the town would feel to her now that she'd been in the city for these past months. She also wanted to visit with Micki and her family and needed to do some thinking. "I don't know when I'll be back exactly."

She felt Jim's body tighten. "It's not because of what we did tonight, is it? You are coming back, aren't you?"

She turned and put her arms around him. "I loved what we did tonight and I'll definitely be back." She slapped him on the hip. "Now it's time for you to be getting home."

He sat up slowly. "Maybe I could stay over?" he said softly.

"Not tonight. I need to do some thinking about me and where my life is going. I don't understand my future just yet."

"I hope I'll be part of your future." She could see the fear and doubts in the slump of his shoulders as he sat on the edge of the bed.

"You are, of course, but so many other things impact it too. I've never made any secret about the fact that I've been with another guy often since before I met you."

"I know, and that's the agreement we've had—no strings and no commitments. It bothers me, but I understand that you need your space."

Ellen leaned forward and kissed Jim's back. "I do. That's part of what I need to think through, away from you and him. Casual sex isn't life for me. It's sort of treading water. I need to find a direction."

"If casual sex isn't for you, we could get married, make it a full-time, permanent thing."

"That's not a reason to get married and we're not ready yet. I'm not sure what I'm ready for, but let's not rush into anything. It might happen, it might not but I never want to lead you on by letting you think that I understand any of this. I need to think and I can't do it here, with you or Kevin."

"If that's what you need, I'll miss you."

She kissed him again. "I'll miss you too."

The following morning she called Kevin and told him that she would be out of town for a few weeks.

"But love, what about the final painting of you? It's almost completed. And what about your landscapes? They are coming along so well. And us?"

She noticed immediately that the painting came first. Ellen glanced around her apartment. Several sheets of heavy cardboard stood balanced against the walls with landscapes clipped to them. All the scenes were woodsy, with babbling brooks and sun-dappled glades. Her work was progressing, but none of them made her happy. Suddenly she realized that nothing made her happy deep inside. The sex was wonderful. Jim and Kevin were both great guys, but this wasn't life. Was Jim her future? "I'll see you when I get back."

"Well, if you must. Have a happy holiday. I'll miss you."

"I'll miss you, too."

She called her sister and told her that she'd be arriving the following afternoon and proceeded to pack a few things in a small suitcase. The holiday gifts she had purchased for her sister, brother-in-law, and her nieces had already been sent home. Where was home?

As Micki drove her into the small town of Fairmont, Ellen looked around. Nothing much had changed, and yet everything had. The small, unmanned firehouse looked so quiet compared with the crowds of people always hanging around in front of New York City firehouses. The Fairmont Mall boasted an eight-movie multiplex; in the city, she could see any one of a hundred movies with just a short bus ride. There was the school complex, elementary, intermediate, and high schools sharing the same now-snow-covered campus with the local community college not far away. The stores were warm and inviting, comfortable and doable. This was Fairmont, not the big city. She had been comfortable here all her life, but not anymore. As she had suspected, she no longer fit in here.

Although she had been to Fairmont for Thanksgiving, Micki's family greeted her like visiting royalty. They shared Micki's famous pot roast, with potato pancakes and applesauce, Ellen's all-time favorite meal. Since it was now only a week before Christmas, the children were wired. They didn't get to bed until after ten and by then Micki's husband was ready to settle down in the bedroom with the TV remote and "let you girls visit."

"So why the sudden visit?" Micki asked when they were comfortably seated on the sofa in her early-American living room. "We expected you on the twenty-fourth."

"It's the Christmas season and I just missed you guys."

Micki cocked her head to one side. "You never could con me, babe. What's up?"

Ellen allowed her body to slump. "I needed to figure lots of things out and one of them was Fairmont. Someone told me recently that I used the word *home* to mean here. I just wanted to know whether that was true, whether here felt like home."

"And does it?"

Ellen stretched her legs out in front of her, crossed at the ankles. "Your home feels like home and probably always will, but this town? It was where I belonged for all the years we were growing up and until I won all that money I thought that Fairmont was the only place in the world for me. That's not true anymore."

Micki sipped her coffee. "So you're moving to the city for good?"

"I think so." She sought her sister's eyes.

"Are you looking for my approval?" Micki asked.

Ellen was surprised, not only at the question but at her inability to give a snap answer. "Maybe I am."

"Well you shouldn't be." Micki set her cup on the coffee table. "I've done quite a lot of thinking over these past months. It worries me that you've always looked to me for guidance. Because I am the 'big sister,' " Micki made quote marks in the air, "we both assumed that I would know what was best, particularly after the folks died. I know what's best for me, or at least I hope I do, and I have to make decisions with Milt, for us and for the girls, but I haven't the foggiest what's best for you any more, assuming that I ever did. You're different now, more self-assured, more confident and I've been aware of that since you arrived. Listen, Ellie, it's your life. You need to make your own decisions regardless of what I think."

Ellen leaned forward and hugged her sister. "Thanks, Micki. I love you, too."

Later, Ellen reclaimed her old car from Micki's driveway and drove to the house that had been her home until recently. Micki had kept the plants watered and the rooms aired so the place was warm and inviting. As Ellen shut the door behind her, she closed her eyes and inhaled. The living room smelled of the furniture oil her mother had always used to polish the top of the upright piano, and the pine candles that had always sat on the hall table. She set her suitcase down and walked slowly into the kitchen. Cookies. Her mother had always had a teddy bear cookie jar on the counter filled with homemade Toll House or sugar cookies. Ellen wandered back toward the living room and touched the long crack in the mirror in the tiny hall, remembering when she and Micki had made it tossing a bean bag in the house despite her mother's warnings. Smiling wistfully she remembered the week that she and her sister had been grounded afterward.

Home. It was quite a concept, one she wasn't sure she understood. This house would always be her home in some ways, yet she felt as though she didn't quite belong. She thought about her little apartment in the city. Was that home? She didn't really belong there either.

And her life. What fit there? Before the lottery, she had been comfortable here. She dropped onto a kitchen chair. Comfortable. There was that word again. Was that what she should be aiming for, comfort? Did Kevin offer comfort? Did Jim? The more she thought, the more confused she became. How much of what she had always done had been settling for just comfortable and easy?

Suitcase in hand, she climbed the stairs and got ready for bed. Where was her life heading? She asked herself question after question as she slipped beneath the log-cabin-design quilt and, sighing, closed her eyes. She pictured her recent evening with Jim and the last time she'd seen Kevin. His brother, Sean, had asked again whether she would pose for him, although she knew that it was not just her posing that he was interested in. Maybe she'd let him. She found herself wondering what he'd be like coupling with her on that same velvet sofa. She closed her eyes, creating the scene.

It was mid-afternoon and the sun shown through the skylight in the studio ceiling creating an oasis of light into which Kevin pulled the sofa. He draped it in a soft blue velour and Ellen quickly removed her clothes. Kevin's totally businesslike hands positioned her on the couch, reclining, with one knee raised, her arm resting lightly across the sofa's back.

"Now," Kevin purred, turning on the radio to a classical station, "I want you to think about your lover. He's just outside the door and you can hear his key in the lock. He's been away for more than a week and you've been yearning for him to return."

Ellen formed the picture in her mind, her lover, who always looked like a cross between Kevin and Jim, about to enter the room and make love with her. She could feel her nipples tighten and her pussy swell.

"The warm sun shines on your skin," Kevin crooned, "and you can feel the heat rise in your body from both outside and within. Now the door is opening, and be comes in and kneels beside you, touching your soft belly, your full breasts, the hair between your legs."

Ellen was lost in her dream, when she heard another voice. "She's just as lovely as I imagined." Her eyes jerked open and she saw Sean at the top of the stairs. "I hope you don't mind," Sean said. "There haven't been any customers for more than an hour and I thought I'd come up and work a bit." He hadn't taken his eyes off Ellen's naked body. "Do you mind?"

Ellen thought about covering herself and realized that she didn't really want to. Rather she reveled in the lust she saw growing in Sean's gaze. "No. I don't mind."

From one of the shelves at the side of the room, Sean pulled a cloth-covered shape and put it on a pedestal table. He removed the drape and Ellen saw that the sculpture was a standing nude that bore a distinct resemblance to her. As she watched Sean's hands stroke the surface of the clay it was as though his hands caressed her flesh. She lay, lost in the sensuality of two men's eyes devouring her nude body. As she looked from Kevin's eyes to Sean's she knew there was nothing professional about their scrutiny now.

"You know, don't you," Sean said, "that this was just an excuse to come up here and be with you." As his thumbs brushed the clay nipples Ellen's nipples became harder and tighter.

"You are so seductive, lying in the light like that," Kevin said,

his voice hoarse, "that I eventually forget about painting and just want to love you."

Slowly, a smile spread over Ellen's face. "Yes," she purred.

Her one-word affirmation was all the two men needed. As one they moved beside her. Sean's hands were still wet from the statue and, as he covered her breasts with his palms, she could feel the traces of slippery clay. Kevin had brought a tube of cadmium yellow paint and squeezed a line over her ribs. Slowly four hands rubbed and stroked, covering her body with water-based sunshine.

Without ever leaving her, they were suddenly naked, too, their bodies fully ready and totally aroused. She took a tube of alizarin crimson and filled her palm. She rubbed Kevin's hard cock with the flame-red paint and skillfully manipulated his shaft. Grinning, Sean filled her other palm with cobalt paint and soon she had a hard cock in each hand.

The moans of the two men filled the studio as she brought them closer and closer to climax. It was strange that, although they were completely passive, neither touching her, she felt filled and complete. She stared at the two cocks, one blood-red and one deep blue, and rubbed, knowing exactly where each man needed to be touched. She cupped Sean's balls and slipped a finger toward Kevin's anus.

She was supremely talented, able to drive them each higher and higher. She knew that she had the power to make them come or leave them suspended over the precipice. "Now," she said, pressing Sean's sac and slowly, inserting a paint-lubricated finger into Kevin's ass.

Two cocks erupted, semen mixing with color, loud roars blending with Mozart. She was the eternal woman, able to please anyone.

In her bed, Ellen touched herself and quickly climaxed and, although Ellen couldn't hear it, from far away, Lucy cheered.

The following morning, Ellen showered and walked slowly downstairs. Smelling freshly brewed coffee, she frowned as she entered the kitchen. "Maggie," she cried, rushing over to hug the older woman. "It's been forever."

"For you maybe. For me it seems like we just parted. Tell me everything that's gone on since I last saw you."

"Everything?"

Maggie picked up a plastic-coated bag and waved it beneath Ellen's nose. "I brought doughnuts. Apple-spice filled. We can eat as you talk."

Over doughnuts and coffee, Ellen filled Maggie in on her escapades over the past weeks. Through the recitation, Maggie remained silent, content to listen to all of Ellen's tales. When Ellen finally ran down, Maggie said, "Tied you to the bed? Is this the Ellen I first met last fall, the one who didn't know about toe-curling, mind-blowing, earth-moving sex?"

"The very same—and the very different." Suddenly Ellen's eyes filled. "Oh, Maggie, I don't know where I belong anymore."

"Do you have to?" When Ellen stared, Maggie continued, Where it is written that you have to know where you fit? Maybe the question you should be asking yourself is what makes you happy?" Maggie paused. "Here's a game I'd like you to play. Fill in the blank. *Blank* makes me happy."

"You make me happy."

"I thank you for the compliment but that's not enough. Again."

"Great sex makes me happy."

"Good. Again."

"Jim makes me happy. Kevin makes me happy."

"Again."

"Micki and her family make me happy."

"Again."

"Okay, okay, let me think."

"That's the idea of this exercise," Maggie said. "Think."

"The city makes me happy. Being on my own and making my own decisions make me happy."

"You haven't mentioned your painting."

Ellen thought. "You're right. Painting forest scenes doesn't make me happy. You know what I want to paint? Purple trees and red skies. Twin moons and black deserts."

"So paint them."

"Kevin would throw me out of class."

"So? Stop doing what you think you should, and do what gives you joy. Paint twin moons and purple trees. You said great sex makes you happy. What about love? You used to think that that would make you happy. A man and a home like Micki's."

"That's not so important now. It will come, I think, but certainly not with Kevin. He's a wonderful interlude, but nothing more than that. And Jim? He's a great guy, but despite his proposal he's not nearly ready. We know what we've got and that's enough for now. I need to find me before I can think about any kind of full-time, permanent relationship."

"Okay. How about your job, does that make you happy?"

"No," Ellen said quickly, "but if I don't work I'll feel like a slug. I have to do something. I can't just sit around all day painting and eating doughnuts." Saying that she reached into the bag and pulled out a second apple-spice doughnut.

"So don't. What would you like to do?"

"Months ago, when Micki and I were talking about what to do in the city, I considered volunteering in a hospital. I think I'd like to do that."

"So do it. You certainly don't need to earn money."

"That's another thing. There's all that money sitting there just earning more money."

"The problem with that is?"

"It's selfish. There are so many people who need. Not the big charities, but people. Individuals. Sick kids and pregnant teens. Children who need to learn how to read."

"Do something about it. You can, you know."

"I could start a foundation with some of that money. Or just give it away to people who need it." She took a big bite of her doughnut and, with her mouth full, continued, "I wouldn't know how to go about any of that."

"There must be people who do and I'm sure with a little searching you could find someone to help you."

"I don't want to get all serious and give up sex and fun."

"You can do everything. You have nothing holding you down."

A familiar voice filled the room. "She's right, you know."

"Lucy, are you eavesdropping again?" Maggie snapped.

"Of course we are," Angela said. "Why do you think you showed up in Ellen's kitchen on this particular morning? Ellen needed a sounding board to help her figure out this thing called life."

"Life isn't easy," Lucy chimed in. "If it were simple we wouldn't have all these 'up or down' decisions to make. Finding a path through the trees is tough."

"And there's usually no one to help you," Angela said.

"Except when you ladies send me down," Maggie said. She took Ellen's hands in hers. "Listen. You're well on your way to becoming something special, a person who has a clear idea of what makes her happy and goes after it. Don't lose that when I'm gone."

"You're leaving?"

"My job here is done." Maggie giggled. "I sound like the Lone Ranger." She lowered the pitch of her voice. "Come on, Tonto, our work here is done."

"But I'm still confused."

"You'll be confused for a long time, but you've got a direction, some ideas. The most important thing you've learned is . . . fill in the *blank*."

"Do what makes me happy, what gives me direction."

"You've got it."

Again Ellen's eyes filled. "I'm going to miss you."

"How about us?" Lucy chimed in.

"Okay," Ellen admitted, "you two also. Without all your help I don't know where I'd be."

Angela answered. "You'd be in the city, in that silly apartment, peeking out at life. Now you're experiencing it. You're flying now, babe. Soar."

Ellen grinned. "I want to get a kitten. A tiny, scrappy, female kitten. Perhaps I'll get two, a white one called Angela, and a coal-black one named Lucy."

"You're making me all misty," Angela said, a catch in her voice.

"You would get weepy," Lucy said. "I think it's cute."

Maggie stood, pulled Ellen to her feet, and wrapped her arms around her friend. "I won't be seeing you again, and if things go the way they have in the past, you'll forget me quickly."

"You've been a great friend, Maggie," Ellen said, tears running down her face.

"You have, too," Maggie said, her eyes moist. "I'm so glad I got to share this time in your life."

"Okay, you two, stop blubbering," Lucy said as her voice slowly faded. "Oh and one last thing. If you decide to keep this place, get that mirror fixed. Cracked mirrors make me crazy."

"I love you all," Ellen said as Maggie walked toward the front door.

"I love you, too," Maggie said, then opened the door and disappeared.

For a long while, Ellen stood in the center of the living room and let the tears fall. Then, when she finally calmed, she found a small pad and began to make plans for the future. Her future.

"So what's next for me, Maggie said, sitting in the computer room with Lucy and Angela.

"Oh, we have plenty of jobs for you." Angela swiveled her computer monitor so Maggie could see. On the screen was a tall, slender, man who looked like a twenty-first-century version of Ichabod Crane. "How would you feet about educating a man for a change? You should be really good at that."

"A man?" Maggie said. "What an idea."

Dear Reader,

I hope you've enjoyed reading *Midnight Butterfly* as much as I enjoyed writing it. I loved creating Ellen and revisiting Maggie, Lucy, and Angela from my earlier novel *Slow Dancing,* Barbara Enright's story. I have a great desire to see what happens on Maggie's next assignment and maybe I'll write that book eventually.

When I wrote *Slow Dancing,* nothing like the tape or CD collections of erotic short stories existed. Since then I've teamed up with the folks at Raven Limited to create just such CD collections, original stories that you can listen to or use for communication as Ellen and Jim did in this book. They are available through my Website at *www.JoanELloyd.com.* Please visit to learn about the CDs, read new erotic short stories I post every month, learn about and read excerpts from all my books, and share information with my thousands of visitors.

I'd love to hear from you any time, so drop me a note and let me know what you particularly enjoyed and what you would like to read about in a future book. Please write me at:

Joan@JoanELloyd.com.